THREE
for
MIDNIGHT

THREE
for
MIDNIGHT

■ ■ ■

Philip MacDonald

DOUBLEDAY & COMPANY, INC.
GARDEN CITY, NEW YORK

FOREWORD

I wonder how many professional storytellers can look back on their own early work with true objectivity. If there are any, I envy them. Because I know I can't. I always fall into the egocentric trap of disliking mine far too much; of feeling (as was once said of a friend of mine who was forever working on the great American novel and never finishing the first chapter) that "it isn't good enough for me to have written."

The only time I'm ever halfway satisfied with any work I've done is for a short while after I've finished it; a depressingly short and evanescent while. A week later any satisfaction with my labors is beginning to fade. In a month I am more than dubious. After a year, I'm convinced the whole thing smells to high heaven, and I can't imagine why anyone would ever trouble to read it.

But I realize that these are conditioned reflexes, and auto-conditioned at that, so I made up my mind to ignore them as I approached the task of going over the three books in this collection. But I still started on the job with trepidation; because (to be euphemistic) the tales were written some time ago* and I was terrified that, in spite of their original success, they might prove hopelessly out of date.

But somehow they didn't; and I was able to confine such editing as I did to matters of cutting, wording and style, of writing *qua* writing. Surprisingly, the stories themselves, as examples of three completely different types of what is now (unfortunately, I think) generically labeled "Mystery Story," seemed to me to hold up pretty well: *The Rasp* as a pure, dyed-in-the-wool Whodunit; *Murder Gone Mad* as a tale of mass-murder, half Whodunit and half (to use a label of my own coining) Howcatchem; and *The Rynox Murder,* called a "light-hearted thriller" at the time of its birth, as one of those razzle-dazzle, now-you-see-it-now-you-don't affairs

* Not only a euphemism; an understatement verging on the classic.

which many of us case-hardened toilers in the field of the *roman policier*† like to throw off once in a while.

The Rasp was my third novel. It was also my first detective story,† and long before I'd finished it I was determined it should be my last. Conceived during a decade which was a Whodunit heyday, a time when it seemed that everyone in the storytelling business was trying his hand at the form, it was begun in a burst of youthful egotism, to show the world not only that I could do this too, but that I could do it better!

However, by the time I'd finished it I wasn't at all sure that I was showing anybody anything. All I knew was that this was hard, *hard* work; I had discovered that if the writer of *romans policiers* believes (as I think he has to) that his books should be novels as well as puzzles; that they must, always, be literate and credible as well as *scrupulously fair to the reader,* the writing of them is pure self-torture!

But—well, *The Rasp* made quite a splash when it came out, first in England and later in the U.S.‡ And I'm still torturing myself for a living, nowadays not only between book covers but also in the dramatic forms of film and television. Although I have, at various and several times, sought relief quite successfully in telling other sorts of story, I seem always to come masochistically back to the sweat and the frustration, the challenge and the agony, of working at what John Dickson Carr has called "the greatest game of all." And it might be worth noting that, when I do, I frequently use as my chief instrument a character (Anthony Gethryn) whom I never imagined, when I tucked him tidily away in matrimony at the end of *The Rasp,* would ever show his inquisitive and somewhat supercilious nose again. . . .

Now for *Murder Gone Mad.* This was my third or fourth detective novel, and is a very different cup of tea from the first. An attempt to break away from the then accepted, and terribly confining, limits of the pure Whodunit (blunt-instrumented corpse in copse or library—eight suspects—least likely murderer) it was suggested by the macabre but very real-life exploits of the greatest mass murderer of the century, the monster of Düsseldorf.

I'm not sure of my memory on this point, but I think I started

---

† If labels must be used, I stubbornly prefer the old ones, unless I happen to invent them myself.

‡ Quite a while (!) after it was written, Ellery Queen did me the honor of including it in his definitive list of the "Cornerstone" detective stories.

the book with the idea that, as well as being a departure from the straight Whodunit form, it would also be easier to write. If I did think this, I was sadly mistaken. It was, in its own demonic way, every bit as tough to do. Because, after all, when the author (or policeman, if it comes to that) is faced with a clever and careful and *motiveless* killer, how *does* he set about uncovering him?

But the book got finished somehow and was very well received,§ so I suppose I did all right by the theme, which is, after all, timeless. An interesting point, however, did occur to me while I was going over it; a point which might be worth some elaboration.

It concerns the present-day preoccupation with the psyche and all its widely bandied but only dimly understood *-iatrys* and *-opaths* and *-ologies*. If I were to be writing this book today, I believe I would feel bound to probe at length into the subconscious past of the murderer (in search, so to speak, of the *psora* and *trauma* of that dark district) so that I could eventually reveal that the whole trouble was caused by the fact that, at an early age, this unfortunate homicidal maniac (like the character in *Cold Comfort Farm*) had seen something nasty in the woodshed.

But, in the days when I did write *Murder Gone Mad* I felt no such compulsion. It was enough, then, that the murderer was mentally unhinged; that the murderer was killing without sane motive; that the murderer was eventually caught. . . .

That was the way we used to do it—and I'm not at all sure we weren't right. . . .

This leaves *The Rynox Murder*. As I have already intimated, it is a much lighter book than the others; lighter in every way. Writing it was really a sort of busman's holiday; and, at the time, I almost had fun working on it, particularly since it satirized several persons and institutions in the London of that time—

I have just caught myself wondering whether the satire, unrecognizable here and now, was the only reason for the book doing as well as it did. And this means, I fear, that I'm back with my conditioned reflexes and had better stop, before I start saying, "It isn't good enough for me to have written," and thereby open the door temptingly wide for any critic who might feel like adding the words, "or anyone else" . . .

PHILIP MacDONALD

§ In 1947, in a critical essay (the same as that from which I quoted him before) Mr. John Dickson Carr actually included *Murder Gone Mad* as one of the all-time ten best detective stories.

THE RASP

TO

THE GUV'NOR

CONTENTS

All the Birds of the Air
  Fell a-sighin' and a-sobbin'
When they heard of the death
  Of poor Cock Robin.

"Who'll dig his Grave?"
  "I," said the Owl,
  "With my little Trowel;
I'll dig his Grave."

"Who *killed* Cock Robin?"
  "I," said the Sparrow,
  "With my Bow and Arrow,
I killed Cock Robin!"

CHAPTER ONE

TOLLING THE BELL

1

The Owl shows its blue and gilt cover on the bookstalls every Saturday morning. Thursday nights are therefore nights of turmoil in the offices in Fleet Street. They are always wearing nights; more so, of course, in hot weather than in cold. They are nights of discomfort for the office-boy and of something worse for the editor.

Spencer Hastings edited *The Owl,* and owned a third of it; and the little paper's success showed him to possess both brains and capacity for hard work. For a man of thirty-three he had achieved much; but that capacity for work was hard tested—especially on Thursday nights. As to the brains, there was really no doubt of their quality. Take, for instance, *The Owl* "specials." After he had thought of them and given birth to the first, *The Owl,* really a weekly review, was enabled to reap harvests in the way of "scoops" without in any way degenerating into a mere purveyor of news.

The thing was worked like this: If, by the grace of God or through a member of the "special" staff or by any other channel, there came to Hastings's ears a piece of Real News which might as yet be unknown to any of the big daily or evening papers, then within a few hours, whatever the day or night of the week, there appeared a special edition of *The Owl*. It bore, in place of the blue and gold, a cover of red and black. The letterpress was sparse. The price was six pence. The public bought the first two out of curiosity, and the subsequent issues because they had discovered that when the red and black jacket was seen Something had really Happened.

The public bought the real *Owl* as well. It was always original, written by men and women as yet little known and therefore unspoilt. It was witty, exciting, soothing, biting, laudatory, ironic, and sincere—all in one breath and irreproachable taste.

And Hastings loved it. But Thursday nights, press nights, were undoubtedly Hell. And this Thursday night, hotter almost than its stifling day, was the very hell of Hells.

He ruffled his straw-coloured hair, looking, as a woman once said of him, rather like a stalwart and handsome chicken. Midnight struck. He worked on, cursing at the heat, the paper, his material, and the fact that his confidential secretary, his right-hand woman, was making holiday.

He finished correcting the proofs of his leader, then reached for two over-long articles by new contributors. As he picked up a blue pencil, his door burst open.

"What in hell——" he began; then looked up. "Good God! Marga—Miss Warren!"

It was sufficiently surprising that the right-hand woman should erupt into his room at this hour in the night when he had supposed her many miles away in a holiday bed; but that she should be thus, gasping, white-faced, dust-covered, hair escaping in a shining cascade from beneath a wrecked hat, was incredible. Never before had he seen her other than calm, scrupulously dressed, exquisitely tidy and faintly severe in her beauty.

He rose to his feet slowly. The girl, her breath coming in great sobs, sank limply into a chair. Hastings rushed for the editorial bottle, glass, and siphon. He tugged at the door of the cupboard, remembered that he had locked it, and began to fumble for his keys. They eluded him. He swore beneath his breath, and then started as a hand was laid on his shoulder. He had not heard her approach.

"Please don't worry about that." Her words came short, jerkily, as she strove for breath. "Please, please, listen to me! I've got a Story—the biggest yet! Must have a special done now, to-night, this morning!"

Hastings forgot the whisky. The editor came to the top.

"What's happened?" snapped the editor.

"Cabinet Minister dead. John Hoode's been killed—murdered! To-night. At his country house."

"You *know?*"

The efficient Miss Margaret Warren was becoming herself again. "Of course. I heard all the fuss just after eleven. I was staying in Marling, you know. My landlady's husband is the police-sergeant. So I hired a car and came straight here. I thought you'd like to know." Miss Warren was unemotional.

"Hoode killed! Phew!" said Hastings, the man, wondering what would happen to the Party.

"*What* a story!" said Hastings, the editor. "Any other papers on to it yet?"

"I don't think they can be—yet."

"Right. Now nip down to Bealby, Miss Warren. Tell him he's got to get ready for a two-page special *now*. He must threaten, bribe, shoot, do anything to keep the printers at the job. Then see Miss Halford and tell her she can't go till she's arranged for issue. Then please come back here; I shall want to dictate."

"Certainly, Mr. Hastings," said the girl, and walked quietly from the room.

Hastings looked after her, his forehead wrinkled. Sometimes he wished she were not so sufficient, so calmly adequate. Just now, for an instant, she had been trembling, white-faced, weak. Somehow the sight, even while he feared, had pleased him.

He shrugged his shoulders and turned to his desk.

"Lord!" he murmured. "Hoode murdered. *Hoode!*"

2

"That's all the detail, then," said Hastings half an hour later. Margaret Warren, neat, fresh, her golden hair smooth and shining, sat by his desk.

"Yes, Mr. Hastings."

"Er—hm. Right. Take this down. 'Cabinet Minister Assassinated. Murder at Abbotshall——"

" 'Awful Atrocity at Abbotshall,' " suggested the girl softly.

"Yes, yes. You're right as usual," Hastings snapped. "But I always forget we have to use journalese in the specials. Right. 'John Hoode Done to Death by Unknown Hand. *The Owl* most deeply regrets to announce that at eleven o'clock last night Mr. John Hoode, Minister of Imperial Finance, was found lying dead in the study of his country residence, Abbotshall, Marling. The circumstances were such'—pity we don't know what they really were, Miss Warren—'the circumstances were such as to show immediately that this chief among England's greatest men had met his death at the hands of a murderer, though it is impossible at present to throw any light upon the identity of the criminal.' New paragraph, please. 'We understand, however, that no time was lost in communicating with Scotland Yard, who have assigned the task of tracking down the perpetrator of this terrible crime to their most able and experienced officers'—always a safe card that, Miss Warren—'No time will be lost in commencing the work of investigation.' Fresh paragraph, please. 'All England, all the Empire, the whole world will join in offering their heartfelt sympathy to Miss Laura Hoode,

who, we understand, is prostrated by the shock'—another safe bet
—'Miss Hoode, as all know, is the sister of the late minister and his
only relative. It is known that there were two guests at Abbotshall,
that brilliant leader of society, Mrs. Roland Mainwaring, and Sir
Arthur Digby-Coates, the millionaire philanthropist and Parliamentary Secretary to the Board of Conciliation. Sir Arthur was an
extremely close and lifelong friend of the deceased and would
affirm that he had not an enemy in the world——' "

Miss Margaret Warren looked up, her eyebrows severely inter-
rogative.

"Well?" said Hastings uneasily.

"Isn't that last sentence rather dangerous, Mr. Hastings?"

"Hm—er—I don't know—er—yes, you're right, Miss Warren.
Dammit, woman, are you ever wrong about anything?" barked
Hastings; then recovered himself. "I *beg* your pardon. I—I——"

There came an aloof smile. "Please don't apologise, Mr. Hastings. Shall I change the phrase?"

"Yes, yes," muttered Hastings. "Say, say—put down—say——"

" '——and are stricken aghast at the calamity which has befallen
them,' " suggested the girl.

"Excellent," said Hastings, composure recovered.

"By the way, did you tell Williams to get on with that padding?
That sketch of Hoode's life and work? We've got to fill up that op-
posite-centre page."

"Yes, Mr. Williams started on it at once."

"Good. Now take this down as a separate piece. It must be
marked off with heavy black rules and be in Clarendon or some
conspicuous type. Ready? '*The Owl,* aghast at this dreadful tragedy,
yet arises from its sorrow and issues, on behalf of the public, a
solemn exhortation and warning. Let the authorities see to it that
the murderer is found, and found speedily. England demands it.
The author of this foul deed must be brought swiftly to justice and
punished with the utmost rigour of the law. No effort must be
spared.' Now a separate paragraph, please. It must be underlined
and should go on the opposite page—under Williams's article.
'Aware of the tremendous interest and concern which this terrible
crime will arouse, *The Owl* has made special arrangements to have
bulletins (in the same form as this special edition) published at
short intervals in order that the public may have full opportunity
to know what progress is being made in the search for the criminal.

" 'These bulletins will be of extraordinary interest, since we are
in a position to announce that a special correspondent will despatch

to us (so far as is consistent with the wishes of the police, whom we wish to assist rather than compete with) at frequent intervals, from the actual locus of the crime, a résumé of the latest developments.'" Hastings sighed relief and leant back in his chair. "That's all, Miss Warren. And I hope—since the thing *is* done—that the murderer'll remain a mystery for a bit. We'll look rather prize idiots if the gardener's boy or some one confesses to-morrow. Get that stuff typed and down to the printers as quick as you can, please."

The girl rose and moved to the door, but paused on the threshold.

"Mr. Hastings," she said, turning quickly, "what does that last bit mean? Are you sending one of the ordinary people down there —Mr. Sellars or Mr. Briggs?"

"Yes, yes, I suppose so. What I said was all rot, but it'll sound well. We just want reports that are a bit different from the others."

She came nearer, her eyes wide. "Mr. Hastings, please excuse me, but you must listen. Why not let *The Owl* be really useful? Oh, don't you see what it would mean if we helped to catch the murderer? Our reputation—our sales. Why——"

"Oh, come now! We've not got an office full of Holmeses. They're all perfectly ordinary fellers——"

"Colonel Gethryn," said the girl quietly.

"Eh, what?" Hastings was startled. "He'd never—Miss Warren, you're a wonder. But he wouldn't take it on. He's——"

"Ask him." She pointed to the telephone at his side.

"What? Now?"

"Why not?"

"But—but it's two o'clock," stammered Hastings. He met the level gaze of his secretary's blue eyes, lifted the receiver from its hook, and asked for a number.

"Hallo," he said two minutes later, "is that Colonel Gethryn's flat?"

"It is," said the telephone. Its voice was sleepy.

"Is—is Colonel Gethryn in—out—up, I mean?"

"Colonel Gethryn," said the voice, "who would infinitely prefer to be called Mr. Gethryn, is in his flat, out of bed, and upon his feet. Also he is beginning to become annoyed at——"

"Good Lord—Anthony!" said Hastings. "I didn't recognise your voice."

"Now that you have, O Hastings, perhaps you'll explain why the hell you're ringing me up at this hour. I may mention that I am in execrable temper. Proceed."

Spencer Hastings proceeded. "Er—I—ah—that is—er——"

"If those are scales," said the telephone, "permit me to congratulate you."

Hastings tried again. "Something has happened," he began.

"No!" said the telephone.

"D'you think you could—I know it's an extraordinary thing to ask—er, but will you—er——"

Miss Margaret Warren rose to her feet, removed the instrument from her employer's hands, put the receiver to her ear and spoke into the transmitter.

"Mr. Gethryn," she said, "this is Margaret Warren speaking. What Mr. Hastings wished to do was to ask whether you could come down here—to the office—at once. Oh, I know it sounds mad, but we've received some amazing news, and Mr. Hastings wishes to consult you. I can't tell you any more over the phone, but Mr. Hastings is sure that you'll be willing to help. Please come; it might mean everything to the paper."

"Miss Warren," said the telephone sadly, "against my will you persuade me."

CHAPTER TWO

ANTHONY GETHRYN

Anthony Ruthven Gethryn was something of an oddity. A man of action who dreamed while he acted; a dreamer who acted while he dreamed. The son of a hunting country gentleman of the old type, who was yet one of the most brilliant mathematicians of his day, and of a Spanish lady of impoverished and exiled family who had, before her marriage with Sir William Gethryn, been in turn governess, dancer, mannequin, actress, and portrait painter, it was perhaps to be expected that he should be no ordinary child. And he was not.

For even after taking into consideration the mixture of blood and talents that were rightly his, Anthony's parents soon found their only child to be possessed of far more than they had thought to give him. From his birth he proved a refutation of the adage that a Jack-of-all-Trades can be master of none.

At school and at Oxford, though appearing almost to neglect work, he covered himself with academic glory which outshone even that of his excellence at racquets and Rugby football. Not only did he follow in the mathematical tracks of his father, but also became known as an historian and man of classics.

He left Oxford in his twenty-third year; read for the bar; was called, but did not answer. He went instead round and about the world, and did not, during the three and a half years he was away, use a penny other than earnings of one sort and another.

He returned home to settle down, painted two pictures which he gave to his father, wrote a novel which was lauded by the critics and brought him not a penny, and followed up with a book of verse which, though damned by the same critics, was yet remunerative to the extent of one hundred and fifty pounds.

Politics came next, and for some six months he filled adequately the post of private secretary to a Member of Parliament suspected of early promotion to office.

Then, on top of his decision to contest a seat himself, the world plunged itself into war. Within twenty-four hours he had enlisted as an infantry private; within three months he was offered, and accepted, an artillery commission; within a year was in hospital recovering from the damage caused by a sniper's bullet, an attack of the newest thing in undiagnosed fevers, and three pieces of shrapnel. . . .

By the middle of the second year, he was in Berlin.

That calls for explanation. Anthony Ruthven Gethryn was in Germany because his uncle, Sir Charles Haultevieux de Courcy Gethryn, was a personage at the War Office. Uncle Charles liked and had an admiration for his nephew Anthony. Also, Uncle Charles was aware that nephew Anthony spoke German like a German, and was, when occasion demanded, a person of tact, courage, and reliability. "A boy with *guts,* sir. A boy with *guts!* And common sense, sir; in spite of all this poetry-writin' and paintin' cows in fields and girls with nothin' on. A damnation *clever* lad, sir!"

So Uncle Charles, having heard the wailings of a friend in the Secret Service division concerning the terrible dearth of the right men, let fall a few words about his nephew.

And that is how, in the middle of a war, Anthony Ruthven Gethryn came to be living and working, not as a prisoner, in the capital of the country against which he and most of the rest of the world were fighting. He was there for eighteen long months, and when Uncle Charles next saw his nephew there were streaks of gray in the dark hair of the thirty-year-old head.

The results of Anthony's visit were of much value. A grateful Government patted him on the back, decorated him, gave him two months' leave, promoted him, and then worked him as few men were worked even during the war. It was queer work, funny work, work in the dark, work in strange places.

When it was all over, he was still in one piece. To show for his service he had a limp (slight), the C.M.G., the D.S.O., a baker's dozen of other orders (foreign: various) and those thick streaks of gray in his black hair. Few save his intimate friends knew either of that batch of medals or of his right to the title of Colonel.

Anthony stayed with his mother until she died, peacefully, and then, since his father—who had preceded his wife by some two years —had left him no more than a few hundreds a year, looked round for work.

He wrote another novel; the public were unmoved. He painted three pictures; they would not sell. He published another book of poems; they would not sell either. Then he turned back to his secretaryship, his M.P. being now a minor minister. The work was of a sort he did not care for, and save for meeting every now and then a man who interested him, he was bored to extinction.

Then, arrived a winter when Uncle Charles fell a victim to malignant influenza, became convalescent, developed pneumonia, and died. To Anthony he left a house in Knightsbridge and an estate from which the annual income was considerably more than comfortable. Anthony leased the house, set up in a flat, and, re- moved from carking care, did as the fancy took him. When he wanted to write, he wrote. When he wished to paint, he painted. When pleasure called, he answered. He was very happy for a year.

But then came trouble. When he wrote, he found that, im- mediately, a picture would form in his head and cry aloud to be put on canvas. Did he paint, verse unprecedented, wonderful, clamoured to be written. Did he leave England, his soul yearned for London.

It was when this phase was at its worst that he renewed a friendship, begun at Trinity, with that eccentric but able young journalist, Spencer Hastings. To Anthony, Hastings unbosomed his great idea—the idea which could be made fact if there were exactly twice as much money as Hastings possessed. Anthony provided the capital, and *The Owl* was born.

Anthony designed the cover, wrote a verse for the paper now and then; sometimes a bravura essay. Often he blessed Hastings for having given him one interest at least which, since the control of it was not in his own hands, could not be thrown aside altogether.

To conclude: Anthony was suffering from three disorders, lack of a definite task to perform, severe war-strain, and not having met the right woman. The first and second, though he never spoke of them, he knew about; the third he did not even suspect.

CHAPTER THREE

COCK ROBIN'S HOUSE

1

The sudden telephone message from Hastings at two o'clock on that August morning and his own subsequent acceptance of the suggestion that he should be *The Owl's* "Special Commissioner," had at least, thought Anthony, as he drove his car through Kingston four hours later, remedied that lack of something definite to do.

He had driven at once to *The Owl's* headquarters, had arranged matters with Hastings within ten minutes, and had then telephoned to a friend—an important official friend. To him Anthony had outlined, sketchily, the scheme, and had been given in reply a semi-official, "Mind you, *I* know nothing about it if anything happens, but get ahead" blessing. He had then driven back to his flat, packed a bag, left a note for his man, and set out for Marling in Surrey.

From his official friend he had gathered that once on the right side of Miss Hoode and his way was clear. As he drove he pondered. How to approach the woman? At any mention of the Press she would be bound to shy. Finally, he put the problem to one side.

The news of John Hoode's death had not moved him, save in the way of a passing amazement. Anthony had seen too much of death to shed tears over a man he had never known. And the

Minister of Imperial Finance, brilliant though he had been, had never seized the affections of the people in the manner of a Joe Chamberlain.

Passing through Halsemere, Anthony, muttering happily to himself: "Now, who *did* kill Cock Robin?" was struck by a horrid thought. Suppose there should be no mystery! Suppose, as Hastings had suggested, that the murderer had already delivered himself.

Then he dismissed the idea. A Cabinet Minister murdered without a mystery? Impossible! All the canons were against it.

He took his car along at some speed. By ten minutes to eight he had reached the Bear and Key in Marling High Street, demanded a room and breakfast, and had been led upstairs by a garrulous landlord.

2

Bathed, shaved, freshly-clothed and full of breakfast, Anthony uncurled his lean length from the best chair in the inn's parlour, lit his pipe, and sought the garden.

Outside the door he encountered the landlord, made inquiry as to the shortest way to Abbotshall, and, placidly puffing at his pipe, watched with enjoyment the effect of his question.

The eyes of Mr. Josiah Syme flashed with the fire of curiosity.

" 'Scuse me, sir," he wheezed, "but 'ave you come down along o' this—along o' these *'appenings* up at the 'ouse?"

"Hardly," said Anthony.

Mr. Syme tried again. "Be you a 'tective, sir?" he asked in a conspiratorial wheeze. "If so, Joe Syme might be able to 'elp ye." He leant forward and added in yet a lower whisper: "My eldest gel, she's an 'ousemaid up along at Abbotshall."

"Is she indeed," said Anthony. "Wait here till I get my hat; then we'll walk along together. You can show me the way."

"Then—then—you are a 'tective, sir."

"What exactly I am," said Anthony, "God Himself may know. I do not. But you can make five pounds if you want it."

Mr. Syme understood enough.

As they walked, first along the white road, then through fields and finally along the bank of that rushing, fussy, barely twenty-yard-wide little river, the Marle, Mr. Syme told what he knew.

Purged of repetitions, biographical meanderings, and excursions into rustic theorising, the story was this:

Soon after eleven on the night before, Miss Laura Hoode had entered her brother's study and found him lying, dead and mutilated, on the hearth. Exactly what the wounds were, Mr. Syme could not say; but by common report they were sufficiently horrible.

Before she fainted, Miss Hoode screamed. When other members of the household arrived they found her lying across her brother's body. A search-party was at once instituted for possible murderers, and the police and a doctor notified. People were saying— Mr. Syme became confidential—that Miss Hoode's mind had been unhinged by the shock. Nothing was yet *known* as to the identity of the criminal, but Mr. Syme gave vent to many a dark suggestion, implicating in turn every member of the household save his daughter.

Anthony dammed the flow with a question. "Can you tell me," he asked, "exactly who's living in the house?"

Mr. Syme grew voluble at once. At the present moment there were Miss Hoode, two friends of the late Mr. Hoode's, and the servants and the young gent—Mr. Deacon—what had been the corpse's secretary. The names? Oh, yes, he could give the names all right. Servants—his daughter Elsie, housemaid; Mabel Smith, another housemaid; Martha Forrest, the cook; Lily Ingram, kitchen-maid; Annie Holt, parlour-maid; old Mr. Poole, the butler; Bob Belford, the other man-servant. Then there was Tom Diggle, the gardener, though he'd been in the cottage hospital for the last week and wasn't out yet. And there was the chauffeur, Harry Wright. Of course, though, now he came to think of it, the gardener and the chauffeur didn't rightly *live* in the house, they shared the lodge.

"And the two guests?" said Anthony. It is hard to believe, but he had assimilated that stream of names, had even correctly assigned to each the status and duties of its owner.

"One gent, and one lady, sir. Oh, and there's the lady's own maid, sir. Girl with some Frenchy name. Duboise, would it be?" Mr. Syme was patently proud of his infallibility. "Mrs. Mainwaring the lady's called—she's a tall, 'andsome lady with goldy-like sort of 'air, sir. And the gent's Sir Arthur Digby-Coates— and a very pleasant gent he is, sir, so Elsie says."

Anthony gave a start of pleasure. Digby-Coates was an acquaintance of his private-secretarial days. Digby-Coates might be useful. Hastings hadn't told him.

"There be Habbotshall, sir," said Mr. Syme.

Anthony looked up. On his left—they had been walking with the little Marle on their right—was a well-groomed, smiling garden, whose flower-beds, paths, pergolas, and lawns stretched up to the feet of one of the strangest houses within his memory.

For it was low and rambling and shaped like a capital L pushed over on its side. Mainly, it was two stories high, but on the extreme end of the right arm of the recumbent L there had been built an additional floor. This gave it a gay, elfin humpiness that attracted Anthony strangely. Many-hued clouds of creeper spread in beautiful disorder from ground to half-hidden chimney-stacks. Through the leaves peeped leaded windows, as a wood-fairy might spy through her hair at the woodcutter's son who was really a prince. A flagged walk bordered by a low yew hedge ran before the house; up to this led a flight of stone steps from the lower level of the lawns. Opposite the head of the steps was a verandah.

"This here, sir," explained Mr. Syme unnecessarily, "is rightly the back of the 'ouse."

Anthony gave him his congé and a five-pound note, hinting that his own presence at Marling should not be used as a fount for bar-room gossip. Mr. Syme walked away with a gait quaintly combining the stealth of a conspirator and the alertness of a great detective.

Anthony turned in at the little gate and made for the house. At the head of the steps before the verandah he paused. Voices came to his ear. The tone of the louder induced him to walk away from the verandah and along the house to his right. He halted by the first ground-floor window and listened, peering into the room.

Inside stood two men, one a little, round-shouldered, black-coated fellow with a dead-white face and hands that twisted nervously; the other tall, burly, crimson-faced, fierce-moustached clad in police blue with the three stripes of a sergeant on his arm.

It was the policeman's voice that had attracted Anthony's attention. Now it was raised again, more loudly than before.

"You know a blasted sight more than you says," it roared.

The other quivered, lifted a shaking hand to his mouth, and cast a hunted look round the room. He seemed, thought Anthony, remarkably like a ferret.

"I don't, sergeant. Re-really I d-don't," he stammered.

The sergeant thrust his great face down into that of his victim. "I don't believe you this mornin' any more'n I did last night,"

he bellowed. "Now, Belford, me lad, you tell me what you're
hidin'. *All* of it—or it'll be the worse for you!"

Anthony leaned his arms on the window-sill and thrust head
and shoulders into the room.

"Now, sergeant," he said, "this sort of thing'll never do, you
know."

The effect of his intrusion tickled pleasantly his sense of the
dramatic. Law and Order recovered first, advanced, big with rage,
to the window and demanded the meaning of the intrusion.

"Why," said Anthony, "shall we call it a wish to study at close
quarters the methods of the County Constabulary."

"And just 'oo may you be?" The face of Sergeant Higgins was
dark with wrath.

"I," said Anthony, "am Hawkshaw, the detective!"

Before another roar could break from outraged officialdom,
the door of the room opened. A thick-set, middle-aged man of a
grocerish air inquired briskly what was the trouble here.

Sergeant Higgins became on the instant a meek subordinate. "I
—I didn't know you were—were about, sir." He stood stiff at
attention. "Just questioning of a few witnesses, I was, sir. This
er—gentleman"—he nodded in the direction of Anthony—"just
pushed his 'ead——"

But Superintendent Boyd of the C.I.D. was shaking the interloper by the hand. He had recognised the head and shoulders as
those of Colonel Gethryn. Once, in war days, he had been "lent" to
Colonel Gethryn in connection with a great and secret round-up in
and about London. For Colonel Gethryn Superintendent Boyd had
liking and a deep respect.

"Well, well, sir," he said, beaming. "Fancy seeing you. They
didn't tell me you were staying here."

"I'm not," Anthony said. Then added, seeing the look of bewilderment: "I don't quite know what I am, Boyd. You may have
to turn me away. I think I'd better see Miss Hoode before I
commit myself."

He swung his long legs into the room, patted the doubtful Boyd
on the shoulder, sauntered to the door, opened it and passed
through. Turning to his right, he collided sharply with another
man. A person this, of between forty and fifty, dressed tastefully
in light gray; broad-shouldered, virile, with a kindly face marked
with lines of fatigue and mental stress. Anthony recoiled from the
shock of the collision. The other stared.

"Good God!" he exclaimed.

"You exaggerate, Sir Arthur," said Anthony.

Sir Arthur Digby-Coates recovered himself. "The most amazing coincidence that ever happened, Gethryn," he said. "I was just thinking of you."

"Really?" Anthony was surprised.

"Yes, yes. I suppose you've heard? You must have. Poor Hoode!"

"Of course. That's why I'm here."

"But I thought you'd left——"

"Oh, yes," said Anthony, "I've left the Service. Quite a time ago. I'm here because—look here, this'll sound rot if I try to explain in a hurry. Can we go and sit somewhere where we can talk?"

"Certainly, my boy, certainly. I'm very glad indeed to see you, Gethryn. Very glad. This is a terrible, an awful affair—and, well, I think we could do with your help. You see, I feel responsible for seeing that *everything's* done that can be. It may seem strange to you, Gethryn, the way I'm taking charge like this; but John and I were—well ever since we were children we've been more like brothers than most real ones. I don't think a week's passed, except once or twice, that we haven't seen—— This way: we can talk better in my room. I've got a sitting-room of my own here, you know. Dear old John——"

3

It was three-quarters of an hour before Anthony descended the stairs; but in that time much had been decided and arranged. So much, in fact, that Anthony marvelled at his luck—a form of mental exercise unusual in him. He was always inclined to take the gifts of the gods as his due.

But this was different. Everything was being made so easy for him. First, here was dear, stolid old Boyd in charge of the case. Next, here was Sir Arthur. As yet they were the merest acquaintances, but the knight had, he knew, for some time been aware of and impressed by the war record of A. R. Gethryn, and had welcomed him to the stricken household. Through Sir Arthur, Miss Hoode—whom Anthony had not seen yet—had been persuaded to accept Anthony, despite his present aura of journalism.

Oh, most undoubtedly, everything was going very well! Now, thought Anthony, for the murderer. This, in spite of its painful side, was all vastly entertaining. Who killed Cock Robin Hoode?

Anthony felt more content than for the last year. It appeared that, after all, there might be interest in life.

In the hall he found Boyd; with him Poole, the butler—a lean, shaking old man—and a burly fellow whom Anthony knew for another of Scotland Yard's Big Four.

Boyd came to meet him. The burly one picked up his hat and sought the front door. The butler vanished.

"I wish you'd tell me, colonel," Boyd asked, "exactly where you come in on this business?"

Anthony smiled. "It's no use, Boyd. I'm not the murderer. But lend me your ears and I'll explain my presence."

As the explanation ended, Boyd's heavy face broke into a smile. He showed none of the chagrin commonly attributed to police detectives when faced with the amateur who is to prove them fools at every turn.

"There's no one I'd rather have with me, colonel," he said. "Of course, it's all very unofficial——"

"That's all right, Boyd. Before I left town I rang up Mr. Lucas. He gave me his blessing, and told me to carry on—provided I was accepted by the family."

Boyd looked relieved. "That makes everything quite easy, then. I don't mind telling you that this is a regular puzzler, Colonel Gethryn."

"So I have gathered," Anthony said. "By the way, Boyd, do drop that 'Colonel,' there's a good Inspector. If you love me, call me mister, call me mister, Boydie dear."

Boyd laughed. He found Anthony refreshingly unofficial. "Very well, sir. Now, if we may, let's get down to business. I suppose you've heard roughly what happened?"

"Yes."

"Much detail?"

"A wealth. None germane."

Boyd was pleased. He knew this laconic mood of Anthony's; it meant business. He was pleased because at present he felt himself out of his depth in the case. He produced from his breast-pocket a notebook.

"Here are some notes I've made, sir," he said. "You won't be able to read 'em, so let me give you an edited version."

"Do. But let's sit down first."

They did so, on a small couch before the big fireplace.

Boyd began his tale. "I've questioned every one in the house except Miss Hoode," he said. "I'll tackle her when she's better, probably this afternoon. But beyond the fact that she was the first one to see the body, I don't think she'll be much use. Now the facts. After supp—dinner, that is, last night, Mr. Hoode, Miss Hoode, Mrs. Mainwaring and Sir Arthur Digby-Coates played bridge in the drawing-room. They finished the meal at eight-thirty, began the cards at nine and finished the game at about ten. Miss Hoode then said good-night and went to her bedroom; so did the other lady. Sir Arthur went to his own sitting-room to work, and the deceased retired to his study for the same purpose."

"No originality!" said Anthony plaintively. "It's all exactly the same. Ever read detective stories, Boyd? They're always killed in their studies. Always! Ever notice that?"

Boyd—perhaps a little shocked by the apparent levity—only shook his head. He went on: "That's the study door over there, sir, the only door on the right side of the hall, you see. That little room just opposite to it—the one you climbed into this morning—is a sort of den for that old boy Poole, the butler. Poole says that from about nine-forty-five until the murder was discovered he sat in there, reading and thinking. *And* he had the door open all the time. *And* he was facing the door. *And* he swears that no one entered the study by that door during the whole of that time."

"Mr. Poole is most convenient," murmured Anthony. He was lying back, his legs stretched out before him.

Boyd looked at him curiously. But the thin face was in shadow, and the greenish eyes were veiled by their lids. A silence fell.

Anthony broke it. "Going to arrest Poole just yet?" he asked.

Boyd smiled. "No, sir. I suppose you're thinking Poole knows too much. Got his story too pat, so to speak."

"Something of the sort. Never mind, though. On with the tale, my Boyd."

"No, Poole's not my man. By all accounts he was devoted to his master. That's one thing. Another is that his right arm's practically useless with rheumatism and that he's infirm—with an absolute minimum of physical strength for his job, so to speak. That proves he's not the man, even if other things were against him, which they're not. You'll know why when I take you into that room there, sir." The detective nodded his head in the direction of the study door.

"Well," he continued, "taking Poole, for the present at any rate, as a reliable witness, we know that the murderer didn't enter by the door. The chimney's impossible because it's too small and the register's down; so he must have got in through the window."

"Which of how many?" Anthony asked, still in that sleepy tone.

"The one farthest from the door and facing the garden, sir. The room's got windows on all three sides—three on the garden side, one in the end wall, and two facing the drive; but only one of 'em —the one I said—was open."

Anthony opened his eyes. "But how sultry!" he complained.

"I know, sir. That's what I thought. And in this hot weather and all. But there's an explanation. The deceased always had them— those windows—shut all day in the hot weather, and the blinds down. He knew a thing or two, you see. But he always used to open 'em himself at night, when he went in there to work. I suppose last night he must have been in a great hurry or something, and only opened one of 'em." He looked across at Anthony for approval of his reasoning, then continued: "But the queer thing is, sir, that open window shows no traces of anything—no scratches, no marks, no nothing. Nor does the flower-bed under it either."

"Any finger-prints anywhere on anything?" said Anthony.

"None anywhere in the room but the deceased's—except on one thing. I've sent that up to the Yard—Jardine's taken it—for the experts to photograph. I'll have the prints sometime this afternoon I should think." Boyd's tone was mysterious.

Anthony looked at him. "Out with it, Boyd. You're like a boy with a surprise for daddy."

"As a matter of fact, sir," Boyd laughed, rather shamefacedly, "it's the *materia mortis,* so to speak."

"So you've found the ber-loodstained weapon. Boyd, I congratulate you. What was it? And whose are the finger-prints?"

"The weapon used, sir, was a large wood-rasp, and a very nasty weapon it must have made. As for the finger-prints, I don't know yet. And it's my firm belief we shan't be much wiser when we've got the enlargements—not even if we were to compare 'em with all the prints of all the fingers for miles round. I don't know what it is, sir, but this case has got a nasty, puzzling sort of feel about it, so to speak."

"A wood-rasp, eh?" mused Anthony. "Not very enlightening. Doesn't belong to the house, I suppose?"

"As far as I can find out, sir, most certainly not." Boyd's tone was gloomy.

"H'mm! Well, let us advance. We've absolved the aged Poole; but what about the rest of the household?" Anthony spread out his long fingers and ticked off each name as he spoke. "Miss Hoode, Mrs. Mainwaring, her maid Duboise, Sir Arthur, Elsie Syme, Mabel Smith, Maggie—no, Martha Forrest, Lily Ingram, Annie Holt, Belford, Harry Wright. Any of them do? The horticultural Mr. Diggle's in hospital and therefore out of it, I suppose."

Boyd stared amazement. "Good Lord, sir!" he exclaimed, "you've got 'em off pat enough. Have you been talking to them?"

"Preserve absolute calm, Boyd; I have not been talking to them. I got their dreadful names from an outsider. Anyhow, what about them?"

Boyd shook his head. "Nothing, sir."

"All got confused but trustworthy alibis? That it?"

"Yes, sir, more or less; some of the alibis are clear as glass. To tell you the truth, I don't suspect any one in the house. Some of the servants have got 'confused alibis' as you call it, but they're all obviously all right. That's the servants; it's the same only more so with the others. Take the secretary, Mr. Deacon; he was up there in his room the whole time. There's one, p'r'aps two witnesses to prove it. The same with Miss Hoode. And the other lady; to be sure she's got no witnesses, but that murder wasn't her job, nor any woman's. Take Sir Arthur, it's the same thing again. Even if there was anything suspicious—which there wasn't—about his relations with the deceased, you can't suspect a man who was, to the actual knowledge of five or six witnesses who saw him, sitting upstairs in his room during the only possible time when the murder can have been done.

"No, sir!" Boyd shook his head with vigour. "It's no good looking in the house. Take it from me."

"I will, Boyd; for the present anyhow." Anthony rose and stretched himself. "Can I see the study?"

Boyd jumped up with alacrity. "You can, sir. We've been in there a lot, taking photos, etcetera; but it's untouched—just as it was when they found the body."

CHAPTER FOUR

THE STUDY

Once across the threshold of the dead minister's study, Anthony experienced a change of feeling, of mental attitude. Until now he had looked at the whole business in his usual detached and semi-satirical way; the reasons for his presence at Abbotshall had been two only—affection for Spencer Hastings and desire to satisfy that insistent craving for some definite and difficult task to perform. He had even felt, at intervals throughout the morning, a wish to laugh.

But, now, fairly in the room, this aloofness failed him. It was not that he felt any sudden surge of personal regret. It was rather that, for him at least, despite the sunlight which blazed incongruously in every corner, some cold, dark beastliness brooded everywhere.

The big room was gay with chintz and as yet unfaded flowers of the day before; the solid furniture was of some beauty—in fact, a charming room. Yet Anthony shivered even before he had seen the shrouded thing lying grotesque upon the hearth. When he did see it, the sight shook him out of the nightmare of dark fancy, and he stepped forward to look more closely.

Came the sound of a commotion from the hall. With a muttered excuse, Boyd went quickly from the room. Anthony knelt to examine the body, turning back the sheet which covered it.

It sprawled upon the hearth-rug, legs towards the window in the opposite wall. The red-tiled edge of the open grate forced up the neck. The almost hairless head was dreadfully battered; crossed and re-crossed by five or six gaping gashes, each nearly half an inch wide and an inch or so deep. Of the scalp little remained but islands and peninsulas of skin and bone streaked with the dark brown of dried blood, among it ribands of gray film where the brain had oozed from the wounds.

The body was untouched, though the clothes were rumpled and twisted. The right arm was outstretched, the rigid fingers of the hand resting among the pots of fern which filled the fireplace. The left arm was doubled under the body.

Pulling the sheet back into place, Anthony stood up; and as he did so, Boyd re-entered. He looked flushed and not a little annoyed.

Anthony turned to him, raising his eyebrows.

"Only a bit more trouble with some of these newspaper fellows, sir. But thank the Lord, I've got rid of 'em now. Told 'em I'd give 'em a statement to-night. What they'd say if they knew you were here—and why—God knows. There'll be a row after the case is over, but there you are. Miss Hoode's agreeable to you, and I don't blame her, but she won't hear of any of the others being let in. I don't blame her for that either." He nodded towards the body. "What d'you make of it, sir?"

"Shocking messy kill," Anthony said.

"You're right, sir. But what about—things in general, so to speak?"

Anthony looked round the room. It bore traces of disturbance. Two light chairs had been over-turned. Books and papers from the desk strewed the floor. The grandfather clock, which should have stood sentinel on the left of the door as one entered it, had fallen, though not completely. It lay face-downwards at an angle of some forty-five degrees with the floor, the upper half of its casing supported by the back of a large sofa.

"Struggle?" said Anthony.

"Yes," said Boyd.

"Queer struggle," said Anthony. He sauntered off on a tour of the room.

Boyd watched him curiously as he halted before the sofa, dropped on one knee, and peered up at the face of the reclining clock.

He looked up at Boyd. "Stopped at ten-forty-five. That make the murder fit in with the times the people in the house have told you?"

"Yes, sir."

"When are you going to have the room tidied?"

"Any time now. We've got the photos."

"Right." Anthony got to his feet. "Let us, Boyd, unite our strength and put grand-dad on his feet."

Between them they raised the clock. Anthony opened the case and set the pendulum swinging. A steady tick-tock began at once.

Anthony looked at his watch. "Stopped exactly twelve hours

ago, did grandfather," he said. "Doesn't seem to be damaged, though."

"No, sir. It takes a lot to put those old clocks out of order."

Anthony went back to the front of the sofa and stood looking down at the carpet.

"No finger-prints, you said?"

"Except on the wood-rasp, absolutely none but those of the deceased, sir. I've dusted nearly every inch of the room with white or black. All I got for my pains were four good prints of the deceased's thumb and forefinger. They're easy enough to tell—long scar on the ball of his right thumb."

Anthony changed the subject. "What time did you get here, Boyd?"

"About four this morning. We came by car. I made some preliminary inquiries, questioned some of the people, and went down to the village at about eight."

"Who's that great red hulk of a sergeant?" said Anthony, flitting to yet another subject. "You ought to watch him, Boyd. When I came along he was indulging in a little third degree."

"I heard it, sir. That's why I came in."

"Good. Who was the timid little ferret?"

"Belford—Robert Belford, sir. He's a sort of assistant to Poole and was valet to the deceased."

"How did he answer when you questioned him?"

"Very confused he was. But his story's all right—very reasonable. I don't consider him, so to speak. He hasn't got the nerve, or the strength."

Anthony stroked his chin. "It's easy enough to see," he said, "that you don't want to be persuaded away from your idea that an outsider did this job."

"You're right, sir," Boyd smiled. "As far as I've progressed yet an outsider's my fancy. Most decidedly. Still one never knows where the next turning's going to lead to, so to speak. Of course, I've got a lot of inquiries afoot—but so far we've less than nothing to go on."

"Anything stolen?"

"Nothing."

Anthony was still gazing down at the carpet before the sofa. Again he dropped on one knee. This time he rubbed at the thick pile with his fingers. He rose, darting a look round the room.

"What's up, sir?" Boyd was watching attentively.

"A most convenient struggle that," murmured Anthony.

"What's that? What d'you mean, sir?"

"I was remarking, O Boyd, that the struggle had been, for the murderer, of an almost incredible convenience. Observe that the two chairs which were over-turned are far from heavy; observe also that the carpet is very far from thin. These light chairs fell, not, mark you, on the parquet edging of the floor, but conveniently inwards upon this thickest of thick carpets. Observe also, most *puissant* inspector, that the articles dislodged from the writing-table, besides falling on the carpet, are nothing but light books and papers. Nothing heavy, you see. Nothing which would make a noise."

"If I follow you, sir," Boyd said, "you mean——"

Anthony raised a hand. "I would finally direct your attention to the highly convenient juxtaposition of this sofa here and our friend the clock. The sofa is a solid, stolid lump of a sofa; it's none of your trifling divans. In fact, it would require not merely a sudden jerk but a steady and lusty pull to move it, wouldn't it?"

The detective applied his considerable weight to the arm of the sofa. Nothing happened.

"You see!" continued Anthony with a gesture. "See you also then the almost magical convenience with which, in the course of the struggle, this lumping sofa was moved back towards grandfather, who stood nearly three feet from the sofa's usual position, which position can be ascertained by noting these four deep dents made in the carpet by the castors. Oh, it's all so convenient. The sofa's moved back, then grandfather falls, not with a loud crash to the floor, but quietly, softly, on to the back of the sofa. Further, those two vases on that table there beside the clock weren't upset at all by the upheaval. Those vases wobble when one walks across the room, Boyd. No, it won't do; it won't do at all."

"You're saying there wasn't any struggle at all; that the scene was set, so to speak." Boyd's eyes were alight with interest.

Anthony nodded. "Your inference is right."

"I had explained things to myself by saying that the carpet was thick and old Poole rather deaf," said the detective, "because he did say that he heard a noise like some one walking about. Of course, he just thought it was his master. I'll wager it wasn't, though. I'm sure you're right, sir. I hadn't noticed the sofa had been shifted. This is a very queer case, sir, very queer!"

"It is. Or anyhow it feels like that. What about the body, Boyd? Aren't you going to have it moved?"

"Yes, sir, any time now. It was going to be moved before you came; then Jardine wanted to take some more photos. After that, you being here, sir—well, I thought if you *were* going to have anything to do with the case you might like to see everything in *status quo,* so to speak."

Anthony smiled. "Thanks, Boyd," he said. "You're a good chap, you know. This isn't the first job we've done together by any means; but all the same, it's most refreshing to find you devoid of the pro's righteous distrust of the amateur."

Boyd smiled grimly. "Oh, I've got that all right, sir. But I don't regard you in that light, if I may say so, though we *may* disagree before this case is over. And—well, sir, I've not forgotten what you did for me that night down at Sohlke's place in Limehouse——"

"Drop it, man, drop it," Anthony groaned.

Boyd laughed. "Very well, sir. Now I'll go and see about having the body moved."

"And I," said Anthony, "shall think—here or in the garden. By the way, when's the inquest?"

"To-morrow afternoon, here," said Boyd, and left the room.

Anthony ruminated. This study of Hoode's, he reflected, was curious, being in itself the end of the long wing of the house and having, therefore, window or windows in all three sides. As Boyd had said, only one of these windows was open, the farthest from the door of the three which looked out upon the terraced gardens and the river at their foot. All the others—two in the same wall, one in the end wall, and two overlooking the drive—were shut and latched on the inside. The open one was open top and bottom.

Anthony looked at it, then back at the writing-table. He seemed dissatisfied, for he next walked to the window, surveyed the room from there, and then crossed to the swivel-chair at the writing-table and sat down. From here he again peered at the open window, which was then in front of him and slightly to his left.

He was still in the chair when Boyd came back, bringing with him a policeman in plain clothes and a man in the leather uniform of a chauffeur. Anthony did not move; did not answer when Boyd spoke to him.

The body covered and lifted, the grim little party, Boyd leading, made for the door. As they steered carefully through it, the grandfather clock began to strike the hour. Its deep ring had, it seemed to Anthony, a note ominous and mournful.

The door clicked to behind the men and the shrouded thing they carried. The clock struck again.

"Good for you, grandfather," muttered Anthony, without turning in his chair to look. "I wish to High Heaven you could talk for a moment or two."

"Bong!" went the clock again.

Anthony pulled out his watch. The hands stood at eleven o'clock. "All right, grand-dad," he said. "You needn't say any more. I know the time. I wish you could tell me what happened last night instead of being so damned musical."

The clock went on striking. Anthony wandered to the door, paused, and went back to the writing-table. As he sat down again the clock chimed its final stroke.

He felt a vague discomfort, shook it off and continued his scrutiny of the table. It was of some age, and beautiful in spite of its solidity. The red leather covering of its top had upon it many a stain of wear and inks. Yet one of these stains seemed to Anthony to differ from the general air of the others. He rubbed it with his fingers. It was raised and faintly sticky. It was at the back of the flat part of the table-top. Immediately behind it rose two tiers of drawers and pigeon-holes. Also, its length was bisected by a crack in the wood.

He rubbed at the stain again; then cursed aloud. That vague sense of something wrong in the room, something which did not fit the essential sanity of life, had returned to his head and spoilt these new thoughts.

The door opened and shut. "What's the matter, sir? Puzzled?" Boyd came and stood behind him.

"Yes, dammit!" Anthony swung round impatiently. "This room's getting on my nerves. Either there's something *wrong* in it or I've got complex fan-tods. Never mind that, though. Boyd, I think I'm going to give you still more proof that there was no struggle. Come here."

Boyd came eagerly. Anthony twisted round to face the table again.

"Attend! The body was found over there by the fireplace. If one accepts as true the indications that a struggle took place, the natural inference is that Hoode was overpowered and struck down where he was found. But we have found certain signs that lead us to believe that the struggle was, in fact, no struggle at all, and here, I think, is another which will also show that Hoode's body was dragged over to the hearth after he had been killed."

Boyd grew excited. "How d'you mean, sir?"

"This is what I mean." Anthony pointed to the stain he had

been examining. "Look at this mark here, where my finger is. Doesn't it look different to the others?"

"Can't say that it does to me, sir. I had a look over that table myself and saw nothing out of the ordinary run."

"Well, I beg to differ. It not only looks different, it feels different. I notice these things. I'm *so* psychic!"

Boyd grinned, watching as Anthony opened a penknife and inserted the blade in the lock of the table's middle drawer.

"I think," said Anthony, "that this is one of those old jump locks. Aha! it is." He pulled open the drawer. "Now, *was* that stain different? Voilà! It was."

Boyd peered over Anthony's shoulder. The drawer was a long one, reaching the whole width of the table. In it were notebooks, pencils, half-used scribbling pads, and, at the back, a pile of notepaper and envelopes.

On the white surface of the topmost envelope of the pile was a dark, brownish-red patch of the size, perhaps, of a half-crown. Boyd examined it eagerly.

"You're right, sir!" he cried. "It's blood right enough. I see what you were going to say. This is hardly dry. It must have dripped through that crack where the stain you pointed out was. And the position of that stain is just where the deceased's head would have fallen if he had been sitting in this chair here and had been hit from behind."

"Exactly," said Anthony. "And after the first of those pats on the head Hoode must've been unconscious—if not dead. *Ergo,* if he received the first blow sitting here, as this proves he did, there was no struggle. One doesn't sit down at one's desk to resist a man one thinks is going to kill one, does one? What probably happened is that the murderer—who was never suspected to be such by Hoode—got behind him as he sat here, struck one or all of the blows, and then dragged the body over to the hearth to lend a touch of naturalness to the scene of strife he was going to prepare. He must be a clever devil, Boyd. There's never a stain on the carpet between here and the fireplace. There wouldn't have been on the table either, only he didn't happen to spot it."

The detective nodded. "I agree with you entirely, sir."

But Anthony did not hear him. The *wrong* something was troubling him again. He clutched his head, trying vainly to fix the cause of this feeling.

Boyd tried again. "Well, we know a little more now, sir, anyhow. Quite a case for premeditation, so to speak—thanks to you."

Anthony brought himself back to earth. "Yes, yes," he said. "But hearken again, Boyd. I have yet more to say. Don't wince, I have really. Here it is. Assuming the reliability, as a witness, of Poole, the old retainer, we know the murderer didn't come into this room through the door. Nor could he, as you've explained, have used the chimney. Remains the one window that was open. Observe, O Boyd, that that window is in full view of a man seated at this table. Now one cannot come through a window into a room at a distance of about two yards from a man seated therein at a table without attracting the attention of that man unless that man is asleep."

"I shouldn't think Hoode was asleep, sir."

"Exactly. It is known that he was a hard worker. Further, if I'm not mistaken, he's been more than usually busy just recently —over the new Turkish Agreement. I think we can take it for granted he wasn't asleep when the murderer came in through that window. That leads us to something of real importance, namely, that Hoode was not surprised by the entry of the murderer."

Boyd scratched his head. " 'Fraid I don't quite get you, sir."

Anthony looked at him with benevolence. "To make myself clearer, I'll put it like this: he either (i) expected the murderer— though not, of course, as such—and expected him to enter that way; or (ii) did not expect him to enter that way, but on looking up in surprise saw some one who, though he had entered in that unfamiliar way, was yet so familiar in himself as not to cause Hoode to remain long, if at all, out of his seat. Personally, I think he didn't leave his chair at all. Is not all this well spoken, Boyd?"

"True enough, sir. I think you're quite right again. I should've seen it." Boyd was dejected. "Of the two views you propounded, so to speak, I think the first's the right one. The murderer was an out-sider, but one the deceased was expecting—and by that entrance."

"And I," said Anthony, "incline strongly toward my second theory of the unconventional entry of the familiar."

Boyd shook his head. "You'd hardly credit it, sir," he said solemnly, "but some of these big men get up to very funny games. I've had over twenty years in the C.I.D., and I know."

"The mistake you're making in this case, Boyd," Anthony said, "is thinking of it as like all your others. From what little I've seen so far of this affair it's much more like a novel than real life, which is mostly dull and hardly ever true. As I asked you before, d'you ever read real detective stories? Gaboriau, for instance?"

"Lord, no, sir!" smiled the real detective.

"You should."

"Pardon me, sir, but you're a knock-out at this game yourself and it makes me wonder, so to speak, how you can hold with all that 'tec-tale truck."

"A knock-out? Me?" Anthony laughed. "And I feel as futile as if I were Sherlock Holmes trying to solve a case of Lecoq's." He put a hand to his head. "There's something about this room that's haunting me! What is the damned thing? Boyd, there's something *wrong* about the blasted place, I tell you!"

Boyd looked bewildered. "I don't know what you mean, sir." Then, to humour this eccentric, he added: "Ah! if only this furniture could tell us what it saw last night."

"I said that to the clock," said Anthony morosely. Then suddenly: "The clock, the clock! Grandpa *did* tell me something! I knew I'd seen or heard something that was utterly wrong, insane. The clock! Good God Almighty! What a fool not to think of it before!"

Boyd became alarmed. His tone was soothing. "What about the clock, sir?"

"It struck. D'you remember it beginning when you were taking the body away?"

"Yes." Boyd was all mystification.

"What time was that?"

"Why, eleven, of course, sir."

"Yes, it was, my uncanny Scot. But grandfather said twelve. I was thinking about something else. I must have counted the strokes unconsciously."

"But—but—are you *sure* it struck twelve when"—Boyd glanced up at the old clock—"when it said eleven?"

Anthony crossed the room, opened the glass casing of the clock-face, and moved the hands on fifteen minutes. They stood then at twelve.

"Bong!" went the clock.

They waited. It did not strike again.

Anthony was triumphant. "There you are, Boyd! Grandpa looks twelve and says one. There's another strand of that rope you're making for the murderer. Miss Hoode came in here at eleven-ten, to find the murder done and the murderer gone. Your time's almost fixed for you. He wasn't here at eleven-ten, but he was here after eleven, because, to put the striking of that clock out as it is, the murderer must have put back the hands after the hour—

eleven, that is—had struck. If he'd done it before the striking had begun, grand-dad wouldn't be telling lies the way he is."

Boyd's expression was a mixture of elation and doubt. "I suppose that's right, sir," he said. "About the striking, I mean. Yes, of course it is; just for the moment I was a bit confused, so to speak. Couldn't work out which way the mistake would come."

"It seems to me," said Anthony, "that the whole reason he faked this elaborate struggle scene was in order that the clock could be stopped under what would seem natural circumstances. But why, having stopped the clock, did he alter it? Two reasons occur to me. One is that he merely wished to make it seem that the murder was done at any other time except when it really was. That's rather weak, and I prefer my second idea. That is, that the time to which he moved the hands has a significance and wasn't merely a chance shot. In other words, he set the thing at ten-forty-five because he had a nice clean alibi for that time. Judging by the rest of his work he's a man of brains; and that would've been a pretty little safeguard—if only he hadn't made that mistake about the striking."

"They all make bloomers—one time or another, sir. That's how we catch 'em in the main."

"I know." Anthony's tone was less sure than a moment before. "All the same it's a damn' silly mistake. Doesn't seem to fit in somehow. I'd expected better things from him."

"Oh, I don't know, sir. He'd probably got the wind up, as they say, by the time he'd got so near finishing."

Anthony shrugged. "Yes, I suppose you're right. By the way, Boyd, tell me this. How did Miss Hoode come to be downstairs at ten past eleven? I thought she was supposed to have gone to bye-bye after that game of cards."

"As far as I know—I haven't been able to see her yet, sir—she came down to use the telephone—not this one but the one in the hall—about some minor affair she'd forgotten during the day. After she'd finished phoning she must've wanted to speak to her brother. Probably about the same matter. That's all, sir."

"It's so weak," said Anthony, "that it might possibly be true." Then, after a pause: "I think I've had about enough of this tomb. What you going to do next, Boyd? I'm for the garden." He walked to the door. "You took the weaker end of my reasoning if you still believe in the mysterious outsider."

Boyd followed across the hall, through the verandah and down the steps which led from the flagged walk behind the house to the lawns below.

Anthony sat himself down upon a wooden seat set in the shade of a great tree. He showed little inclination for argument.

But Boyd was stubborn. "You know, sir," he said, "you're wrong in what you say about the 'insider.' You'd agree with me if you'd been here long enough to sift what evidence there is and been able the way I have to see *and* talk to all the people instead of hearing about them sketchy and second-hand as it were."

Anthony looked at him. "There's certainly something in that, Boyd. But it'll take a lot to shift me. Mind you, my predilection for the 'insider' isn't a conviction. But it's my fancy—and strong."

Boyd fumbled in his breast-pocket. "Then you just take a good look at this, sir." He held out some folded sheets of foolscap. "I made that out before you got here this morning. It'll tell you better what I mean than I can talking. And I only sketched the thing to you before."

Anthony unfolded the sheet, and read:—

SUMMARY OF INFORMATION ELICITED

1. MISS LAURA HOODE.—Played cards until 10 o'clock with the deceased, Sir A. D.-C., and Mrs. Mainwaring. Then went to bed. Was seen in bed at approximately 10.30 by Annie Holt, parlour-maid, who was called into room to take some order as she passed on her way to the servants' quarters. Miss Hoode remembered, at about 11.05, urgent telephone call to be made. Got up, went downstairs to phone, then thought she would consult deceased first. Entered study, at 11.10, and discovered body. [*Note.*—By no means a complete alibi; but it seems quite out of the question that this lady is in any way concerned. She is distraught at brother's death and was known to be a devoted sister. They were, as always, the best of friends during day.]

N.B.—It appears impossible for a woman to have committed this crime, since the necessary power to inflict blows such as caused death of deceased would be that of an unusually powerful man.

2. MRS. R. MAINWARING.—Retired at same time as Miss Hoode. Was seen in bed by her maid, Elsie Duboise, at 10.35. Was waked out of heavy sleep by parlour-maid, Annie Holt, after discovery of body of deceased.

3. ELSIE DUBOISE.—This girl sleeps in room communicating

with Mrs. Mainwaring's. The night was hot and the door between the two rooms was left open. Mrs. Mainwaring heard
the girl get into bed at about 10.40. The parlour-maid had
to shake her repeatedly before she woke.

4. SIR A. DIGBY-COATES.—Went upstairs, after cards, to
own sitting-room (first-floor, adjoining bedroom) to work at
official papers. Pinned note on door asking not to be disturbed,
but had to leave door open owing to heat. Was seen, from
passage, between time he entered room until time murder was
discovered, at intervals averaging a very few minutes by
Martha Forrest (cook), Annie Holt (parlour-maid), R.
Belford (man-servant), Elsie Duboise, Mabel Smith (housemaid), and Elsie Syme (housemaid). The time during which
the murder must have been committed is covered.

5. MR. A. B. T. DEACON (Private Secretary to deceased).—
Went to room (adjoining that of Sir A. D.-C.) to read at
approximately 10.10. Was seen entering by Mabel Smith,
who was working in linen-room immediately opposite. She
had had afternoon off and was consequently very busy. Stayed
there till immediately (say two minutes) before murder was
discovered. She can swear Mr. Deacon never left room the
whole time, having had to leave door of linen-room open owing to heat.

6. WOMEN SERVANTS.—These are Elsie Syme, Mabel Smith,
Martha Forrest, Annie Holt, Lily Ingram. All except the
first two account for each other over the vital times, having
been in the servants' quarters (in which the rooms are inter-
communicating) from 10.15 or so onwards. Elsie Syme, who
was downstairs in the servants' hall until the murder was
discovered, and Mabel Smith, may be disregarded. They have
no one to substantiate their statements, but there is no doubt
at all that they are ordinary, foolish, honest working-girls.
(See also note after details re Miss Hoode.)

7. ALFRED POOLE (Butler).—Has not a shred of alibi.
Was seated, as usual, in his den opposite study all the evening. After 10 spoke to no one; was seen by nobody. May,
however, be disregarded as in any way connected with murder. Will be very useful witness. May (in my opinion) be
trusted implicitly. Not very intelligent. Very old, infirm, but
sufficiently capable to answer questions truthfully and
clearly. Was devoted to deceased, whose family he has served
for forty-one years.

8.   ROBERT BELFORD (Man-servant).—Has certain support
for his own account of his actions; but not enough probably
for fuller test. Nothing against him, and last man in world
for crime of this type. Might possibly poison, but has neither
courage nor strength enough to have murdered deceased.
Seems nervous. *May* know more than he admits, but unlikely.
9.   OTHER MEN-SERVANTS.—Harry Wright, chauffeur, and
Thomas Diggle, gardener. Both not concerned. Diggle is in
hospital. Wright, who lives in the lodge by the big gates, was
off last night and with reputable friends in Marling village.
He did not return until some time after murder had been
discovered. The three lads who work under Diggle live in
their homes in the village. All were at home from eight
o'clock onwards last night.

Anthony, having reached the end, read through the document
again, more slowly this time. Boyd watched him eagerly. At last
the papers were handed back to their owner.

"Well, sir," he said. "See what I mean?"

"I do, Boyd, I do. But that doesn't necessarily mean I agree,
you know."

Boyd's face fell. "Ah, sir, I know what it is. You're wondering
at an old hand like me trying to prove to you that nobody in the
house could've done it, when all the time most of 'em haven't
got what you might call sound alibis at all. But look here, sir——"

Anthony got to his feet. "Boyd, you wrong me! I like your
guesses even better than your proofs. Guesses are nearly always
as good as arithmetic—especially guesses by one of your experience.
I didn't say I didn't agree with you, did I?"

"You didn't *say* so, sir, so to speak!"

"And I didn't mean it either." Anthony laughed. "My mind's
open, Boyd, open. Anyhow, many thanks for letting me see
that. I know a lot more detail than I did. I suppose that's a basis
for a preliminary report, what?"

Boyd nodded, and fell into step as Anthony turned in the direction of the house.

CHAPTER FIVE

THE LADY OF THE SANDAL

1

Anthony was still in the garden. Anthony had found something. Clouds of pipe-smoke hung round his head in the hot, still air. Anthony was thinking.

He was alone. Boyd, indefatigable, had gone at once into the house, bent upon another orgy of shrewd questioning. This time his questions would have, in the light of what the study had told, a more definite bearing.

What Anthony had found were two sets, some eighteen inches apart, of four deep, round impressions each roughly the size of a shilling. They were in the broad flower-bed which ran the whole length of the study wall and were directly beneath the sill of the most easterly of the three windows—the farther closed window, that is, from the open one through which it seemed that the murderer must have effected entrance to the study. The flower-bed, Anthony noticed, was unusually broad—so broad, in fact, that any person, unless he were a giant, wishing to climb into any of the three windows, would perforce tread, with one foot at least, among the flowers.

He stooped to examine his find. Whoever, in the absence of Mr. Diggle the gardener, had so lavishly watered the flower-bed on the previous day received his blessing. Had the soil not been so moist, those holes would not have been there.

Anthony thought aloud: "Finger-holes. Just where my fingers would go if I was a good deal narrower across the shoulders and squatted here and tried to look into the room without bringing either of my feet on to the bed."

He stepped deliberately on to the flower-bed and bent to examine the low sill of the window. There was a smudge on the rough stone. It might be a dried smear of earthy fingers. On the other hand, it might be almost anything else. But as he straightened his back a bluish-black gleam caught his eye.

He investigated, and found, hanging from a crevice in the rough edge of the sill, a woman's hair. It was a long hair, and jet black.

"That explains the closeness of those finger-marks," he muttered. "A woman in the case, eh? Now, why was she here, in front of the closed window? And was she here last night? Or this morning, quite innocent like? The odds are it was last night. One doesn't crouch outside a Cabinet Minister's window in daylight. Nor at all, unless one's up to no good. No, I think you were here last night, my black beauty. I love little kitten, her hair is so black, and if I don't catch her she'll never come back. Now where did you come from, Blackie dear? And have you left any other cards? O, Shades of Baker Street!"

He stepped back on to the path and knelt to examine the stone edging to the flower-bed. In the position she must have been in, the woman would most probably, he argued, have been on one knee and had the foot of the other leg pressed vertically against this edging.

She had; but Anthony was doubly surprised at what he found. For why, in this dry weather, should the mark of her foot be there at all? And, as it was there, why should it look like a finger-print a hundred times enlarged?

He scratched his head. This was indeed a crazy business. Perhaps he was off the rails. Still, he'd better go on. This all *might* have something to do with the case.

More closely he examined this footprint that was like a finger-print. Now he understood. The mark had remained because the peculiar sole of this peculiar shoe had been wet and earthy. There had been no rain for a week. Why was the shoe wet? And why —he looked carefully about—were there no other such marks on the flagstones of the path? Ah, yes; that would be because in ordinary walking or running the peculiar shoes did not press hard enough to leave anything but a wet patch which would quickly dry. Whereas, in pressing the sole of the foot against that edging to the flower-bed, much more force would have to be used to retain balance—sufficient force to squeeze wet clayish earth out in a pattern from that peculiar sole.

But what about the wetness? He hadn't settled that. Suddenly his mind connected the peculiarity of that imprint with the idea of water. A rope-soled sandal. When used? Why, swimming. Here Anthony laughed aloud. "Sleuth, you surpass yourself!" he murmured. "Minister murdered by Bathing Belle—only not at the seaside! Cock Robin's murderer not Sparrow as at first believed, but one W. Wagtail! Gethryn, you're fatuous. Take to crochet."

He started for the verandah door. Half-way he stopped, suddenly. He'd forgotten the river. But the idea was ridiculous. But, after all—well, he'd spend ten minutes on it, anyhow. Now, to begin—assuming that the woman *had* come out of the river and had wanted (strange creature!) to get back there—he would work out her most probable route and follow it. If within five minutes he had found no more signs of her, he'd stop.

After a moment's calculation he started off, going through the opening in the yew hedge, down the grass bank to his right and then crossing the rose garden at whose far side there began a pergola.

At the entrance to the pergola he found, caught round a thorny stem of the rose-creeper that fell from the first cross-piece of the archway, four long black hairs.

Anthony controlled his elation. These might not, he thought, be from the same head. But all the same it was encouraging. It fitted well. Running in the dark and a panic, she hadn't ducked low enough. He could see her tearing to free her hair. Well, he'd get on. But really this mad idea about swimming women *couldn't* be true.

From the other end of the pergola he emerged on to a lawn, its centre marked by a small but active fountain. A gravelled path, along which he remembered having walked up to the house, ran down at the right of the grass to the gate on the river-bank through which he had entered. He paused to consider the position; then decided that one making in a hurry for the gate would cut across the grass.

He found confirmation. Round the fountain's inadequate basin was a circle of wet grass, its deep green in refreshing contrast to the faded colour of the rest. At the edge of the emerald oasis were two indistinct imprints of the sandal and its fellow, and two long smeared scars where the grass had been torn up to expose the soil beneath. Farther on, but still within the circle, were two deeper, round impressions; beyond them, just where the wet grass ended, was another long smear.

Anthony diagnosed a slip, a stagger, and a fall. Not looking for more signs—he had enough—he hurried on to the little gate. The other side of it, on the path which ran alongside the blustering pigmy of a river, he hesitated, looking about him. Again he felt doubt. Was it likely that any one would swim the Marle at night? Most decidedly it was not. In the first place there was, only some three hundred and fifty yards or so downstream to his right, a perfectly good bridge, which joined the two halves of the village of Marling. In the second place, the Marle, though here a bare twenty yards wide, seemed as uncomfortable a swim as could well be, even for a man. Always turbulent, it was at present actually dangerous, still swollen as it was by the months of heavy rain which had preceded this record-breaking August.

"No!" said Anthony aloud. "I'm mad, that's what it is. But then those *are* bathing sandals. *And* didn't I just now tell Boyd he was making a mistake in not treating this business like a detective story?"

He stood looking over the river. If only he could fit any sort of reason——

One came to him. He laughed at it; but it intrigued him. It intrigued him vastly. There was a house, just one house, on the opposite bank. It was perhaps thirty yards higher up the stream than the gate by which he was standing.

Suppose someone from that house wanted to get to Abbotshall quickly, so quickly that they could not afford to travel the quarter-mile on each side of the river which crossing by the bridge would involve. Taking that as an hypothesis, he had a reason for these natatory shenanigans. The theory was insane, of course, but why not let fancy lead him a while?

The very fact that the woman was so good a swimmer as she must be, made it probable that she would be sufficiently water-wise to make use of, rather than battle helplessly against, the eight-mile-an-hour stream. Very well, then, before taking to the river, on her way back she would have run upstream along this bank to a point some way above the house she wished to return to on the opposite bank.

Still laughing at himself, Anthony turned to his left and walked upstream, his eyes on the soft clay at the river's edge. When he had passed by fifty yards the house on the other side, he found two sandal-marks. They were deep; the clay gave a perfect impression.

He was surprised but still unbelieving. Then, as he stood for a moment looking down into the dark water only a few inches below the level of his feet, a gleam of white caught his eye. Curious, he squatted, pulled up his sleeve and thrust his arm into the water, groping about the ledge which jutted out from the bank some inches below the surface. His fingers found what they sought. He rose to his feet and examined his catch.

A small canvas bathing-sandal. From its uppers dangled a broken piece of tape. The sole was of rope.

"Benjamin," said Anthony to his pipe, "I'm right. And I've never been so surprised in my life. Where's my 'insider' now?"

2

Anthony had crossed the river. Behind him lay Marling's wooden bridge, before him the house which must shelter the swimming lady. In his hip-pocket rested the sandal, wrung free of some of its wetness and wrapped in a piece of newspaper found by the hedge.

He walked slowly, framing pretexts for gaining admission to the house. His thoughts were interrupted by a hail. He swung round to see Sir Arthur Digby-Coates coming at a fast walk from the direction of the bridge.

Sir Arthur arrived out of breath. "Hallo, my boy, hallo," he gasped. "What are you doing here? Calling on Lucia? Didn't know you knew her."

"I don't. Lucia who?"

"Mrs. Lemesurier. That's her house there. Just going there myself."

"I'll walk along to the gate with you," said Anthony. He saw a possible invitation. He began to make talk. "I wasn't going anywhere; just strolling. I wanted to get away from Abbotshall and think. After I left the study, I drifted through the garden and crossed the river without knowing I'd done it." Not even to Sir Arthur was he saying anything yet of his discoveries.

The elder man picked his remarks up eagerly. "You've hit on something to think about, then? That's more than I've done, though I've been racking my brains since midnight. That detective fellow don't seem much better off either."

"Oh, Boyd's a very good man," Anthony said. "He generally gets somewhere."

"Well, I hope so." Sir Arthur sighed. "This is a terrible business, Gethryn. Terrible! I can't talk much about it yet—poor old John. Did you know him at all?"

"No. Shook hands with him once at some feed, that's all."

"You'd have liked him, Gethryn. He—we'd best not talk about it. God! What an outcry there'll be—is already, in fact."

"Yes," said Anthony. "A blow to England and a boon to Fleet

Street. Look here, don't let me keep you. I hope Mrs.—Mrs. Lemesurier appreciates the beauty of her house."

"Charming, isn't it? Gleason built it, you know." He paused, and Anthony feared his bait unswallowed.

They had arrived at the gate to the garden. Over the hedge showed lawns, flowers, and the house. Anthony had not been merely diplomatic when he had praised its beauty. It was a building in the best modern manner and in its way as good to look upon as Abbotshall.

Anthony made as if to leave.

But Sir Arthur had swallowed the bait. "See here, Gethryn," he said; "why not come in with me? The inside's more worth seeing than the out. And I'd like you to meet Lucia and her sister. They'd be glad to see you too. They were expecting another to lunch besides me—young Deacon, John's secretary. He wouldn't come. He's very busy, and being young, I suppose he feels it'd be a sin to enjoy himself in any way to-day. Silly, but I like him for it. He don't know the necessity yet for doing anything to keep sane." He laid a hand on Anthony's arm. "Do come along."

Anthony allowed himself to be persuaded. They walked through the garden and then round the house to the front door. They were shown by a cool, delightful maid to a cool, delightful drawing-room.

Through the French-window, which opened on to the garden they had approached by, there burst a girl. Anthony noted slim ankles, a slight figure, and a pretty enough face. But he was disappointed. The hair was of a deep reddish-gold.

Sir Arthur presented Mr. Anthony Gethryn—he knew of Anthony's dislike of the "Colonel"—to Miss Dora Masterson.

The girl turned to the man she knew. "But—but where's Archie? Isn't he coming, too?"

Sir Arthur's face lost its conventional smile. "No, my dear. I'm afraid he's not. He—he's very busy." He hesitated. "You will have heard—about Mr. Hoode?"

The girl caught her breath. "Yes. But only just now. You must think it awful of me not to have asked you at once; but—but I hardly believed it. It wasn't in any of the papers we had this morning. And I've only just got up; I was so tired yesterday. Travers, the parlour-maid, told me. Loo doesn't know yet. I think she's got up—or only just; she stayed in bed this morning too." The girl grew agitated. "Why are you looking like that? Has—is Archie in—in trouble?"

Sir Arthur laughed, and then grew grave again. "Lord, no, child! It's only that he's busy. You see, there are detectives and—and things to see to. I'm rather a deserter, I suppose, but I thought I'd better come along and bring Mr. Gethryn with me. He arrived this morning, very fortunately. He's helping the police, being—well, a most useful person to have about." He paused. Anthony, to conceal his annoyance at this innocent betrayal, became engrossed in examination of a water-colour of some merit.

Sir Arthur continued: "It is a terrible tragedy, my dear——"

"What! What is it?" came a cry from the doorway behind them. The voice would have been soft, golden, save for that harsh note of terror or hysteria.

Sir Arthur and the girl Dora whipped round. Anthony turned more slowly. What he saw he will never forget.

"A woman tall and most superbly dark," he quoted to himself later. She was tall, though not so tall as her carriage made her seem. Night-black hair dressed simply, almost severely, but with art; eyes that seemed, though they were not, even darker than the hair; a passionate mouth in which, for all its present grimness, Anthony could discern humour and a gracious sensuality; a body which fulfilled the promise of the face.

Dora was beside her. "Loo darling! Lucia!" she was saying. "It—it's terrible, but—but it's nothing to do with us. What's upset you so? What's the matter, darling?"

Sir Arthur came forward. Simply, straightforwardly, he told of Hoode's death. "It's an awful blow for me," he concluded, "but I wouldn't have frightened you for worlds, Lucia."

From where he stood discreetly in the background, Anthony saw her force a smile at the young sister hovering solicitous about her.

"I—I don't know what made me such a fool," she said. And this time her voice was under control.

She became suddenly aware of the presence of a stranger. Anthony was presented. The clasp of her hand sent a thrill up his arm and through his body. He reproached himself for possessing, in the thirties, the sudden emotions of sixteen.

The two sisters withdrew. Lunch, they said, would be ready in five minutes.

Sir Arthur dropped into a chair and looked across at Anthony with raised eyebrows.

"A touch overwrought," said Anthony.

"She can't be well. Most unusual for Lucia to be anything but mistress of herself." He fell silent for a moment; then a smile broke across the tired face. "Well, what impression has she made, Gethryn?"

"My feelings," Anthony said, "are concerned with Mr. Lemesurier. I wonder is he worthy of his luck?"

Sir Arthur smiled again. "You'll have a job to find out, my boy. Jack Lemesurier's been dead four years."

A gong announced lunch. At the foot of the stairs Mrs. Lemesurier encountered her sister.

Dora was still solicitous. "Feeling better, darling?" she asked.

Lucia grasped her sister's arm. "Who—who was that man with Sir Arthur?" Her voice rose. "Who is he? Dot, tell me!"

Dora looked up in amazement. "What *is* the matter, dear?"

Lucia leant against the balusters. "I—I don't know exactly. I— I'm not feeling well. And then this—" Again she clutched at her sister's arm. "Tell me! They say Mr. Hoode was killed last night. But how? Who—who shot him?"

The door of the drawing-room opened behind her. Anthony emerged. His poker-playing is still famous; he gave no sign of having heard.

3

If lunch was a success it was due to Anthony Gethryn. Until he came to the rescue there was an alternation of small-talk and silence so uncomfortable as to spoil good food and better wine.

The situation suited him well enough. He talked without stint; he had what is known as "a way with him." Soon he extorted questions, questions which he turned to discussion. From discussion to smiles was an easy step. Sir Arthur's face lost some of its gloom. Dora frankly beamed.

Only the woman at the head of the table remained aloof. Anthony took covert glances at her. He could not help it. Her pallor made him uncomfortable. He blamed himself. He saw that she was keeping herself under an iron control, and fell to wondering, as he talked to the others, how much more beautiful she would be were this fear or anxiety lifted from her shoulders.

But was she beautiful? He stole another look, purely analytical. No, she was not: not, at least, if beauty were merely perfection of feature. The eyes were too far apart. The mouth was too big. No, she was better than beautiful. She was herself, and therefore—

Anthony reproved himself for the recurrence of adolescent emotions. His thoughts took a grimmer turn. He thought of that spongelike mess that had been a man's head.

He slid into another story. The silence which fell was flattering. It was a good story. Whether it was true is no matter.

It was a tale of Constantinople, which Anthony knew as his listeners knew London. He had, it seemed, been there, almost penniless, in nineteen hundred and twelve. It was a tale of A Prosperous Merchant, A Secret Service Man, A Flower of the Harem, and A Globe-Trotter. Its ramifications were amusing, thrilling, pathetic, and it was at all times enthralling. Its conclusion was sad, for the Flower of the Harem was drowned. She could not swim the distance she had set herself.

"Of course," said Anthony, "she was a fool to try it. Think of the distance. And the tide was strong. It'd be impossible even for an athletic, full-grown woman." He is to be congratulated upon making so ridiculous a statement in so natural a tone.

"Oh! Mr. Gethryn, surely not," cried Dora excitedly. "Why Lucia——"

A spurt of flame and a crash of breaking china interrupted her sentence. Reaching for a cigarette, Mrs. Lemesurier had overturned spirit-lamp and coffee-pot.

"Not bad at all," thought Anthony, as he rose to help. "But you won't get off quite so easily."

Order was restored; fresh coffee made and drunk. The party moved to drawing-room and thence to garden.

Anthony lingered in the pleasant room before joining the others on the lawn.

He took a seat beside his hostess. The deck-chairs were in the shade of one of the three great cedars.

"A delightful room, your drawing-room, if I may say so." His tone was harmlessly affable.

The reply was chill. "I'm glad you like it, Mr.–Mr. Gethryn."

Anthony beamed. "Yes, charming, charming. It has an air, a grace only too rare nowadays. I admired that sideboard thing immensely; Chippendale, I think. And how the silver of those cups shows up!" He let the smile fade.

"I'm afraid I was so interested that I had to examine those cups and their inscriptions," he murmured. "Very rude of me. But to have won all those! You must be a wonderful swimmer, Mrs. Lemesurier."

A pulse in her throat beat heavily. "I have given it up—long ago," she said simply. Her eyes—looked at him steadily.

Anthony spurred himself. "Of course," he said, smiling, "there's no opportunity for pleasure swimming about here, is there? Except the Marle. And one would hardly tackle that for pleasure, what? The motive would have to be sterner than that."

The blood surged to the pale face, and then as suddenly left it. Anthony was seized with remorse. His mind hunted wildly for words to ease the strain, but he could find none. The sandal in his pocket seemed to be scorching him.

She rose slowly to her feet, crossed to where her sister sat with Sir Arthur some yards away, said something in a low voice, and walked slowly across the grass towards the house.

He went to join the others. As he reached them, there was a strange little cry from behind him, and he whipped round to see a yellow-clad figure crumple and fall, close to the windows of the drawing-room.

Anthony reached her before the girl or the elder man could move. As they came up,

"Dead faint," he said. "Nothing to be frightened about, Miss Masterson. Shall I carry her in?"

"Oh, please!" Dora picked nervously at her dress. "It—it *is* only a faint, isn't it?"

She was reassured. Anthony gathered the still body in his arms and bore it into the room.

He withdrew to the background while Sir Arthur and the girl ministered. He cursed himself. He wanted to take himself away, but couldn't move. His heart hammered at his ribs. Only by an effort did he manage to mask his face with its usual impassivity.

Colour had come back to Lucia's face. The lids of her eyes flickered.

Sir Arthur stepped back from the couch, and Anthony touched him on the arm. "I think we're superfluous, you know," he said.

The other nodded. "You're right. I told Dora I'd send a doctor, but she doesn't seem to think it's necessary. Come on."

They slipped from the room, and in two minutes were walking back along the river-bank towards the bridge.

CHAPTER SIX

THE SECRETARY AND THE SISTER

1

They had walked for perhaps two hundred yards before the elder man broke the silence.

"I hope Lucia will be all right," he said. "Probably it was the heat. It's a scorcher to-day."

Anthony nodded. He was in no mood for talk.

"Dora was telling me," continued Sir Arthur, "that Lucia had been feeling queer since last night. They hardly saw her after dinner. She vanished to her room and locked herself in. But apparently she'd been all right this morning until lunch-time."

Anthony began to take notice. Here was more confirmation—though it was hardly needed.

They were drawing near the bridge now. Another silence fell. Again it was Sir Arthur who broke it.

"You're very silent, my boy," he said. "Perhaps you've got something to think about, though. Something definite, I mean." His tone changed. "God! What I would give to get my hands on the—the animal that killed John! I shan't sleep till he's caught!"

Anthony looked at him curiously. "The great difficulty so far," he said, "is failure to find any indication of motive. I mean, you can't do anything in a complicated case unless you can do *some* work from that end. A motiveless murder's like a child without a father—damn' hard to bring home to any one. Suppose I suddenly felt that life wouldn't be worth living any longer unless I stabbed a fat man in the stomach; and I accordingly went to Wanstead and assuaged that craving on the darkest part of the Flats, and after that took the first train home and went to bed. They'd never find me out. The fat man and I would have no connection in the minds of the police. No, motive's the key, and so far it's hidden. Whether the lock can be picked remains to discover."

Sir Arthur smiled. "You're a curious feller, Gethryn. You amuse while you expound." He grew grave again. "I quite see what you mean: it's difficult, very difficult. And I can't imagine any one having a grudge against John."

Anthony went on: "Another thing; the messiness of the business indicates insanity on the part of the murderer. With homicidal mania there might be no motive other than to kill. But myself, I don't think the murderer was as mad as all that. Look at the care he took, for all his untidiness. No, the murderer was no more mad than the rest of the affair. It's all mad if you look at it—in a way. Mad as a Hatter on the first of April. And so am I, by God!" His voice trailed off into silence.

They had crossed the bridge now. Sir Arthur, instead of turning directly to his right to return to Abbotshall by the riverside path, chose the way which led to the village. Anthony drifted along beside him in unheeding silence. He was thinking.

Yes, "mad" had been the right word to use. There didn't seem to be any common sense about the thing. Even She was mad! Why swim to Abbotshall? The saving in time, he calculated, could have only been a matter of ten minutes or so. And she couldn't—well, she must have been in hell's own hurry. But the sandals indicated a bathing-dress, and surely the time taken to change into that might have been spent in covering the distance on dry land. And what had she been there for, outside that window of the study? She—surely She had nothing to do with that messy crime—must be interrogated. Oh, yes! His heart beat faster at the thought of seeing her again.

He rebuked himself for thus early and immorally losing interest in his task, and returned to consciousness of his surroundings. He found himself in Marling High Street.

Sir Arthur disappeared, suddenly, into a low-browed little shop, whose owner seemed, from his wares, to be an incongruous combination of grocer, tobacconist, draper and news-agent. Anthony stood looking about him. The narrow street, which should have been drowsing away that blazing August afternoon, carried an air of tension. Clumps of people stood about on its cobbles. Women leaned from the windows of its quaint houses. The shop outside which he waited, and two others across the road, flaunted shrieking news placards.

" 'Orrible Murder of a Cabinet Minister!" Anthony quoted with a wry face. "Poor devil, poor devil. He's made more stir by dying than he ever did in his life."

Sir Arthur emerged, a packet of tobacco in one hand, a sheaf of newspapers in the other. With fleeting amusement Anthony noticed the red and black cover of an *Owl* "special." They walked on.

The elder man glanced down at the papers in his hand. "It's a queer thing, Gethryn," he said, "but I somehow can't keep away from the sordid side of this awful, terrible tragedy. Up at the house I keep feeling that I must get into that study—that room of all places! And I came this way really to buy newspapers, though I cheated myself into thinking it was tobacco I wanted. And I can't help nosing about while the detectives are working. I expect I shall bother you." His voice was lowered. "Gethryn, do you think you'll succeed? He was my best friend—I—my nerves are on edge, I'm afraid. I——"

"Great strain." Anthony was laconic. Conversation did not appeal to him.

He tried to map out a course of action, and decided on one thing only. He must see and talk with the Lady of the Sandal again. For the rest, he did not know. He must wait.

They walked on to the house in silence. At the front door was a car. Boyd was climbing into it. He paused at the sight of Anthony. Sir Arthur passed into the house.

Boyd was excited, respectably excited. "Where've you been, sir? You've missed all the fun."

"Really?" Anthony was sceptical.

"Yes. I don't mind telling you, sir, that the case is over, so to speak."

"Is it now?"

"It is. You were quite right, sir. It *was* some one belonging to the house. I can't tell you more now. I'm off back to town. I'll see you later, sir."

Anthony raised his eyebrows. Things were going too fast. Had Boyd found out anything about Her?

"Shalt not leave me, Boyd." He raised a protesting hand. " 'The time has come, the Walrus said——' You're too mysterious. Be lucid, Boyd, be doosid lucid."

The detective glanced at his watch with anxiety. He seemed torn between the call of duty and desire to be frank with the man who had helped him.

"I'll have to be very short, then, sir," he said, pushing the watch back into his pocket. "Ought to have started ten minutes ago. This is very unofficial on my part. I'm afraid I must ask you——"

"Don't be superfluous, Boyd."

"Very well, sir. After I left you in the garden this morning, I asked them all—the household—some more questions, and elicited the fact that one of what you called the 'cast-iron' alibis was a dud, so to speak. It was like this, sir: one of the maids had told me she'd seen Mr. Deacon—that's the deceased's secretary—go to his room just after ten. That coincided with what he told me himself, and also with what Sir Arthur Digby-Coates said. Now, this girl spent the time from ten until about a minute before the murder was discovered working—arranging things and what not, I take it—in the linen-room. Apparently it took her so long because she'd been behindhand, so to speak, and was doing two evenings' jobs in one. This linen-room's just opposite Mr. Deacon's room, and the girl said last night that she knew he hadn't come out because, having the door of this linen-room open all the time, she couldn't have helped but see him if he had.

"But she told a different tale this morning, sir, when I talked to her after you'd left me. I wasn't thinking about Deacon at all, to tell you the truth, when out she comes with something about having made a mistake. 'What's that?' I said, and told her not to be nervous. Then she tells me that she hadn't been in the linen-room all that time after all. She'd left it for about ten minutes to go down-stairs. She was very upset—seemed to think we'd think she was a criminal for having made a slip in her memory." Boyd laughed.

Anthony did not. "What time was this excursion from the linen-closet?" he asked.

"As near as the girl can remember, it was ten minutes or so after she saw Deacon go into his room, sir."

"And I suppose, according to you, that this Deacon left his room while the girl was away, slipped out of the house, waited, climbed into the study window, killed his employer, climbed out again, hid somewhere till the fuss was over, got back unseen to his room, and then pretended he hadn't ever left it."

Boyd looked reproach. "You're being sarcastic, sir, I know; but as a matter of fact that's very nearly exactly what he did do."

"Is it? You know, Boyd, it doesn't sound at all right to me."

"You won't think that way, sir, when I tell you that we *know* Deacon's our man." Boyd lowered his voice. "Colonel Gethryn, those finger-prints on the weapon—the wood-rasp—are Deacon's!"

"Are they now?" said Anthony irritably. "How d'you know? What did you compare 'em with?"

Boyd looked at him almost with pity. "Got every one's marks this morning, sir." He looked again at his watch.

"One moment," said Anthony. "Found anything like a motive?"

The watch went back into its pocket. "We have, sir. Yes, you may well look surprised—but we have. And the motive's a nice little piece of evidence in itself. A chance remark Sir Arthur made when I was talking to him before luncheon-time put me on to it. Yesterday morning he happened to walk with the deceased into the village. The deceased went into the bank, and, luckily, Sir Arthur went in with him. Mr. Hoode drew out a hundred of the best, so to speak—all in ten-pound notes. We didn't know of this before, because Sir Arthur had mentioned it to the Chief Constable —Sir Richard Morley—last night, and Sir Richard had somehow not thought it important enough information to pass on." Boyd's tone conveyed his opinion of the Chief Constable of the county. "Well, sir, I had a search made. That hundred was missing. But we found it!"

Anthony ground his heel savagely into the gravel.

"I suppose it was secreted behind the sliding panel in Deacon's room, all according to Cocker?"

"Don't know anything about any sliding panel, sir; nor any Mr. Cocker. But Deacon's room is just where we did find it. I verified the numbers of the notes from the bank."

"What's Deacon say about it?"

The detective barked scornfully. "Said Mr. Hoode gave it to him for a birthday present. Lord, a birthday present! So probable, isn't it, sir?"

"Why the withering irony, Boyd? It's so improbable that it's probably true."

Boyd snorted. "Now, sir, just think about it! Turn it over in your mind, so to speak. Deacon's alibi turns out all wrong. His movements last night fit the time of the murder. A hundred pounds drawn from the bank by the deceased are found stuffed into a collar-box in Deacon's room—a good hiding-place, but not one to put a 'birthday-present' in. *And,* sir, Deacon's finger-prints are found on the weapon which the murder was done with! Why! it's a case in a million, so to speak. Wish they were all as easy."

"All right, Boyd; all right. I'll admit you've some justification. Yes—I suppose—queer about those finger-prints! Very queer!"

Boyd smiled. "In fact, they settle the business by themselves, as you might say." His kindly face grew grave. "It's quite clear, sir, I think. That murder—one of the worst in my experience—was done for the sake of a paltry hundred pounds!"

Anthony was not moved. "And your culprit, I presume," he said, "languishes in Marling's jail."

"If you mean have we arrested Deacon, sir, we have not. He doesn't know anything about us having found his finger-prints. And I'm afraid I must ask you, sir, officially, to say nothing to him about what I've told you. You see, this is one of those cases where contrary to the general rule we should like the coroner's jury to pass a verdict against our man and then arrest him. I'm having him watched until the inquest to-morrow, and we'll nab him after." Out came the watch again; a look of horror crossed its owner's face. "I must really get off now, sir. I'm terrible late as it is. Got to report up at the Yard. Good-day, sir, I'll see you to-morrow if you're still here. And thank you for your help. It was you and what you said in your study about it being an 'insider,' so to speak, that put me on the right track, though I did take your other view at first. Now I see—as I've done in the past, sir—that you generally know."

Anthony concealed a smile at this attempt to gild the pill. "So I put you on the right track, did I?" he said softly. "Or the wrong, my friend; or the wrong! I don't like it. I don't like it a little bit. It's too rule-of-thumb. The Profligate Secretary, the Missing Bank-Notes, the Finger-printed Blunt Instrument! It's not even a good shilling shocker. It's too damnation ordinary, that's what it is!"

If Boyd heard him he gave no sign, but hurried back to the waiting car.

Anthony watched it out of sight. He communed with himself. No, he didn't like it. And where did She come in? And why, in the name of a name, had she said: "Who shot him?" when the poor devil had had his head battered in?

"That rather lets her out as regards the actual bashing," he said, half-aloud. "That's a comfort, anyhow. But it's perplexing, very perplexing. 'Do I sleep, do I dream, or is Visions about?' I think, yes, I think a little talk with the murderous secretary would do me good—always remembering the official injunction not to tell him he's going to be hanged soon."

2

Archibald Basil Travers Deacon—his parents have much to answer for—was in the drawing-room. He sprawled in an easy-chair beside the open windows. A book lay face-downwards upon his knees.

Anthony, entering softly, had difficulty in persuading himself

that this was the man he sought. He had expected the conventional
private secretary; he found a man in the late twenties with the face
of a battered but pleasant prize-fighter, the eyes of a lawyer, and
the body of Heracles.

Anthony coughed. The secretary heaved himself to his feet. The
process took a long time. The unfolding complete, he looked
down upon Anthony's six feet from a height superior by five inches.
He stretched out a hand and engulfed Anthony's. A tremendous
smile split his face.

He boomed softly: "You must be Gethryn. Heard a lot about
you. So you're here disguised as a bloodhound, what?"

They sat, and Anthony produced cigars. When these were well
alight,

"Queer show, this," said Deacon.

"Very," Anthony agreed.

Silence fell. Openly they studied each other. Deacon spoke first.

"Boyd," he said, settling a cushion behind his great shoulders,
"is quite wrong."

"Eh?" Anthony was startled.

"I remarked, brother, that your Wesleyan-lookin' detective
friend was shinning up the wrong shrub."

"Indeed," said Anthony. "How?"

"Your caution, brother, is commendable; but I think you know
what I mean. Chief Detective-Inspector, or whatever he is, W. B.
Boyd of Scotland Yard's Criminal Investigation Department—bless
his fluffy little bed-socks—is labourin' under the delusion that I, to
wit Archibald Etcetera Deacon, am the man who killed John
Hoode. You apprehend me, Stephen?"

Anthony raised his eyebrows. "How much do you know, I
wonder?"

"All depends on your meanin'. If you're asking whether I know
anything about how the chief was done in, the answer's 'nothing.'
But if you mean how much do I know of Scotland Yard's suspicion
of me, that's a different story."

"Number two's right," said Anthony. "Fire ahead."

"Comrade Boyd," said the secretary, "is a tenacious, an indefatigable old bird, and he's found out some funny things. But what
he doesn't see is that they're only funny and no more. First, I didn't
contradict him—very foolish of me, that—when it was obvious that
he thought I'd been in my room last night from ten until after they
found the chief done in in his study. I didn't contradict him because the mistake seemed as if it would get me out of a very com-

promising position. You see, at about a quarter-past ten I left my room, went downstairs, out of the front door, and enjoyed a cheery stroll on my lonesome. When I came back I found the whole damn' place in an uproar, the murder having been already discovered. There was such a general shemozzle that nobody noticed me come in until I got there, what! My—what's the officialese for it?—'suppression of the truth' gave Boyd clue number one.

"Clue number two was the money. And the money was what had made me seize on an alibi when it was handed to me on a plate —the alibi, I mean. You see, it was so hellish awkward, this money business, and I let old Bloodhound Boyd fog himself because I wanted time to think. It was like this: the chief and I really were very good friends indeed—he was a damn' good fellah—though we did growl at each other occasional-like; and I believe the poor old lad was really attached to me; anyhow the money made it seem like that. He was a very canny old Haggis, you know, but he was subject to fits of extraordinary generosity. I mentioned some days ago—forget how it came up—that Wednesday was my birthday. Well, last night, or rather yesterday afternoon about five—when I took some papers in to him in the study, he wished me many happy returns of the day before, apologised for having forgotten the ceremony, and shoved an envelope into my mit: in that envelope were ten crisp little tenners, all nice and new and crumply-lookin'. Of course I did the hummin' and haain' act, but he'd have none of it.

"'No, my boy,' he says, 'you keep it. Must let an old fellah like me do what I want.' So I scraped at the old forelock and salaamed. Thought it was damned decent of him, you know. As I was clearin' out, though, he stopped me, coughin' and hum-hummin' and lookin' all embarrassed. 'Deacon,' he said, 'er-um-er-um —don't you mention that little memento to—to any one, will you?' 'Not if you'd rather I didn't, sir,' says I. He gave a sickly sort of grin and muttered. But I understood him all right. He meant his sister. She's one of those holy terrors that's not a bad sort really. I always knew she kept a pretty tight fist on the purse-ropes, though. P'r'aps that's why he didn't give me a cheque."

Anthony took the cigar from his mouth. "And Boyd," he said, "finds out that Hoode had this money in the house, institutes a search, and finds it in your collar-box, which looks like an ingenious hiding-place but was really just an accidental safe. He also finds out that you weren't in your room last night during all the time that you let him think you were, and that you entered the house—

probably by the verandah door—just after the body was found. He looks at you and connects your obvious strength with the ruts in Hoode's skull. He sees your titanic length of leg and argues that you're the only person in the house likely to be able to step through that open study-window without marking the flower-bed by treading on the flowers. He does a sum, and the answer is: x equals the murderer and Archibald Deacon equals x. That's what you know, isn't it?"

"You have it all, old thing, all! *Quel lucidité!*"

"But you haven't," said Anthony, thinking of the finger-prints and his promise to Boyd. "There's more in it than that, I'm afraid." He puffed at his cigar. "By the way, you didn't do it, did you?"

"No," said Deacon, and laughed.

Anthony smiled. "I shouldn't have believed you if you'd said yes. You can't give me a line, I suppose? Any private suspicions of your own? I've a bag of data, but nothing to hang it on."

"The answer, old thing, is a lemon. Nary suspicion. But what's all this about data? Found anythin' fresh?"

"Oh, well, you know"—Anthony waved vague hands. "Possibly yes, possibly no, if you follow me. I mean, you never can tell."

Deacon smiled. "Kamerad!" he said. "Served me right. But that's me all over, I'm afraid. Damn nosey! But you must admit I'm an interested party."

"I do," Anthony said; then suddenly leaned forward. "Have you told me *all* you know?" he asked. "And are you going to tell me anything you don't *know*, but merely feel?"

Deacon was silent for perhaps a minute. "I can't tell you anything more that I *know*," he said at last and slowly. "And as to the other, what exactly are you driving at? D'you mean: do I definitely suspect any one as being the murderer?"

Anthony nodded. "Just that."

"Then the answer's no. But I'll tell you what I do feel very strongly, and that's that it isn't any one belonging to the house."

"So you think that, do you?" said Anthony. "You know, I've heard that before about this affair."

Deacon sat up. "Oh! And what do *you* think? The reverse?"

Anthony shrugged non-committal shoulders.

"But it's absurd," said the secretary. "Quite utterly impossible, my dear feller!"

"Is it?" Anthony raised his eyebrows. "Ever read detective stories, Deacon? Good ones, I mean. Gaboriau, for instance. If you do, you'll know that the 'It' is very often found among a bunch of 'unlikely and impossibles.' And one of my chief stays in life is my well-proved theory that Fiction is Truth. The trouble is that the stories are often more true than the real thing. And that's just where one goes wrong, and sometimes gets left quite as badly off the mark as the others. I'm beginning to think I may be doing that here."

Deacon scratched his head. "I think you're ahead of me," he said.

"Never mind, I'm ahead of myself. A long way ahead."

"Well, says I, I hope you catches yourself up soon."

"Thanks." Anthony got to his feet. "Is it possible for me to see Miss Hoode this afternoon?"

"'Fraid not. Our Mr. Boyd saw her this morning, and she's given orders that that was enough."

"Well, I prowl," said Anthony, and walked to the door. "By the way, on that walk of yours last night, that awkward walk, did you meet any one? or even see any one?"

"No. And that's awkward, too, isn't it? Nary human being did I pass."

Anthony opened the door. "Any time you think I'd be useful, let me know," he said, and passed into the passage.

Deacon's voice followed him. "Thanks. When you're wanted I'll make a noise like a murderer."

Walking down the passage which led to the great square hall, Anthony pondered. It seemed impossible that this gigantic imperturbability was a murderer. But how to explain the finger-prints? And Deacon did not know of those prints. What would he do when told of them?

"The man's in a mess," he said to himself. "This week's problem: how to extricate him? The solution will be published in our next week's issue—per-haps!"

He came out into the hall. The utter silence of the house oppressed him. Any sound, he thought, would be welcome, would make things seem less like a nightmare.

He turned to his left, making for the verandah door. His fingers on its handle, he paused. Behind him, to his right, was the door of the study. His ears had caught a sound, a rustling sound, from that direction. He looked about him. No one was near, in sight even. The two men Boyd had left on duty had disappeared.

Quietly, he crossed to the study door. He laid his ear against it. He heard the click of a lock, a light lock, then a rustle of paper, then soft footsteps.

He crossed the hall to the foot of the stairs in three jumps. A barometer and a clock hung on the wall. He studied them.

He heard the study door open, slowly, as if the one who opened were anxious not to be noisy. Then came a rustle of skirts. He stepped out from the shadow.

Half-way between the study and where he stood by the foot of the stairs was a woman. Her hand, which had been at the bosom of her dress, fell to her side.

Anthony moved towards her. Closer, he saw her more plainly— a tall, square-shouldered grenadier of a woman, with a sexless, high-cheekboned, long-nosed face. The features, the sand-coloured hair, were reminiscent of the dead minister.

"Miss Hoode?" Anthony bowed. "My name is Gethryn. I believe Sir Arthur Digby-Coates has explained me."

"Yes." The woman's tones were flat, lifeless as her face. She essayed cordiality. "Yes, indeed. I told him I was glad, very glad, to have your help. I need to apologise for not having spoken to you before, but—I—but——"

Anthony raised a hand. "Believe me, madam, I quite understand. I would like, if it is not an impertinence, to express my condolence."

The woman bowed her head. "Thank you," she said; pressing a hand to her heart. "I—I must leave you. Give orders for anything you may want."

Anthony watched her mount the stairs and disappear. "My good woman—if you really are a woman—what's your trouble? Sorrow? Or fear? Or both?" he thought. "And why were you in the study? And why were you so secret about it? And above all, what did you hide in your flat bosom when you saw me? Two whats and two whys."

He stood filling his pipe. Assuredly this fresh mystery must be investigated. And so must that of the lady that swam rivers in the night and blinded her pursuer's eyes and assaulted his heart in the morning. If it had not been for Her all this would have been great fun; but now—well, it was anything but amusing. She must know something, and since Boyd had seen fit to suspect the one obviously innocent person, it was Anthony Ruthven Gethryn's business to find out what she knew. What was so disturbing was the unreasonableness of the affair. Nothing seemed to have motive behind it. Of course, there was reason for everything—the Lady of the Sandal's swim over the river, the secret ravishing of the study by the bosom-less, sexless sister of the corpse, even the appearance of an innocent man's finger-prints on the murderer's weapon—but were they sane reasons? At present it seemed as if they could not be, and what could be more hopeless than the search of a sane man for the motives of lunatics!

Anthony shook himself, chided and took himself in hand. "Gethryn," he murmured, "do something, man! Don't stand here saying how difficult everything is. Well, what shall I do? Have a look at the study? All right."

He still had the hall to himself. Quietly, he entered the study and closed the door behind him.

He surveyed the room. He strove for memory of the sounds he had heard just now when Laura Hoode had been there and he outside.

There had been a fumbling, a click, a pause and then the rustling of paper. The writing-table was the most likely place. The drawers, he knew, were all locked, but perhaps the gaunt sister had duplicate keys. The originals were in Boyd's official possession.

But it was unlikely that sister would have keys. He looked thoughtfully at the table. Something of a connoisseur, he judged it as belonging to the adolescence of the last century.

A desk more than a hundred years old! A mysterious, sinister woman searching in it! "A hundred to one on Secret Drawer!" thought Anthony, and probed among the pigeon-holes. He met with no success, and felt cheated. His theory of the essential reality of story-books had played him false, it seemed.

Loath to let it go, he tried again; this time pulling out from their sheaths the six small, shallow drawers which balanced the pigeon-holes on the other side of the alcove containing the ink-well. The top drawer, he noticed with joy, was shorter by over an inch than its five companions. He felt in its recess with long, sensitive fingers. He felt a thin rim of wood. He pressed, and nothing happened. He pulled, and it came easily away. The Great Story-book Theory was vindicated.

He peered into the unveiled hollow. It was filled with papers, from their looks recently tossed and crumpled.

"Naughty, naughty Laura!" said Anthony happily, and pulled them out.

There were letters, a small leather-covered memorandum-book, a larger note-book and a bunch of newspaper-cuttings.

He pulled a chair up to the table and began to read. When he had finished, he replaced the two little books and the letters. They were, he judged, unimportant. The newspaper-cuttings he retained, slipping them into his wallet. The illegality of the proceeding did not apparently distress him.

He replaced the little drawers, careful to leave things as he had found them. On his way to the door, he paused to examine the little polished rosewood table which stood beside the grandfather clock and was the fellow of that which supported the two tall vases he had spoken of to Boyd. A blemish upon its glossy surface had caught his eye.

On close inspection he found a faint scar some twelve inches long and two wide. This scar was compounded of a series of tiny dents occurring at frequent and regular intervals along its length and breadth.

Anthony became displeased with himself. He ought to have noticed this on his first visit to the room. Not that it seemed important—the wood-rasp had obviously been laid there, probably by the murderer, possibly by some one else—but, he ought, he considered, to have noticed it.

He left the room, passed through the still empty hall and so into the garden. Here, pacing up and down the flagged walk outside the study, he became aware of fatigue. The lack of a night's sleep and the energies of the day were having their effect.

To keep himself awake, he walked. He also thought. Presently he halted and stood glaring at the wall above the windows of the study. As he glared, he muttered to himself: "That bit of dead creeper, now. It's untidy. Very untidy! And it doesn't fit!"

Ten minutes later Sir Arthur found him, heavy-eyed, hands in pockets, still looking up at the wall, and swaying ever so little on his feet.

"Hallo, Gethryn, hallo!" Sir Arthur looked at him keenly. "You look fagged out, my boy. This won't do. I prescribe a whisky and soda." He caught Anthony's arm. "Come along."

Anthony rubbed his eyes. "Well, I grow old, I grow old," he said. "Did you say a drink? Forward!"

CHAPTER SEVEN

THE PREJUDICED DETECTIVE

Thornton, Mrs. Lemesurier's parlour-maid, was enjoying her evening out. To Mrs. Lemesurier and her sister, drinking their coffee after dinner, came Thornton's second-in-command.

"Please, ma'am," she said, "there is a gentleman."

"What? Who?" Lucia pushed back her chair.

"There is a gentleman, ma'am. In the drawing-room. He says might he see you. Very important, he said it was. Please, ma'am, he didn't give no name." The girl twisted her apron-strings nervously.

"Shall I go, dear?" Dora asked placidly. Inwardly she was frightened. She had thought her sister recovered from her attack of the afternoon, but here she was, again.

Lucia Lemesurier rose to her feet. "No, no. I'd better see him." She walked slowly from the room.

Outside the drawing-room door she paused, fought for composure, and entered. Anthony came forward to meet her.

"What do you want? What have you come here for, again?" Her voice was pitched so low that he could barely catch the words.

"You know," said Anthony, "we're getting melodramatic. Please sit down." He placed a chair.

Mechanically she sank into it. Her eyes never left his face.

"Now," said Anthony, "let us clear the atmosphere. First, please understand that I've no object here except to serve you. I wasn't quite clear about that this morning, hence my clumsy methods. The next move's up to you. Suppose you tell me all about it."

She kept her eyes on his. "All about what? Really, Mr.—Mr. Gethryn, I don't understand all this. I don't understand it at all."

"Quite good!" Anthony approved. "But it won't do, you know. I repeat, suppose you tell me all about it."

She tried escape by another way. "Did you—do you—really mean that about—about serving? Is it true that you want to help me?" Now her voice was soft with a different softness! "If it is, I assure you that you'll do it best by—by"—she hovered on the brink of admission—"by not asking me anything, by not trying any more to—to——" Her voice died away.

Anthony shook his head. "No. You're wrong, quite wrong. I'll show you why. Last night John Hoode was murdered. During the night you swam across the river, crept up to the house, and crouched outside the window of the room in which the murder was done. Why did you do all this? Certainly not for amusement or exercise. So, unless a coincidence occurred greater than any ever invented by a novelist in difficulties, your visit was in some way connected with the murder. Or, at any rate, some of the circumstances of the murder are known to you."

"No! No!" Lucia shrank back in her chair.

"There you are, you see." Anthony made a gesture. "I was putting the point of view of the police and public—what they would say if they knew—not giving my own opinion.

"The sleuth-hounds of fiction," he went on, "are divinely impartial. The minions of Scotland Yard are instructed to be. But I, madam, am that *rarissima avis,* a prejudiced detective. Ever since this case began I've been prejudiced. I've been picking up new prejudices at every corner. And the strongest, healthiest, and most unshakable prejudice of them all is the one in favour of you. Now, suppose you tell me all about it."

"I—I don't understand," she murmured, and looked up at him wide-eyed. "You're—bewildering!"

"I'll go further, then. Suppose I say that even if you killed Hoode and tell me so, I won't move in any way except to help you, will—you—tell—me—all—about—it?"

Her eyes blazed at him. "Do you really think I did it?"

"Oh, woman, Illogicality should be thy name!" Anthony groaned. "I was merely endeavouring, madam, to show how safe you'd be in telling me all that you know. Listen. I'm in this business privately. I oblige a friend. If I don't like my own conclusions, I shall say nothing about them. I seek neither Fame nor Honorarium. I have, thank God, more money than is good for me." He was silent for a moment, and then added: *"Now,* tell me all about it."

She looked up at him; and went on looking. There was a moment when he saw nothing, felt nothing, but the dark twin pools of her eyes and the golden lights deep down in the darkness.

"I believe you," she said at last. "I *will* tell you."

The white hands twisted in her lap. She said: "I—I hardly know where to begin. It's all so—it doesn't seem real, only it's too dreadful to be anything else——"

"Why did you go to Abbotshall last night? And why, in Heaven's name, since you did go there, did you choose to swim?" Anthony conceived that questions would help.

"There wasn't time to do anything else," she said, seeming to gather confidence. "We'd been out all day—Dora and I and some friends. I—when we got back—Dora and I—there was only just time to change for dinner. As I came in I saw some letters in the hall, and remembered I'd not read them in the morning—we'd been in such a hurry to start. Then I went and forgot them again till after dinner.

"It wasn't till after half-past ten that I thought of them. And then, when—when I read the one from Jimmy, I—I—" She covered her face with her hands.

"Who," said Anthony sharply, "is Jimmy?"

The hands dropped to her lap again. He saw the long fingers twist about each other.

"Jimmy," she said, "is my brother. I love him very much! Only —only he's not been quite the same since he got back from Germany. He—he's ill—and he's—he's been d-drinking—and—he was a prisoner there for three years! When they got him he was wounded in the head and they never even—even——"

"That letter," Anthony was firm.

She choked back a sob. "I—I read it. I read it, and I thought I'd go out of my mind! He said he was going—going to kill Hoode— that night! To shoot him!"

"Your brother? What had he to do with Hoode?" Anthony was at once relieved and bewildered. He knew why she had said, 'Who shot him?' But why should Brother want to shoot?

She seemed not to have heard his question. "I tried hard—ever so hard—to persuade myself that the letter was all nonsense, that it was a practical joke, or that Jimmy was ill or—or anything. But I couldn't. He—he was so precise. The train he was coming by— and everything. The——"

"What had your brother to do with Hoode?"

"He was his secretary until Archie took his place—about six months ago. I—I never knew why Jimmy left, he wouldn't tell me. He wouldn't tell me, I say!"

Anthony shifted uneasily in his chair. There had been a note of hysteria in the last words.

Suddenly she was on her feet. "He did it! He did it!" She flung her hands above her head. "Oh, Christ!" She began to cry, and laugh at the same time. Her face was distorted.

Anthony jumped at her, took her by the shoulders, and shook. Her flesh seemed to burn his fingers. With every movement of his arms her head jerked like a puppet's.

He shook harder, and she came back to herself. She gasped, and sat straight, and looked at him.

"I'm s-sorry, p-please," she said.

Anthony's hands fell to his sides. He went back to his chair. He said, after a moment:

"Then you were so impressed by the sincerity of your brother's letter that you determined you must try to stop him. Is that right?"

She nodded.

"But why, in God's name, didn't you walk or run, or do anything rather than swim?"

"There wasn't time. You see, it—it was so late—as I explained— before I read the—the l-letter that I knew th-that Jimmy was probably almost there. There wasn't time to—to—to——"

"I see. Judging that you'd save at least ten minutes by crossing the river here, you pretended you were going to bed, probably removed the more clinging of your garments—if you didn't put on a bathing-dress—put on a pair of bathing-sandals to make running easy without hindering swimming, slipped out of the house quietly and beat all previous records to Abbotshall by at least ten minutes. That right?"

"Yes." Besides other emotions there was wonder in her tones.

"Good. Now, when you were kneeling outside the window of Hoode's study, what did you see?"

Her eyes closed. Her throat moved as she swallowed. She said:

"I saw a man lying face-downwards by the fireplace. There was blood on his head. It was a bald head. I saw a clock half-fallen over; and chairs too. And I came away. I ran to the river."

"Do you know," Anthony asked slowly, "what time it was when you got back here?"

"No," said the lifeless voice.

He was disappointed. Nothing new here, except, of course, the brother. And of this business of Brother James he did not yet know what to think.

With his silence, Lucia's momentary impassivity left her. "What shall we do?" she whispered. "What shall we do? They'll find out about Jimmy—they'll find out. I *know* they will, I——"

"So far, the police know nothing about your brother." Anthony was soothing. "And if they did, they wouldn't worry their heads about him. You see, they've found a man they're sure *is* the murderer. There's quite a good *prima facie* case against him, too."

Relief flooded her face with colour. For a moment she relaxed; then suddenly sat upright again.

"But—but if they're accusing some one else, we must tell them about—about—Jimmy." Her face was white again.

"You go too fast, you know," said Anthony. "Don't you think we'd better find out a few more people who *didn't* do it before we unburden ourselves to the Law?"

She laid eager hands on his arm. "You mean—you think Jim didn't—didn't do it?"

Anthony nodded. "More prejudice, you see. And I know the man the bobbies have got hold of had nothing to do with it either. Again prejudice. Bias, lady, bias! There's nothing like it to clear the head, nothing! Now, I need a telephone, and your brother's address?"

Unhesitatingly she gave it. "The phone's in here." She pointed to a writing-table at the far end of the room.

As he turned to go to it, she clutched again at his arm. "Isn't it dangerous to use the telephone?" she whispered. "Isn't it? The girls at the exchange—if you use his name——"

"Credit me with guile," smiled Anthony.

He crossed the room, sat by the table and pulled the instrument towards him. She stood beside him, her fingers gripping the back of his chair. He lifted the receiver and asked for a city number.

"Is it a trunk-call?" he added. "No? Good!"

To Lucia, her heart in her mouth, it seemed hours before he spoke again. Then—

"Hallo. That *The Owl* office?" he said. "It is? Well, put me on to Mr. Hastings, please. At once. You can't? My child, if I'm not put through *at once* you'll go to-morrow! Understand?" A pause. To Lucia it seemed that the heavy thudding of her heart must be filling the room with sound. She pressed a hand to her breast.

Then Anthony's voice again. "Ah, that you, Spencer? Oh, it's the unerring Miss Warren, is it? Yes, Gethryn speaking. He is, is he? When'll he be back? Or won't he? Oh, you're all always there until after midnight, are you? Well, when he comes in, will you please tell him—this is important—that I've run across some one who knows where our old friend Masterson, Jimmy Masterson, is. Hastings will want to see him at once, I know. He and I have been trying to find Masterson for years. And say that I want to find out what Jimmy was doing last night. Tell Hastings to ask him or find out somehow where he was. It's a great joke.

"The address is 84, Forest Road, N.W. 5. Now, Miss Warren, if you wouldn't mind repeating the message?" A pause. Then: "That's exactly right, Miss Warren, thanks. You never make mistakes, do you? Don't forget to tell Hastings he simply must go there this evening, whether the work'll allow him or not. And he's got to ring me up here—Greyne 23—and tell me how he got on. And, by the way, ask him from me if he remembers his Cicero, and tell him I said: *Haec res maxim est: statim pare.* Got it? I won't insult you by offering to spell it.

"Thanks so much, Miss Warren. Good-night."

He replaced the receiver and rose from his chair. He said:

"That message was to a friend whose discretion is second only to my own. Nothing there any long ears at the exchange could make use of, was there? All so nice and above board, I thought. And I liked the canine Latin libellously labelled 'Cicero.' That was to make sure he understood that the affair was urgent. The need for discretion he'll gather from the way the message was wrapped up.

"And I'm afraid you'll have to put up with me until I've had an answer. That ought to be about midnight." He sat down, heavily, upon a sofa. He closed his eyes.

Lucia was watching him. "Mr. Gethryn," she said softly.

"Yes?" Anthony's eyes opened. "Sorry."

"You look *so* tired! I feel responsible. I've been difficult, haven't I? But I'm not going to be any more. And—and isn't there anything I can do? You *are* tired, you know."

Anthony smiled and shook his head.

Suddenly: "Fool that I am!" she exclaimed; and was gone from the room.

Anthony blinked wonderingly. He found consecutive thought difficult. This sudden recurrence of fatigue was a nuisance. "Haven't seen her laugh yet," he murmured. "Must make her laugh. Want to hear. Now, what in hell do we do if Brother James turns out to be the dastardly assassin after all? But I don't believe he is. It wouldn't fit. No, not at all!"

His eyes closed. With an effort, he opened them. To hold sleep at bay he picked up a book that lay beside him on the couch. He found it to be a collection of essays, seemingly written in pleasant and even scholarly fashion. He flicked over the leaves. A passage caught his eye. "And so it is with the romantic. He is as a woman enslaved by drugs. From that first little sniff grows the craving, from the craving the necessity, from the necessity—*facilis descensus Averno.* . . ."

The quotation set his mind working lazily. So unusual to find that dative case; they nearly all used the almost-as-correct but less pleasant '*Averni.*' But he seemed to have seen '*Averno*' somewhere else, quite recently, too. Funny coincidence.

The book slipped from his hand to the floor. In a soft wave, sleep came over him again. His eyes closed.

He opened them to hear the door of the room closed softly. From behind him came a pleasant sound. He sat upright, turning to investigate.

Beside a tray-laden table stood his hostess. She was pouring whisky from decanter to tumbler with a grave and most attractive preoccupation. Anthony, barely awake, murmured something, and she turned in a flash. "You were asleep," she said, and blushed under the stare of the green eyes.

"I told you I was psychic." Anthony looked at the tray. "I always know when spirits are about."

She laughed; and the sound gave him more pleasure even than he had anticipated.

She lifted the decanter again. "Say when," she said, and when he had said it: "Soda?"

"Please—a little." He took the glass from her hand and tasted. "Mrs. Lemesurier, I have spent my day in ever-increasing admiration of you. But now you surpass yourself. This whisky—prewar, I think?"

"Yes." She nodded absently, then burst out: "Tell me, why are you doing all this for me—taking all this trouble? Tell me!"

To-night Anthony's mind was running in a Latin groove. "*Veni, vidi, vicisti!*" he said, and drained his glass.

CHAPTER EIGHT

THE INEFFICIENCY OF MARGARET

1

Miss Margaret Warren, severely exquisite as to dress, golden hair as sleek as if she were about to begin rather than finish the day's work, sat at her table in Hastings's room.

Before her was the pad on which, ten minutes ago, she had written Anthony's message. She knew it by heart. As the minutes passed she grew more troubled at her employer's absence. Here—it was obvious—was something which ought to be done without waste of time; and time had already been wasted. She knew Colonel Gethryn well enough to be sure that the talk about a "great joke" had been camouflage. No, this was all something to do with the murder. Had he not said with emphasis that Hastings was to ring him up as soon as he had found this man Masterson? He had, and all had to know, it seemed, where this man Masterson had been on Thursday night, the night Hoode had been killed. . . .

"I don't believe," thought Margaret, "that either of them know this man Masterson at all. That's all part of the camouflage, that is. And then there's that bit of terrible Latin. I thought better of Colonel Gethryn, I did. Still, there it is: 'This matter is of the greatest importance. Obey immediately.' Cicero indeed!"

She glanced at her watch. A quarter of an hour wasted already!

An idea came to her. Hastings had gone out for food. In that case he might, if he had indeed gone there, still be at that pseudo-Johnsonian haunt, The Cock. Thither she sent a messenger, hotfoot. He was back within five minutes. No, the boss wasn't there.

"Damn!" said Miss Warren.

She looked again at her watch. Twenty past ten. She put on her hat—the little black hat which played such havoc with the emotions of the editor. The copy of Anthony's message she placed on Hastings's table, together with another hastily scribbled note. Then she ran down the stairs and out into Fleet Street.

After three attempts, she found a taxi whose driver was willing to take her so far afield as Forest Road, N.W. 5.

The journey, the driver said, would take 'arfenar or thereabouts. Margaret employed it in constructing two stories, one to be used if this man Masterson turned out to be over fifty, the other if he were under. They were good tales, and she was pleased with them. The "under-fifty" one involved an Old Mother, Mistaken Identity, and an Ailing Fiancée. The "over-fifty" one was, if anything, better, dealing as it did with A Maiden from Canada, A *Times* "Agony," Tears, A Lost Kitten, and A Railway Journey. Both tales were ingeniously devised to provide ample opportunity for innocently questioning this man Masterson as to his whereabouts on the night of Thursday.

The taxi pulled up. The driver opened the door. "'Ere y'are, miss. Number fourteen."

As she paid the fare, Miss Warren discovered her heart to be misbehaving. This annoyed her. She strove to master this perturbation, but met with little enough success.

The taxi jolted away down the hill. The road was quiet; too quiet, Margaret thought. Also it was dismal, too dismal. There were too few lamps. There was not even a moon. There didn't seem to be any lighted windows. A nasty, inhospitable road.

She perceived No. 14 to be a "converted" house. A great black building that might once have housed a merchant prince, but was now the warren of retired grocers, oddities, solicitors, and divorcees.

Margaret mounted the steps, slowly. The porter's lobby in the hall was empty. From one of a series of brass plates she divined that flat 6B was the burrow of one James Masterson. Flat 6B, it seemed, was on the first floor. The lift was unattended. She walked up the stairs.

Frantically she reviewed her stories, testing them at every point. She wished she hadn't come, had waited till Hastings had got back!

Facing the door of flat 6B, Miss Margaret Warren took herself in hand, addressed rude remarks to herself, and applied firm pressure to the bell-push.

There was no sound of footsteps; there was no hand on the latch—but the door swung open.

Margaret fell back, stifling a scream. A small squeak broke from her lips.

"Don't be a fool, Margaret," she told herself sternly. "Haven't you heard of contraptions to open doors? Hundred per cent. labour-saving."

But her heart was thudding violently as she entered the little hall.

From a room on her right came a man's voice, querulous, high-pitched.

"Who's that," it said. "Come in, damn you! Come in!"

She turned the handle, and entered a bedroom well furnished but in a state of appalling disorder. A dying fire—the temperature that day had been over ninety in the shade—belched out from the littered grate occasional puffs of black smoke. The bed-clothes were tossed and rumpled; half of them on the floor. A small table sprawled on its side in the middle of the room. Crumpled newspapers were everywhere, everywhere. Huddled in an arm-chair by the fireplace was a man.

His hair was wild, his eyes bright, burning with fever. A stubble of black beard was over the thin face. Over his cheek-bones was spread a brilliant flush. A man obviously ill, with temperature running high.

One must sympathise with Margaret. She had expected any scene but this. Again fear seized her. What a fool she had been to come! What a fool! This man Masterson was ill; yet she couldn't feel sorry for him. Those over-bright eyes fixed on hers were so malevolent somehow.

She stammered something. Her mouth was so dry that coherent speech seemed impossible.

The man got out of his chair. Dully, she noticed how great was the tax on his strength. He clutched at the mantel for support. Dislodged by his elbow, a bottle crashed down and splintered on the tiles of the hearth. The smell of whisky, which always made her feel sick, combined with apprehension and the heat of the room to set Margaret's senses dancing a fantastic reel.

Clutching the mantelpiece, the man attempted a bow. "You must pardon my appearance," he said, and his voice made the girl shrink back, "but I am—am at your service. Oh, yes, believe me. What can I have the great pleasure of—of doing for you? Eh?"

He started to move towards her, aiding his trembling legs by scrabbling at the wall. Margaret felt a desire to scream; choked the scream back. She tried to burst into speech, to say something, anything, to tell one of her stories that she had been so proud of. She failed utterly.

The man continued his spider-like approach.

"Go back! Go back!" Margaret whispered. She was shaking.

But the man had left the wall, and without its support had fallen to his knees. His head lolling with every movement, he crawled to the over-turned table and searched among the litter of newspaper beside it.

Margaret cast longing eyes at the door. She tried to move, but her legs would not obey her. Fascinated by the horror of the thing, she looked down at the man. Her eye caught heavy headlines on the tumbled papers.

"*Abbotshall Murder! Cabinet Minister Assassinated! Horrible Atrocity! Is it Bolshevism?*" they shrieked in letters two inches high.

And the man—this man Masterson—had found what he wanted. He sat grotesquely on the carpet, holding in both hands the butt of a heavy automatic pistol. The barrel pointed straight at Margaret's head. A queer, sick feeling came over her. She felt her knees grow weak beneath her.

"Sit down. Sit down, will you!" The man's tones were harsh, cracked—the voice of one ill to the point of collapse.

2

Spencer Hastings stood disconsolate on the threshold of the editorial chamber. He had supped with a friend who was an artist. The artist had talked. Spencer Hastings had been later than he had intended in returning to the office. When he did—she had gone.

"Damn it! Oh, damn it!" he said fervently.

One must sympathise with him. He was ashamed, bitterly ashamed, of himself. For the ten thousandth time he thought it all over. Hell! He was badly in love with the woman, why didn't he grab hold of her and tell her so? Why was it that he couldn't? Because he was afraid. Afraid of her aloof beauty, her completeness, her thrice-to-be-damned efficiency—how he loathed that word! If only she weren't quite so—so infernally and perpetually equal to the situation!

Yes, he was afraid, that's what it was! He, Spencer Sutherland Hastings, sometime the fastest three-quarter in England, sometime something of an ace in the Flying Corps, renowned in old days for his easy conquest of Woman, he was afraid! Afraid forsooth of a little slip of a thing he could almost hang on his watch-chain! Disgusting, he found himself!

He flitted dejectedly about the room. Should he go home? No, he'd better do some work; there'd be an easy time coming soon.

He crossed the room and sat down at his table. Two slips of

paper, both covered with Margaret's clear, decisive handwriting, stared up at him.

He read and re-read. Here was more Efficiency! Undoubtedly she had put its real meaning to Anthony's message. In his mind alarm replaced that mixture of irritation and reverence. "I thought this should be attended to at once, so have gone to the address given by Colonel Gethryn," she had written. Aloud, Hastings heaped curses upon the loquacity of the artist with whom he had supped.

He read the message and the note a third time, then jumped to his feet. For her to go, alone and at such a time, to the house of a man who might be a murderer! Of course, Anthony might only be after a possible witness, but——

He seized his hat and made for the stairs and Fleet Street.

3

Margaret lay huddled in the uncomfortable chair. For perhaps the hundredth time she choked back the scream which persisted in rising in her throat. Every suppression was more difficult than its predecessor.

Still, though she seemed to have been looking down it for an eternity, the black ring which was the muzzle of the automatic stared straight into her eyes.

The man had not moved. He was crouched upon the floor, no part of him steady save the hands which held the pistol. And he went on talking. Margaret felt that the rest of her life was a dream; that always, in reality, he had been talking and she listening.

And the talk—always the same story. "You're clever, aren't you? Very clever, eh? 'Who killed Hoode?' you said to yourselves—you and your friends. I don't know you, but you're Scotland Yard, that's what you are. Well, if you want to know *I did!* See? But, my golden child, I'm not going to tell any one! Oh, no! Oh, no!"

There was much more of words but none of sense. He went on talking, and always the burden of his whispering, his half-shouting, his mumbling, was the same. "I killed Hoode! But I'm not going to tell any one, oh, no! Thought he could play about with me, did he? Get rid of the man who was helping him, eh? Fool!"

Once she had tried to rise, intending a wild dash for the front door she knew had not shut behind her. But the pistol had been thrust forward with such menace that ever since she had been as still as stone. Her right leg, twisted beneath her, was agony. Her head seemed bursting.

At last there came a pause in the babbling talk. The man began to struggle to his feet. Margaret shrank back still farther into her chair. Even as he heaved himself upright the gun never wavered from her.

Another scream rose in her throat, only to be fought back. He was up now, and coming towards her with wavering steps. Even in her terror she could see that his fever had increased. She prayed for his collapse as she had never prayed before.

He was close, close! Margaret shut her eyes, screwing up the lids.

She heard a rush of feet outside the door. Some one burst into the room. Slowly, unbelieving, she opened the blue eyes. Hastings stood in the doorway.

A black mist flickered before her. Through it, as if she were looking through smoked glass, she saw him walk swiftly, his right hand outstretched as if in greeting, up to the unsteady, malevolent figure in the dressing-gown.

The mist before her eyes grew thicker, darker. When it had cleared again, Hastings had the pistol in his hand. As she watched, the numbness of fear still upon her, the man Masterson crumpled to the floor.

With a great effort she rose from the chair. On her feet, she stumbled. She felt herself falling, gave a weak little cry, and was caught up in Hastings's arms.

Now that safety had come she broke down. Her body shook with sobs. Then came tears and more tears. She burrowed her face into Hastings's shoulder, rubbing her cheek up and down against the smooth cloth of his coat.

Hastings, his heart beating too fast for comfort, looked down. All he could see was the little black hat. The shaking of her body in his arms, the very fact that in his arms she was, deprived him of speech. They remained locked together. From the floor behind them came a hoarse, delirious babbling. Neither man nor woman heard it.

The sobbing grew quieter. A great resolve swelled in Hastings's bosom.

"I w-want a—a hanky," said a small voice from his shoulder.

From his breast pocket he whipped a square foot of white silk. A little hand snatched at it. Its work completed, she smiled up at him, then endeavoured to withdraw from his arms. Hastings held on.

"Please," said the small voice, "will you let me go?"

"No!" roared Hastings. "No! Never any more!"

Slowly, she raised her head to look at him again. Immediately, thoroughly, satisfyingly, he kissed her. For a moment, a fleeting fraction of time, it seemed to him that the soft lips had answered the pressure of his.

But then she broke free. *"Mr. Hastings!"* She stamped her foot. "How dare——"

A grin of delight was on his face. "'Sno use," he murmured. "'Sno use any more. I'm not frightened of you now!" He snatched at her again.

From the floor there came again that hoarse mutter. Again they didn't hear it.

"And you know you've been in love with me for years," said Hastings.

"Oh! I have *not!*" She was all indignation. Suddenly it went. "Yes, I have, though—for months, anyway. Oh, Jack, Jack, why didn't you do this before?"

"Frightened," said Hastings. "Wind up."

"But—but whatever of?"

"You—and your damned sufficient efficiency. Yesterday I swore to myself I'd pluck up the nerve to tell you as soon as I caught you, red-handed, making a mistake. And you see I have——"

Her eyes flashed. "What d'you mean? *Mistake!* I like that! When I've caught the murderer——"

They both swung round, remembrance flooding back. The owner of the flat lay beside the over-turned table, a shapeless heap in the dark dressing-gown.

Margaret shivered. "Mistake, indeed!" she began.

"Well, you did. This is a man's job. You ought to've waited till I came back. God! how you frightened me! Suppose this outer door here hadn't been ajar."

"But, Jack——"

Hastings forgot murders. "Why d'you call me that?" he asked.

"Because I couldn't always be saying 'Spencer.' I'd feel like a heroine in a serial. And don't interrupt. I was going to say: Never mind, we've got the man. Won't Colonel Gethryn be pleased?"

Hastings came back to earth. "By God!" he said. "So that's the murderer, is it? Well, he's a very ill criminal. How d'you know he is one, by the way?"

"He confessed. He was sort of delirious. Kept saying he'd done it, but wasn't going to tell any one. Horrid it was!"

Hastings rubbed his chin. "I wonder," he said. "I wonder. Come on, we're going to have a nice diplomatic talk with that porter I saw downstairs. And don't forget we mustn't let him get a line on what we're after."

4

The hands of the clock in Lucia Lemesurier's drawing-room stood at five minutes to midnight.

There came a lull in the conversation which Anthony had kept flowing since he had sent his message to Hastings. A wandering talk it had been, but he had achieved his object. Save for a certain look about her eyes, there was now nothing to tell of the strain Lucia had been under. She had even laughed, not once but many times. Watching her, Anthony thought: "She's almost too good to be true." And then he thought: "I'm a fatuous, infatuated ass—and I revel in it!"

For a moment his eyes closed. Behind the lids came a picture of her face—a picture strangely more clear than any given by actual sight.

"You," said Lucia, "ought to be asleep. Not tiring yourself out to make conversation for an hysterical woman who can't control her emotions."

"The closing of the eyes," Anthony said, opening them, "merely indicates that the great detective is thrashing out a knotty problem. Who, what and where is the Sparrow?"

"The Sparrow?" Her eyebrows were lifted.

"Yes. Don't you remember 'Who killed Cock Robin'? Probably the first detective story you ever read. And it was the Sparrow who did the dirty work. Which brings me to another problem: was a certain thing done genuinely or was it done to look as if it had been done genuinely, or was it done in the way it was on purpose to look ungenuine? The answer, at present, is a lemon."

Again she smiled. "It sounds awful," she said. Then, with a change of tone: "But—but my brother? You were saying——"

Piercing, blaring, came the angry ring of the telephone.

They reached it together. As Anthony lifted the receiver, he pointed to the extra earpiece, and she snatched it from its hook in time to hear: "That you, Gethryn?"

"Yes. What did you find?" Anthony snapped.

"The man your message referred to—er—said it was he who had pulled off that deal you were asking about."

Anthony flashed a glance at the woman beside him. He put a hand over hers on the table. Into the telephone he said: "Go on, go on!"

"*But,*" said the telephone. "The chap's out of his head. Must have dreamed it all. I found out he couldn't possibly have had anything to do with the thing. Why on earth he thought *he'd*—er—put this deal through, I can't say—unless the explanation is that he got the idea that he would do it when he began to be so ill, put in a goodish bit of brooding, and then, when it *was* done and he heard about it, got all mixed and thought he was really the—er—manipulator of the business. Anyway, it's certain he couldn't've had anything to do with it at all. Take it from me."

Lucia sank weakly into a chair, still clasping the black disc to her ear.

"You're *sure?*" said Anthony to the telephone.

"See it wet, see it dry. The man lives by himself. He's been ill. I got that from the porter of the flats. This porter told me J.M. hasn't been outside his front door for a week. The story's right enough. You've only got to look at the chap to see he's too ill to have been trotting about. There's not a doubt. You disappointed?"

"God, no! Hastings, my brother, I kiss your hands. And commend you. From what I know, your explanation of why J.M. thought what he did is right. But tell me, how ill is he?"

"Baddish, but nothing fatal. Er—as a matter of fact, the doctor's with him now. Severe flu, I think it is, plus old-standing shell-shock or something like that probably."

Lucia stirred uneasily in her chair.

"Oh, the doctor's with him, is he? Now, what doctor?" Anthony said.

"Well—er—as a matter of fact—er"—bubbled the telephone in embarrassed accents—"I—we—we've taken him back to my place. D'you know the man?"

"I'm, well, interested in him."

"Well, he's all right now, you know. You see, we—I felt rather sorry—fellow's seedy and no one to look after him. We felt rather that we owed him something for false suspicion, what? Hope you don't mind my taking charge."

"Mind? I'm very grateful! But why the hesitancy, the embarrassment? Why all this we—I—us business?"

"Because I've done it!" roared the telephone ecstatically. "I've asked her. I'm going to be married. She——"

"One moment. The admirable Miss Warren, I gather?"

"Yes!" cried the telephone. "Congratulate me!"

"I pound your spirit on the back. Tell the lady this is the only mistake I've ever known her to make. I'll offer my felicitations in person to-morrow. Now listen. I want you to come down here to-morrow—you'll find it best to do it by car—and attend the inquest. It's being held at the house—Abbotshall—and it begins at eleven A. M. If you bring Miss Warren with you, please ask her to take a complete shorthand note of the proceedings. After the inquest go to the Bear and Key in Marling and ask for me. I shall want to pump you. Got that?"

"Very good, sergeant."

"If you see me at the house during the inquest don't speak to me, or do anything to attract attention to me."

"Right."

"Good-bye, and again congratulations." Anthony hung up the receiver.

He turned to Lucia. She smiled up at him, limp from reaction and relief. He brought her a drink, and she took it obediently looking up at him over the rim of the glass.

When she had finished, "Feeling better?" he asked.

Her eyes flashed gratitude. "Thanks to you. Oh! you don't know how—what a horrible, *awful* day I've had!"

"I can guess," Anthony said.

"Oh, I know; I know you can! How can I ever thank you?"

"Thank me? Why, you know, it seems I've done nothing much yet except make a fool of myself running down blind alleys."

"Done nothing!" She was indignant. "Why, if it hadn't been for you I'd never have known Jimmy was safe. I'd just have gone on and on thinking horrors to myself." Suddenly all the fire died out of her. "And I think I should have died," she said.

Anthony said: "You overwhelm me," and thought how true that was. He stood up.

"I must go," he said. "May I suggest that I get my friend Hastings to drive you up to town to-morrow to see your brother. That'll be some time in the afternoon, after the inquest."

"Mr. Gethryn, you think of everything, everything!" She smiled; and Anthony caught his breath.

He made a move in the direction of the door; then paused. "Mrs.

Lemesurier," he said, "you can't, I suppose, tell me anything I haven't already picked up about the Abbotshall *ménage?*"

She shook her head. "I'm sorry; I can't. Except Sir Arthur—and he's only a guest—I hardly know anything about them. Mr. Hoode I met twice. I've never seen his sister. I dare say I should have known them quite well by this time if Jim hadn't left Mr. Hoode in that odd way. But after that—well, it was awkward, and we just haven't mixed."

"D'you know this Mrs. Mainwaring at all?"

"Not at all, except from the illustrated papers."

"Oh. So she's what Zenith might call a Society Snake, is she? Well, well. Not a tennis champion as well, is she, or anything athletic?"

"Oh, no. I'm sure she isn't. Why?"

Anthony smiled. "Merely my 'satiable curtiosity." He turned to the door. "I really must go now."

She stopped him, laying a hand on his arm. "Mr. Gethryn, one minute. I'm like the elephant's child, too, simply bursting with curiosity. Who *did* do it?"

Anthony laughed. "I haven't the faintest idea—yet. On the subject of who didn't do it I could talk for hours. 'But whose the dastard hand that held the knife I know not; nor the reason for the strife.' "

"But you're going to find out, aren't you?"

"I have hope, lady."

The black eyes held the green ones for a long moment. "I think," she said at last, "that you're the most extraordinary man I've ever met. Some day, you must tell me how you knew everything I did last night. I believe you were watching me; only you couldn't have been."

"I," said Anthony, opening the door, "I am Dupont, I am Lecoq, I'm also Hewitt, Holmes and Rouletabille. Good-night."

She was left staring at the closed door. When she opened it to peer into the hall, he had gone.

CHAPTER NINE

THE INQUEST

1

At ten o'clock the next morning they brought a note to Lucia, radiant from a nine hours' sleep.

"MY DEAR MRS. LEMESURIER"—she read—"Hastings and I will call for you at some time between four and five this afternoon.

"Do not attend the inquest this morning, and above all prevent your sister from doing so. No doubt this warning is unnecessary, but I thought safer to issue it. For it is highly probable that the coroner's jury will return a verdict of murder against Archibald Deacon.

"Do not worry about this. Deacon had nothing to do with this messy business. (The great god Bias again, you see.) At the moment, however, things look bad for him. But I repeat: do not worry. Also, prevent your sister (I understand there is an alliance) from doing so more than is unavoidable. I promise things shall be straightened out.

"Yours optimistically,
"ANTHONY GETHRYN."

"P.S.—I find that yesterday I omitted to return to you a bathing-sandal which I found. I ought to have sent it with this letter; but have decided to keep it."

Lucia, after the first shock, obeyed orders. Fond as she was of her sister and her sister's lover, she found worry, for this morning at least, impossible. After the events of yesterday, she somehow discovered herself possessed of a childlike faith in the power of Anthony Gethryn to work necessary miracles.

She told Dora; then spent the morning to such purpose that the girl's fears were in some measure allayed.

2

At ten minutes to eleven Anthony left the Bear and Key and walked slowly in the direction of Abbotshall. He was tired and very tired. In spite of his fatigue he had barely slept. There had been so much to think about. And also so much which, though nothing to do with this work of his, had yet insisted on being thought about.

He entered the house at five minutes past the hour. Proceedings were being opened. The coroner and his jury had just seated themselves round the long table set for them in the study.

All about was an air of drama, heightened by the intensity of public feeling and the fact that the court was set on the actual scene of the crime. Marling felt the eyes and ears of the world bent in its direction. It rather enjoyed the feeling, but nevertheless went sternly, and with due solemnity, about its duty.

Anthony nodded to Boyd, shook hands with Deacon, ignored Hastings and Margaret Warren, already seated at the press table, and ran an eye over the jury.

The sight depressed him. "Mutton!" he murmured.

The coroner rapped the table, cleared his throat, and opened the court.

Five minutes later Superintendent Boyd turned to address a remark to Colonel Gethryn. But Colonel Gethryn was no longer there. Nor, apparently, was he anywhere else in the room. Boyd shrugged his shoulders.

Anthony was in the hall. In the far corner, by the front door, stood a knot of servants. They were clearly absorbed in their talk. On the steps were two policemen, their blue backs towards him. Slowly, Anthony mounted the wide, curving staircase. Once out of sight from below, his pace quickened to a run.

On the first floor he found his hopes realised. It was depopulated. As he had calculated, the whole household was downstairs.

3

The court adjourned at fifteen minutes to two. Hastings and a different, softer, Margaret Warren were given lunch by Anthony in his sitting-room at the Bear and Key.

The meal over, Margaret was given the one comfortable chair,

Hastings sat on the table, and Anthony leaned against the mantelpiece.

"Now, my children," he said, "I have congratulated you, I have filled your stomachs. To work. What of the crowner's quest?"

"Adjourned till three-thirty," said Hastings. "When, after a quarter of an hour's cosy talk, they'll bring in a red-hot verdict of willful murder against the hulking private secretary. We needn't go back, I think. There's one of our men there. He'll take the rest of the report; and it's all over except the shouting."

Anthony nodded. "No, you needn't stay."

"*I*," said Margaret, "don't think the secretary had anything to do with it. Not with those sort of eyes—he couldn't."

Hastings laughed.

"I agree with you, Miss Warren," Anthony said. "And it was the eyes which made me think that way."

Hastings exploded. "Now, wait a minute——"

"Quiet, dog!" Anthony waved him to silence. "I am Richard on the Spot. The case is mine, and I say that Archibald Deacon's a non-starter. Children, I am about to question you. Make ready."

Hastings cast his smile. Margaret produced a notebook.

Anthony said: "So far, the case against Deacon is, I assume: one, that in his possession were found bank-notes for a hundred pounds proved as having been drawn by Hoode from his bank on the morning of the murder; two, that his explanation that this money was given to him by Hoode as a birthday present was neither regarded as at all probable nor supported by any witness; three, that his explanation as to his whereabouts during the time within which the murder was committed was both unsatisfactory and entirely uncorroborated; four, that he attempted to mislead officers of the law by means of an alibi which he knew to be false; five, that in view of his size, strength, length of leg, and the fact that every one else for miles round appears to be accounted for, he seems the most likely person; and six, that his finger-prints were found on the wood-rasp with which the deed was done."

"Look here," said Hastings, "if you were at the inquest, what's all the palaver about?"

"I wasn't, and you'll see. Some of this I knew already, some I guessed. Wonderful, isn't it?"

Margaret leaned forward. "But who do you think did do it, Mr. Gethryn? Do you suspect any one?"

"Every one in the world," said Anthony. "Except Deacon, you, James Masterson, and one other. But I look first at the household;

just as a matter of interest." He ticked off names on his fingers. "The butler Poole, the chauffeur Wright, Martha Forrest the cook, Robert Belford the other man-servant; Elsie Syme, Mabel Smith, housemaids; Lily Ingram the kitchen-maid, and one Thomas Diggle, gardener. Also the sister of the corpse, Sir Arthur Digby-Coates, and Mrs. Mainwaring. And there we have the ''ole ruddy issue, incloodin' the 'eads.'"

"Shades of Pelman!" Hastings was moved to exclaim.

"And," said Anthony benignantly, "what about 'em all? Their stories, their behaviour?"

Margaret consulted the notebook. "The servants," she said, "were all right. Most obviously all right—except the man Belford. The girls no one could accuse of murder, they're too timid and their stories were all connected enough. In most cases they fitted in with each other naturally enough. The cook was in bed before ten-thirty, and slept through the whole thing. The chauffeur was talking to friends outside the lodge. The butler was apparently in his little room all the evening. He can't prove it by witnesses, but you couldn't suspect an old man like that. He's not strong enough for one thing; and he's obviously dreadfully upset by the death of his master. Mrs. Mainwaring seemed all right. She went to bed early, and was seen there by both Miss Hoode and the maid Smith—the one that was afterwards in the linen-room. After the murder was discovered she was found fast asleep. Sir Arthur Digby-Coates is quite all right. He was in his own sitting-room—it has his bedroom on one side of it and the secretary's on the other, apparently—from ten-fifteen until the body was found by Miss Hoode and the old butler rushed up and fetched him. During that time he was seen by various people, including Deacon, at very short intervals. As for Miss Hoode, she deposed—that's the word, isn't it?—that she was in bed by half-past ten, reading. At about eleven she suddenly remembered something about an invitation to some one—she wasn't very clear in her evidence—and went downstairs to use the telephone and to speak to her brother. After that, well, you know what happened. That's all."

Anthony smiled. "And very good, too. I congratulate you, Miss Warren. 'So there, in a manner of speaking, they all are.' Of course, it's all very untidy, this evidence. Very untidy!"

"I know, Mr. Gethryn. But then, you see, it wasn't as if they were all on trial. I mean, all this about where they were and that sort of thing came out mixed up with other things. It wasn't cross-examination with everything on the point and nowhere else. And if people don't know there's going to be a murder, they can't very well all get up nice, smooth alibis, can they?"

Anthony laughed. "Just what I said, Miss Warren. They can't. Now, about ferret-face—Belford, I mean. You seem to think his evidence wasn't as good as the others'. What did he do? Or say?"

Hastings took up the tale. "Nothing very unusual in itself. But his manner was all wrong. Too wrong, I thought, to be merely natural nervousness. Margaret thinks the same. It wasn't that he said anything one could catch hold of; he was just fishy. He made rather a bad impression on the court too. In fact, I think there'd have been a lot more of him later if the case against your limpid-eyed pet hadn't come out so strong.

"Damn it all!" he went on, after a moment's silence, "in any other circumstances I'd be quite willing to bow to your vastly greater experience, Gethryn. And to Margaret's womanly intuition and all that sort of thing. But this is a bit too much. When you get such a lot of circumstantial and presumptive evidence as there is against this man Deacon and then add to it the fact that his finger-prints were the only ones on the weapon the other feller was killed with, it does seem insane to blither: 'He couldn't have done it! Just look at his *sweet* expression!' and things like that!"

"I dare say," Anthony said. "But then Miss Warren and I are *so* psychic, you see."

"But the finger-prints, man! They——"

Anthony became sardonic. "Ah, yes! Those eternal finger-prints. Hastings, you're an incorrigible journalist. Somebody says 'finger-print' to you, you shrug—and the case is over. The blunt instrument bears the thumb-mark of Jasper Standish, *ergo* Jasper's was the hand which struck down the old squire. It's so simple! why trouble any more? Hang Jasper! Hang him, damn him, hang him!"

"But look here, that's not——"

Anthony lifted his hand. "Oh, yes, yes. I know what you're going to say. And I know I'm talking like a fool. The finger-print system is wonderful; but its chief use is tracing old-established criminals. If you consider the ingenuity exercised by this murderer in everything else, doesn't it strike you as queer that he should leave the damning evidence of finger-marks on only one thing, and that the actual weapon? Why, he might as well have stuck his card on Hoode's shirt-front!"

Hastings looked doubtful. "I see what you're driving at," he said, "but I'm not convinced. Not yet, anyhow. And we've rather got away from Belford. Not that there's any more to say, really. He merely struck us as being rather too scared."

"What you really mean, I think," said Anthony, "is that in your opinion Belford was very likely in it with Deacon."

Margaret laughed. "That's got you, Jack. You shouldn't funk."

Anthony said: "Let us leave ferret-face for the moment. Was there no one else you thought behaved suspicious-like?"

Margaret fingered the notebook in her lap. Hastings looked at her.

"You shouldn't funk, Maggie," he said.

"Pig!" said Margaret. "And *don't* call me Maggie! It's disgusting!"

"What *is* all this?" Anthony asked.

Margaret looked up at him. "It's only that I told this person Miss Hoode made me uncomfortable."

"You've watered it down a good bit," Hastings laughed.

"Well, all I meant was that she seemed so contradictory. Not in what she said, you know, but in the way she looked and—and behaved. It was funny, that feeling I had. At first I thought she wasn't suffering over her brother's death, but was just worn out with fear and with trying to—to hide something. And then after that I began to think she was sorry after all, and that all the queer things about her were due to grief. And then after that again I sort of half went back to my first ideas. That's all."

"I think," said Anthony, "that you're a remarkable young woman. You ought to set up in the street of Baker or Harley, or both." His tone was more serious than his words; Margaret coloured.

"Did they," asked Anthony, after a pause, "exhibit the wood-rasp at the 'quest?"

Hastings nodded. "And a nasty weapon it must have made, too."

"I must get a look at it somehow," Anthony said. Then added, half-aloud: "Now, why does that mark worry me?"

"What's that?"

"Nothing, nothing." Anthony stretched himself. "Enough for to-day, children. Hastings, there is a lovely lady who wishes to visit your flat, and this to-night. She is the sister of our old friend J. Masterson. I promised she could see him if she went up to town this evening."

"Of course. J. Masterson, by the way, is doing pretty well. Temperature much lower; though he's very weak still, of course. Does nothing but sleep. Doctor saw him again this morning, and says his trouble is really nothing worse than 'flu, aggravated by inattention and complicated nervous thingumitights due probably to shell-shock."

"I see. It'll be all right about his sister seeing him this evening?"

"Of course." Hastings's smile was replaced by a blank sort of look. "Er—by the way, if this lady lives down here, perhaps I had —could drive her up now, what?"

"I was going to ask whether you would," Anthony said, after a pause, "but I've changed my mind. Don't look too relieved." His reasons for this sudden change of plan were mixed; it is certain they were not purely philanthropic.

"I gather, then," said Hastings, "that having left a competent subordinate to take down the dregs of the inquest, the lady Margaret and I may now get back to town."

They descended to the waiting car. Before it began to move,

"Miss Warren," said Anthony, "would you be so kind as to have that report of this morning's proceedings typed and sent down to me here to-morrow; it'll be so much better than the public ones."

"I'll do it at once," said Margaret.

The car moved forward. Anthony waved his thanks, turned on his heel and re-entered the inn.

4

Within half an hour he was in Lucia's drawing-room. Outside the gate was his big red car.

Lucia kept him waiting barely two minutes. When she came he noticed with irritation the schoolboyish unruliness of his heart. There was for him some new, subtle quality in her beauty to-day. Something dark and wonderful and wild.

She gave him her hand. "I heard the car. I haven't kept you waiting, have I?" she asked.

Anthony shook his head. She glanced curiously round the room.

"No," he said. "Hastings hasn't come. He had to get back. That's my car outside. If you'll allow me to, I'll take you up to town now. If you're ready, shall we start?" He turned to the door.

"I'm sorry," she said as he opened it, "that Mr. Hastings couldn't come."

Anthony, jarred, cheered himself with the thought that there had been a laugh in her voice. He glanced at her face. It told him nothing.

Her travelling-bag was carried out and placed in the car.

"I'm driving myself," said Anthony. "Will you sit in front?"

She smiled at him and took the seat beside the driver's. Annoyed with the disturbance aroused in his breast by that smile, Anthony drove out of the gate and down the narrow road to the bridge at a speed quite illegal. Then he slowed ashamed of himself.

"I'm sorry," he said. "Too fast?"

"Not a bit," she said; and laughed. "I feel quite safe with you, if you want to know."

Anthony glowed.

Presently she asked:

"How did the inquest go? I've heard nothing. Was it—was it as bad as you said it might be?"

"I wasn't there myself," said Anthony, his eyes on the road, "but from what I've been told, I'm afraid it was."

"But you said you *were* there."

"At the house, yes. At the inquest, no."

She said: "You do love being mysterious, don't you?"

"*Touché!* I believe I do, you know. I've been discovering a lot of youthful traits in myself lately." Something in his tone made her look up at him. His profile showed grim; it seemed leaner than ever. He said, after a pause:

"I went to Abbotshall because I wanted to play burglars on the first floor. And the best time to do it was when everybody was downstairs at the inquest. That's all."

"Did you burgle successfully? I mean, did you find what you wanted to find?"

"I found. Some of what I found I'd expected to find; some not." His tone was final and silence fell again. The big car's speed increased. Soon they were among London's outskirts.

"Where are you going to stay?" Anthony asked.

"Brown's Hotel. May I go there first, please?"

To Brown's he took her, and waited with the car till she reappeared. During the journey to Hastings's flat in Kensington there was little opportunity for conversation. Once, threading skillfully through a press of traffic, he began to whistle, under his breath, the dirge of Cock Robin.

Then Hastings's flat was reached. Introductions over, they were left alone in Hastings's study while Hastings went to prepare the invalid.

Anthony picked up his hat. "I must go," he said.

"Where?"

"Back to Marling."

Lucia stared. "Did you only come up to bring me?"

"Yes," he said, after a pause.

"How *awfully* nice of you! But ought you to have wasted all that time?"

"All pleasure," Anthony said oracularly, "is gain. Did you warn your sister that Deacon would probably be arrested after the inquest?"

"I did. And I tried to persuade her not to worry. So I obeyed orders, you see."

"Did you believe there was no cause for worry?"

"Yes," she said.

Anthony bowed. "Good-night," he said, and was gone.

CHAPTER TEN

BIRDS OF THE AIR

1

It was a few minutes after half-past four when Anthony descended to the street and re-entered his car. He drove fast; always, when he found himself disturbed, he sought consolation in speed. It was preferable to be on a horse; but the car was better than nothing.

On the journey he thought much. One half of his mind was occupied with a problem of x and y; the other with a quantity more obscure even than x. It was that second half of his mind which conceived doubts of the worthiness of Anthony Ruthven Gethryn. The sensation was new.

As he drove through the gates of Abbotshall and up the drive, the clock over the stables struck. A quarter to six! If the distance from Kensington to Marling is what they say it is, he had fractured every speed law in the kingdom.

He stopped the car. Round the corner of the house, running, came Sir Arthur Digby-Coates. Though the thick, gray-flecked hair was unruffled by the wind of his speed, there was yet an agitation, a wildness about him, his fluttering tie, his clothes, most unusual.

He panted up to the car. "Gethryn, Gethryn! Just the man I was wanting! Where've you been?"

"London." Anthony was almost surly. He had been dreaming a dream.

"My God!" Sir Arthur pulled at his collar as if he were choking. "Look here! I must talk to you. But not here. Not here! Come in! Come in! My room'll be best. Come on!"

Anthony was dragged into the house and up the stairs and into Sir Arthur's room. They sat, in chairs drawn up to the window. In his, Anthony lay back, but the elder man hunched himself like a nervous schoolboy, sitting on the edge of his chair with his feet thrust backwards and then outwards until they protruded behind and beside each of the front legs. It was an old trick of his when preoccupied, and never ceased to amuse Anthony.

It was some time before Sir Arthur spoke. He seemed in his agitation to have difficulty in finding words. His hands twisted about each other.

"God!" he burst out at last. "What *are* we to do?"

"About what?"

"About this awful, this horrible mistake." Suddenly he jumped to his feet and stood over Anthony. "Why—is it possible—haven't you heard? About Deacon?"

Anthony shook his head.

"Why, man, they've arrested him! The coroner's jury passed a verdict against him. And the police have arrested him. Arrested him!"

"Quite natural, when you think of it," said Anthony.

Sir Arthur stared at him. "D'you mean you think he did it?" he roared. "That boy!"

"No. I'm sure he didn't."

Sir Arthur sighed loud relief. "Thank the Lord for that! But, Gethryn, how was it you hadn't heard about this? And if you hadn't, how was it you weren't surprised? Weren't you at the inquest?"

"Only roughly speaking," said Anthony. "And I wasn't surprised because I knew on what evidence the police were working. Pardon me if I seem flippant—I'm not really—but what we've got to do is to find out who really did kill Cock Robin. That's the only way of getting Deacon off. The police take Deacon to be the Sparrow. You and I believe that he isn't; but we've got to admit that the case against him is good, extraordinarily good. His size and strength fit the part of the murderer. And above all his finger-prints were found on the Bow and Arrow. That last will want a deal of explaining, especially to an English jury, who don't, as a rule, know that real life's more like a fairy story than Hans Andersen."

"I know, I know," Sir Arthur groaned. "Those finger-prints. He must have touched the—the—what do they call the thing?"

"Wood-rasp. A file for wood."

"Ah, yes. He—I suppose he *must* have touched it. Must have. But I'll swear the boy had nothing to do with—with John's death. And he said he'd never seen the thing. And I believe him!"

"So he'd never even seen the thing," Anthony said. "Now that's interesting. Most interesting!"

But Sir Arthur was not listening. "What I'm feeling so—so damnably," he burst out, "is that my evidence helped to make things look worse for the boy."

"How?"

"Because they took mine first; and in describing that awful night I mentioned, like the idiot I am, that Deacon had come into my room at a quarter to eleven. You see, he'd asked me the time, and I'd told him: that's what made me remember. Then later it all came out about the clock in the study, and now every one says the boy put the hands back because he knew he had an alibi. Oh! It's all a ghastly, damnable mistake!"

"It is; and we shan't mend it by sitting here and talking." Anthony got to his feet. "By the way, before I go, tell me: what is Mrs. Mainwaring, who is she, that this poor swine don't see her? If it comes to that, why is she here at all?"

Sir Arthur made a wry face. "Why you haven't seen her I can't tell. Why she's staying here is, I'm sorry to say, for the notoriety. Any decent person would have left the house at once. I'm disgusted; I used almost to like the woman. I would have left, but Laura wished me to stay. And she's so apathetic that she won't get rid of the Mainwaring."

"I must see the lady," said Anthony.

Sir Arthur looked at him with curiosity, but found no enlightenment.

"In fact," said Anthony, "I must see both ladies."

Sir Arthur looked at him again, with no result.

"A last question," Anthony said: "what—without prejudice—do you think of the man-servant, Robert Belford of the ferret face?"

"I wondered whether you'd ask about him," Sir Arthur said eagerly. "I didn't like to say anything because I really know nothing against him at all. Never had anything to do with him, in fact. He used to valet John, and would have me, only I don't use valets. It's simply that I can't bear the fellow; his looks are enough to make any one suspicious. And he's been more furtive than ever—since the —the murder."

"H'm," grunted Anthony.

"It's really very ungrateful of me," said Sir Arthur, "to say anything against the man. He was one—or really two—of the witnesses to the fact that I was sitting here in this chair from ten until after —until poor old John was found. But still, joking aside, I have a very real feeling that Mr. Belford at least knows more than he has told."

"H'm. Yes," Anthony said. "And now for Miss Hoode. Where can I find her?"

"I think she's downstairs somewhere, but I'm not sure. I say, Gethryn, you're not going to—to cross-examine her, are you? I mean I don't think she'll want a lot of talk about——"

"No," Anthony said, crossing the room, "probably she won't."

Sir Arthur opened his mouth to speak; but was left staring at the closed door.

As he shut it behind him, Anthony caught sight of a black-clad figure disappearing round the corner by the stairhead. It was a back he had seen before. It wore an air of stealthy discomfort; and the speed with which it had vanished was in itself suspicious.

Anthony laughed. "Belford, my friend," he thought, "if you *have* done anything naughty, you're simply asking to be found out." He went on and down the stairs.

2

This evening, thought Anthony, as he stood facing her by the open windows of the drawing-room, Laura Hoode was even less prepossessing than she had seemed on the day before. She had risen at his entry, and though the thin, sharp-featured face was calm, he somehow felt her perturbation.

She waved him to a chair. He sank into it, draping one long leg over its fellow.

"What do you want of me, Mr. Gethryn?" The voice was as lifeless as the woman, and Anthony shivered. The sexless always alarmed him.

"A great deal, Miss Hoode." In spite of his aversion his tone was blandly courteous.

"I cannot imagine——"

"Please—one moment," said Anthony. "As you know, I came down here to Marling to find out, if possible, who killed your brother. A——"

"That task," said the woman, "has already been performed."

"Not quite, I think. In my opinion, young Deacon had no more to do with the murder than I. Each minute I spend in this house increases my certainty. This morning I found something I had been looking for, something that may throw a light where one is badly needed, something which you must tell me about."

She drew herself yet more upright on her straight-backed chair.

"Mr. Gethryn," she said, "I like neither your manner nor your manners."

"Unfortunately," said Anthony grimly, "neither manner nor manners matter just now. I started on this business half out of boredom, half because a friend asked me to; but now—well, I'm going to finish it."

"But—but I don't understand at all what you are talking about." The woman was plainly bewildered, yet there seemed in her tone to be an uneasiness not born of bewilderment alone.

Anthony took from his breast-pocket a thick packet of letters. The paper was a deep mauve, the envelopes covered with heavy, sprawling characters. The bundle was held together by a broad ribbon, this too of deep mauve. He balanced the little bundle in the palm of his hand; then looked up to see white rage on the bony, dull face of the woman. The rage, he thought, was not unmixed with fear; but not the kind of fear he had expected.

"These," he said, "are what I want you to explain. To explain, that is, who they are from, and why you took them from your brother's desk and hid them again in your own room."

She rose to her feet; moved a step forward. "You—you——" she began, and choked on the words.

Anthony stood up. "Oh, I know I'm a filthy spy. Don't imagine that I think this private inquiry agent game is anything but noisome. It has been nasty, it will be nasty, and it is nasty, in spite of the cachet of Conan Doyle. I know, none better, that to rifle your room while you were at the inquest this morning was a vile thing to do. I know that brow-beating you now is viler—but I'm going to find out who killed your brother."

"It was that boy," said the woman, white-lipped. She had fallen back into her chair.

"It was not that boy. And that's why I shall go on thinking and spying and crawling and bullying until I find out who it really was.

Now, tell me why you stole those letters." He moved forward and stood looking down at her.

An ugly, dull flush spread over her face. She sat erect. Her colourless eyes flamed.

"You think—you *dare* to think *I* killed him?" she cried in a dreadful whisper.

Anthony shook his head. "Not necessarily. I shall know better what I think when you've told me what I want to know."

"But what have those foul scratchings to do with—with John's death?" She pointed a shaking finger at the little package in his hands.

"Nothing, everything, or just enough," said Anthony. "You're asking me the very questions which I want you, indirectly, to answer."

She said: "I refuse," and closed tightly the thin-lipped mouth.

"Must I force your hand?" he asked. "Very well. You must tell me what I want to know, because, if you don't, I shall go to Scotland Yard, where I have some small influence, and lay these letters and the story of how I found them before the authorities. You must tell me because, if you don't, you will lead me to believe that you do, in fact, know something of how your brother met his death. You must tell me because, if you don't"—he paused, and looked at her until she felt the gaze of the greenish eyes to be unbearable —"because, if you don't," he repeated, "the contents of these letters and their implication are bound to become known to others beside you and me. You will tell me because to keep that last from happening you would do anything."

Even as he finished speaking he knew that last shot had told, fired in the dark though it had been. The woman crumpled. And in her terror Anthony found her more human than before.

"No, no, no!" she whispered. "I'll tell. I'll tell."

Anthony stood, waiting.

"Did you read those—those letters?" The words came tumbling from her lips in almost unseemly haste.

Anthony nodded assent.

"Then you must know that this woman—the *evil* person who wrote them was John's—John's—mistress."

Again he nodded, watching curiously the emotions that supplanted each other in the nondescript face of his victim. Fear he had seen and anxiety; but now there were both these with horror, indignation, tenderness for the dead, and a fervour of distaste for anything which savoured of "loose living." He remembered what he had been told of the lady's rigid code of life, and understood.

She went on, more confidently now that she had once brought herself to speak of "unpleasantnesses" to this strange man who watched her with his strange eyes.

"You see," she said, "nearly a year ago I found out that John was—was associating with this—this woman. I will not tell you how I found out—it is too long a story—but my discovery was accidental. I taxed my brother with his wickedness; but he was so—strange and abrupt—his manner was violent—that I had to leave him with my protest barely voiced.

"Afterwards I tried again and again to make him see the folly, the horror of the sin he was committing—but he would never listen. He would not listen to me, to me who had looked after him since he left school! And I was weak—sinfully weak—and I gave up trying to influence him and—and tried to forget what I had learnt. But those letters kept coming and then John would go away, and I —oh! what is the use——" She broke off, covering her face with her hands.

Anthony felt a growing pity; a pity irrationally the stronger for his own feeling of sympathy with the dead man in what must have been a sordid enough struggle against colourless Puritanism.

She dabbed at the red-rimmed eyes with a handkerchief and struggled on.

"There is not much more to tell you except—except that I—stole those letters for the very reason which you used to—to force me to tell you about them. It is wicked of me, but though John did sin, had been living a life of sin, I determined to keep him clean in the eyes of the world; to keep the knowledge of the evil that he did from the sordid newspapers which would delight in making public the sins of the man they are lamenting as a loss to the nation. And he *is* a loss to the nation. My poor brother—my poor little brother——" She leant her head against the back of her chair and wept, wept hopelessly, bitterly. The tears rolled slowly, unheeded, down the thin cheeks.

Anthony felt himself despicable. A great surge of pity—almost of tenderness—swept over him. Yet the thought of the big, big-hearted, cleanly-sane man who might be hanged held him to his work.

"Do you know," he asked, leaning forward, "the name of this woman?"

"Yes." Her tone was drab, hopeless; she seemed broken. "At least, I know that which she goes by."

Anthony waited in some bewilderment.

"She is a dancer," said the woman, "and shameless. They call her Vanda."

"Good God!" Anthony was startled into surprise. He was a fervent admirer, from this side the footlights, of the beautiful Austrian. He reflected that politicians were not always unlucky.

He got to his feet. The woman started into life.

"The letters!" she cried. "Give me the letters!"

He handed them to her. "My only stipulation," he said, "is that they're not to be destroyed until I give the word." He looked at her searchingly. "I know that you won't attempt to be rid of them until then. And please believe, Miss Hoode, that you have my sincere sympathy, and that there will be no idle talk of what we two know."

"Oh, I believe you," she said wearily. "And now, I suppose you are happy. Though what good you have done Heaven alone knows!"

Anthony looked down at her. "The good I have done is this: I have added to my knowledge. I know, now, that you had nothing to do with your brother's death. And I know there is a woman in the business and who she is. She may not be concerned either directly or indirectly, but the hackneyed French saying is often a useful principle to work on."

The pale eyes of Laura Hoode regarded him with curiosity. He felt with surprise that she seemed every minute to grow more human.

"You are an unusual person, Mr. Gethryn," she said. "You spy upon me and torture me—and yet I feel that I like you." She paused; then went on: "You'll tell me that you know that the young man Deacon did not kill my brother; you tell me that although I have behaved so suspiciously you know also that I had nothing to do with—with the crime. How do you know these things?"

Anthony smiled. "I know," he said, "because you both told me. I know that neither of you did it as you would know, after talking to him, that the bishop hadn't really stolen the little girl's sixpence, even though all the newspapers had said he did. Now I must go. Good-night."

As he entered the hall from the passage, a woman rushed at him. She was tall, and suspiciously beautiful. She drooped and made eyes. She was shy and daring and coy.

"Oh!" she gasped. "Is it Colonel Gethryn? *Is* it? Oh, you *must* be? Oh, Colonel, how *thrilling* to meet you! How *too* thrilling!"

Mrs. Roland Mainwaring pleased Anthony not at all. It is to be deplored that he was at no pains to conceal his distaste.

"Mrs. Mainwaring?" he said. "Madam, the thrill is yours."

She stood blocking his path. Perforce he stood still.

"Oh, colonel, *do* tell me you don't think that *sweet* boy—oh! the beastly police—it's all *too,* too horrible and *awful!*"

Anthony laughed. The thought of Deacon as a *"sweet boy"* amused him. The lady regarded his mirth with suspicion.

Anthony became ponderously official. "Your questions, madam, are embarrassing. But my opinions are—my opinions; and I keep them"—he tapped his forehead solemnly—"here."

Awe-stricken eyes were rolled at him. "Oh, colonel," she whispered. "Oh, colonel! How *won-derful!*" Then, coyly: "How lucky for little me that I'm a poor, weak woman!"

"I have always," said Anthony gravely, "believed in equal rights for women. They occupy an equal footing with men in my—opinions." He bowed and brushed past her, crossing the hall.

CHAPTER ELEVEN

THE BOW AND ARROW

Without a glance behind him at the beautiful lady, Anthony made for the study, entered it, and closed the door behind him.

The great room bore an aspect widely different from that of his first visit. Down the centre ran the long trestle table of the coroner's court. Two smaller ones were ranged along the walls. The far end of the room was blocked with rows of chairs.

Anthony realised, with something of surprise, what a big room it was. Then he banished from his mind everything save his immediate purpose, and turned to the little rosewood table which stood between the door and the grandfather clock.

He bent to see more clearly the scar on the table-top; the scar which he had noticed on his second visit to the room and which had, in some vague way he could not define, been persistently worrying him during the day. It was an even more perfect impression of the wood-rasp than he had remembered it to be, an orderly series of indentations which made a mark two inches wide and over a foot in length.

That something kept jogging in his mind; something about the mark that was indefinably wrong because the mark itself was so undoubtedly right.

Beside him the door opened. He straightened his back and turned to see Sir Arthur.

"Hallo, Gethryn. Can I come in? Thought you might be in here. Turn me out if you'd rather be alone."

"No, no," said Anthony. "Come in. I'm here because I wanted to look at something and because it was the best way of escape. What sweetness! I feel quite sticky, I do!"

Sir Arthur smiled. "Dodo Mainwaring, eh? I caught a glimpse of her. What d'you think?"

Anthony raised one eyebrow.

"Exactly," said Sir Arthur. "If that woman doesn't go soon I won't wait for Laura, I'll pack her off myself."

"Ah, yes," Anthony said vaguely, looking down at the table. "I say, have you seen the Bow and Arrow?"

"Eh? What?"

"The wood-rasp."

Sir Arthur shivered. "Oh, yes. Yes, I have. It was an exhibit at the inquest."

"What was the size of it?"

"Well, I believe it's about the biggest made. Usual short, thick handle with a blade of about a foot long and perhaps two inches wide."

Anthony pointed to the table. "Did it make this mark?" he asked.

"Of course. Why, all that came out at the inquest. Weren't——"

"I've got it!" cried Anthony, and slapped his thigh.

"What's that? What's that? Have you thought—found something?"

"I have and I have. Now, another thing: was the handle of the thing old and battered and worn at the edges and filthy and split?"

Sir Arthur smiled. "No; I'm afraid you're wrong there, Gethryn. It was almost brand-new."

"Exactly!" said Anthony. "Exactly. All polished and convenient. Oh, ours is a nice case, ours is!"

"My dear boy, I'm afraid you go too fast for me." Sir Arthur was puzzled.

"That's nothing," Anthony said. "I go a damn sight too fast for myself sometimes."

"But what are you driving at? What's all this about the wood-rasp?"

"I won't give you a direct answer—it's against the rules of the Detectives' Union—but I invite you to bring your intellect to bear on the position of this scar here. You'll see that it's roughly twelve inches by two and lies ten inches from all four edges of the table —right in the middle, in fact. Then think of the nice new handle on the wood-rasp." Anthony appeared well pleased. " 'O frabjous day, Calloo callay!' Rappings from Doyle!"

Sir Arthur shook his head. "I suppose you're not mad?" he said, smiling.

" 'No, not mad, said the monkey.' "

There fell a long silence, broken at last by the elder man.

"God!" he cried in a whisper. "Let's get out of this room. Gethryn, it's horrible! Horrible! Where poor old John was killed— and here we are cracking *jokes!*" He took Anthony by the arm and pulled him to the door.

They went into the garden through the verandah. By the windows of the study Anthony stopped and stood staring at the creeper-covered wall; staring as he had stared on the afternoon before. Sir Arthur stood at his elbow.

"Splendid sight, that creeper," said Anthony. *"Ampelopsis Veitchii,* isn't it?"

"So you're a botanist? It may be what you say. I'm afraid it's just creeper to me."

Anthony, turning, saw Boyd walking towards them, and waved a hand.

"Damn!" Sir Arthur growled. "The Scotland Yard man. He arrested the boy. Officious fool!"

"Oh, Boyd's a good chap. I like Boyd. He's done his best. On the evidence he couldn't do anything but take Deacon."

"I know, I know," said Sir Arthur impatiently. "But all the same, he——" He broke off, turning to go.

Boyd came up to them. "Good evening, gentlemen."

"Evening, Boyd," said Anthony.

Suddenly, "By Gad!" Sir Arthur cried, and turned a bewildered face upon them. "I didn't think of that before!"

"Think of what, sir?" asked Boyd.

"Why, something that may change everything! Look here, that's the window of my sitting-room up there—the one over the window of the study which you say the murderer must have got in by!"

Anthony was silent. Boyd said stolidly: "Well, sir?"

"But don't you see, man? Don't *you* see, Gethryn? I was sitting up in my room, by that window, all the time. I should have been bound to hear something. Bound to!"

"But you didn't, sir," said Boyd.

"Ach!" Sir Arthur turned on his heel and flung away from them and into the house.

"He thinks you've taken the wrong man, Boyd," said Anthony.

"I know, sir. Do you?"

Anthony laughed. "I do, I do. By the way, can I see him?"

"You can, sir. He asked for you. That's really what I came up for. That and the walk."

"Thanks. I'll take you down in the car. How long before Deacon's moved to the county jail?"

"He'll be going to-morrow sometime, sir. Afternoon or evening."

They walked in silence to the car. Anthony drove out of the gates and down the hill very slowly. Boyd sighed relief: he knew "the colonel's" driving of old.

"I'm afraid, sir," he said at last, "that this case has been a disappointment to you, so to speak."

Anthony looked round at him. "Why so fast, Boyd? Why so fast?" After a moment he added: "Pumps not working too well to-day, are they?"

The detective gave a rumbling chuckle. "I suppose it was a bit obvious, sir," he said. "But you're puzzling me, that you are."

"What am I that I should flummox one of the Big Four? Oh, Fame! Oh, Glory! I stand within your gates."

Boyd reddened. "Oh, don't josh, sir. What I mean is, here are we with as clear a case as ever there was, and yet there are you, a gentleman who's no amateur, still searching around and—and trying to *make* another criminal, so to speak."

"It's not a bit of good trying to get me to explain what I'm doing, Boyd, because I don't know myself. I'm groping—and it's devilish dark. There is a little light, but I don't know where it's coming from—yet. But I will." He fell silent; then added in a different tone: "Look here: we'll take it that I'm mad and the law is sane. But will you help me in my madness? Just one or two little things?"

"As far as I can, sir," Boyd said solemnly, "of course I will."

"You're a good fellow, Boyd," said Anthony warmly, "and you

can start now." He stopped the car and turned in his seat. "Where's the Bow—I mean the wood-rasp?"

"At present it's at the station. Where we're going. To-morrow it'll be taken up to the Yard."

"Can I see it this evening?"

"You can, sir, seeing that you're an old friend, if I may say so."

"Excellent man!"

"Look here, sir," Boyd took a wallet from his pocket; from the wallet some photographs. "You might care to see these. Enlargements of the finger-prints."

Anthony took the six pieces of thin pasteboard and bent eagerly to examine them. They had been taken, these photographs, from three points of view. They showed that the handle of the rasp had been marked by a thumb and two fingers—all pointing downwards towards the blade.

"And these were the only marks?" Anthony said.

"Enough, aren't they, sir?"

"Yes," murmured Anthony. "Oh, yes. What lovely little marks! How kind of Archibald!"

"What's that, sir?"

"I was remarking, Boyd, on the kindly forethought which Mr. Deacon showed for Scotland Yard. He couldn't bear to think of you wasting your time detecting all the wrong people, so he left his card for you."

"I don't know what you're getting at at all, sir." Boyd shook his head sadly.

Anthony handed back the photographs and started the car. In less than a minute they had finished the descent and turned the corner into the village of Marling. Boyd caught his breath and clung to his seat. The High Street streamed by them. At its far end Anthony pulled up, outside the little police-station. Marling was proud of its police station, an offensive affair of pinkish brick. To Anthony, coming upon it in the midst of the little leaning houses, the low-browed shops and thatched cottages, it was like finding a comic postcard of the Mother-in-law school in an exhibition of pleasing miniatures.

He shivered, and dragged Boyd inside. Here he was received by the local inspector. At a word from Boyd the inspector produced keys, opened locks and at last laid on the table the wood-rasp.

It was, as Sir Arthur had said, the biggest of its kind—a foot-long bar of serrated iron, looking like a file whose roughnesses have been ten times magnified. To the points of these roughnesses clung little scraps of stained and withered flesh, while in the corresponding hollows were dark encrustations of dried blood. The handle was new, of some light-coloured wood, and was perhaps four inches long and three and a half in circumference.

"Now that's not at all pretty," said Anthony, with a grimace. "Can I pick it up? Or would that spoil the marks?"

Boyd said: "Oh, that's all right, sir. The coroner's jury have passed it about. And we've got the official record and the photos."

Anthony took it from the table; peered at it; shook it; weighed it in his hand.

Boyd pointed to the blade. "Not much doubt that's what did the trick, is there, C—Mr. Gethryn?"

"Never a doubt," said Anthony, and shook the thing with vigour. There was a sudden clatter. The blade had flown off, struck the table, and fallen to the floor.

"Bit loose," said Anthony, looking at the handle in his fingers. He stooped and picked up the blade, holding it gingerly.

"Those blows that broke in the deceased's skull," said Boyd, "must've been hard enough to loosen anything, so to speak."

"Possibly." Anthony's tone was not one of conviction. "Aha! Now what are *you* doing here, little friends?" He picked, from a notch in the thin iron tongue upon which the handle had been fitted, two threads of white linen. "And you, too, what are you?" He stopped and picked up from the floor a small, thin wedge of darkish wood. "There should be another of you somewhere," he murmured, and peered into the handle. He shook it, and there dropped out of the hollow where the tongue of the blade had been another slip of wood, identical with the first.

He turned to the two men watching him. "Boyd, I give these, the threads and the woods, into your official keeping. You and the inspector saw where they came from." He took an envelope from his pocket, slipped his discoveries into it and laid it upon the table beside the dismembered rasp.

The inspector looked at the man from Scotland Yard, and scratched his head.

"That's all, I think," Anthony said. "Can I see the prisoner now?"

CHAPTER TWELVE

EXHIBITS

The door of the cell clanged to behind Boyd. From a chair, Deacon unfolded his bulk to greet Anthony. They shook hands.

"Wasn't long before I yelled for you," the criminal grinned. "Take the chair. I'll squat on the gent's bedding."

Anthony sat, running his eye over the cell. There was the chair he sat on, the truckle bed, a tinware wash-stand, a shelf, a dressing-case of Deacon's, and, in one corner, a large brown-paper parcel.

"Pretty snug, brother, isn't it?" Deacon smiled. "I languish in comfort. 'D've been pretty glad of this at times during the recent fracas in France. I say, wouldn't you like to write the story of my life? *Some Criminals I Have Known: Number One—The Abbotshall Murderer.* You know the sort of thing."

Anthony laughed. "Well, you take it easily enough. I'm afraid I should alternate fury and depression."

For a moment Deacon's blue eyes met his; and in them Anthony saw a kind of despairing horror. But only for the half of a second. And then the old laughing look was in them again. More than ever, Anthony felt admiration and a desperate desire to get this large man out of this small cell; to make him free again—as free as the hot, gleaming streak of the setting sun which pierced the little barred window and painted a line of gold on the drab floor. But to get him out one must work.

"What about those finger-prints?" he asked suddenly.

"You have me," said Deacon, "on the hip. That's *the* most amazing bit of jiggery pokery about all this hocus pocus. What about 'em to you?"

"They certainly savour," Anthony said, "of hanky panky. In fact, since I know they're yours and that you didn't kill Hoode, I know they must be. Now, have you seen that wood-rasp?"

"Yes. At the inquest."

"Never before?"

"Not as I knows on, guv'nor. In fact, I'd almost swear to 'never.'"

But then I'm the most amazing ass about tools. A fret-saw or a pile-driver, they're all one to me."

"Did you notice the handle?" Anthony asked.

"With interest; because they said it had my paw-marks on it."

"Ever seen that before? By itself, I mean."

Deacon shook his head. "Never." He fell silent, then said: "I suppose those prints *couldn't* be any one else's, could they?"

"I'm afraid they couldn't," said Anthony.

Deacon looked at him. "I say, Gethryn, are we mad? Or is this all a bloody nightmare? I tell you, I didn't kill the boss, and yet the thing he's killed with is all over the marks of my fingers! And as far as I know I never even saw the gadget before! It doesn't work out, does it?"

"It's got to," Anthony said. "I'll damned well make it. Now, what d'you know about the incomparable Vanda?"

Deacon whistled. "How did you get hold of that?" he asked, wonderingly.

"You know my methods, my dear Deacon. But what d'you know about Vanda? Beyond the fact that she's a wonderful dancer."

"I don't really *know* anything; but I've a shrewd little suspish she was the boss's mistress."

"She was. But as you didn't actually know anything, I gather you can't help me further there."

" 'Fraid not. For one thing my suspicion was founded on something that happened by accident, and for another I've not the foggiest idea of what you're driving at."

"They *will* all say that!" Anthony sighed. "And it's just what I want some one to tell *me*. Never mind, we'll get on with the exhibits. Have you ever seen this?" He took from a swollen hip pocket a small paper package, unfolded it, and handed the contents to Deacon.

They were a coil of filthy, black-smeared silk cord. Curiously, the prisoner shook it out, letting one end fall to the floor. He saw now that it was knotted at regular intervals along its length, which was a full sixteen feet.

"Never saw it in my natural." He looked up at Anthony. "What is it?"

"Obviously a length of silk cord," Anthony said, "with, as you would probably say, knobs on."

"I mean, where did you find it? What bearing's it got?"

"I found it," said Anthony slowly, "in your bedroom at Abbotshall."

"What?"

"In your room. On a ledge inside that wonderful old chimney; about six inches higher than the mantelpiece. That accounts for the filth. You can see the rope was white once, and not so long ago."

Deacon frowned at the floor. "Well, it's either been there up the chimney since I went to the house—last May, that is—or else it's been planted there. I never set eyes on it before."

"Good!" Anthony coiled up the cord, wrapped it up in the paper, and returned the parcel to his pocket.

"But what's the beastly bit of string *mean?* What's it got to do with me or you or anything in this business? Tell me that!"

"Shan't," said Anthony. "I'm not sure yet myself. You'll have to wait."

Deacon shrugged his great shoulders. "Right-o. Next, please."

Anthony's hand went to his breast pocket. From a leather wallet he took a bunch of newspaper cuttings.

"These," he said, "I found in a really-truly secret drawer in your late chief's desk. Know anything about 'em? Or why they were there?"

In silence, Deacon read each slip. When he had finished,

"Well?" Anthony said.

"They mean nothing in my young life. These three rags—*The Searchlight, The St. Stephen's Gazette,* and the weekly one, *Vox Populi*—always were dead agin the boss. I can't make head or tail of what you're driving at, Gethryn, I can't really!"

Anthony groaned. "There you go again. Never mind that, but tell me, did you know Hoode was keeping these cuttings?"

"No."

"Did he ever mention the persistent attacks of these three papers?"

"No."

"No? Pity." Anthony got to his feet. "I must move. Anything you want? Books? Food? Tobacco?"

Deacon smiled. "Nothing, thanks awfully. Our Arthur—old Digby-Coates, you know—has done all that. Brought me down a sack of books, a box of cigars, and arranged for decidedly improved victuals to be brought over from the White Horse by quite a neat line in barmaidings. Also, he's fixed up the solicitors and trimmings. They're going to try to get Marshall, K.C."

"Excellent! Marshall's about the best counsel there is. There's nothing you want, then."

"Nothing. Shall I see you to-morrow?"

Anthony nodded. "You will. Early afternoon, probably, as I hear they're moving you later. Good-night; and don't forget I'm going to get you out of this—somehow."

They shook hands. A minute later Anthony was walking slowly back towards his inn up the cobbled street. The sun was sinking behind the gables of a twisted house at the top of the rise, and the road which had been gold was splashed with blood-red blotches.

He shivered. In all this morass of doubt, where every one was sure except Anthony Ruthven Gethryn, he felt alone. Not even the golden-dark background to his thoughts which was the perpetual image of the Lady of the Sandal could compensate for the blackness of bewilderment—the blackness through which he could see light but not the way to it.

Then his thoughts turned to Deacon, his cheerfulness, his ease of manner, his courage which surely masked a hell of distress. Suddenly the admiration which he felt somehow cheered him. His step quickened.

"By God!" he muttered, "that's a man and a half——" and broke off sharply. He had collided with something softly hard. A girl, running. A girl with wild, red-rimmed eyes and hatless, dishevelled, golden head.

Before he could voice apology; almost before he was aware of the collision, she had passed him and was stumbling down the uneven little road with its splashes of crimson painted by the dying sun. From a doorway a slatternly woman peered out, curious with the brutal, impersonal curiosity of the yokel.

Anthony struggled to adjust his memory. Ah, yes! It was the sister. Her sister. Dora Masterson. He turned; caught up with four long strides; laid a hand upon the girl's shoulder. She shook it off, turning to him a face disfigured by desire for more tears, tears that would not come.

"You were going to the police-station, Miss Masterson?" Anthony asked.

She nodded.

"You mustn't—not like this." He took her gently by the arm. "You could do nothing—and you'd make him feel as if things were unbearable."

"I must see him." She spoke dully, an unnatural pause between each word.

"Not now," said Anthony firmly. "Not when I want your help." He wondered if the lie showed through his words; cursed that he should have to hamper himself with an hysterical girl.

She swallowed the bait. "Help you?" she asked eagerly. "About —about Archie? How can *I* do that?"

"I can't tell you here. You must come up to the inn." He led her back up the hill.

CHAPTER THIRTEEN

IRONS IN THE FIRE

1

Up in his little, low-ceilinged, oak-panelled sitting-room in the Bear and Key, Anthony sat the girl in the one arm-chair. She refused whisky so pleadingly that he ordered tea. When it had come and the bearer departed, he sat on the table and watched her drink.

"Now," he said, "suppose you tell me all about it," and was immediately smitten with memories of another occasion when he had used the phrase.

Dora Masterson said simply: "I was frightened. Oh, so horribly, *horribly* frightened!"

Anthony was puzzled. "But why just now? Surely you must have felt like this as soon as you heard?"

"N-no. Of course it was—terrible! But Lucia told me what you said, Mr. Gethryn—and she—she seemed to so absolutely *believe* that you would make everything all right that I—I tried to believe too."

Anthony's heart gave a leap that startled him.

The girl went on, struggling for control. "But—but it was when I heard about the end of the inquest—that he was actually in—— Oh, it's too awful! It's too *terrible!*" She swayed about in the big chair, hands hiding her face, the slim shoulders twisting as if her pain were bodily.

Again was Anthony puzzled. Something in the tone told him that here was something he had not heard of. And this tendency to hysteria must be stopped.

"What d'you mean? Explain!" he said sharply.

She sat upright at that, her face working. "I mean that—that— if only I hadn't been a senseless, vicious little fool; if—if only I hadn't be-behaved like a b-beastly schoolgirl, Archie wouldn't—wouldn't be in that awful place! Oh! why was I ever born!" She pressed her hands to her face and doubled up in the chair until her forehead rested on her knees.

"I'm afraid I don't understand yet," said Anthony.

She raised her head. "Weren't you at the inquest?" she asked, dabbing at her swollen eyes with the back of a hand like the schoolgirl she had named herself.

"Not exactly," said Anthony, and wondered how many more times he would have to answer this question.

"Why, then you—you don't know that—that Archie s-said he went out for a walk during the time when the—the Thing must have been done. And the *beasts* d-don't believe him because nobody at all saw him while he was out!"

"I still don't——"

She broke in on his sentence with a flood of speech, springing to her feet.

"Oh, you fool, you fool!" she cried. "*I* ought to have seen him! *I, I, I!* I was to have met him down there on the bank, this side, by the bridge. We'd arranged a walk! And then because *I* thought *I* was some one; because *I* thought he had been rude to *me* that afternoon, I must needs think *I* would punish *him!* And I didn't go! I didn't meet him! I stayed at home! Christ help me, I stayed at home!"

Anthony was shocked into sympathy. "My *dear* chap," he said. "My *dear* chap!" He went to her and dropped a hand on her shoulder. "You poor child!"

Wearily, she sank against him. The reddish-golden head fell on his shoulder. But she made no sound. She was past tears.

For a moment they stood thus, while he patted the slim shoulder. Then she drew herself upright and away from him.

"You must sit down," he said.

She looked up at him. "Please forgive me," she said. "I didn't mean to—to make such a fool of myself. And I was very rude." She sat down.

Anthony waved aside apology. "What we've got to do," he said, smiling down at her, "is to do something."

"Yes, yes, I know. But what, what? Oh, you said I could help, but I believe you only did it out of kindness. But if I could really help—how much less—less awful I should feel!"

Anthony conceived a liking for this girl; a liking born not altogether of sympathy. But he wondered, with half-humorous desperation, how he was to provide what she wanted and yet not waste time.

"Consoler-in-Chief to the Birds of the Air, I am," he said to himself; then aloud: "You can help, Miss Masterson, by listening to me think. In this business, I'm like a mad poet without hands or tongue. I mean, I've found out more than the other fellows—the police—but it's all odds and ends and tangles—little things, queer in themselves, that men would tell me might be found anywhere if one only troubled to look for 'em. But I say they're not; that they fit!"

The girl was sitting upright now, alert, gazing at him intently. "Think, then," she whispered.

"Now for it," thought Anthony, "and God send it'll take her in —and quickly."

Aloud, he began: "Reconcile for me—put these things into order and make 'em mean something—if you can. Innocent finger-prints on a weapon which performed a murder. An innocent person—not the one of the finger-prints—stealing letters from the corpse to hide the fact that the corpse had a mistress. An attempt to make a clock give an alibi, the attempt being so clumsily carried out that it seems very ill in accord with other indications of the murderer's ingenuity. Secret drawer in corpse's desk full of newspaper-cuttings, all of 'em vicious attacks on corpse when alive. Finger-prints——"

"Mr. Gethryn!" the girl interrupted harshly; "you're making fun of me! No, that's not fair; you're just playing with me to make me think I can help. No doubt you mean to be kind—but I *hate* it!"

Anthony for once was crestfallen. The truth of the accusation was so complete as to make an answer impossible. He found himself in the indefensible position of one "who means well." He groped wildly for words, but was saved; for, suddenly, Dora sprang to her feet.

"Those cuttings!" she cried. "Did you mean—do you *really* want to know anything about them?"

Anthony was surprised. "Most certainly I do. I don't know exactly what I want to know, but that means I want to know everything."

"Well, go and see Jim—my brother—now, at once!" She stamped her foot at him. "When he was secretary to Mr. Hoode he was full of those attacks in the press. I remember we thought he was rather silly about them. He used to say there was something more than mere—what did he call it?—policy behind them, and swore he'd make Mr. Hoode take notice of them. I *think* it was what they eventually quarrelled about, but I'm not sure, because he'd never tell me. He wouldn't even tell Loo. But if you want to know anything about those papers, Mr. Gethryn, Jimmie's more likely to be able to tell you than any one else!"

Anthony looked at her and said: "The best apology I can make to you is to go up to town now. Your brother ought to be well enough by this time. He's got to be!" He paused; then added with a smile: "You know you wouldn't have found me out if I'd been less preoccupied. I'm a bit tired, too."

Dora, forgetting herself, looked at him closely. "Why—why, you look almost *ill!*" she cried, "p'r'aps you—oughtn't to go to-night."

"Oh, I'm going right enough," Anthony said; "and now. And I'm not ill; that's only my interesting pallor. You must go home— and don't worry."

She cried: "How can I *help* worrying? Worrying till I wish I'd never been born! Unless there's a miracle——"

"Chesterton once wrote," Anthony interrupted her, "that 'the most wonderful thing about miracles is that they sometimes happen.' And he's a great and wise man."

The girl flashed a tremulous smile at him and passed out of the door.

2

At ten minutes past ten the great red Mercedes drew up outside the block of flats where Spencer Hastings lived. Anthony had broken his own record of that afternoon for the Kensington-Marling journey.

Stiffly, he clambered to the pavement, noted with curiosity that his hands were shaking, and ran up the steps. As he went he wondered would he see Lucia. He arrived at the door of No. 15 more out of breath than the climb should have made him.

It was she who opened it, and at the sight of her the shortness of his breath was ridiculously increased.

Hastings, she told him, was at his office: his housekeeper, too, was out, being on holiday. She was talking fast, and Anthony didn't have to speak. She was pale, and there were dark marks under her eyes. She was troubled, she said, about her brother's progress: his fever was back, and although he was sleeping, she had sent for the doctor again. She wanted to go back to Marling to look after her sister, but she couldn't. Not while Jim was like this.

They were by this time in the little drawing-room; and as yet Anthony had done nothing save stare.

He said: "Er—good evening. Hastings out?"

She opened her eyes. "But—but I've just told you that Mr. Hastings is at his office!"

"Of course. Ah, yes," said Anthony.

"Did you want to see him?"

Anthony recovered himself.

"No," he said shortly. "Mrs. Lemesurier, I must talk to your brother." It was, he thinks now, the great fatigue which had accumulated during the past days and the strain of that flying drive which led him to speak with such curtness.

"Talk to Jim? Oh, but you can't," Lucia said. Her tone was gentle and rather aloof and very firm.

"Oh, but I must," Anthony said. His loss of temper is regrettable.

The dark eyes blazed at him. "You can't," she said.

Anthony said, slowly: "Mrs. Lemesurier, I am, as best I know how, trying to clear of the charge of murder a man I believe innocent. I've got to a point where a five minutes' conversation with your brother will help me. Your brother—you have told me yourself—can't be considered as dangerously ill. I must see him."

This time it was her eyes that fell. Anthony was angry—with himself. And a man angry with himself is often invincible.

But she had not capitulated, he saw. She crossed to the inner door and stood with her back to it.

Anthony picked his hat from the table and walked slowly towards her, smiling as he walked. It was not a nice smile. It crept up one side of his face and stopped before it reached his eyes. A black smile. There are men in odd corners of the world who would counsel, out of personal experience, that when one sees that smile one had better get out.

He came close to her, still smiling. For a moment she faced him; then faltered; stood to one side and let him pass.

He closed the door softly behind him and began his search for the sick-room, and found it at once.

A shaded lamp arranged to leave the bed in shadow was the only light. In the bed lay a man. Peering at his face, Anthony could trace a certain faint resemblance. He sat on the chair by the bed and waited.

"Who the devil are you?" said a weak voice.

Clearly, but with rapidity, Anthony explained his presence.

"I'm sorry," he said in conclusion, "to disturb a sick man, and I'll get the business over as quickly as possible. But I've got to find out all I can, you see."

"Quite, quite." Masterson's voice was stronger now. Though flushed with fever, he was shaven and clean, vastly different from Margaret's bogey.

"How can I help?" he asked after a silence.

Anthony told him. Bored at first, Masterson woke to sudden interest at the mention of the newspaper-cuttings.

"So he *did* keep 'em!" He lifted himself in the bed to rest on one elbow.

Anthony pushed the little bundle of slips into the thin hands. Eagerly, the sick man read each.

"Some of these are new," he said. "After my time with Hoode, I mean. But these three—and this one—I remember well. Dammit, I ought to! These are what we had that infernal row about."

"How?"

"Well, you see, I'd been watching these three papers for a long time, and I'd come to a definite conclusion that there was one man behind all the attacks. I told Hoode so, and he laughed at the idea! That made me as mad as hell. I've always had a foul temper, but since the war, y'know, it's really uncontrollable. I mean I actually can't help it."

"I know," Anthony nodded.

"That's all. I cursed him for a blind, pig-headed, big-headed fool, and he sacked me. He couldn't very well do anything else. I still feel very bitter about it; though not quite so much now he's dead. He was such a brilliant cove in some ways, but so blasted silly in others. Simply wouldn't listen to what I had to say—and I was sweating to benefit him!"

" 'Zeal, all zeal, Mr. Easy!' " said Anthony.

"Exactly; but zeal's a damn good thing at times, 'specially in private secretaries, and being turned down like that made me brood. I really couldn't help it, you know. After I got the sack I brooded to such an extent that I simply went to pieces. Drank too much. Made an idiot of myself. I say, Lucia's told me all about things, and I want to thank——"

"You can do that best," Anthony interrupted, "by keeping on about Hoode and these press-cuttings. I've made some conclusions about 'em myself, but you know more."

A deeper flush came to the cheek of the man in bed. He turned restlessly.

"When I come to think of it," he said nervously, "I don't *know* a great deal. Mostly surmise, and from what I've heard of you I should say you're better at that game than I am."

Anthony grew grim. "Some one's been exaggerating. You fire ahead. The sooner you do, the sooner I'll be able to get away and leave you in peace."

Masterson said hesitantly: "All right. When I first saw the things coming out one by one I didn't think anything about 'em. But after a week or so—it may have been a month—something queer struck me. At first I couldn't place it. Then after collecting a few of the articles, I tumbled. It seemed to me that one man was behind 'em. More, that one man was writing 'em—and for three papers of very different politics and apparently belonging to different people!"

Anthony was pleased. "You support me. I thought the author seemed to be one man, though I've not had time to study the things carefully. I went so far as to think—the authorship being the same and the papers so different in views—that one man controlled all three." He fell silent a moment, then added slowly: "One might consider, you know, whether the controller and the writer——"

But Masterson interrupted. "Look here," he said, sitting up in obvious excitement, "how did you spot the unity of authorship business?"

"Similarity of style, I think." Anthony was reflective. "I've got quite an eye for style. Two or three times the fellow tried to disguise it. By doing that he gave the game away completely."

"Oh, but there was more than that!" cried the other, fumbling with shaking hands at the sheaf of cuttings. "Wait till I find—ah! Now, look at this. 'The Minister of Imperial Finance, in his efforts for advancement of self, would do well to remember that hackneyed line of Pope: "A little learning is a dangerous thing."' Did you see that?"

Anthony opened his eyes. "I did. And thought how refreshing it was to see the quotation given right. They nearly all get it wrong, though you'd think any one could see that Pope couldn't have been such a fool as to say a little knowledge was dangerous. Knowledge is always useful; learning isn't—until you've got plenty. But go on: what about it?"

Masterson was searching feverishly. "Tell you when I've found—here we are! Listen. Er-um Finance—policy—rumty-tumty—'when Greek joins Greek, then comes the tug-of-war!' There you are again. How many times d'you see that given right?"

"Never," said Anthony. "They all say 'meets.'"

"There you are, then. It all goes to prove what you felt and I'm certain about." He tapped the bundle of cuttings with a lean finger. "All these were written by the same man; there's not a doubt in my mind. Style—similarity in style, I mean—isn't proof; but this orgy of correctitude *plus* that similarity is. At least it's good enough for me. There are plenty more instances if you want them. There's one I remember well—a leader in *Vox Populi*. It was a more vicious attack on Hoode even than the others, and it was so damn' well done that it was almost convincing. It said, apropos of him: *'facilis descensus averno.'* What about that?"

Anthony sat up. " *'Averno'* is very rare," he said slowly. "But it's a better reading. I saw it. I wondered. I wondered a lot."

There was a silence. The two looked at each other.

"Masterson," Anthony said at last, "you're very useful, you know. Most useful. Wish you weren't sick a-bed. Now here's another point. We've fixed the author of these articles as one man; but what about the motive force behind the author. I'm inclining to the view that as these papers differ so widely in everything else they are controlled by some one whose only interest in them was to do Hoode a bad turn. Agree?"

Masterson nodded emphatically.

"Right." Anthony leaned forward, speaking softly. "But did this motive force hire some one to write for it, or was its distaste for the unfortunate Robin Hoode so great that it wrote itself, being unwilling to forgo the pleasure of, so to speak, giving birth to a new litter of scorpions three times a month or more? Briefly, are you with me in thinking that author and motive force are probably one and the same?"

"By God, I am!" Masterson said.

Anthony smiled. "Well, thank God I've found another lunatic! That's what we are, you know. Think of our theory! It is that some one had such a hatred of Hoode that the secret purchase of three newspapers was needed to assuage it. That's what we've said; we're thinking more. But we're frightened to say what it is because it'll sound so silly."

"I know. I know." Masterson's tone was almost fearful. "I say, we *can't* be right! It isn't sense! Now I come to think of it there are dozens of other theories that'd fit. There might be more than one person. The whole thing might be political. The——"

Anthony raised a hand for silence. "Fear not. Of course you can fit other theories. One always can; that's the devil of this bloodhound business. The only way to work is to pick a likely-looking path and go down it. I've chosen one to get on with. As you say, it's not sense; but then nothing else is. It's sad and bad and very mad and very far from sweet. But there it is. So we'll all go mad. I'm starting now." He got to his feet.

"Here, wait a minute!" Masterson cried. "Don't go. I—I might be able to help you."

"My dear fellow, you have already—immeasurably! For one thing you've crystallised my determination to go mad and stay mad——"

"Oh, I know all about that!" Masterson exhibited some irritation. "But I mean really help. I was just going to tell you. When I was with Hoode, before I told him about this business, I went to one of those filthy private inquiry agents. I was so absolutely certain, you see. I told this chap to find out, if he could, who the enemy was. Or rather I told him to find out who really owned the three newspapers. He thought I was mad, said he could do it in a day— but he didn't! I think he imagined he'd only got to look it up or get some one from Fleet Street to tell him. Of course, that didn't work, he only gave me the three figureheads that're shown to the trusting world. But when I laughed at him, and explained a little, I think he got his back up and really went for the job."

"D'you mean to say——" began Anthony.

"No, I don't! Before I heard any more I had the row with Hoode—I didn't tell *him* about the 'tec, of course; I was too angry —and dropped the whole business and paid this chap off. He was very fed up—kept trying to see me, and writing. Of course—well in the state I was in, I refused to see him and chucked his letters into the fire. But he was so very eager! He *might* know something, I think!"

Anthony was elated. "He might indeed. Masterson, you're a treasure! What's the name?"

"Pellet, he calls himself. Office is at 4, Grogan's Court, off Fleet Street, just past Chancery Lane."

"Excellent! Now I'm going." Anthony held out his hand. "And thank you. Hope I've done you no harm."

"Not a bit. Feel better already. Let me know how you get on. Going to sleep again now," said the invalid, and did, before Anthony had reached the door.

In the passage, Anthony hesitated. Should he go straight from the flat or should he tell her first that he was going? Then, as he reached it, the door of the drawing-room opened.

The passage was dimly lit, and she did not see him until he spoke.

"Your brother," he said, "is asleep. By the look of him he's in for a good twelve hours. He's none the worse and I'm even more full of information than I'd hoped to be. So everything in the garden is lovely!" All his anger was gone, and he felt suddenly and most surprisingly unsure of himself. As ever, he did not seem able to get away from her eyes though now he wanted to.

If she was wanting them to hurt, she was certainly succeeding. He found it difficult to recognise them, just as he found it difficult to recognise her voice when she spoke.

"I'm happy you're so pleased," she said.

And then she said: "You know, it isn't what you *do*, it's that manner of yours. That ineffable superiority!"

She walked past him, and out of the door which led to her brother's room.

The door closed behind her. . . .

CHAPTER FOURTEEN

HAY-FEVER

1

Anthony headed his car for Fleet Street. At twenty-five minutes past eleven he burst into the room of *The Owl's* editor.

The editor and his secretary were rather close together. The shining golden hair of the secretary was noticeably disordered.

"Er—hallo!" said Hastings.

Anthony said: "Get hold of private 'tec called Pellet; 4, Grogan's Court. Find out what he knows about the ownership of *The Searchlight, The St. Stephen's Gazette,* and *Voz Populi.* He was commissioned for same thing some time ago by J. Masterson. Never mind how much he costs. I'll pay. If Pellet doesn't know anything, find out yourself. In any case give me the answer as soon as is damn' well possible. Got that? Right. 'Night. 'Night, Miss Warren." The door banged behind him.

Margaret Warren snatched some papers from her table and followed. She caught him in the entrance hall.

"Mr. Gethryn!" she said, breathless. "Here's the report—asked—for—inquest.—Just finished—typed. You may—want it."

Anthony raised his hat. "Miss Warren, you're wonderful." He took the papers from her hand. "Many thanks. Hope I don't seem rude. Very busy. Good-night—and good luck." He shook her hand and was gone.

Slowly, Margaret went back to her editor. He was found pacing the room, scratching his head in bewilderment.

"Yes, darling, he was a bit strange, wasn't he?" Margaret said.

"He was." Hastings spoke with conviction. "I've known that man for fifteen years and I've never seen him all hot and bothered like that before. He's usually calmest when he's got most to do."

Margaret patted his cheek. "But, you silly infant, he wasn't like that because of the work he was doing. It was something much, much more important than that—or I'm a Dutchman!"

Hastings was alarmed. "Not that! Anything but that! What was it, then?"

"A woman, of course. *The* woman! Heaven, am I tied to an idiot?"

2

From Fleet Street, Anthony drove straight to the Regency, over whose great frontage flaring placards and violently winking electric signs announced that the great, the incomparable Vanda was gracing with her art this mecca of vaudeville. As he reached it the audience were streaming out from its great glass doors.

He anticipated difficulty, and approached the stage-door keeper with a five-pound note and a gabble of Viennese English. He was Herr Von und Zu Unpronounceable, a cousin and friend of the great, the incomparable Vanda. He *must,* it was of an imperativeness, see her. Further, the good keeper of the door really must accept this so little piece of paper.

The good keeper did; then proceeded laboriously to explain that the Vanda was not in the theatre. Hadn't been there at all that day. *And* there 'adn't been half a row about it, neither! She had wired to say she couldn't appear. Why? Gawd perhaps knew; certainly nobody else did. When would she reappear? The keeper of the door reely couldn't say. P'r'aps to-morrer. P'r'aps never. Good-night to *you,* sir.

Anthony went to his flat, surprised his man, and ordered a drink, a bath, fresh clothing, a drink, and supper.

At the meal, his hunger surprised him. Then he remembered that since the lightest of lunches he had eaten nothing. Having made up the deficiency, he lit a cigar, sat in a chair by the open window and read through, not once but many times, the typed report of the inquest.

Somewhere a clock struck one. Anthony put down the report, clasped his head with his hands, and plunged into thought. Presently he found his mind to be wandering, strictly against orders—wandering in a direction forbidden. He swore, got to his feet, and crossed to the writing-table. At this he employed himself with pen and paper for almost two and a half hours.

At last he put down his pen and read through what he had written. The clock struck four. He finished his reading, said: "H'mm! Those blasted gaps!" and went to bed.

3

He had barely two hours' sleep, for by a quarter past six he was breaking his fast. At twenty minutes past seven he was driving his car slowly through London.

This morning he took the journey to Marling slowly: he was thinking.

For the first third of the journey his thoughts were incoherently redundant. They were of a certain scene in which Anthony Ruthven Gethryn had lost his temper; had behaved, in short, abominably, and this to the one person in the world for whose opinion he cared.

It cost him an effort greater than might be supposed to wrench his thoughts out of this gloomy train, but at last he succeeded.

This puzzle of his—some of it fitted now, only there were several idiotic pieces which, unfitted, made nonsense of the rest. He flogged his unwilling brain for the rest of the journey.

He backed the Mercedes into the garage of the Bear and Key at twenty-five minutes to ten. By five minutes to the hour he was walking with his long, lazy stride up the winding drive of Abbotshall.

Drawing near the house he saw that the great oaken door stood open, letting a shaft of morning sunlight paint a golden track across the polished floor of the wide hall. He entered, flung his hat on to a chair, and turned in the direction of the stairs.

He had set foot upon the third step when from behind and below him came a noise—a rasping roar of a noise. To his overtired brain and overheated imagination it seemed a noise evil and inhuman. He swung round. The hall was as he had left it, empty of all save furniture. He descended the three steps; stood looking about him; then walked towards the front door. Before he could reach it, the noise came again, louder this time. The same roaring, rasping sound. But this time it had for a tail a snuffling choke which came, obviously, from the throat of a man.

Anthony laughed at himself. Noiselessly, he retraced his steps, passed the foot of the stairs, and halted outside the door opposite that of the study. It stood ajar, giving him a glimpse of the little room which he remembered as being the lair of the butler.

Anthony waited. In a moment came the roar again, now recognisable as half-cough, half-sneeze. Anthony pushed the door wide. Facing it, huddled in a chair, was the butler. His gray head was on a level with his knees. In one claw of a hand he clutched a bandanna handkerchief with which he dabbed every now and then at his streaming eyes.

Anthony stood unmoving in the doorway. Presently another spasm shook the old man.

"Bad cold, that," Anthony said loudly.

There was no answer. The coughing gasps went on; gradually grew less frequent. The thin shoulders ceased to shake.

"Bad cold, that," said Anthony again.

This time he got an effect. Poole leapt to his feet, fumbling hurriedly to hide in a tail pocket the capacious handkerchief.

"Your pardon, sir!" he gasped. "Did you want me, sir?"

"I only remarked that yours was a bad cold."

"Thank you, sir. Thank you. Not that it's a cold, sir, exactly. It's this hay-fever. And very troublesome it is, sir, for an old fellow like me!"

"Must be." Anthony was sympathetic. "D'you have these attacks many times a day?"

"I used to, sir. But this summer it does seem to be improving, sir. Only takes me every now and then, as you might say." The old man's voice showed gratitude for this concern about his ailment.

But Anthony's interest in hay-fever was not yet abated. "This the first bad fit you've had for some time?" he asked.

"Yes, sir. Quite a while since I was so bad, sir. It didn't trouble me at all yesterday, sir."

Anthony drew nearer. "D'you happen to remember," he said

slowly, "whether you—er—sneezed like that at all on the evening your master was killed?"

Poole exhibited agitation. "Whether I—the master——" the thin hands twisted about each other. "Forgive me, sir—I—I can't remember, sir. I'm a foolish old fellow—and any mention of—of that terrible night sort of seems to—to upset me, sir." He passed a hand across his forehead. "No, sir, I really can't remember. I'm an old man, sir. My memory's not what it was. Not what it was——"

But Anthony was listening no longer. He was, in fact, no longer there to listen. He had suddenly turned about and sprung into the hall. As Mr. Poole said later in the servants' hall: "I'd never of believed such a lazy-looking gentleman could of moved so quick. Like the leap of a cat, it was!"

Had he followed into the hall, he would have had more matter for gossip. For by the door of the verandah Anthony stood clutching, none too gently, the skinny shoulder of Robert Belford—the man-servant he had christened "Ferret-face."

"A word in your pointed ear, my friend," he said, and tightened his grip. "Now where shall we chat? The garden?" He pulled his trembling captive, whose face was a dirty gray with fear, out through the verandah and on to the terrace.

"Suppose," Anthony said, dropping his hand, "suppose you tell me why in hell you listen to my conversations with other people."

"I wasn't listening." The man's voice was sullen, yet at the same time shrill with fear.

"Why take the trouble?" Anthony asked plaintively. "Besides, it's wicked to tell stories, Belford. Wicked! Unhappy is the burden of a fib. We will, I think, get farther from our fellows and you shall tell me all about everything. I've been watching you, you know."

With these last words, true but intentionally misleading, a black shadow of hopelessness seemed to fall upon the prisoner.

"All right," he mumbled wearily, and followed meekly, but with dragging feet, while his captor led the way down the steps and across the lawn and into the little copse which faced the eastern end of the house.

As he walked, Anthony thought hard. He was something more than mystified. What in heaven, earth or hell was this little person going to tell him? Another old boot turning into a salmon, what? Father Gethryn, confessor! Well, every little helps.

When the house was hidden from them by the trees, he stopped. He sat on a log and waved Belford to another. Then he lit his pipe and waited. To his surprise, the little servant, after clearing his throat, began at once. Much of his nervousness seemed to drop from him, though he still looked like a man in fear.

"I'm rather glad this has happened, sir," he said, "because I was going to come to you anyway."

"You were, were you?" thought Anthony. "Now why?" But he went on smoking.

"I couldn't of stood it much longer, sir, reely I couldn't! And ever since you stopped that great brute of a sergeant from popping it across me, sir, I've been tryin' to make up me mind to tell you." He paused as if expecting an answer; but getting none, plunged on. "I wasn't upstairs *all* the time that night, like I said I was at the inquest!" Again he paused.

Anthony went on smoking. Here, if he wanted the story quickly, silence was best.

Belford swallowed hard. His face, as he went on speaking, turned from muddy gray to dead white.

"I—I come downstairs, sir, after I'd finished in the master's room. And when I got to the 'all I heard old Poole starting on one of them sneezin' fits. And—and, sir, I went into the study and I saw the master lyin' there on the rug—just like they found 'im! And—and I shut that door behind me quick—old Pooley was still coughin' and chokin' his head off—and I nipped back up the stairs, sir. It's God's truth, sir! It is——"

This time the pause was so long that Anthony knew speech necessary.

"Are you trying to explain," he said, "that though you did go into the study that night you didn't have anything to do with the murder?"

"Yes, sir, yes." The man's eagerness was pathetic. "That's just it, sir! I didn't have nothink to do with it, sir, *nothink!* So 'elp me God!"

"What did you go into the room for?" Anthony shot out the question. "Must've been for something you didn't want found out or Poole's hay-fever wouldn't have been so important to you?" The logic, he knew, was faulty. But the thrust told.

Belford hung his head. "Yes, sir, it was what you say. I thought —one of the girls told me—the master was in the billiard-room. And I knew as 'e always kept money somewhere in the study. I was goin' to pin—steal it if I could. I was desprit, sir. Desprit!"

Anthony was puzzled. "But if you came out without stealing anything, why didn't you rouse the house when you saw Mr. Hoode was dead?"

"I don't know, sir. Except that it all come as such a shock like
—my sneaking in there while old Poole was sneezin'—and then finding—that, sir. You see, when I nipped out, the old man was still
sneezin' with 'is 'ead on his knees. And I *knew* as he hadn't spotted
me. And I bolted away to think. An' the more I thought, the more
I feels as if I couldn't—hadn't better like—tell anybody.

"I can see, now, sir, 'ow blasted silly it were—me having done
nothink wrong. But there it was, sir, I meant to tell, but as I'd gone
in there to steal and 'ad sneaked in in the way I did—well, it made
me feel as if they'd all jump on me immediate as the murderer.
Specially as I never goes into the study in the ordinary way. You
do see 'ow it was, don't you, sir?"

"I do," Anthony said. "But I also see that you're a fool. A fool
for not rousing every one at once; a fool for not keeping quiet after
you'd decided to say nothing about it."

Belford's little eyes opened wide. "But you—you were on me,
sir! You suspected me like—thought I was the murd'rer!"

Anthony shook his head. "Not really, Belford. You know, you
looked too guilty to be true. I nabbed you just now because I don't
like eavesdroppers. Also because anything fishy in this house interests me at present."

"I may be a fool," cried Belford suddenly, "but I feel better
now I've got it off my chest like. Reely I do, sir! I kept sayin' to
meself as how I wasn't guilty of anythink, and yet I 'ad the conscience awful! I've bin trying to tell you for twenty-four hours, sir,
but when I 'eard you askin' Poole if 'e'd 'ad a 'tack of that hay-
fever on the night the master was killed, I got frightened again and
was goin' to bolt. Only you copped me." He was silent a moment,
then burst out: "Mr. Deacon didn't do it, sir. He couldn't of!
You know that, sir?"

Anthony did. But he wanted to turn this tragicomic confession
of nothing into evidence of importance, though he had but little
hope of success.

"What time," he asked with affected carelessness, "*did* you go
into the study?"

"I was only just in and out like a flash, sir. But when I got back
to the stairs, the clock there said five past eleven, sir—I remember
it perfect. I wasn't lookin' for the time reely, only some'ow I saw
it and couldn't forget it like."

Anthony repressed elation. "Thanks," he said, and got to his
feet.

Belford jumped up. "Are you—going, sir?"

Anthony nodded.

"But what—what are you goin' to—to do about me? About what I told you, sir?"

Anthony looked down benignly. "Nothing."

Belford's mouth fell open. "Nothing! *Nothing?* But——"

"What I mean, Belford, is this. I'll keep you out of trouble. You've told me one thing that makes all your confession of nothing worth while. You may, later on, have to give evidence; but that's the worst you'll have to do as far as I'm concerned. And don't worry. And for the Lord's sake don't walk about as you've been doing lately, looking like Charles Peace with a bellyache."

The little man smiled all over his wizened face. Anthony looked at him curiously. Somehow, when talking to him as a man and not a servant, one found something so far from being sly as to be almost lovable.

Anthony gave the narrow shoulders a reassuring pat and strolled away, making for the house. He had covered perhaps twenty yards when he stopped, turned on his heel, and walked back.

Belford was seated again on his log. His face was buried in his hands. Anthony stood looking down at him.

"What's the matter?" he asked.

The other dropped his hands with a cry, bounding to his feet. "I—beg your pardon, sir. You—I——"

Anthony soothed him. "Steady, man, steady. Take your time. Lots of it."

Belford looked up at him, tried to speak, failed, and hung his head again.

"Just now," Anthony said, "you told me something about being desperate. What is it? Money?"

Belford nodded. "You're right, sir," he muttered. "It's—it's my wife, sir. Been very ill, she has. And is still. I was goin' to ask the master to 'elp me; but when it come to the point, I couldn't. That's why I was after pinchin', sir. I would 'ave asked 'im, I would reely, sir; but I knew he'd ask Miss Hoode about it, and that'd 'ave made it 'opeless. You see, sir, the missus was in service here before we was married—and, well, sir, she 'ad—'ad to leave in a nurry. And through me! You understand, sir—our nipper——" He broke off, looking up appealingly. "We're very fond of each other, sir," he finished. "And it's 'ard to see 'er so ill like!"

"How much d'you want?" Anthony felt for his note-case. "Here, you'd better have twenty now. And I'll fix you up properly to-morrow. Now, for God's sake, man, pull yourself together!" he added sharply.

For Belford's shrivelled, sharp-featured little face was working in a way which was not good to see. Gratitude is sometimes more uncomfortable to watch than baser emotions.

Anthony thrust the notes into one limp hand and beat hurried retreat.

Belford stood where he was left. His lips moved soundlessly. The banknotes in his hand crackled as the stubby fingers clenched upon them. Presently he raised his head and looked with blurred vision along the path through the trees.

"Gawd!" he said, the refinement of the servants' hall now completely gone. "Gawd! What a bloke! What a *bloody* good bloke!"

Anthony took the terrace steps three at a time. He was elated. The elation was short-lived; before he had reached the house, despair had taken its place. After all, this playing at detectives was foolery. Why, such a day as this, with its hot, clean peace, its drowsiness, its little scented breeze—was it not a day for a lover to lie at the feet of his mistress? Was it not a day for hot, sun-warmed kisses?

He shook himself, laughing bitterly. "Affected ass!" he said to himself.

Sir Arthur came out of the house. "Lovely day, Gethryn. Early, aren't you?"

"It is and I am. I am also a detective of the greatest. Do I look it?"

Sir Arthur grew eager. "What d'you mean? Have you got anything? Found out anything important?"

Anthony nodded. "Yes, twice."

"But what, man? What?"

"One, the butler suffers from hay-fever. Two, the murder was committed at as near eleven o'clock as I am to you."

"Damn it all, Gethryn," said the elder man, "I don't think it's quite fair to pull my leg like that. Not about this. I don't really!"

"You're right, it isn't. I'm sorry." Anthony was contrite. "But you know, I'm not as silly as I sound. You must think I'm telling you things you knew before; but I'm not really. What I think these things mean, I'm not going to say just yet. Not to any one."

"I see. That's all right, Gethryn. You must forgive me if I seem touchy." Sir Arthur smiled forgivingly.

"Seen Deacon lately?" Anthony asked.

"This morning. In fact, I've just come back. He's wonderful, that boy!"

"He is," agreed Anthony. "I'm just going to see him now. Walk to the gate with me, will you? I want you to help me."

"My dear chap, with pleasure!" He put his arm through Anthony's as they walked.

"I want to know," said Anthony, as they reached the end of the house, "whether any one in any way connected with the household does any playing about with carpenter's tools. Amateurs, professionals, or both."

"Funny you should ask that, Gethryn. I've been thinking about that. But it's no help. You see, the place is full of 'em—carpenters, I mean. There's Diggle, the gardener, he's really an excellent rough-job man. Then there's the chauffeur, he made that shed over there—and a splendid bit of work it is. And John, well, it was his one hobby as it is mine. You know that set of three small tables in the drawing-room?"

"I did notice them. They puzzled me rather. Couldn't place 'em."

"John made those," said Sir Arthur, with a touch of pride, "nearly twenty years ago. I remember I was very jealous at the time. I couldn't ever have done anything so good, you see. I was a bit better than he at the finer sorts of work, though." He broke off, seeming to fall into a reverie. After a while he added: "No, Gethryn, I'm afraid this line's no good to us. That wood-rasp doesn't belong to Abbotshall."

"You're sure?" Anthony asked.

"Well, it isn't mine, it didn't belong to John, it isn't Diggle's—he was questioned by the police, you know—and it certainly isn't the chauffeur's."

"Humph!" Anthony seemed annoyed.

They walked on to the gate in silence. Anthony nodded an adieu and set off down the white, dusty road with his long horseman's stride.

CHAPTER FIFTEEN

ANTHONY'S BUSY DAY

1

He covered the distance to the village in a time very creditable for so hot a day. As he passed the Bear and Key, a knot of men stopped their conversation to eye him with thirsty interest. He smelt reporter and passed by, giving silent thanks to the efficiency of Boyd. Now that the case seemed, to the public at least, as good as over, there was no real danger; but had the news-hungry hordes been let loose at first to overrun Abbotshall, Heaven alone knew how impossible things would have been.

For the case of the murdered minister had seized violently on public imagination. It was so like, so very like, the books the public had read yesterday, were reading to-day, and would read to-morrow and to-morrow. Great Britain (and Ireland) was divided now into two camps—pro and anti-Deacon. The antis had a vast majority. Many of them held that to waste time on a trial which would be purely formal was disgraceful. The wretch, they said, should be hanged at once. Not a few were convinced that hanging was too merciful. It was all very funny, really, thought Anthony, and wished he could laugh. But whenever he tried to realise how funny it was, he thought of Deacon, and then found that it wasn't funny at all.

On this morning, though, he was at least on the road to high spirits, and walked on down the twisting, cobbled street towards the police-station, whistling beneath his breath. The whistle bewailed the cruel death of Cock Robin.

Still whistling, he ran up the steps of the police-station. As he passed through the doorway the whistling stopped, cut off in the middle of a bar. He stepped to one side, away from the door. Coming towards it were Lucia Lemesurier and her sister.

Neither at once saw Anthony. Then, with a gracious smile to officialdom, Lucia turned and looked full at him. He raised his hat and looked grim. He didn't mean to look grim; he was merely trying to behave well in a police-station to a lady he loved and had offended. Lucia flushed and bowed coldly and walked down the steps. She hadn't meant to do any of these things; but the man *did* look so forbidding. "Conceited idiot!" she said to herself, referring to Anthony and not meaning it in the least.

"Hell!" said Anthony under his breath, and went rather white.

Dora Masterson held out her hand. "Good-morning," she said, and looked curiously at him.

From somewhere he dragged out a smile.

" 'Morning. Feeling better?"

She beamed at him. "Oh, ever so much! Archie seems so—so exactly as if everything was the same as usual. He's wonderful! And I haven't forgotten what you said about miracles. You will do one, won't you?" With another smile she ran down the steps and after her sister.

Anthony emerged from thought to find a constable looking at him with barely veiled curiosity. He essayed a cheerful manner. Perhaps the officer would be so good as to let him see Mr. Deacon. If the officer remembered, Superintendent Boyd——

In less than two minutes he was alone with the prisoner.

Deacon put down the book he was reading.

"Hallo-allo! More visitors for the condemned man. Good job you're early. I believe they're moving me to the county clink about eleven."

Anthony sat down upon the bed. "How are you?" he said. He said it to gain time. His thoughts, once so carefully ordered, had been thrown into much confusion. That bow had been so extremely distant.

"To tell you the truth," Deacon said slowly and heavily, "I feel absolutely rotten! It's beginning to get on my nerves—all this!" He made a sweeping gesture. "It—I feel——" He broke off and laughed. "Conniptions won't do any good, will they? And it's only what I might have expected. Nurse always told me my middle name was Crippen."

Admiration and sympathy cleared Anthony's head. "When's the magistrate's court?" he asked abruptly.

"The balloon, I believe, goes up at 10 A. M. the day after to-morrow."

Anthony muttered: "Day after to-morrow, eh? Well, it may," and relapsed into silence.

Deacon half rose, then sat down again. "After you left me last night," he said, after a pause, "I had a visit from Crabbe—the solicitor Digby-Coates got. We had a long talk, and he's going to prime Marshall, who's going to come and see me to-morrow himself. So all the legal business is fixed up."

"Good," said Anthony. "What I came for this morning was to ask you two questions. Are you ready?"

"Aye ready!"

"Have you any money? Beside the salary you got from Hoode, I mean."

"About two hundred and fifty a year," said Deacon. "When Cousin James dies of port it'll be about three thousand."

"That's good. You made that point with the solicitor, I hope. It tends to destroy that insane theft theory."

"I told the bloke all right. But it won't count much, I'm afraid. You see, I've been awfully broke for quite a time now. One thing and another, you know. However!" He shrugged.

Anthony said: "Now the second question. And it's really important! Think carefully before you answer. When recently—say within the last week—have you had in your hands *any* implement of *any* kind with a wooden handle four inches long and about three and a half round? Think, man, think!"

2

Ten minutes later, Anthony was running up the High Street towards his inn. Arrived there, he found a telegram. It read: "Authentic astounding revelations by Pellet what next Hastings."

Anthony wrote on a telegraph form: "Wait with you afternoon office keep Pellet Gethryn." The form he gave to the barman with a ten-shilling note and instructions for immediate despatch, and then set off for Abbotshall at a fast walk.

As he entered the gates, a car—an unfamiliar green Daimler, a woman seated primly beside the chauffeur—left them. In spite of the heat it was closed. Peering, Anthony saw the only occupant of the tonneau to be a woman. She was veiled. He deduced the languishing Mrs. Mainwaring and her Gallic maid. The sight appeared to amuse him. He walked on to the house humming beneath his breath.

Sir Arthur, he was told by a rejuvenated Belford, was believed to be in his own sitting-room.

Anthony mounted the stairs. He found Sir Arthur's door ajar, on it pinned a notice in red ink: "Please do not disturb." From where he stood, all Anthony could see was the big arm-chair drawn

up to the window, the top of an immaculate head above its back
and some six inches of trouser and a boot-sole by each of its front
legs.

Anthony chuckled, knocked, and entered. Sir Arthur rose, turning a frowning face towards the intruder. As he saw who it was, a
smile replaced the frown.

"You looked," said Anthony, "like some weird animal, sitting
like that. Hope I haven't disturbed you."

"Not a bit, my boy, not a bit. Very glad to see you." He picked
up some sheets of paper from the chair. "As a matter of fact, I was
just jotting down a few notes. I'd like you to read them—not now,
but when they're finished." He hesitated; then added rather shyly:
"They're just some ideas I've had about this awful business. Somehow, I can put them more clearly in writing. I want to give them to
Marshall before the boy's tried, but I'd like you to see them first.
There might possibly be some points which have escaped you,
though I expect not."

"I'd like to look at 'em very much," Anthony said. "Get them
done as quick as you can, won't you? Now, what I interrupted you
for: is there in the house a good collection of reference books?"

"There is. Right-hand book-case in the study. You'll find anything you want from sawdust to Seringapatam. John got together
the most comprehensive reference library I've ever seen."

"Good!" Anthony turned to the door. "No, don't trouble to
come, I'll find 'em!"

It was, as Sir Arthur had said, a most comprehensive collection.
Anthony locked the study door and sat at the big writing-table,
now back in its old place, surrounded by the volumes of his choice.
They were many and varied.

He worked for an hour, occasionally scribbling notes on a slip
of paper. At last he rose, stretched himself, and returned the books
to their shelves. Again sitting at the table, he studied his notes.
They appeared to afford him satisfaction. He folded the paper and
took out his note-case. As he opened it, the bunch of newspaper-
cuttings fluttered down to rest upon the table.

He picked them up and slid them, with the notes he had scribbled, back into the case. As he did so a line of the topmost cutting
caught his eye. It was the quotation from the *Æneid* which Masterson had referred to and which then had titillated some elusive
memory. Now where, recently, had he seen this unusual and me-
ticulous dative case?

His mind wrestled with forgetfulness; then, suddenly tired, refused to work longer on so arduous a task. As minds will, it switched abruptly off to the matter with which it most wished to be occupied. Before Anthony's eyes came a picture of a dark, proud face whose beauty was enhanced by its pallor. He thought of her as he had seen her that morning; as he had seen her that first time; as she had sat in her drawing-room that night—the night he had made her tell him all about it.

His mind, remorseful perhaps, made a half-hearted attempt to get back to that tiresome business of the correct quotation from Virgil. Suddenly, it connected the work and the woman. The great light of recaptured memory burst upon him.

He jumped for the telephone; asked for Greyne 23; was put through at once; thought: "Wonder who'll answer?" then heard the "Hallo" of a servant.

"Miss Masterson in?" he asked.

"Yes, sir. What name shall I say?"

He told her. Waiting, he grew excited. If by any chance he was right, here was yet more confirmation of his theory.

Dora Masterson's voice came to his ears. "Hallo. Is that Mr. Gethryn? I——"

Anthony interrupted. "Yes. I wonder whether you can help me. The second time I was in your house I picked up a book. Little green book. Soft leather binding. Essays. Pleasantly written. One was called 'Love at First Sight.' Author's name on title-page was a woman's. D'you know the book I mean?"

"Is it one called *Here and There?*"

"Yes, now who wrote it? Was it really a woman? And is that her real name? I meant to ask at the time, but forgot."

3

At twenty minutes to two that afternoon, Anthony stopped his car outside *The Owl* office. He had broken no record this time; his mind had been much occupied on the journey. The interviews he had held with Belford, Mabel Smith, and Elsie Syme before leaving Abbotshall had given him food for thought.

He found Hastings in his room, with him a little, dapper, sly-eyed man. "Discreet Inquiries. Divorces, Watching, etc.," thought Anthony.

"This," murmured Hastings, "is Mr. Pellet."

"Ah, yes." Anthony sat down heavily. He was tired and very

hungry. He had not eaten since breakfast. Mr. Pellet displeased him.

"Mr. Pellet," said Hastings, "has some information which should interest you. I have paid him fifty pounds. He wants another two hundred."

"He would," Anthony said. "And if he's got what I want he shall have it."

"Thath right," said Mr. Pellet with a golden smile.

"It may be." Anthony fixed him with a glittering eye. "Let us hear you, Mr.—er—Pellet."

Mr. Pellet cleared his throat, produced a packet of papers, wiped his hands on a pink silk handkerchief and began.

"About theeth three newthpaperth," he said—and went on for one hour and fifty-seven minutes by the clock on Hastings's table.

He got his two hundred pounds.

4

There was a matinée at the Regency. At half-past four, Anthony was at the stage-door.

The stage-door keeper remembered that five-pound note and the foreign gent. He was civil. Yes, Madarm Vander was in the theatre. She had, indeed, just finished her performance. He would see if Mr. Von und Zu could be admitted. That gentleman scribbled on a card, placed the card in an envelope, and sealed the envelope. As balm for tender feelings, he gave the doorkeeper a flashing foreign smile and a pound-note.

He was kept waiting not more than three minutes. After four, he was ushered into the most sacred dressing-room in Europe.

From a silken couch in a silken corner a silken, scented vision rose to meet him.

Anthony saw that they were alone. He bowed, kissing the imperious hand. He was regarded with approval by tawny, Slavonic eyes.

She peered at the card in her hand. "Who air you," she said, "that write to me of—of John?"

Anthony proceeded to make himself clear.

It was nearly six o'clock when he left the theatre.

5

By half-past six Anthony was in his flat. At seven he bathed; at eight dined. From eight-thirty to nine he smoked—and thought. From nine until midnight he wrote, continuing his work of the night before. Save for occasional reference to notes, he wrote for those three hours without a pause. From midnight until one he considered what he had written. Then, after a long and powerful drink, he unearthed from its lair his typewriter.

It was lucky, he reflected, that two years ago he had wearied at last of professional typists and taken a machine unto himself.

From one-thirty in the morning until five—three whole hours and a half—he typed. There were two reasons why the work took him so long: the first, that he had not used the machine for six months; the second, that in copying what he had written he was constantly polishing, correcting, altering, improving.

At five he discarded the typewriter, took pen and paper and wrote a letter. This, together with the typewritten document, he placed in a large envelope. He stamped the envelope; was about to leave the flat and post it; then changed his mind. It should be sent by special messenger as early as one could be found awake.

He did not go to bed, feeling that if he did, nothing could wake him for at least twelve hours. He had another drink, another bath, and, when he had roused his man, a breakfast.

CHAPTER SIXTEEN

REVELATION AND THE SPARROW

1

His meal over, he left the flat, going first to a District Messengers' office and then back to the garage for his car.

He knew the road to Marling so well by this time that he could almost have driven blindfold, and he has said that on this morning he once or twice found himself to have been sleeping at the wheel.

It is certain, anyhow, that he barely saw where he was going. Such thought as his tired brain could compass was not of murders and murderers, but of Love, a Lover and a Lady.

It was, if one is to believe him, at the cross-roads beyond Beachmere that he made up his mind to see Her, to drive straight to the house on the bank of the Marle.

He looked at his watch. The hands pointed to ten. He settled down in his seat, and his right foot grew heavy on the accelerator.

His spirits mounted with the speed. The car tore its way into Marling and down the cobbled slope of the High Street, swung to the left, took the little bridge at a bound, raced on, turned the corner next on the left after the river bank on two wheels, ploughed up the little lane, and pulled up at the gates of the house which was graced with Her presence.

Or should have been. For the parlour-maid informed him that her mistress and her mistress's sister were out. For the day, she thought. She was not sure, but she imagined the ladies to have gone to London.

Anthony, his fatigue heavy upon him, walked slowly back to his car. For a moment he sat idle in the driving-seat; then suddenly quickened into life. Though their ultimate destination might indeed be London, the women would surely stop on their way through Greyne. For in Greyne's jail was Deacon.

So to Greyne he drove at speed. He missed them by five minutes.

Had Anthony Gethryn been a man of common sense he would have returned at once to his Marling inn, fallen upon his bed, and let sleep have her way with him. But he was not, so he stayed with Deacon. Deacon was obviously—in spite of his flippancy—delighted at this visit. Anthony stayed with him until two o'clock, when Sir Edward Marshall, K.C., arrived in person for consultation with his latest case, and then set out for Marling. This he did not reach for two hours, fatigue and preoccupation having cost him no fewer than three wrong turnings.

At the inn was waiting the reply to the letter he had sent by District Messenger that morning. It had come, this reply, in the form of a seemingly ordinary message over the inn's telephone. It was what he had expected, but nevertheless it made it necessary for him to think.

And think he did, sitting on the hot grass bank at the edge of the little bowling-green behind the inn, for as long as it takes to smoke one cigar and two pipes. Then he sought the bar, to slake a savage thirst.

He ordered a meal to be served at seven. To pass the hour that must elapse before this and to throw off the lassitude brought on by his fatigue and the oppression of the day's heavy, airless heat, he sought the bathroom and much cold water.

After the bath he felt better. He returned to his quarters whistling. Crossing his sitting-room to get to the bedroom which opened out of it, he saw something he had not noticed when going bathwards. The whistling ceased abruptly. On the table in the centre of the room lay an envelope. His name was on it, in hurried, pencilled scrawl. The writing was feminine.

He ripped it open, read, and jumped for the door. The pink-cheeked chambermaid came running. She would not have believed this quiet gentleman could shout so loud, nor so angrily.

Anthony, his lank black hair dishevelled, his long, lean body swathed in a bath-gown, towered wrathfully above her.

"When did this note arrive?" He waved the envelope in her face.

The girl fingered her apron. "Oh, sir! It came this morning, please, sir. Lady left it, sir. Just after ten, it was. Mrs. Lermeesherer, sir."

"I know, I know!" Anthony snorted. "But why in Satan's name wasn't I told about it when I got back this evening?" He went back into his room, slamming the door and feeling not a little ashamed of himself.

The little chambermaid clattered downstairs to discuss with her colleagues the strange effect of a note upon a gentleman hitherto so pleasant.

Anthony clad himself with speed; then ran downstairs to the telephone. The answer to his first call was disappointing. No, Mrs. Lemesurier was not back; would not be, probably, until eight.

He rang off, swore, bethought him of his work, made sure that the door of the telephone cabinet was closed, lifted the receiver and asked for another number.

It was ten minutes before he went slowly to his dinner. He ate little, fatigue, preoccupation, and the stifling heat of the evening combining to deprive him of appetite. Over coffee he re-read his letter. It is a tribute to his self-restraint that he had delayed so long. It was a short letter, running thus:—

"DEAR MR. GETHRYN,—I am sorry you were out: I wanted to apologise for my unpardonable behavior. I can't think what made me so foolish; and quite see now that you had to talk to Jim and also that he was none the worse for the interview—in fact I hear from Mr. Hastings, who rang up early this morning, that he is ever so much better!

"If you are not too busy and would care to, do come and see us this evening. I would ask you to dinner, but we shall probably be late and have a very scrappy meal.

"Yours gratefully,
"LUCIA LEMESURIER."

There is a peculiar and subtle and quite indefinable pleasure that comes to a man when the woman he loves first writes to him. However curt, however banal the letter, there is no matter. It is something from her to him; something altogether private; something she has set down for him to read; something not to be shared with a sordid world.

Anthony lost himself in this sea of subtle delight, varying pleasure with self-recrimination for having exhibited such boorishness and for being so ridiculously, so youthfully in love. "For, after all," he told himself, "I haven't known her for a week yet. I've spoken with her not a dozen times. I am clearly a fool!"

Unpleasant thoughts broke in upon him. He looked at his watch; then jumped to his feet and made his way upstairs to his rooms. He reached them mopping his forehead. He could not remember a day in England so oppressive.

He took his hat and turned to leave the room. As he did so a rush of wind swept in through the open window, and a long, low angry mutter of thunder came to his ears. Then, with a rush, came the rain; great sheets of it, glistening in the half-dusk.

Anthony put on a mackintosh, substituted a cap for the hat, and left the inn. He did not take his car. Even as he turned out of the yard into the cobbled street, the thunder changed from rumble to sharp, staccato reports, and three jagged swords of lightning tore the black of the sky.

Anthony strode on, hands thrust deep into pockets, chin burrowed into the upturned collar of the trenchcoat.

2

Mr. Poole the butler—Anthony once said that he sounded like a game of Happy Families—was in a state of nervous agitation verging upon breakdown. The events of the past few days had shaken him to such extent that he would not, he was sure, "ever be the same man again."

He sat in the little room opposite that which had been the master's study. He shivered with age, vague fears, and fervent distaste for the storm whose rain beat upon the windows, whose sudden furies of wind shook the old house, whose flashes of lightning played such havoc with the nerves.

Mr. Poole was alone. Miss Hoode had retired. Sir Arthur was reading in the billiard-room at the other end of the house. Belford was on three days' holiday, his wife, it seemed, being an invalid. The other servants were certainly either in bed or huddled together moaning as women will at the violence of the storm.

Mr. Poole was alone. All manner of lurking terrors preyed upon him. There were noises. Sounds which seemed like the master's voice. Sounds which seemed like the rustling of curtains, whispering and soft footsteps. Elusive sounds as of doors opening and shutting. Mr. Poole trembled. He knew his fears groundless; imaginings born of the roaring rattle of the Universe. But nevertheless he trembled.

Suddenly there came a knocking on the great front door. This knocking was not loud, yet it seemed to the old man the more terrible for that. For there is always something terrible about a knock upon a door.

For a full minute he strove to leave the shelter of the little, cheerful, glowing room. At last he succeeded, struggling through the beastly mysteries of the dimly lighted hall to open with trembling hands the great oak door.

Anthony stepped over the threshold; stripped off dripping cap and mackintosh.

"A dirty night, Poole," he said.

"It is indeed, sir! Indeed it is, sir!" The old man's voice was hysterical with relief.

Across the hall to them came Sir Arthur, sturdy, benign, hair as smoothly brushed as ever.

"Oh, it's you, is it, Gethryn?" he said. "I wondered who was knocking. You must have very pressing business to bring you up here on a night like this. Aren't you wet?"

"Nothing to speak of. I wanted to talk with you. It's important —and urgent."

Sir Arthur grew eager. "My dear boy, of course. Where shall we go? Billiard-room?"

"All right."

They turned, but before they had crossed the hall,

"Tell you what," Anthony said, "the study'd be better. Not so near the servants, you know."

"You're right," Sir Arthur agreed.

The study had that queer stillness which comes to a room at one time in constant use and then suddenly deserted save for the morning activities of a servant with duster and broom. It had an air of almost supernatural lifelessness, increased, perhaps, by the fact that now everything was in its accustomed place; the same pictures on the walls; the table; the chairs; the very curtains cutting off the alcove at the far end of the room hanging in the old slightly disordered folds.

A silence fell upon both men while they found chairs and drew them up to the table, under the light.

Sir Arthur spoke first. "Out with it, now, Gethryn. You've excited me, you know." He rubbed his hands. "I've always thought you'd do something; go one better than those damn' fools of policemen!"

Anthony leant back in his chair. "This," he said, "is a most unusual business. I said so at the beginning, and, by God, I say so now! You might say that I have solved the mystery. After I've told you, that is. And in another way, as you'll see, it's more of a puzzle than ever."

Sir Arthur leant forward. "Go on, man, go on! Do you mean to say you actually know who killed John?"

"I do not." Anthony laid his head against the back of his chair and closed his leaden, burning eyes.

Sir Arthur started to his feet. A crash of thunder drowned his words. Followed a zig-zag of lightning so vivid as to seem more a stage-effect than an outburst of nature. Outside, the rain fell heavily, solidly—a veil of water. The furious blast of wind which had come hard on the heels of the great peal died away in a plaintive moan.

Anthony opened his eyes. "What did you say? Before that barrage, I mean."

Sir Arthur paced the room. "What did I say?" he exploded. "I said that if you hadn't found out who did it, I couldn't see the use of coming here and gabbling about mystery. Damn it, man, we're not in a two-shilling novel! We've got to get Deacon off, that's what we've got to do! *And* find the murderer! Not sit here and play at Holmes and Watson. It's *silly,* what we're doing! And I expected great things of you, Gethryn!"

"That," Anthony said placidly, "was surely foolish."

Sir Arthur made impatient sounds in his throat; but lessened the pace of his prowling. Under the graying hair his broad forehead was creased in a tremendous frown.

Anthony lit a cigarette. "But I may yet interest you," he went on. "You said, I think, that you wished to lay your hands on the murderer."

"I did. And by God I meant it!"

Anthony looked up at him. "Suppose you sit down and then I'll tell you all about it."

"Sit down!" Sir Arthur shouted. "Sit down! God above, you'll be telling me to keep calm next!" He flung himself into his chair. "Here I am then. Now get on!" He buried his face in his hands; then looked up to say: "You must forgive me, Gethryn; I'm not myself. I've been more on edge the last few days—a lot more—than I've let any one see. And to-night, somehow, my nerves have gone. And when you came with news I thought it meant that you'd caught the real murderer and that the boy would get off—and—and everything!"

"I was going to tell you," Anthony said, "that the murderer of John Hoode will never be caught. To get him is impossible. Please understand that when I say impossible I mean it."

"But why, man? Why?" cried Sir Arthur.

"Because," said Anthony slowly, "he doesn't exist."

"What?" Sir Arthur was on his feet again at a bound.

Anthony lay back in his chair. "I can't bear it! I can't bear it!" he said plaintively. "You know, you're very violent to-night. I can't talk if you will jump about so."

The elder man groaned apology and sat again in his chair. His eyes, bewildered, sought Anthony's.

Anthony said: "Sorry if I seem too mysterious. But you must let me elucidate in my own way. Here goes: I have said that the murderer of John Hoode doesn't exist. I don't mean that the murderer's dead or that Hoode committed suicide. I mean that John Hoode was never killed; is not, in fact, dead."

Sir Arthur's lips moved, but no sound came from them. His chair was outside the circle of light and it was by the vivid violet illumination of a quivering glare of lightning that Anthony saw the pallor the shock of his revelation had caused. Following the lightning came peal after peal of thunder.

As it died away, Anthony saw that the other was speaking. He had not moved in his chair, but his strong, square hands were twisting about each other.

"What are you telling me?" he whispered. "Are you mad? John not dead! John not dead! Why, it's idiocy—stark idiocy!"

Anthony shook his head. "It isn't. Whatever it is, it isn't that. Wait till I have told you more. It's a long tale and a strange one."

Sir Arthur moistened his lips with his tongue but did not speak.

The thunder, after the outburst of a moment before, seemed to have ceased entirely. No sudden furies of wind shook the house. The only sounds in the room were the tick-tick of the grandfather clock and the soft hish-hish of the rain against the closed windows.

Anthony drew a deep breath, and began:—

"My first impression of this affair was, as you know, that it was a straightforward murder, committed by some member of this household. Later, I had good reason to search this table here, and it was from the time of that search that I began to revise my theories. In this table I found—as I had expected—a drawer hidden from the casual eye. From that drawer I took some letters, a collection of newspaper-cuttings, a memorandum book, and other papers. You'll see them all in due course.

"The letters gave me my first inkling there was something more obscure about the case than I had thought. So I went to the lady who had written those letters. From her I got the first pieces of the story, not without difficulty. I also went to see a man who had once been Hoode's secretary. He was obliging, and clever. He had seen things, heard things, while he served Hoode, that had set him thinking. He thought so much that he employed, on his own initiative, a private detective. I have seen the detective. The detective, even after he was told to drop the business, went on detecting. You see, he had become interested. He is not a nice man. He smelt scandal and money. He, without knowing it, has helped me to piece together the whole amazing story—the story which shows how it was that John Hoode was not killed." Anthony paused, taking a last puff at his cigarette.

Sir Arthur, gray of face, hammered with his fists on the leather-padded arms of his chair.

"But the body!" he gasped. "The body! It was there!" He glanced wildly over his shoulder at the fireplace. "I saw it! I tell you I saw it!" His voice gathered strength. "And the inquest, the arrests, the identifications! And the funeral! Why, you fool!" he cried, "the funeral is to-morrow. All England will be there! And you tell me this absurd story. What in God's name has come to you that you can play pranks of this sort? Haven't we all suffered enough without this?" The man was shaking.

Anthony sat up. "Wait!" he said. "And let me finish. I said that John Hoode had not been murdered. I didn't say that no murder had been done. Murder was done. I know it. You know it. The world knows it. But what you and the world don't know is that the body upon which the inquest was held, the body which is to be buried to-morrow, is *not* the body of John Hoode!"

Sir Arthur glared at him. "What does this *mean?*" he said. "I don't understand! I—I——"

Sleep was creeping insidiously upon Anthony. He wished the storm had not stopped. Its violence had at least helped to keep him awake, helped to conquer this deadly fatigue.

He began again: "The story is this. And though it's as mad as Hatta and the King's Messenger, it's true. John Hoode's mother, as you probably know, was, before marriage, a Miss Monteith. His father, as you must know also, was John Howard Beauleigh Hoode. Now, do you know that your John Hoode is very like—to look at, I mean—one of his parents and not the other?"

"Yes, yes. He and his father were—well, like twin brothers almost."

"Exactly. John Howard Beauleigh Hoode had a way of passing on his features. John Howard Beauleigh Hoode was married to Miss Adeline Rose Monteith in '73. In '72 John Howard Beauleigh Hoode's mistress, the daughter of Ian Dougal—he was a smith in Ardenross—gave birth to a son. That son, named also John, was maintained and educated at his father's expense; but he turned out as complete a waster as any man well could be. John Hoode—your John—didn't know of his half-brother's existence until John Howard Beauleigh Hoode's death. When he did find out—from his father's executors, I imagine—John—your John—was good to his bastard brother; and when he first saw him, he was astounded by the likeness. Looking at him was like looking into a mirror.

"The result of his kindness was the expected. Ingratitude, surliness, constant demands for money and yet more money; finally threats and blackmail——"

"No, no, no!" groaned Sir Arthur, his face in his hands. "It's all lies, lies! I knew John. He told me everything, everything!"

"Not he," Anthony said. "I've all the papers. Some of them here." He tapped his breast-pocket. "Birth certificates. Copy of John Howard Beauleigh Hoode's will, and so on. It's all by the book. Well, things went from bad to worse and from worse to intolerable for your John. These threats—I'll show you some letters later—wore his nerves, his health, to shreds. He tried every way of kindness—and failed." Anthony paused to moisten his parched lips.

"Finally," he went on, "John—your John—found his work for the State to be suffering. He is, as I see him, an upright, conscientious, kindly man, but determined. He made up his mind. He would help once more, but once more only. He sent for the other John. He told him when and how to come, how to approach the house, how to get into this room by that window, all without being seen.

"The other John came at the appointed time and knocked on the window. Your John helped him in. The other John, as always, was rotten with liquor. Your John told of the determination he'd come to that this was to be the last time if the other John didn't amend his ways. Then came trouble. Perhaps half-brother had drunk more than usual. Anyhow, he attacked your John. Sodden with drink though he was, he was the more powerful man. But John —your John—managed somehow to tear himself free. Not knowing what he did, he picked up the poker and struck; not once, but many times——"

"But what—— Good *God*——!"

Anthony overrode the interruption. "Wait till I've finished. Appalled at what he had done, he stood looking down at his bastard half-brother's body. It sprawled there on the hearth in its untidy, shabby, mud-stained clothes. It wasn't, I conceive, a pretty sight. Then John—your John—did what better men had done before him. He lost his head. Completely!

"He locked the door, after listening to make sure no-one had heard the struggle. He stripped to the skin. He stripped the body of his brother. Somehow, he forced himself not only to put on his brother's stained and dirty clothes, but (my God, what a ghastly task!) to dress the body in his own.

"And when it was all done, John—your John—took himself away. Through that window there. To drift through the darkness.

"And the next day he lay in a Whitechapel doss-house, with all the world thinking him dead."

Anthony's voice trailed off into silence. His head fell back against the chair, and his eyes almost closed. He seemed to be resting for a moment, as if gathering his strength to go on.

But he did not. Because the other man jumped suddenly to his feet.

"It's a lie!" he roared. "It's a lie!" He smashed his fist down upon the table. "A lie, I tell you! What's that?" He turned sharply to face the end of the room.

"What?" Anthony rose to his feet.

"Nothing, nothing." He came close to Anthony. "What you tell me is lies! All lies! Lies and more lies, you——" His voice rose with each word.

Suddenly, amazingly, Anthony shouted too. "It's true, and you must believe it! Your help is wanted." He thrust his thin, dark face at the other's. "It's the truth! Truth! D'you understand? I know! I know because, because *Hoode told me himself—to-day! He's coming here to-night! Now!*"

Sir Arthur flung his arms above his head. "Lies, lies, lies!" His voice rose to a harsh, unnatural scream. "All lies! God rot him! Christ torture his soul in hell! He's dead! He's dead! You fool! *I* know, *I, I!* You know nothing!" His hands seemed to be reaching higher, clawing. "You fool!" he screamed again. "He's dead. *I* know! *I killed him!* I climbed down and killed him——"

Anthony sat down on the edge of the table. "That'll be all, I think," he said.

The curtains over the alcove at the end of the room parted. From behind them came three men: the first tall and of middle-aged immaculateness, the second an obvious detective-inspector, the third negligible save for the pencil and notebook he carried.

Sir Arthur turned, crouching like an animal, to see the invasion. In a flash he whipped round and leapt at Anthony's throat, his arms outflung, his fingers crooked. Anthony, still sitting, had little time to avoid the rush. He raised a knee sharply. Sir Arthur fell to the floor, where for a time he rolled in agony.

The obvious detective-inspector bent over him. There was a click of handcuffs.

The immaculate man advanced to the table. "Very good indeed, Gethryn," he said.

"Thanks," Anthony said. "I suppose you're satisfied now, Lucas?"

"Eminently, Gethryn, eminently!" Mr. Lucas beamed.

"Then that's all right." Anthony's tone was heavy. "Now what about young Deacon? Can you unwind the red tape quickly?"

Mr. Lucas leant forward. "If you like," he said, "I can arrange for him to get away to-night. It's all most unofficial; but I can manage it. Speak to the Commissioner on the phone and all that sort of thing, you know."

Anthony's face relaxed into a smile. "Good for you. You might have Deacon told that if he likes I can arrange for the Bear and Key to fix him up for to-night."

"I'll tell him myself," said the other. "You're really rather a wonder, Gethryn! We ought to have you as a sort of super-super-intendent. Or you might do well on the stage. At one time just now you almost took *me* in with that grisly tale and manner of yours. And what a yarn it was, too. Just enough to make that half-crazy devil think he'd killed the wrong man. Enough, I mean, to make him wonder whether you hadn't got half the tale right and had only gone astray about who actually did the bashing." Lucas chuckled reminiscently. "I say," he added, "it was a good thing no-body heard us getting in here through the window. It would've spoilt the whole thing. The storm effect helped everything along nicely, though, didn't it?"

"It did," Anthony said. "I didn't arrange that, you know."

Mr. Lucas smiled. "No, I suppose not; though I'm so full at the moment of wonder and admiration that if any one told me you had, I don't know that I'd disbelieve 'em." He turned to look at the prisoner. "God!" he exclaimed. "Look at that!"

For Sir Arthur was sitting quietly at the feet of the plain-clothes man. His face was empty, vacuous. He was staring down at his manacled hands, while both his forefingers traced the intricate pattern of the carpet.

Anthony looked, then turned away with a shiver. Lucas dropped a hand on his shoulder.

"Never mind, Gethryn," he said, after a moment. "It isn't your fault."

Anthony shook off the hand. "Damn it, I know that! Only the whole thing is so filthy. It might be said, I know, that I sent him over the edge. But it wouldn't be true. He did that himself. Hatred, ingrowing hatred of a better man: that's the cause."

Lucas was thoughtful. "It complicates things, this madness."

"It does. What'll happen?"

"Usual, I suppose. The case'll be tried. He'll be convicted—and sent to Broadmoor, where he'll die, or recover in a year and be let out to kill some one else. We're so humane, you know!" Lucas was bitter. "Anyhow, you won't be bothered any more, except for the trial, at which you'll figure prominently. Oh, yes! Great glory will be yours, Gethryn. Think what a press you'll have!"

Anthony grunted disgust.

Lucas went on: "Lord! *What* a stir this is going to make. Millionaire M.P. arrested for murder of Cabinet Minister! It won't be nice for us at the Yard either. Not at all nice! Getting hold of an innocent man and all that. Police shown the way by amateur!" He groaned. "Never mind, *The Owl* shall be the first to publish anything. I arranged that before I came down. And then they'll have that report of yours to get out, too. What envy will tear Fleet Street! Of course, that report can't come out yet, you know. At least, I don't think so; not before the trial——"

Anthony started. "Lucas," he said, "there's something we've forgotten to verify." He put a hand up to his head.

"Gad! So we have. Let's see."

Together they stooped over the prisoner. He did not look up at them.

"Rotten business!" Anthony muttered. "Indecent when the man's like this." He put his hand on Sir Arthur's head. His fingers groped for a moment; then came away. With them came that immaculate head of graying hair.

"Wonderful *toupé!*" Lucas stretched out his hands for it. "I'd never have noticed it. And I thought they were always obvious. Well, that's the last confirmation of your theory, Gethryn." He peered at Anthony. "Lord! You look worn out, man!"

Anthony said heavily: "I am. Think I'll get back to bed at my pub."

Lucas glanced at his watch. "Yes, do. Get off now: it's only ten past eleven. Shall——"

"What time did you say it was?"

"Eleven-ten."

"Gad! I thought I'd been here at least five hours. Only eleven-ten! And I'm sitting here!" Anthony made for the door.

Lucas grabbed at his arm. "Here, what's to do?"

"Got to go and pay a call." Anthony wrenched himself free and got to the door, paused to say over his shoulder: "Don't tell Deacon to come to my pub. Just let him go. He'll get where I want him," and was gone.

Lucas stared after him. "Fool ought to be in bed," he muttered. "Clever devil, though, but odd!" He turned to the business on hand.

Sir Arthur still sat on the floor, playing his game. His fingers wandered ceaselessly over the carpet. His head, bald save for a sand-coloured tonsure, was sunk between his square shoulders.

CHAPTER SEVENTEEN

BY 'THE OWL'S' COMMISSIONER

The letter which Anthony, in the early hours of that morning, had despatched by District Messenger; the letter which had brought so important a person as Mr. Egbert Lucas down to Abbotshall, had run as follows:—

"MY DEAR LUCAS,—As you know, I have been playing at detectives down at Marling. I have finished my game; the rest is up to you.

"What I have found, how I have found it, and my opinion of the meaning of what I have found, you will discover set out in the enclosed document, typed by my very own fingers. You may—I cannot tell—think my conclusions wrong, and say that in real life, even as in fairy tales, a set of circumstances, a collection of clues, may equally lead to the innocent as to the guilty. For me, however, I am convinced. To put it in my own diffident way: I *know* I am right!

"So please read the enclosed. If you agree with me, as I think you will, you will yet find that the evidence is insufficient: and you will be right. I will, therefore, endeavour to arrange for a confession by the guilty person to be given in the (unsuspected) presence of officers of your able department. In order for this to be done, will you give orders for some of your men—three, including a shorthand writer, would be enough—to meet me at the cross-roads on the London side of Marling at about nine to-night? I will then get them covertly into Abbotshall and dispose them in advantageous but covert positions. This may, I know, be irregular, but you can take it that I can manage things without any one in the house knowing until the business is over. Once your men are where I shall put them, I shall enter the house by a more orthodox way. The rest will follow.

"This is asking a lot of you, but, after all, you know me well enough to be reasonably certain that I am less of a fool than many. So, if you agree with my conclusions as set out in the report, please arrange this. Whether you agree or not, ring me up, before seven to-night, at my pub in Marling (Greyne 29). If I am not there leave a message: 'All right' or 'Nothing doing,' as the case may be. Whichever your answer is, I will ring you up when I have received it.

"My main reason—or one of my main reasons—for doing all this work was to do Hastings's little paper, *The Owl,* a good turn. The report is really for them, though I don't know when and to what extent you will allow them to publish it. But I rely on you to see that *The Owl* gets as much journalistic fat as it can digest. No other paper must hear a whisper until you've allowed Hastings to make a scoop out of the 'Dramatic New Developments.'

"Yours,
"A. R. GETHRYN."

"P.S.—Don't forget that if you decide to let me try to arrange this confession, I may fail. I don't think I will; but I might."

Coming to the end of this letter, Mr. Egbert Lucas had whistled beneath his breath, instructed his secretary that on no account was he to be disturbed, and had settled down—he has the most comfortable chair in the Yard—to read the typewritten report.

Unfolding it, he murmured: "Unexpected chap, Gethryn. This ought to be interesting."

He read:—

"THE MURDER OF JOHN HOODE

"Upon the morning of the 20th of August, I drove to the village of Marling in Surrey. By 9.30 A. M. I had gained admission to the house Abbotshall.

"Owing to circumstances which need not be set down here, and also, in a great measure, to the courtesy and assistance of Superintendent Boyd of Scotland Yard, I was able from the beginning to pursue unhampered my own investigations. The result of these I give below.

"(For reasons which must, I think, be obvious, I have divided this report into four parts. Also, I would point out that, for reasons equally evident, the steps in my deduction, reasoning—call it what you will—are not necessarily given here in their chronological order.)

I

"Immediately upon my arrival at Abbotshall, I spoke at some length with Superintendent Boyd, who gave me the history of the affair as obtained by him through close questioning of the inmates. It appeared then that with the exception of the butler, these one and all had alibis, complete in some cases and in others as nearly so as could be expected of persons who had not known beforehand that they were like to be accused of murder. (Later, of course, it was revealed—see reports of the inquest—that Mr. Archibald Deacon's alibi did not exist in fact.)

"Superintendent Boyd and I at once agreed that to suspect the alibiless Poole (the butler) was folly. He had been, obviously and by common report, devoted to his master. Moreover, he is physically incapable—even were he out of his mind—of dealing such blows as caused the death of the murdered man.

"After our conversation, Superintendent Boyd and I together made an examination of the study, the room in which the murder was done. Together we came to the following conclusions,[1] all of which were explained by the superintendent in his evidence at the inquest. Since, therefore, these points are by this common knowledge, I will not go into the processes by which they were arrived at, but will merely enumerate them as follows:—

"(i)   That when Hoode was struck, either by the first or all the blows, he was seated at his table.

"(ii)   That the appearance of the room had been carefully arranged to convey the impression that a struggle had taken place.

"(iii)   That the murderer was well known to Hoode, and was, in all probability, an inmate of the house.

"(iv)   That the murderer had worn gloves for most of the time during which he was in the study, there being no finger-prints except Hoode's anywhere save on the wood-rasp.

"(v)   That the blows which killed Hoode must have had tremendous strength behind them.

"(vi)   That, in all probability, the murderer entered by the window. (I fully endorsed, at that stage of the inquiry, the opinion of the Police that Poole's evidence was reliable.)

[1] Colonel Gethryn is unusually modest here.

"It will be seen that the cumulative implication of these six points tends to strengthen considerably the case against Deacon, which even without them is by no means weak circumstantially. It is now, therefore, that the keynote of my report must come.

"I met and spoke with Deacon for the first time on the afternoon of the day I arrived at Abbotshall. It needed but three minutes with him to convince me that here was a man who had not been, was not, and never could be a murderer. I cannot defend this statement with logic. It was simply conviction. Like this: In a party of, say, twelve persons there will be eleven about none of whom I could say definitely: 'That one is incapable of stealing the baby's marmalade'; but in the twelfth I may find a man—perhaps unknown to me before—of whom I can swear before God or man: 'He *could not* have stolen the baby's marmalade—not even if he had tried to! He is incapable of carrying out such a crime.'

"Deacon was a twelfth man. Before I had seen him, my views were beginning to differ from those of Scotland Yard: after I had seen and spoken with him they became directly opposed. It became my business to prove, in spite of all difficulties, that this man, whatever the appearances, had had no hand in the death of John Hoode. In what follows, they who read will find, I hope, absolute proof of his innocence; or if not that, at least a battering-ram to shake the tower of their belief in his guilt.

"Knowing that Deacon was not the murderer, I nevertheless realised that his innocence—so strong was the case against him—could only be established by definite proof that some one else was. That is to say: a negative defence would be useless.

"It will be seen, then, that the divergence of my opinions from those of the Crown began almost at the outset of my investigation.

"Let us go back to the study at Abbotshall. On each of the numbered points I gave earlier, I agreed with Superintendent Boyd. Where I began to—had to—disagree was concerning their implication of Deacon. Points (i), (ii), (iii), and (iv) can be left alone; they will fit my murderer as well as, or better than, they fit Deacon. The remaining two, however, must be dealt with more fully.

"We will take (v) first. The obvious fact that strength far above the normal was behind the blows that killed Hoode was a perfect link in the chain of circumstantial evidence against the gigantic Deacon. But at the inquest, Dr. Fowler, the divisional surgeon, said: 'The wounds were inflicted so far as I can judge, either by a man three times stronger than the average or by a person of either sex who was insane and had the super-normal strength of the insane.'

"Having to find an alternative to Deacon and having determined to cling to my theory that the murderer was an inhabitant—permanent or temporary—of the house, my choice of Dr. Fowler's alternative was a man or woman mentally unbalanced. This choice was not, as it might at first seem, a drawback; rather was it the reverse. For one of my first impressions had been that there was something of terrible senselessness about the whole affair, and this impression had increased a thousandfold when I saw the battered head of the dead man. Madness was my first thought then. Those blows—*four* of them, mark you! when the first had been obviously sufficient—surely spoke of insanity; either the lust for blood and destruction of a confirmed homicidal maniac or *the consummation of a hatred so deadly, so complete in its possession of the hater, as to constitute insanity of itself.*

"The second was the theory I adopted. For, believing the murderer to be an inmate of the house, it was clear that I must look for one whose insanity was not of a type apparent to the world.

"Now for point (vi)—the entry by the window. As I have said, I agreed with the police that the murderer did enter by the window; but there our agreement ceased. It is a point in the Crown's case against Deacon that his are the only legs in the house long enough to enable their owner to clear the flower-bed in stepping from the flagged path to the low sill of the study window. This, I am sure, is, as evidence against Deacon, more than useless. I have not taken measurements, but it is obvious that even for his long legs, a step right *into* the study would be impossible. This being so, the fact that he could step *on to* the window-sill is of no importance whatever. For one thing, it would have been extremely difficult for him to retain balance; for another, if he had retained his balance, the necessary scrabbling at the window and the twisting and turning he would have had to perform to get legs and then body into the room would have attracted Hoode's attention before he could see enough of the intruder to recognise him. And then the theory, agreed by the police, that Hoode did not rise from, or anyhow did not remain long out of, his chair, falls to the ground.

"Now let us get back to my murderer. Yes, he got in by the window; but he left the flower-bed unmarked. Now, as he is a member of the household we know that his legs cannot be as long as Deacon's. How, then, did he approach the window?

"He must have (*a*) jumped over the flower-bed and into the

room; (*b*) stepped on the flower-bed, but, on leaving, repaired or disguised the damage he had done; or (*c*) *got his feet on to the sill and his whole self into the room without having crossed the flower-bed.*

"It is almost impossible that he should have done (*a*); (*b*) is unlikely, since after the murder the murderer had no time to spare. (This is proved later.) One is left, then, with the conviction that the real answer lies in (*c*). This means either that the murderer erupted through the floor or walls of the study or that *he descended the wall of the house and entered the open study window without ever reaching the earth in his journey.* (Entrance through the door is barred. Remember, we are taking Poole's evidence on that point as reliable.)

"As the murderer was presumably flesh and blood and there was no hole in walls or floor, I fastened on the 'descent' theory, which was subsequently confirmed by an examination of the wall outside and above the open study window. Over this wall—over the whole house, in fact—the commonest and creepiest of creepers creeps. I refer to *Ampelopsis Veitchii*. A large drainage-pipe runs to earth beside the study window in question, and for a space of perhaps half a foot on each side of it throughout its length the creeper has been cleared away. But half-way between the top of the window through which the murderer entered the study and the first-floor windows above it, a shoot of creeper has pushed its way out into the cleared space beside the pipe. This shoot drew my attention because it was black and shrivelled.

"*Ampelopsis Veitchii,* though one of the commonest forms of creeper, is also one of the most tender. A sharp blow upon the main branch of a shoot means death to that shoot within a few hours. The dead piece of creeper I refer to was, I thought at first, at that point on the wall where it might have been struck by the feet of a man of middle height climbing out of either of the first-floor windows over the open one of the study at the moment when he was clutching the sill with one or both hands and hanging with arms bent.

"It was, I saw, clearly impossible for the murderer to have dropped from the upper window on to the sill of the open study window and so miraculously to have retained his balance that he did not fall on to the flower-bed. Also—in spite of the novelists—there are few drain-pipes which can be used to climb by. This drain-pipe is no exception. Fingers could not be clasped round it; neither would it support more than a five or six-stone weight. It was clear, therefore, that the murderer, in descending the wall, had used something to climb down—probably a rope. (Descent of the wall was another confirmation of the theory that the murderer was a member, permanent or temporary, of the household.)

"It will have been noticed that I have used the masculine personal pronoun to describe the murderer. Dr. Fowler's statement at the inquest, which I quoted earlier, would allow, given insanity, of equal rights to women. But I *felt,* from the beginning, that John Hoode had been killed by a man, and I worked throughout on that assumption. At every turn little things told me that this was a man's work; and I was finally satisfied when I accepted the theory of descent by the wall.

"I will bring to an end here the first part of this report. But before starting upon the next, I will summarise the conclusions already shown, give them life with a touch of imagination, and let you see the picture.

"The murder was committed by a man who, if not completely mad, was at least insane in his hatred of Hoode. He was at the time of the murder an inmate of Abbotshall. He effected entrance to the study that night by letting himself down from the more easterly of the first-floor windows over the most easterly of the study windows. He spoke to Hoode, jokingly explaining his unceremonious entry. By some pretext (it would, you know, be easy enough) he got behind Hoode as he sat at his big table. Then he struck.

"His object achieved, he carries out the plan he has been hatching for weeks. He sets the scene, overturning chairs, spilling papers, dragging the body to the hearth—and all as quietly as you please. He steps back, to regard with pleasure the result of his labours.

"He overturns the clock, having moved the sofa to rest it upon. He moves back the hands of the clock until they stand at 10.45. A quarter to eleven, mark you! Not ten to, not twenty to, not twenty-three and a half minutes to—but a quarter to!

"He gives a hasty glance round the room. Everything is in order. He thrusts his head cautiously from the window. All is as he had calculated: there is nobody about; the night is sufficiently dark. He goes up his rope again and through that first-floor window.

II

"Having established our criminal as at least a monomaniac and an inhabitant—permanent or temporary—of the house, let us go further into detail.

"First, as regards the finger-prints of which so much has been heard and so few have been seen.

"Every one is satisfied that the murderer wore gloves, because nowhere else in the study, where he must have handled one thing after another, were any finger-prints found. They are found, these important pieces of evidence, upon the one object where their presence is utterly damning—and there only!

"The spirals, whorls, and what-nots which compose these marks correspond exactly with those to be found in the skin and thumb and first two fingers of Archibald Deacon's right hand. *Ergo,* say Police and Public, Archibald Deacon is the murderer. But I say that these finger-prints go a long way to prove (even without the rest of my evidence) that Deacon *cannot* be the murderer.

"Here is the one really clever murder (of those discovered) committed within the last fifteen years. Yet, if one takes the popular view, one has to believe that the murderer, who was wise enough to wear gloves during the greater part of the time he was in the study, actually removed one of them and carefully pressed his thumb and fingers upon the highly receptive surface of his weapon's handle before leaving that weapon in a nice easy place for the first policemen to find!

"Surely the fallacy of blindly accepting as the murderer the man who made those prints is obvious? Consider the *position* of the marks. They point down the handle, towards the blade! It is almost incredible that at any time would the murderer have held the weapon as a Regency buck dandled his tasselled cane.

"My difficulty was to reconcile with Deacon's innocence of the murder the presence of his finger-prints upon the tool with which it was committed. That the prints were his I had too much respect for the efficacy of the Scotland Yard system to doubt.

"A possible solution came to me from memory of a detective story[1] I once read, in which the murderer, something of a practical scientist, made, by means of an ingenious and practicable photographical process, a die of another man's thumb-print. This he used to incriminate the innocent owner of the thumb.

"For a while I cherished this theory, so vivid was my recollection of the possibility of the method; but I was never really satisfied.

[1] *The Red Thumb Mark,* by R. Austin Freeman.

Then, suddenly, I found the explanation which I was afterwards to prove true.

"*Instead of going to the immense trouble of making a stamp or die, why not obtain beforehand upon the desired object the* actual *finger-prints of the chosen scapegoat?*

"After consideration, I accepted this idea. It fitted well enough with my murderer—a fellow of infinite cunning. I proceeded with the work of reconstruction. Thus:—

"Since Deacon had no knowledge of the crime, the murderer must have induced him, in circumstances so ordinary or usual as to be likely to escape his memory, to take hold of the wood-rasp by its handle at some time before the murder; perhaps eight hours, probably not more. For this clever murderer would realise the difficulty of retaining the finger-prints unspoiled.

"When, after obtaining the finger-prints, he had got rid of Deacon, he must have removed with gloved hands—taking care not to touch those parts of the handle where the prints must be—the handle he had loosened before Deacon had held it. Then that handle must have been packed (say in a small box with cork wedges) in such a way as to ensure that its carriage in the pocket for the descent of the wall and subsequent activities could be effected without those beautiful marks being spoiled. The reassembling of the tool must have been done after the murder; and the whole Deacon-damning bit of evidence then planted for the police to find.

"In the study, on a later visit, I found confirmation of the accuracy of my deductions. It will be remembered that when the wood-rasp was produced at the inquest, it was proved to the satisfaction of the court that it was indeed the weapon which had caused Hoode's death. This proof lay pre-eminently in the condition of the blade, which was far from nice. But it was also pointed out by the police, to make the jury's assurance doubly sure, that on a little rosewood table in the study there was a scar on the polish, known not to have existed before, which had obviously been made by the blade of just such a wood-rasp as this wood-rasp. Superintendent Boyd gave it as his opinion that the murderer had laid the wood-rasp on this table after he had killed Hoode, and while he was arranging the appearance of a struggle.

"I agree with the superintendent—but only up to a point. Where he was wrong was in assuming that the scar had been made by the murderer having put down on the table the *whole* wood-rasp.

"That scar is of exactly the same length as the *blade* of the rasp,

and is in the centre of the table, having on every side of it some
six inches of unscarred table-top.

"Do you see? That scar *could not have been made by the
complete tool!* The handle is two and a half to three inches in
circumference, and if it had been joined to the blade would, by
reason of its far greater thickness, *have allowed no more than an
inch or so of the blade's tip to touch and scar the table.* Had the
complete rasp been laid down at an edge of the table with the
handle projecting into space, the full-length scar would have been
possible. But the scar, as I have described, is in the middle of the
table, and could therefore only have been made by the blade without its handle.

"Here, then, was the justification of my theory. Further proof
came later. With full official permission I examined the wood-rasp.
It was as it had been found. I held it in my hand. I shook it—and
the blade flew off. Two small wooden wedges fell to the floor. I
picked a shred of linen from the tang of the blade.

"Obviously, the use of the little wedges had been to hold the
tang of the blade in the enlarged socket of the handle. And the
fact that the socket had been enlarged, added to the inadequacy
of the wedges, is surely proof enough that the blows which killed
Hoode were struck with the blade alone. There is, however, yet
more—the shred of linen. It came, I should say, from a handkerchief, the use of which had been, I take it, to get a better grip of
the thin tang when striking. The glove the murderer was undoubtedly wearing probably proved insufficient to ensure against a slipping grip. So he wrapped a handkerchief about his gloved hand.
An inequality in the surface of the steel caught some loose thread.
This he did not notice when hastily ramming handle and blade
together after the kill.

"The wedges and the shred of linen are in the keeping of Superintendent Boyd, to whom I gave them at the time of my discovery.
I could not, my case being incomplete, explain then their significance.

"My next step was to question Deacon. To my surprise and
consternation I found that although he was a man for whom tools
had neither interest nor meaning and for whom therefore the
handling of any such implement might be so much out of the
ordinary as to impress itself upon his memory, he had no recollection of ever seeing, before the inquest, any wood-rasp. He
even suggested that until now he had not known such a tool to
exist.

"I will not deny that Deacon's emphatic assertion that he had never even seen the rasp until it was exhibited at the inquest gave me a shaking. It did, and a bad one. I tested all the links in my chain, only to find each sound and the whole most obviously right—until this blind alley.

"Then it struck me, and I laughed at myself as those who read are probably already laughing at me. I saw that I was committing the grave error of underrating my man. I saw that so far from having received a check I had really been advanced.

"The finger-prints were on the handle of the rasp, and the handle—had I not been at much pains to prove it?—had been separated from the blade by the murderer. The murderer—being an intelligent murderer—would certainly never have been such a fool as to let the fearsome and so-likely-to-be-remembered blade within Deacon's sight. No, it was far more likely that he had disguised the handle as the handle of something else.

"Having got thus far, I progressed at speed. As what could he have disguised the handle? With efficacy, only as that of another tool. But he probably knew Deacon as a man who had no truck with tools. How, then, did he get the so-ordinary surroundings necessary to prevent awkward memories arising afterwards in the mind of Deacon? The answer is that they were there, ready-made, to his hand. In order to avoid obscurity, I will elucidate this.

"The indication all through had been that the murderer was a man accustomed to the use of carpenter's tools. The murderer was an inmate of the house. Put one and two together and you will see that he would very possibly be known to the household as one who was 'always messing about at that there carpent'ring.' Deacon was also of the household, and would therefore see nothing unusual in, say, being asked to 'hold this chisel (or gouge, or anything else you like) for just half a second.' If this seems farfetched, remember that from the beginning I felt the murderer as one who had been preparing his work for some long time.

"It was almost at the moment when I reached this stage of thought that a number of hitherto insufficiently substantiated suspicions which had been steadily massing in my mind suddenly rearranged themselves in such a manner as to become extra links in my chain of reasoning rather than the wild plungings of a mind tired of logic. This merging of reason with intuition left me certain that I should know who I was trying to prove guilty if Deacon gave me the name of the man against whom these suspicions of mine had been directed in answer to the question: 'Who, at any time within the last twenty-four hours preceding the murder, induced you to hold in your right hand an implement with a short, thick wooden handle of the same appearance as the handle you have seen in the wood-rasp?'

"You see, I had already learned that of the Abbotshall *ménage* four men frequently used, and had consequent access to, carpenter's tools. These were the gardener, the chauffeur, the murdered man, and the guest from whom I had the information.

"Hoode, the gardener, and the chauffeur I disregarded. The first because he was not his own murderer; the second because at the time of the murder he was in bed at the Cottage Hospital in Marling; and the third because he has respectable and trustworthy friends to swear that he spent the evening of the crime in their company.

"Remained the guest—that enthusiastic amateur Dædalus—and he the man that from the beginning had excited those nebulous suspicions I have mentioned. He was living in the house at the time when the murder was committed. He was, by his own showing, an amateur carpenter of experience and enthusiasm. (Early he simulated ignorance as to the name of a wood-rasp. Later, by his voluntary statement, he showed that he could not have been ignorant of it. This was the only slip he made when talking with me.)

"Before I took opportunity to ask Deacon the all-important question, I did much and thought more. With one exception, these thoughts and actions are proper to the next part of this report, and accordingly are dealt with there. The exception is this:—

"I became aware that of the two first-floor windows of Abbotshall which (see Part I.) are over the window through which the murderer entered the study, the more easterly must have been the one used by the murderer. For I saw what I had not seen at first, that it would be almost an impossibility for a man descending by a rope from the other window to swing his legs, at the end of the descent, on to the sill of the study window, since that window is not exactly, as one would find in a house younger and less altered than Abbotshall, between the two first-floor windows above it but has most of its length beneath the more easterly. Moreover, although a man descending from the less easterly window might possibly have struck with his foot that one shoot of creeper in the cleared space beside the drain-pipe (see Part I.), he would also be bound to do damage to the main body of the creeper—and that is uninjured.

"It was, in fact, obvious that the murderer had come out of the room with the more easterly window. (I was annoyed with myself for not having seen this sooner.)

"That window is to the room occupied as a sitting-room by Sir Arthur Digby-Coates.

"My suspect amateur carpenter was Sir Arthur Digby-Coates.

"When at last I put to Deacon my question of who had given him any implement with a wooden handle to hold, the answer was: 'Sir Arthur Digby-Coates.'

"(*Note.*—Before going on to Part III, it might be well to explain briefly the circumstances in which Deacon was induced to leave the prints of his fingers on the handle. Deacon, when I asked him my question, explained that on the morning of the day of the murder he passed by Digby-Coates's sitting-room. The door was open. Digby-Coates called to him to come in. He entered to find, *as on several previous occasions,* that Digby-Coates was amusing himself with the completing of an excellent carved cabinet he had been engaged on for many weeks. Digby-Coates was in difficulties, having, he explained, too few hands. Deacon was asked to stand by. He did so, and assisted the enthusiast by handing from the carpenter's bench near the window, one tool after the other. Among them was one, he just remembered, with a handle such as I had described and such as he remembered the wood-rasp handle to be now that he came to think of it.)

"So there you are. When I heard the story I felt, I confess, no little admiration for Digby-Coates. He is so thorough! You see, this was not the first time Deacon had given such assistance. And he knew Deacon thought little and cared less about the whole business of cabinet-making.

III

"It is evidence purely of trivialities which has put Deacon in a cell awaiting trial; yet I am convinced that did I attempt to establish his innocence merely by the means I have employed so far, the very people who already accept his guilt as certain would accuse me of having nothing but trivialities upon which to base my version of the affair. Further, it could be said—and would be— that I have read between the lines writing which wasn't there; that I have so ingeniously twisted the interpretation of what are, in fact, merely ordinarily meaningless signs as to make them appear a grim and coherent indictment against another man.

"So I must strengthen my case; for the truth is that this evidence of trivialities is good, but not nearly good enough. It must have a backing to it.

"Now, there is, if you look at it, a complete absence of any backing to the case against Deacon. 'What about the money?' you say. 'What about that hundred pounds belonging to Hoode? There's motive for you!' 'Nonsense!' say I. Deacon was paid six hundred pounds a year. He had also an allowance from his only living relative. He had been, it is true, a little shorter of money than usual lately; but to suggest that he would commit a murder for a hundred pounds is absurd. A man in his position could have raised the money in a thousand safer and less energetic ways. No, Deacon's story that the money was a birthday gift from Hoode is, besides being more likely, true. Further, it is easy of proof that Deacon and Hoode were on the best of terms: for corroboration apply to the Ministry of Imperial Finance and the households of Abbotshall and 12 Seymour Square. Further still, look at Deacon's record and see how rash it is to condemn him murderer with nothing more to go upon than those too-beautiful finger-prints and a few ragged pieces of circumstantial evidence, *the two best of which were supplied—oh! so ingeniously—by Sir Arthur Digby-Coates*. For it was from him that the police first learnt that Hoode had drawn a hundred pounds in notes from his bank. And it was through him that it became known that Deacon had asked him the time at ten forty-five on the night of the murder—the time to which the hands of the clock in the study had been moved by the murderer.

"There being no backing to the case of the Crown against Deacon, I saw that if I could find a stout one for mine against Digby-Coates I should score heavily.

"The first thing to be found was motive. What, I asked myself, could it be? Money? No. Digby-Coates is a wealthier man by far than ever was Hoode. Revenge for some particular ill turn? Hardly that, since Hoode, though a politician, bore all his life the stamp of honesty and straight dealing. A woman? I was not prepared to accept one as the sole cause. She might, of course, be contributory, but I wanted something more likely. Middle-aged men of the social and intellectual standing of these two do not often, in this age of decrees nisi and cold love, go about killing each other over a woman if she is only the first blot upon the fair sea of their friendship.

"I was forced back, in this search for motive, upon the deductions I had made from those little material signs, and remembered that I had determined, before ever I thought of putting a name to the murderer, that John Hoode was killed by a man insane; not mad in the gibbering, straws-in-the-hair sense, but mentally unbalanced by a kind of ingrowing, self-nourishing hatred.

"I took this as my starting point and asked myself how I could find corroboration of and reason for this hatred having existed in the heart of a man ostensibly the closest friend of its object. The answer was: look at their past history; as much of it as is available in books of record. I did so, using Hoode's own books.

"I found soon enough reason for the hatred. Look as I looked. You will see that always, always, always was Digby-Coates beaten by the man he killed. Were the race one of scholarship or sport, politics or social advancement or honours, the result was the same. Hoode first; Digby-Coates second. Look in the *Who's Who, Hansard,* the records of Upchester School and Magdalen, the Honours Lists. Look in the minds of the men's colleagues and contemporaries. Look at this, the slightest extract from the list:—

John Hoode.	*Arthur Digby-Coates.*
Captain of Upchester (last three years at school).	Senior Monitor (same three years).
Won John Halket scholarship to Magdalen.	Second on list.
Rowed 2 in Oxford boat (third year).	Rowed 6 in trials (third year).
Gaisford (fourth year).	Newdigate (fourth year).
Minor office (Admiralty) after three years in Parliament.	Still merely M.P. after six months longer in Parliament.
President of Board of Trade.	Still M.P. (He was, I believe, offered at this time a minor Parliamentary Secretaryship; but refused.)
K.C.M.G., C.V.O., etc.	K.B.E.
Minister of Imperial Finance (from the date of the forming of the Ministry).	Almost at same time accepted Parliamentary Secretaryship to Board of Conciliation.

"One could go on for pages, for ever telling this story of races won by a stride—Hoode the winner, Digby-Coates his follower-up —and that stride getting longer and longer as time went on.

"But at last came the race for the Woman—the race whose loss snapped the last cord of sanity in the mind of the loser.

"I discovered *la femme's* existence in this way: I searched Hoode's desk in suspicion of a hidden drawer. I found one and in it a diary (of no use save to corroborate the fact of some of those races), and a bunch of newspaper-cuttings. But I knew— how is no matter—that something was missing from that drawer.

"What that something was I did not know. I only knew that it was most probably of importance. So I searched the house— and found it. A packet of letters from the lady in the case. As I was by then up to the neck in the unspeakable nasty work of the Private Inquiry Agent, I read them. Who the woman is will not be set down here. It is my hope that not even in court shall I have to give her name.

"I found her and talked with her. Put briefly, her replies were that I was correct in assuming that she had been Hoode's mistress, and that I was also right (this was a shot in black dark) in as- suming that she knew Sir Arthur Digby-Coates. She did not, it seemed, have any affection for the gentleman. She made it plain to me, under some pressure, that Sir Arthur had wished her to stand in the relation to him that she subsequently did to John Hoode. But (a shrug of distaste) Sir Arthur had been sent packing—and quickly.

"Isn't that enough, when added to those other and perpetual defeats of the past five-and-thirty years, to show the reason for hatred in the mind of the egoist? Consider the history of the mat- ter. First, boyish jealousy and a determination to win next time; then the gradual process of realisation that strive as he would he would never reach a common goal before his rival; then the slow at first but increasingly fast transition from healthy jealousy to dislike, from dislike to utter hatred. Then, at last, with the crowning loss of the woman, the monomania takes a firmer hold and be- comes a fire so fierce that only the complete elimination of the hated man will quench it.

"So much for reasons why Digby-Coates should have hated Hoode. Now for corroboration that such hatred actually existed.

"I wrote just now of certain newspaper-cuttings which I found in the hidden drawer of Hoode's desk. These were a bunch of twenty-four, taken from various issues (all bearing dates within the last two years) of *The Searchlight, The St. Stephen's Gazette,* and *Vox Populi*. Every one of the cuttings was a prominent article attacking the Minister of Reconstruction in no half-hearted way.

"Being one who prefers news without sensationalism, I had never before read a line from any one of these three papers. I came to these extracts, therefore, with a mind not only open but blank, and was immediately struck by the strange unanimity of the three newspapers in regard to John Hoode. For, as all the world must know, whether they read them or not, the trio's politics are widely varying. Their attacks upon the murdered man were made upon different grounds, it is true, but the very fact that the attacks were made, and made so viciously, struck me as unusual. It seemed to me that in the ordinary way the fact of one attacking would be enough to make at least one of the others defend. Further, the grounds upon which the attacks were made appeared to my un-biased mind as flimsy compared with the whole-hearted virulence of the writing.

"From wondering and re-reading, I came upon a thing even stranger: the unmistakable and mysterious similarity in the style of the composition. This similarity was to me, who have made something of a study of other men's methods, even more pro-nounced when attempts had been made to disguise or vary the manner of writing. After ten minutes' examination of those cut-tings, I was prepared to swear that one man had been conducting the anti-Hoode campaign in three papers whose views on every other matter from vaccination to the Vatican are as wide apart as Stoke Poges and Seattle. I pictured a man of some scholastic attainment who was unable to write in fashion other than pre-ciously correct and so set in his style as to be incapable of varying it, no matter how hard he tried.

"I took the cuttings and my conviction to Deacon. He could not help me, so I went to his predecessor as Hoode's private secretary. From him I obtained confirmation of my theory. He, too, had suspected that not only was one man behind these press attacks, but that this man was also the actual author. He showed me something I had only half-noticed till then; something which went further than mere similarity of style. Throughout the articles, he pointed out, quotations occurred. They were, some of them, unusual quotations. But usual or unusual, one and all were correct! They were correct in some cases to the point of pedantry —if correctness can be so described. And they were thus correct in these three widely differing and highly sensational weekly papers, whose literary standards have always been a byword with those who hate journalese, *cliché,* and the dreadful mutilation, humiliation and weakening of the English language.

"It was when this former secretary of Hoode's pointed this out to me that I recollected having recently been puzzled by a memory which would not be remembered. In one of the cuttings I had come across a quotation from Virgil, in which a dative case had been used rather than the all-prevalent but less correct genitive, and had been haunted at the time of reading with a sense of having seen this same rarity only recently. Suddenly it came back to me. It had been in a book of essays I had dipped into—a book of essays which, on inquiry made later, turned out to be from the pen of Sir Arthur Digby-Coates, writing under a feminine *nom de guerre.*

"That, I admit, is not much to go upon. But more was to come. This forerunner of Deacon had—before he quarrelled with Hoode and left him—on his own initiative employed a private detective and sent him to unearth this enemy of Hoode's who seemed to command and write for three incendiary newspapers. You see, this secretary was sure that there was an enemy of some importance at work. At first he said nothing to Hoode, but at last told of his suspicions. He was laughed at. He returned to the charge—and they quarrelled. He left Hoode's employment without having told him of the private detective. Being, with some excuse, more than a little disgruntled, he paid the detective, telling him to stop the work and go to hell.

"But, luckily, the private detective had smelt a Big Thing, and consequently Big Money. He went on working. He finished his job. I got into touch with him. He has been paid, and the result of his labours has been forwarded to Scotland Yard.

"His proofs are more than adequate. He has established, mainly through the corruptibility of a discharged employee, that Digby-Coates was beyond doubt the hidden owner of those three newspapers and also the composer of all these elaborate pæans of hate which appeared in them from time to time, and were directed against the man who was his friend and whose friendship he so cleverly pretended to return. (One cannot but admire the ingenuity with which Digby-Coates foisted more or less respectable and quite foolish figureheads upon the world—including the rest of the Press —as owners of the papers on the purchase and upkeep of which he must have spent nearly half his great fortune.)

"But it was in writing the attacks himself that he overstepped and left a loophole through which curious persons could wriggle.

Had he left the writing to different men and rested content with being the power behind the machine, he would have increased by a thousand his chances of remaining undiscovered. I suppose his hate was so strong that to leave the work to others was beyond him.

"Before ending the third part of this report, I would draw attention to what has thus far been established—established, I hope, to the satisfaction of even the most rigorous anti-Deaconite.

"It has been shown that there is both reason for and corroboration of Digby-Coates's hatred of Hoode.

"It has been shown not only that all the evidence against Deacon can be used equally well against Digby-Coates, but also that there is in fact more of this evidence of material signs against Digby-Coates than there is against Deacon.

"Above all, we have in the case against Digby-Coates two things (which might be called one thing) that there have never been against Deacon. The first is motive—although it is nothing more (nor less) than the crazy hatred of a half-madman. *The second is reliable evidence that ill-will existed before the murder.*

IV

"If I were (God forbid!) delivering this report as a lecture, I am sure there would be a little fat man in a corner bounding up and down with ill-suppressed irritation. At this stage he would be unable to restrain himself any longer and would ask passionately why the hell I was wasting my time and his by faking up a case against a man who had a chilled-steel alibi—the perfect, unassailable defence of a man who is seen by various people at such times and in such a place as to make it impossible for him to have committed the crime.

"I would assure the fat little man—as I assure those who read—that I would in due course deal with and demolish that alibi, pointing out at the same time that it was the very perfection of the thing which had bred some of my first suspicions of its owner. It was too good, too complete, in a household where every one else had only ordinary ones; it was a Sunday-go-to-meeting alibi; the alibi of a man who at least knew that a crime was going to be committed.

"But more of that later. For the moment I will take two points which, though they might be considered proper to the first part of this document, I have seen fit to reserve until now.

"The first concerns a rope. I have explained that I found it necessary to search the house. During that search, which was not only for the missing letters from the drawer in Hoode's writing-table, I went into Deacon's bedroom. This is next to, and on the west side of, the room used by Digby-Coates as a sitting-room, study, and, occasionally, carpenter's shop. (He has had a bench fitted up there for him, as I mentioned earlier.)

"In the grate in Deacon's bedroom was a little pile of soot which at once attracted my attention, as being unusual in so scrupulously tended a house as Abbotshall. I investigated. On the ledge which runs round the interior of the chimney at the point where—on a level with the mantelpiece outside—it suddenly narrows, I found a coil of silk cord of roughly the thickness of a man's little finger. It was double-knotted at intervals of two inches throughout its length, which was sixteen feet. (By the time this report is read the rope will be in the hands of the authorities. They would have had it sooner, only I was not giving away information until my case was complete.)

"That pile of soot in the grate was not of long standing. The cord was new. I knew at once that I had found the rope by which my criminal had descended the wall. But how did it get where I found it?

"I saw that the only answer which would fit the rest of my case was that the rope had been put there by Digby-Coates. Since I knew Deacon to be innocent and I had nowhere found any evidence to show that Digby-Coates had an accomplice, it could have been nobody else. And it was so easy for him, occupying as he did the room next to Deacon's.

"I am aware that here I am treading on dangerous ground—from the point of view, that is, of the logical anti-Deaconite—but I say nevertheless that this business of the rope strengthens my case and goes to give yet further indication of Digby-Coates's deliberate plan to fasten his guilt upon Deacon. Silk rope of so excellent a quality is not common, and I think that Scotland Yard should have little difficulty in tracing its purchase. So convinced am I that they will find Digby-Coates at the other end of the trail that, if I could be of any use, I would willingly help them. Without the rest of my investigations, the finding of that rope would only have hastened Deacon's journey to another and thicker one. But with them it has a very different effect.

"Now for the second matter which was to be dealt with before the alibi:

"It will be remembered that a great point against Deacon was that the hands of the overturned clock in the study stood at 10.45.

The coroner, in reviewing the case at the end of the inquest, argued thus: At a quarter to eleven Deacon had entered the room of Sir Arthur Digby-Coates and inquired the time. That he had done so was apparent both from the evidence of Sir Arthur and of Deacon himself. All the other evidence pointed to Deacon. Was it not then only reasonable to assume that Deacon, after committing the murder and arranging the room to look as if a struggle had taken place, had pushed those hands back to 10.45, knowing that at that time he had been with so reputable a witness as Sir Arthur Digby-Coates? The whole thing was clear, said the coroner, answering his own question and practically directing the already willing jury to pass a verdict against Deacon.

"The coroner added that he could not say whether, if his assumption were correct, which he was sure it was, Deacon had asked the time of Sir Arthur Digby-Coates in order to be able, by moving the clock, to establish an alibi, or whether that request for the time had been an accident and the moving of the clock hands a subsequent idea brought about by memory of the 'time' incident. In any case, added this erudite official, the omission to make a corresponding alteration in the chiming served to show how the cleverest criminal will always make some foolish mistake which will afterwards lead to his capture.

"How true! How trite! And, in this instance, how utterly wrong! Observe. Both Digby-Coates and Deacon are highly intelligent men. Suppose either of them wishing to show by moving back the hands of a clock that the clock stopped at a time earlier than it did in fact: would either make the ridiculous, childish mistake of forgetting the striking? I think not!

"Observe again. Two men know that one asked the other the time. Why, then, is the subsequent utilising of that incident to be attributed to only one of them? Clearly it can apply equally to both!

"Here again the evidence which has been used against Deacon can be used at least equally well against Digby-Coates.

"This clock business, I say, is only further proof of the great ingenuity of Digby-Coates. It was the cleverest stroke of all. Deacon innocently, naturally, asks him the time. At once Digby-Coates, having already made up his mind that to-night was the night, is seized with an idea whose brilliance is surprising even to himself. Deacon, the man he has already chosen as scapegoat, is playing into his hands.

"Suppose (I can see his mind working) that he slew Hoode

just on the hour, and then made sure, after the clock in the study had struck, that its works, though undamaged, would not go on working, and then moved the hands back till they stood at 10.45. The disorder of the striking when the clock was set going again would reveal to investigators the fact that the hands had been moved and that the clock had stopped not before the hour but after it. Why, these investigators would ask, had the hands been moved to that particular place—10.45? Soon they would find out— he, clever fellow! helping them without seeming to—that at this moment on the night of the crime Deacon had asked him the time. 'Ah-ha!' would say the investigators, 'Mr. Deacon, to whom so much else points, has been trying to make alibis for himself!'

"But how, he thinks, can he carry out this great, this wonderful scheme? Ah, yes! Let him put himself in Deacon's place; let him think what Deacon would do if he was killing Hoode. If he stopped the clock, he wouldn't draw too much attention to it, so—so—ah, yes!—he would try to make it look as if there had been a struggle and would derange the tidy room accordingly!

"That, I am convinced, is the way Digby-Coates reasoned. To put it briefly, he had to arrange the study to look, not as if a struggle had really taken place, but as if some one had tried their best to *make it look like that*. That is to say, while giving the air of a genuine attempt to mislead, he must yet make sure that investigators were not, in fact, misled; the first thing, for instance, that he had to do was to ensure that attention was drawn to the clock, but in such a way as to make it seem that endeavours had been made to draw attention *from* it.

"Clever, you must admit. Clever as hell! And successful, as those who have followed the case must know. He got the effect he wanted—that of a man who had tried to mislead. The police know that 'struggle' scene for a fake. But I hope I have shown that it was a double fake. If you think I have imbued my criminal with more ingenuity than any murderer would possess, remember that I, too, am a man, and therefore a potential murderer. Remember also something of which I have given more tangible proof— the finger-print game he played on Deacon. Remember that it was through him that the police first learnt of the money Hoode had drawn from his bank, and the fact that at 10.45 on the night of the murder Deacon had asked him the time!

"And now for that alibi:

"That the murderer was in the study after the clock which, by the way, was correct by the other clocks in the house, had struck eleven, is proved by the fact of the striking of that clock being one hour behind.

"Miss Hoode entered the study and found the body at about ten minutes past eleven.

"The murderer, then, left the study at some time between two minutes past the hour at the earliest and ten minutes past.

"So soon as I was certain that the murderer was Digby-Coates, I saw that before my case against him was complete I must disprove his alibi; also I realised that this could best be done by ascertaining much more definitely at what time he left the study to climb back up the wall and into his room. That eight minutes between eleven-two and eleven-ten was too wide a margin to work in.

"The more I pondered this task the more difficult it seemed. Then, by the grace of God, there emerged, in circumstances which need not be set down here, a new witness whose evidence put me in possession of exactly the information I needed.

"This witness is Robert Belford, a man-servant, and therefore a permanent member of the Hoode household. He is a highly-strung little man, and refrained at first from telling what he knew through very natural fear of being himself suspected of the murder of his master.

"Before Belford's emergence I had come to the conclusion—though I couldn't see then how this was going to help—that the acceptance of old Poole as a trustworthy witness had been a mistake. I discovered, you see, that he suffers from that inconvenient disorder hay-fever.

"When in the throes of a seizure he can neither see, hear nor speak; is conscious, in fact, of nothing save discomfort. That these seizures last sometimes for as long as a minute and a half I can swear to from having watched the old man struggle with one.

"Immediately after my discovery of the existence in him of this ailment, I questioned Poole; with the result that at last he remembered having suffered a paroxysm on the night of the murder at some time during that part of the evening before the murder when his master was in the study and the rest of the house was quiet. He had not remembered the incident until I asked him. His memory, as he says, is not what it was, and in any case the event was not sufficiently out of the ordinary to have stayed in his head after all the emotions of that crowded night.

"But it was during, or rather at the beginning, of that minute and a half or two minutes during which the old man could do

nothing but cough and sneeze and choke and gasp with his head
between his knees, that Belford—the new witness—had entered the
study—by the door!

"When he got into the room he saw immediately the body of
his master. In one horrified second (I have said that he is an
intensely nervous, highly-strung little man) he took it all in; corpse,
disorder, and all the other details of that brilliant and messy
crime. *And there was, he swears, no one else in the room.* The
only place in which a man could have hidden would have been
the alcove at the far end of the room, but the curtains which,
as a rule, cut that off from view, were drawn aside.

"Belford, after that one instant of horror, fled. As he closed
the door behind him, he noticed that Poole, in his little room across
the hall, was still wrestling with his paroxysm. Belford retreated.
He was terrified the murder might be laid at his door were he seen
coming from the room. It was, to say the least, unusual that he
should enter the study when his master was working there. Nobody, he felt, would believe him if he told them he had gone there
to ask a favour of the dead man. He crept up the dark hall and
crouched on the stairs.

"His position was directly under the clock which hangs there;
and here you have the reason for what has possibly seemed metic-
ulousness on my part in describing this minor incident. He
became aware, without thinking, of what that clock said. He stared
up at it blankly. But, as often happens, this mechanical action
impressed itself on his memory. He swears—nothing will shake
his evidence—that the time was *five minutes past eleven.*

"There you have it. Digby-Coates, as I have shown, cannot
have left the study before eleven-two. At some point between
eleven-four and eleven-five Belford finds the study empty of life.

"I split the difference and took eleven-three as the time at
which Digby-Coates left the study—by the window. He must
have been, I argued, snugly back in his room by four minutes
past at the latest. He is still an active and very powerful man, and
the climb could not have taken him long.

"Having, after hearing what Belford had to tell me, thus been
enabled to know at least a part of the time which must prove a
weak spot in the alibi, I reviewed that itself. Before I do so,
here, however, there is one more point which I must settle.
It concerns the hay-fever of the aged Mr. Poole. As the attack of
this malady which let Belford into the study unobserved failed
to stay in his memory, it might be thought that he may have had

another attack, enabling another man to enter the study without being seen. That idea, which is sure to be entertained, is, I submit, of no value. One attack is ordinary enough; but the old man tells me that he has been 'better lately.' Two of those painful seizures would have stayed in his mind. Besides, there is the silk rope and other evidence to prove descent by the wall. Also, the crime was obviously premeditated, and no murderer of such skill as Hoode's would rely upon the hay-fever of an aged butler, even if he knew of its existence.

"Now for the facts of the alibi. It will be remembered that Digby-Coates had, on the night of the murder, retired to his own sitting-room at a few minutes after ten. The night was hot. He opened the window to its fullest extent; also flung the door open. This was (I use his own words, spoken at the inquest) 'in order to get the benefit of any breeze there might be.' Further, since he 'wished to be alone in order to go through some important papers,' he pinned upon that open door a notice: 'Busy—do not disturb.'

"After he had gone to his room, the first incident with which we need concern ourselves occurred at 10.45, when Deacon made that famous request for the time. At that moment Digby-Coates was pacing the room, and Deacon, disregarding or not seeing the notice on the door, put his question from the passage.

"About seven minutes later, Belford, walking down the passage, saw Digby-Coates standing in the doorway.

"The next we hear is from Elsie Syme, one of the housemaids, who 'saw Sir Arthur sitting in his big chair by the window' as she passed his door. (The quotation is from her reply to a question of Superintendent Boyd's.) So far as can be ascertained, this was not more than five minutes after Belford had passed by—making the time about 10.57.

"Next comes another housemaid, Mabel Smith, who had been working in the linen-closet, which is opposite the door of Deacon's room. She said that returning from the journey she had made downstairs (and by forgetting which she had furnished Deacon with that false alibi which he rather foolishly tried to make use of) she had noticed Sir Arthur 'sitting in his room.' The time then, as guessed at by the girl and more definitely confirmed by Elsie Syme, who knew what time she had left the servant's hall, was between eleven and one minute past.

"Next comes Belford again. You remember that he entered the study at a point between three and four minutes past eleven.

On his way there from the upper part of the house he passed Digby-Coates's room and 'saw Sir Arthur by the window.' Since he went straight to the study, the time at which he passed Digby-Coates's door cannot have been earlier than 11.03.

"After this we have Elsie Syme again. This time she is on her way to bed. Passing along the passage she again 'saw Sir Arthur sitting by the window.' The time in this instance is a little harder to get at, but cannot have been more than six minutes past the hour.

"Last we have the evidence of old Poole, who, after entering the study on hearing Miss Hoode scream, immediately fled to fetch his dead master's friend. He found Sir Arthur sitting with a book, his arm-chair pulled close up to the open window. This, since Miss Hoode entered the study at approximately ten minutes past eleven, was probably at 11.13 or thereabouts.

"That is the alibi, and a very good one it is, too—too good. It was, of course, never recognised as being an alibi, since Digby-Coates was never suspected by police or public as being the murderer; but the very fact of its being there (it trickled out mixed up with unimportant and verbose evidence, and was very cleverly referred to by Digby-Coates himself on every possible occasion) must have had its sub-conscious effect. (I should perhaps explain here that, as Digby-Coates was never suspected and the alibi was therefore the nebulous but effective thing I have described, the times I have given were not mentioned otherwise than generally: such exactitude as appears above is the result of Superintendent Boyd's and my own questioning, of which more came later.)

"I have shown that according to the witnesses, none of whom I could suspect of anything but honesty, Digby-Coates was seen there in his room at times which made it impossible that he should have done the murder. Yet I *knew* he was the murderer. Therefore some at least of these witnesses who had sworn to seeing him were mistaken.

"I had, then, to find out (*a*) which witnesses were thus in error, and (*b*) how they had been induced to make their common mistake.

"I got at (*a*) like this:

"Digby-Coates, I reasoned, *must* have begun his preparations immediately after Belford saw him standing in the doorway of his room at eight minutes to eleven. To descend the wall; to enter the study; to hold Hoode in chaffing conversation for a moment to allay his curiosity regarding the unusual method of entry; to kill him; to reassemble the wood-rasp; to set the 'struggle' scene; arrange the clock; to climb back up the wall again; and all as noiseless as you please, cannot have taken him less than eight minutes at the very least. As I have shown, he was in all probability back in his room by four minutes past the hour (if not earlier) and it will be seen, therefore, that he must have begun descent of the wall by four minutes to at the latest.

"The witnesses I was after, therefore, were those who thought they had seen him between four minutes to and four minutes past the hour.

"Of these, as you can see from my statement of the alibi, Elsie Syme is the first, Mabel Smith the second, and Belford the third. (Elsie Syme, it is true, might be considered as barely coming within my rough-and-ready time-limit, but you must remember that all the times I fixed were calculations and not stop-watch records.)

"Separately, I questioned the three servants. It was not an easy task. I had to handle them gently, and I had to impress upon them the vital necessity to forget the conversation as soon as they had left me.

"Their answers to my first important question were the same, though each was with me alone when I put it.

"I said: 'You say you saw Sir Arthur at such and such a time in his room on the night of the murder, and that he was sitting in his chair and that that chair was by the window. Are you certain of this?'

"They said: 'Yes, sir,' and said it emphatically.

"I played my trump card. I played it in some fear; if the answers were not what I expected, my case fell.

"I said: 'Now tell me: *exactly how much of Sir Arthur did you see?* What parts of him, I mean.'

"They goggled.

I tried again: 'Was the chair that big arm-chair? And was it facing the window with its back to the door?'

" 'Yes, sir,' they said.

"I said: 'Then all you saw of Sir Arthur was——'

"They replied, after some further help but with conviction, that all they had seen was the top of his head, part of his trousers, and the soles of his shoes. Belford, who is an intelligent man, expanded his answer by saying: 'You see, sir, we're all so used-like to seein' Sir Arthur sittin' like that and in that chair as we just naturally thinks as how we'd seen all on 'im that night.' Which,

I think, is as lucid an explanation of the mistake as could well be given.

"I must explain here how I came in possession of this trump card of mine. It was through two casual observations, which at first never struck me as bearing in any way upon the matter I was investigating. The first was the annoying, almost impossible tidiness of Digby-Coates's hair. It did not appear to be greased or pomaded in any way, and yet I never saw it other than as if he had just brushed it, and with care. The second was his curious trick of sitting on the edge of a chair with his feet thrust first backwards through the gateway formed by the front legs and then outwards until each instep is pressed against the back of each of those front legs. It is a trick most boys have, but it is unusual to find it persisting in a man of middle-age. Digby-Coates does not, of course, always sit like that, but frequently.

"What changed these two chance observations—the sort of thing one idly notices about any man of one's acquaintance without really thinking about them—into perhaps the most important minor step in my case was a glimpse I had of Digby-Coates from the very point from which the servants who made his alibi had seen him. He was sitting as they had seen him sit (though I did not know this until I questioned them) in the big arm-chair, which was facing the window. All I could see from the passage was the long, solid back of the chair, the top of the well-tended head, six inches of each trouser-leg, and the soles of two shoes. On the open door was a notice: 'Busy—Please do not disturb.'

"The scene was, in fact, a replica of what I had gathered it to be on the night of the murder. I fell to thinking, and suddenly the most annoying pieces of my jig-saw puzzle fell into place. I went in and spoke to him. I looked, more carefully than ever before, at his head, and came to the conclusion that he was bald, but wore the most skilfully made *toupé* I had ever seen. I remembered that he had told me that he never used a valet. I pictured him—he is the type—as one to whom the thought that any one else knew what he looked like minus hair was abhorrent.

"When I discovered the *toupé*, I knew that I could smash the alibi if only the unknowing alibi-makers gave me, honestly, the answers I wanted.

"As you know, they did. I consider the matter clear, but I know it. Perhaps I had better show what Digby-Coates did that night; how he set his stage and played out his one-act show.

"He retires to his room, knowing that Hoode is in his study,

Deacon busy or, as often of late, out, Miss Hoode and Mrs. Mainwaring in their beds, and some of the servants, as he wishes them, moving about the house—he has studied their movements and knows that on this night of the week there is work to do which keeps them later than usual. Luckily for him, the night is hot. It gives the necessary excuse for leaving his door as well as his window open. Upon that open door—which is not back against the wall, but only half open—he places a notice: 'Busy—Please do not disturb.'

"(Observe the cunning of this notice. He had, I found from the servants, placed such a notice on the open door on two previous occasions. This, I am sure, he had done for a two-fold reason: (i) to see whether it would really keep out intruders, and (ii) to ensure, when eventually he placed it there on the night he chose for the killing of Hoode, that though the household were not become sufficiently accustomed to it to avoid a glance at it and subsequently into the room, the sight of the notice was yet familiar enough to ensure that it was not remarkable as being without precedent. He had, you see, for the sake of his alibi, to make certain that people passing (i) would look into his room; (ii) would not come in; and (iii) would not think the notice anything out of the ordinary.)

"Having placed his notice he draws his arm-chair up to its *familiar* position facing the window. Then he has to wait. Sometimes he sits. Sometimes, the waiting too hard upon even such nerves as his, he paces the room.

"All goes well. Every one, everything, plays into his hands. The very man he has chosen to incriminate draws the noose, by that request for the time, tighter round his own neck. The leaden-footed minutes, what with this incident, that of Belford, and the increasing certainty of success, begin to pass more swiftly. People go their ways past his door but do not enter.

"At last it is time. He gets his knotted rope, secures it to the leg of the carpenter's bench Hoode has had fitted for him. The bench is clamped to the floor; no doubt but that it can stand the strain.

"Now, with a wary eye upon the door, he takes from its hiding-place the replica of the *toupé* which is on his head, pads it out with a handkerchief, and sets it on top of a pile of books on the seat of the chair. The pile is just of the height to show the hair over the chair-back to one looking into the room from the passage. He knows, he has tested it many times. (He may, possibly, have used the *toupé* from his head. But I think not. He must have had more than one; and he wouldn't wish to have anything unusual in his appearance when he faced Hoode.)

"A pair of dress trousers pinned to the chair, the lower ends of the legs slightly padded and twisted one round each of the chair's front legs, and a pair of patent-leather shoes set at the right angle, complete the picture.

"(So simple as to sound comic, isn't it? But if one thinks, one can see that in that simplicity lies that same touch of genius which characterises the whole of the other arrangements of the crime. To utilise his own little tricks, such as that way he had of sitting on a chair like a nervous schoolboy, that is genius. He knew that all they could have seen of him from that doorway, if he had really sat in his favourite position in that chair, would have been the top of his head, the ends of his trousers, and his shoes. He knew also that they were so accustomed to seeing only hair, trousers, and shoes when he was really there, that if they saw hair, trousers, and shoes they would be prepared to swear they had seen *him*.)

"When the time comes, at last, he drops his rope of silk from the window and descends, his heart beating high. The moment he has waited for, schemed for, gloated over; the moment has come at last.

"It was the sheer daring of the scheme that made this the well-nigh perfect crime it was, and here the maniac hatred he had of Hoode helped him enormously. I cannot conceive any but a man insane running the tremendous risk of discovery which he took with such equanimity. Nor would any but a man with the great clarity of mind only attained by the mad have ever dreamed of carrying out a crime so adult by means of the schoolboy trick of the dummy. It was an application of the bolster-in-the-dormitory-bed idea which nearly succeeded by virtue of its very unlikelihood.

"I have little more to say, though it would, of course, be possible to go much further in endeavouring to show the subtler shades of motive for each separate link of Digby-Coates's plot, and to go into such questions as whether he chose Deacon as scapegoat merely for convenience in drawing suspicion away from himself or whether he had some darker reason; but the time for that sort of thing is not now.

"One more word. I wish to make it plain that as a case I know this report to be less complete than is desirable. I know that it might be impossible to hang Digby-Coates simply on the strength of what I have set down. I know that in all probability the Crown would say that, unless the case were strengthened, it could not be regarded as enough even to try him on. I know the later stages of the report are mainly conjecture—guess-work if you like.

"I know all this, I say, but I also know that if there is any justice in England to-day I have shown enough of the true history of John Hoode's death to bring about the immediate release of Archibald Deacon.

"*I* know that Arthur Digby-Coates is guilty of the murder of John Hoode, and, having gone so far towards proving this beyond doubt, I intend to see him brought to trial.

"The only way to bring this about is to give my work the substantial backing of a confession by the murderer. This I intend to obtain.

"I cannot but think that, if I succeed, my work is finished and the agreement of even the most sceptical assured.

"A. R. GETHRYN."

CHAPTER EIGHTEEN

ENTER FAIRY GODMOTHER

1

Dinner that night had been a melancholy business for the sisters. During the day the anodyne of action had brought them at times almost to cheerfulness; but from the moment when they had left the chambers of the great Marshall's junior, their spirits had begun steadily to evaporate.

Of the two, perhaps Lucia suffered the most. She was older. She had not the ingenuousness which enabled Dora to take at their face value the reassurance of barristers and the like. And she suffered, though she would barely admit it to herself, from a complication of anxieties.

As the evening grew old so she grew angry and more angry—and always with Lucia Lemesurier. She felt contempt for herself, worrying, at a time like this, over a petty quarrel with a man she barely knew. Yet, yet—well, he might have *answered* that note if he couldn't come.

She took herself in hand. This must stop! She looked across the room to where Dora lay coiled upon a sofa, a book held before her face.

Lucia conceived suspicions. She investigated, to find them well-founded. The book was upside down; the face behind it was disfigured by tear-laden, swollen eyes.

Contrite, Lucia attempted consolation, and was in a measure successful.

"Feeling better, dear?" she said at last.

Dora nodded. "Sorry I'm such a fool. Only it's—it's—I can't help thinking, wondering—oh, what's the good? Everything's going to be all right. It's got to be! It *must* be!"

"Of course it will." Lucia stroked the red-gold hair.

Dora sat upright, hands to her face.

"Don't know why I'm behaving in such a *damn'* silly way!" she burst out. "You ought to shake me, darling, instead of being so sweet. Look at Archie. He's wonderful! And he'd hate it if he knew I was slobbering here like a schoolgirl. He says it'll be all right! And so does Colonel Gethryn."

Lucia drew away; she seemed about to speak, but then was silent.

But Dora went on. Dora was no fool, and Dora was interested. A good thing for Dora; for a moment she forgot her fears. She said:

"Weren't you surprised when Archie told us this morning about Mr. Gethryn really being Colonel Gethryn? And all those wonderful things he did in the war with the Secret What-d'you-call-it?"

"No," said Lucia absently. Then hurried mendaciously to correct herself. "Yes, I mean." She felt a hot flush mount to her face. This did not lessen her annoyance with herself.

Came a silence, broken at last by the younger sister.

"I," she said, with a gallant attempt at frivolity, "am going to repair to my chamber, there to remove traces of these ignoble tears." She hurried from the room.

Lucia stared a moment at the closed door; then sank back into the softness of the couch. Her thoughts were again a jumble.

Would everything, as she had so confidently said, be "all right"? Would miracles indeed be worked by—by *Colonel* Gethryn? How absurd the "Colonel" sounded! Colonels, surely, were purple, fat, and white-moustached, not tall, lean, "hawky" persons with disturbing green eyes.

She was startled from her reverie. Had she heard anything? Yes, there it was again—a tapping on the window. The thunder had stopped now, and the sound came sharply through the soft hissing of the rain.

There is always something sinister in a knocking upon a window. With a jump one exchanges the dull safety of ordinary life for the uncomfortable excitement of the sensational novel. Lucia, her nerves wrecked by the emotions of the past week, sprang to her feet and stood straining her eyes, wide, startled and black as velvet shadows, towards the French windows.

The tapping came again, insistent. She took hold of her courage, crossed the room, and flung them open.

Anthony stepped across the sill. He was, as he had left Mr. Lucas ten minutes before, without hat or mackintosh. He seemed, as indeed he was, serenely unconscious of his appearance. But the pallor of fatigue, the blazing eyes, the labouring breath, the hatless head shining with wet, the half-sodden clothes, all had their effect upon Lucia.

Anthony bowed. "Enter Fairy Godmother," he said. "Preserve absolute calm. The large Mr. Deacon is a free man. Repentant policemen are busy scouring his 'scutcheon. I think it not unlikely that he will be here within an hour or so."

Lucia was left without breath. "Oh—why—what——" she gasped.

He smiled at her. "Please preserve absolute calm. My nerves aren't what they were. What do we do next? Tell little sister, I imagine."

"You—I—I——" she stammered, and rushed from the room.

Anthony, having first covered the seat with a convenient newspaper, sank into a chair.

He communed with himself. "Lord, I'm wet! How can I be melodramatic as well? I must curb this passion for effect. Still, it kept her off any expressions of gratitude and the like. Good God! Gratitude!"

The door burst open. There was a flurry of skirts. Dora, transfigured, rushed at him as he rose, words pouring from her.

He waved hands to stem the flood. Arms were thrown about his neck. Warm lips were pressed to his cheek. Another flurry—and she was gone.

The door opened again. This time it was Lucia. With relief, her sense of humour had returned in full strength; there is nothing more steadying than one's sense of humour.

Anthony was still on his feet. She looked first at him and then at the damp pages of the *Telegraph* covering the chair. She began

to laugh. He was well content; the most seductive, the most pleasant sound in his experience.

He stood smiling at her. The laughter grew. Then, with an effort,
she controlled it.

"I'm sorry. Only I couldn't help it. Really I couldn't!" Her tone
was contrite.

"And why should you?" Anthony asked. "But I hope you appreciate my tender care of your cushions."

She seated herself, waving him back to his chair. "Oh, I do! I
think it was wonderful of you to—to think about my furniture at a
time like this. But then you're by way of being rather a wonderful
person, aren't you?"

"You deceive yourself," said Anthony. "A matter of common
sense plus imagination; that's all. The mixture's rare, I admit, but
there's no food for wonder in it."

She smiled at him. "Now, please, you must tell me all about
everything."

Anthony groaned.

"Pleeease."

"Must I?" He raised feeble hands.

"Of course, you silly person, I don't really mean 'everything.'
How could I when you're so tired, so awfully tired! But you come
here all strange and mysterious and dramatic and simply tell us
that Archie's all right. How *can* one help being curious? Why is
he all right? Have you only persuaded them that he didn't do it?
Or have you shown them the person that really did?"

"The second," Anthony said.

"Who? Who?" she had risen in her excitement.

Anthony looked up at her, and forgot the question.

She stamped her foot. "Oh, you irritating man!" she cried, and
shook him by the shoulder. "Tell me at once!"

"It was—Digby-Coates," said Anthony slowly, wondering how
she would take it.

She took it in silence. Whether astonishment or other emotions
had affected her he could not at the moment discern. Her next
words told him.

"I suppose"—her tone was thoughtful—"that I ought to be
surprised. And horrified. But somehow I'm not. I don't mean, you
know, that I ever suspected him or anything like that. But I'm
just not awfully surprised, that's all."

It dawned upon Anthony that if he were not to seem a boor

he must make an effort at intelligence. He strove to quiet the exuberant agility his heart was exhibiting.

He did his best. "You didn't like him, I gather," he said.

She shook her head. "No. Not that I really disliked him. I just wasn't quite comfortable whenever he was with me. You know. I always had to be nice, of course. Before my husband died they were always together. You see, they had the same tastes. They were about the same age, too." She relapsed into silence.

"So they were much of an age, were they?" Anthony said to himself. "Now, that's illuminating. Coates is over fifty." He was about to speak aloud, but was forestalled.

"What on earth must you think of me?" Lucia cried. "Here are you, that've done all these miracles for us, all tired and wet, and I'm sitting here as if this was afternoon tea at the Vicar's." She ran to the bell. "First, you must have a drink. Whisky? That's the second time I've forgotten my hospitality when you've been here."

Anthony got his drink. When he had finished the second,

"You," she said, "must go back to your inn. And you'll have to walk, poor thing. My little car's been out of action for a fortnight and I've sent away the one we hired for to-day. But the walk may do you good. You'll get warm."

Anthony set down his tumbler. "Exit Fairy Godmother."

Her eyes reproached him. "That's not fair," she said. "You know it isn't! What I *want* to do is to offer you a bed here. Well, there's a bed, but nothing else. No razor. No pyjamas. You'd be uncomfortable. And you've simply *got* to take care of yourself to-night!"

Anthony rose. "Forgive me. It seems my fate always to be rude to you. And you're quite right." He moved towards the door.

She followed him. She touched him on the arm.

"One more question before you go." She smiled at him again. "Was I—am I—oh! I mean, is my evidence part of your case? You know, about my being outside the window that night—what I saw——"

"Two of my main objects," Anthony said, "have been to get Deacon off and to keep you and your brother out. I think I've done both. I thought at one time that I couldn't round off the business without dragging you in. But the gods were good and dropped into my hands a little man who knew as much and a deal more than you. I exulted. I still exult. Like Stalky, I gloat!" He thumped his chest with an air. "I know everything; but I shan't tell. I know so much that I could tell you almost to a minute what time it was when you looked through the window of Hoode's study—and that's more than you know yourself. But I won't tell. Your secret, lady, is safe with me!"

"I think," she said slowly, "that you are a wonderful—Fairy Godmother! And now you must go, or you'll have pneumonia. And if you did, you might never hear those thanks I'm going to give you"—she smiled, and he saw with wonder that the dark eyes were glistening with tears—"*after* I've apologised for behaving as I did the other night." She paused; then burst out: "And, please, will you shake hands?"

Anthony looked at the hand held out towards him. The last shreds of self-control went flying.

"No, by God, I won't!" he shouted.

She found herself caught up in long arms that crushed her. She fought against them for an instant. "No!" she gasped. "No!"

But then she stopped fighting. She looked up into his face.

"Oh, yes," she said. "Yes! Don't let me go—ever!"

MURDER GONE MAD

CHAPTER ONE

There had been a fall of snow in the afternoon. A light, white mantle still covered the fields upon either side of the line. The gaunt hedges which crowned the walls of the cutting before Holmdale station were traceries of white and black.

The station master came out onto the platform from his little overheated room. He shivered and blew upon his hands. The ringing click-clock of the "down" signal arm dropping came hard to his ears on the cold air.

The six-thirty came in with much hissing of steam and a whistling grind of brakes. The six-thirty reached the whole length of Holmdale's long platform. The six-thirty looked like a row of gaily lighted, densely populated little houses. The doors of the six-thirty began to swing open, and a dark tide of humanity flowed out onto the platform and surged up the stairs.

At the head of the stairs the flood split into two streams, one flowing right and east and the other left and west. Two streams flowed across the bridge and down other stairs. At the foot of each staircase stood a harassed porter snatching such tickets as offered themselves and glancing, like a distracted nursemaid, at hundreds of green, square pieces of pasteboard marked "Season."

The flood poured through the booking hall and out through the double doors into the clear, cold night. In the gravelled, white-fenced forecourt there waited, softly chugging, two bright-lighted omnibuses looking like distorted caravans. Each of these omnibuses was built to hold twenty-seven passengers. Each, not less than two minutes after the flood had begun to break about their wheels, rolled off through the night with fifty at least. The rest of the flood, thinning gradually into trickles and then, at last, into units, went off walking and talking. Their voices carried on the cold, dark air, and the sound of their boot soles rang on the smooth iron road.

2

"Coo!" said Mr. Colby. "Sorry we couldn't get the bus, ol' man!"

"Not a bit. Not a bit," mumbled Mr. Colby's friend, turning up the collar of his black coat.

"Not," said Mr. Colby, "that I mind myself. Personally, Harvey, I rather look forward to a nice crisp trudge. Seems somehow to blow away the cobwebs."

"Yes," said Mr. Harvey. "Quite."

Mr. Colby, having shifted his umbrella and attaché case to his right hand, took Mr. Harvey's arm with his left.

"It's only a matter," said Mr. Colby, "of a mile and a bit. Give us all the more appetite for our supper, eh?"

"Quite," said Mr. Harvey.

"I wish," said Mr. Colby, "that it wasn't so dark. I'd have liked you to have seen the place a bit. However, you will to-morrow morning."

Mr. Harvey grunted.

"There are two ways to get to my little place," said Mr. Colby. "One's across the fields, and the other's up here through Collingwood Road. Personally, I always go over the fields but I think we'll go by Collingwood Road to-night. The field's a bit rough for a stranger if he doesn't know the ground." Mr. Colby broke off to sniff the cold air with noisy appreciation. "Marvellously bracing air here," said he. "Didn't you feel it as you got out of the train? You know we're nearly five hundred feet up and really right in the middle of the country. Yes, Harvey, five hundred feet!"

"Is that so?" said Mr. Harvey.

"Yes, five hundred feet. Why, since we've been here, my boy's a different lad. When we came, a year ago, his mother—and his old dad too, I can tell you—were very worried about Lionel. You know what I mean, Harvey, he was sort of sickly and a bit undersized, and now he's a great big lad. Well, you'll see him yourself. . . . Here we are at Collingwood Road."

"Collingwood Road, eh?" said Mr. Harvey.

Mr. Colby nodded emphatically. In the darkness his round, bowler-hatted head looked like a goblin's.

"We don't live in Collingwood Road, of course. We're right at the other side of the place. More on the edge of the country."

Mr. Harvey unburdened himself of a remark. "A good idea," said Mr. Harvey approvingly, "these garden cities."

"Holmdale," said Mr. Colby with some sternness, "is not a garden city. You don't find any long-haired artists and such in Holmdale. Not, of course, that we don't have a lot of journalists and authors live here, but if you see what I mean, they're not the cranky sort. People don't walk about in bath gowns and slippers the way I've seen them at Letchworth. No, sir, Holmdale *is* Holmdale."

Perhaps the unwonted exercise, coupled with the cold and bracing air, had induced an unusual belligerence in Mr. Harvey. "I always understood," said Mr. Harvey argumentatively, "that the place's name was Holmdale Garden City."

"When you said *was*," said Mr. Colby, "you are right. The place's name *is* Holmdale, Harvey. Holmdale pure and Holmdale simple. At the semi-annual general meeting of the shareholders, it was decided that the words Garden City should be done away with. I supported the motion strongly; very, very strongly! And fortunately it was carried." Mr. Colby laughed a reassuring, friendly laugh, and once more put his left hand upon Mr. Harvey's right arm. "So you see, Harvey," said Mr. Colby, "that if you want to get on in Holmdale you mustn't call it Holmdale Garden City."

"I see," said Mr. Harvey. "Quite."

They were now at the end of Collingwood Road—a long sweep, flanked by small, neat, undivided gardens and small, neat-seeming, shadowy houses. Beneath a street lamp, Mr. Colby stopped to look at his watch.

"Very good time," said Mr. Colby. "Harvey, you're a bit of a walker! I always take my time here, and I find I've beaten last night's walk by fully half a minute. Now we haven't far to go. We shall soon be toasting our toes and perhaps having a drop of something."

"That," said Mr. Harvey warmly, "will be very nice."

They crossed the narrow, suddenly rural width of Marrowbone Lane and so came to the beginning of Heathcote Rise.

"At the top here," said Mr. Colby, "we turn off to the right and then we're home."

"Ah!" said Mr. Harvey, and very soon found himself being steered through a hedge-lined lane into a rectangle composed of small and uniform houses looking out upon a lawn dotted with raised flower beds. Round the lawn were small white posts having a small white chain swung between them. All the square ground-floor windows showed pinkly glowing lights. Mr. Harvey wondered for a moment whether all the housewives of the Keep—he knew his friend's address to be No. 4, The Keep—had chosen their curtains together.

"Here we are! Here we are! Here we are!" said Mr. Colby in a sudden orgy of exuberance. He had stopped before a small and crimson door over which hung by a bracket a very shiny brass lantern. He released the arm of Mr. Harvey and fumbled for his key chain, but before the keys were out the small red door opened.

"Come in, do!" said Mrs. Colby. "You must both be starved!"

They came in. The small hall was suddenly packed with human bodies.

"This," said Mr. Colby looking at his wife and somehow edging clear, "is Mr. Harvey. Harvey, this is Mrs. Colby."

"Very pleased," said Mr. Harvey, "to meet you."

"So am I, I'm sure," said Mrs. Colby. She was a plump and pleasant and bustling little person who yet gave an impression of placidity. Her age might have been anywhere between twenty-eight and forty. She was pretty and had been prettier. She stood looking from her husband to her husband's friend and back again.

Mr. Colby, whose Christian name was George, was forty-five years of age, five feet five and a half inches in height, forty-one and a half inches round the belly, and weighed approximately one hundred and forty-seven pounds. He had pleasing and kindly blue eyes, a good forehead and a moustache which seemed, although really it was not out of hand, too big for his face.

Mr. Harvey was forty years old, six feet two inches in height, thirty inches round the chest, and weighed, stripped, one hundred and thirty-three pounds. Mr. Harvey was clean-shaven. He was also bald. His face, at first sight rather a stern, harsh, hatchet-like face, was furrowed with a myopic frown and two deep-graven lines running from the base of his nose to the corners of his mouth. When Mr. Harvey smiled, however, which was quite frequently, one saw, as just now Mrs. Colby had seen, that he was a man as pleasant and even milder natured than his host.

"This," said Mr. Colby throwing open the second door in the right-hand wall, "is the sitting room. Come in, Harvey, ol' man."

Mr. Harvey squeezed his narrowness first past his hostess and then his host.

"You coming in, dear?" said Mr. Colby.

His wife shook her head. "Not just now, Father. I must help Rose with the supper."

"Where's the boy?" said Mr. Colby.

"Upstairs," said the boy's mother, "finishing his home lessons. It's the Boys' Club Meeting after supper and he wants to get the work done first."

"If we might," said Mr. Colby with something of an air, "have a couple of glasses . . ."

Mrs. Colby bustled away. Mr. Colby went into the sitting room with his friend. Mr. Colby impressively opened a cupboard in the bottom of the writing desk and took from the cupboard a black bottle and a siphon of soda water. Mrs. Colby entered with a tray upon which were two tumblers. She set the tray down upon the side table. She raised the forefinger of her right hand; shook it once in the direction of her husband and once, a little less roguishly, at Mr. Harvey.

"You men!" said Mrs. Colby.

Mr. Colby and his guest lay back in their chairs, their feet stretched before the fire. In each man's hand was a tumbler. They were very comfortable, a little pompous, and entirely happy. To them, when the glasses were nearly empty, entered Master Lionel Colby: a boy of eleven years, well built, and holding himself well; a boy with an engaging round face and slightly mischievous, wondering blue eyes which looked straight into the eyes of anyone to whom he spoke. Lionel obviously combined in his person, and also probably in his mind, the best qualities of his parents. He shook hands politely with Mr. Harvey. He reported, with some camaraderie but equal politeness, his day's doings to his father.

"Home work done?" said Mr. Colby.

Lionel shook his head. "Not quite all, Daddy. I came down because Mother told me to come and say how-do-you-do to Mr. Harvey."

Mr. Colby surveyed his son with pride. "Better run up and finish it, son. What you going to do at the Boys' Club to-night?"

The round cheeks of Lionel flushed slightly. Lionel's blue eyes glistened. "Boxing," said Lionel.

The door closed gently behind Lionel.

"That," said Mr. Harvey with genuine feeling, "is a fine boy, Colby!"

Mr. Colby made those stammering, slightly throaty noises which are the middle-class Englishman's way when praised for some quality or property of his own.

"A fine boy!" said Mr. Harvey again.

"A good enough lad," said Mr. Colby. His tone was almost

offensively casual. "Did I happen to tell you, Harvey, that he was top of his class for the last three terms and that the headmaster, Dr. Farrow, told me himself that Lionel is one of the best scholars he'd had in the last twenty years? Not, mind you, Harvey, that he isn't good at games. He's captain of the second eleven and they tell me he's going to be a very good boxer. I must say—although it isn't really for me to say it—that a better, quieter, more loving lad it'd be difficult to find in the length and breadth of Holmdale."

"A fine boy!" said Mr. Harvey once more.

3

At nine o'clock in the Trumpington Hall, Master Lionel Colby had the immense satisfaction of proving himself so immeasurably superior to his opponent, a boy three years older and a full stone heavier than himself, that Sergeant Stubbs stopped the bout.

"I only wish," said Lionel to himself, "that Dad and Mum had been there." "I'm sorry," said Lionel aloud to his cronies, with a self-condemnatory swagger quite delicious, "I didn't realize I was hitting so hard."

At nine o'clock in the Holmdale Theatre—a building so modern in conception, so efficient in arrangement, and so pleasantly strange in decoration that earnest Germans made special trips to England to see it—the curtain was going down upon the first act of the *Yeomen of the Guard* as performed by the Holmdale Mummers. There were in the audience somewhere between two hundred and fifty and three hundred people, two hundred and twenty-two of whom were relatives of the cast.

At nine o'clock, in the library of the Hospice, which was the large house of Sir Montague Flushing, K. B. E., the chairman of the Holmdale Company Limited, Sir Montague himself was concluding a small and informal speech to those six of his fellow directors who had, that night, dined with him. Sir Montague was saying:

". . . and so I think that we may, gentlemen, very fairly congratulate ourselves upon drawing near to the conclusion of a very successful year . . .

At nine o'clock in the Baden-Powell Drill Hall, Mr. William Farthingale had amassed so many points in the Progressive Whist Drive, organized by the Holmdale Mothers' Protective Aid Society, that it seemed almost certain that he would run away with the first prize of a massive pair of ebony and silver-backed hairbrushes. At nine o'clock in No. 3, Pettifers Lane, Mrs. Sterling was, not without grumbling, cooking the late supper of her husband, who worked at the Holmdale Electricity Supply Company. At nine o'clock in No. 14, Prester Avenue, Mrs. Tildesly-Marshall was announcing to the guests in her drawing room that Mr. Giles Freshwater would now sing—Miss Sophie May accompanying— Gounod's "Ave Maria," after which we will have a little bridge. At nine o'clock in Claypits Road, Miss Ursula Finch, the part proprietor and sole editor of the *Holmdale Clarion,* locked up the *Clarion's* office. At nine o'clock in the office of No. 10, Broad Walk, Dr. Arthur Reade was assuring the wife of Mr. Fox-Powell, the solicitor, that there would be no addition to the family. At nine o'clock in Links Lane, Albert Rogers was kissing Mary Filli- more. At nine o'clock in the parlour of The Cottage in High Collings, Mr. Julius Wetherby was having his nightly quarrel with Mrs. Julius Wetherby. At nine o'clock in The Laurels Nursing Home, which was on the corner of Collingwood Road and Minters Avenue, Mrs. Walter Stilson, wife of the Reverend Walter Stilson, was being delivered of a son. At nine o'clock in the draw- ing room of No. 4, Tall Elms Road, Mrs. Rudolph Sharp, having been assailed three times that day by an inner agony, was drafting, for the eye of her solicitors, a codicil to her will. And at nine o'clock down by the station, Percy Godly, the black-sheep son of Emanuel Godly, the tea broker, was missing the last train to London.

It was not until ten-fifteen that Mrs. George Colby first evinced signs of perturbation. She and her husband and the long and saturnine-seeming Mr. Harvey had just finished their last rubber of wagerless dummy.

Mrs. Colby got suddenly to her feet. Her chair fell with a soft crash to lie asprawl upon the blue carpeted floor. Mrs. Colby said:

"George! I—I—don't like it! What can 've happened to him? George, it's a quarter-past ten!"

Mr. Colby looked at his watch. Mr. Colby looked at the clock upon the mantelpiece. Mr. Colby consulted Mr. Harvey. Mr. Colby, after two minutes, came to the conclusion that a quarter-past ten was irrevocably the time.

"Don't you remember, dear," said Mr. Colby, "that time when he didn't come back until just before ten. The boxing had gone on rather longer than usual. You remember I wrote a stiff P. C. to Mr. Maclellon about it——"

"I know. I know," said Mrs. Colby, stooping down and picking up her chair. "I know, but it isn't a few minutes to ten now, George. It's a quarter *past!*" She suddenly left off fumbling with her chair and as suddenly was gone from the room. The door slammed to behind her.

"I expect," said Mr. Harvey, looking at his host, "that the lad's up to some harmless mischief. A fine lad that, and, personally, Colby, I've no use for a boy that hasn't a bit of the devil in him. I remember when *I* was a lad——"

"Clara," said Mr. Colby, "gets that worked up." He looked at his watch again. "All the same, Harvey, ol' man, it's late for the nipper. Have a drink? I'd go out, only I expect Clara's gone. She'll find him all right, playing Tig at the end of the street or something."

The door opened again. A small rush of air blew cool upon the back of Mr. Colby's neck. Mr. Colby turned. He saw Mrs. Colby. She wore a coat about her plump and admirable shape and a hat pulled anyhow upon her head. But she did not go out. Instead, she dropped in the chair which just now she had left, and, gripping her hands with tightly interlocked fingers one about the other, sat breathlessly still and said:

"I don't feel up to it, George. You go and see."

George looked at his Clara. "Tired, my dear?" said George. "We'll go instead, eh, Harvey?"

"A breath of fresh," said Mr. Harvey facetiously, "is just what the doctor ordered."

There was a hard, black frost. After the warmth of the little parlour, the cold air outside caught at their breath. They both coughed.

"A snorter of a night!" said Mr. Colby.

"It is that," agreed Mr. Harvey.

They turned left out of the little red door. They turned up the path to the narrow passage which joins The Keep to Heathcote Rise. Out of the passage Mr. Colby turned to his right.

"The Trumpington Hall," said Mr. Colby, "is just up here. Matter of three or four hundred yards."

"Ah!" said Mr. Harvey. "Quite."

They did not get so far as the Trumpington Hall.

There are two street lamps in the quarter-mile length of Heathcote Rise. The first was behind Mr. Colby and Mr. Harvey as they left the mouth of The Keep. The second was about two hundred yards from the mouth of The Keep. They were walking upon the raised side path, and as they came abreast this lamp, Mr. Colby, as seemed his habit when passing street lamps, paused to take out the great silver watch. Mr. Harvey, halting too, happened to glance over Mr. Colby's plump shoulder and down into the road.

"My—*God!*" said Mr. Harvey.

"What's that!" said his companion sharply. "What's that!"

But Mr. Harvey was gone. With an agility which would at any other time have been impossible to him, he had jumped down into the road and was now halfway out into the broad thoroughfare. Mr. Colby, despite the cold, bony fingers of fear clutching at his vitals, scrambled after him.

Mr. Harvey was on his knees in the middle of the road, but he was within the soft yellow radiance cast by the lamp. He was bending over something.

Mr. Colby came trotting. Mr. Colby halted by Mr. Harvey's shoulder.

Mr. Harvey looked up sharply. "Get away!" he said. "Get away!"

But Mr. Colby did not get away. He was standing like a little, plump statue staring down at the thing beside which Mr. Harvey knelt.

"*Oh!*" said Mr. Colby in a whisper which seemed torn from him. And then again: "*Oh!*"

What he looked at—what Mr. Harvey was looking at—was Lionel.

He lay an odd, twisted heap on the black road. Mr. Harvey picked up one of Lionel's hands. It was cold, like the road upon which it was lying.

CHAPTER TWO

The next day—Saturday—was a windless day of hard frost and bright sunshine. The sort of day, in fact, which had been used to fill the placid heart of Mr. Colby with boyish joy. But now Mr. Colby's heart was black.

Mr. Colby sat, a huddled and shrunken little figure, at the table in his tiny dining room. The chair upon the other side of the table was occupied by Miss Ursula Finch, the editor and owner of the *Holmdale Clarion*. Miss Finch was small and neat and brisk. Miss Finch's age might have been thirty-three but probably was ten years more than this. Miss Finch was severely smart in a tweedy, well tailored manner. Miss Finch's pencil was busy among the rustling pages of her notebook, for Miss Finch was her own star reporter. But the eager, piquant face of Miss Finch was clouded with most unbusinesslike sympathy. And although her questions rattled on and on and her pencil flew, the eyes of Miss Finch were suspiciously bright.

It seemed suddenly to Mr. Colby that he could not stand any more. Miss Finch had asked him a question. He did not answer it. He sat staring across the little room at the yellow distempered wall. First, all those policemen asking questions: *What time did he leave? What time did you expect him back? Where was he going? What was he doing? Why was he doing it? What time did you start to look for him? Did anyone go with you to look for him? Where did you find him? How did you find him? Do you know anyone who bears enmity against yourself or him? If so, why? If not, why not? How? Who? Where? What? When?* And now this woman—although she was nicer than the policemen—now this woman, asking *her* questions. The same questions really, only put differently, and more, as a man might say, intimate. . . .

Mr. Colby thought of the bedroom immediately above this room where he sat; the bedroom where, on the double bed, Mrs. Colby lay a huddled and vacantly staring heap.

Mr. Colby got to his feet. His chair slid back along the boards with a grating clatter. He said:

"I'm sorry, miss. I can't tell you any more. I want—I want——" Mr. Colby shut his mouth suddenly. He sat down again with something of a bump and remained sitting, his folded hands squeezed between his knees. He looked at the floor.

Miss Finch shut her notebook with a decisive snap and put round it its elastic band. She rose from her chair. Automatically Mr. Colby, a well mannered little person, got to his feet. Miss Finch came round the table in an impulsive rush. "I ought," said Miss Finch, "to have something awful done to me for worrying you, Mr. Colby, upon such a dreadful day as this must be for you. But I *would* like you to understand, Mr. Colby, that however much of a ghoulish nuisance I may seem, I may really be doing *something* to help. It may not seem like that to you at the moment. But it really is. You see, Mr. Colby, nowadays the Press, by throwing what you might call a public light on things, helps authorities to—to—to find the monsters responsible for——"

"Oh, *please!*" said Mr. Colby, holding out his hand as if to protect himself from a blow.

Miss Finch, with an impulsive gesture, seized the hand in both of hers and pressed it. "You *poor* man!" she said.

Mr. Colby withdrew his hand. Mr. Colby opened the door for Miss Finch. In the hall Miss Finch halted and collected her stubby umbrella and tucked it martially beneath her left arm. She said:

"If there *is* anything I can do for you or Mrs. Colby—in a purely private capacity, I mean, Mr. Colby—I *do* hope you will let me know. . . . You wouldn't like me, I suppose, to run up and sit with Mrs. Colby for a little while? It would only be a little, because I'm so busy. . . ."

Mr. Colby shook his head dumbly. He opened the street door and shut it, a second later, upon the well tailored back of Miss Finch. He wandered back to his dining room and sat down once more at his dining table and sighed and swallowed very hard and put his head in his hands.

2

"Do they," asked Sir Montague Flushing of his manservant, "insist upon seeing me personally?"

Spender bowed gravely. "Yes, sir."

"And you have put them in . . . ?" said Sir Montague.

"In the library, sir."

Sir Montague blew out his cheeks and frowned. Sir Montague paced up and down the carpet. He said at last, half to himself:

"These newspaper men are a public nuisance!"

"Should I tell them that you are too busy to see them, sir?"

"No," said Sir Montague. "No. No. No. What papers did you say they came from?"

"One of the—er—gentlemen, sir," said Spender, "stated that he represented the *Evening Mercury*. The other was from the *Wire*."

"I see. I see," said Sir Montague.

(Extract from the *Evening Mercury,* dated Saturday, 24th November)

THE HOLMDALE MURDER
etc., etc.

(From our Special Correspondent)

Holmdale, Saturday.

Stranger and stranger grows the mystery of the murdered schoolboy whose body was found at 10 o'clock last night in the middle of a peaceful roadway in Holmdale Garden City. The problem that faces the police is no small one. The boy—Lionel Frederick Colby, of 4, The Keep, Holmdale—had left home at about 7:30 P. M. to visit the Boys' Club, whose meetings are held in the Trumpington Hall. He had been in good spirits when he left home and had arrived at twenty-five minutes to eight at the Boys' Club. Here he had spent the evening in the usual way, and had notably distinguished himself in the boxing competition which was held that night. He left the hall with a number of companions when the club meeting closed at 9:20. Halfway back towards his home—The Keep, which is off Heathcote Rise, is not more than five or six minutes' walk from the Hall—Lionel remembered, according to two of his friends who had been interviewed by the police, that he had left his gymnasium shoes and sweater behind, His companions had tried to dissuade him from going back, telling him that he would not find the place open. Lionel, who was a boy of great determination, stated that he had promised his mother not to forget the sweater, as she wanted to wash it the next day. One of the boys, Charles Coburn (13) of 28, Lochers Avenue, Holmdale, stated to the police that he remembered Lionel saying that he would be able to climb in at a window. He left Coburn and the other boys in the middle of Heathcote Rise at approximately 9:25. At about a quarter-past ten, Mr. Colby, the boy's father, together with a guest (Mr. Harvey) went out to see whether they could find Lionel. They walked down Heathcote Rise towards Trumpington Hall, but halfway on this journey—beside a street lamp —they made the appalling discovery.

POLICE THEORIES

As was reported in earlier editions, the wound which caused Lionel Colby's death had apparently been made by a very sharp implement, probably a long knife. The stomach had been slit open from bottom to top. Death must have been instantaneous. The night was hard and frosty, and it was not possible therefore to find any trace such as footmarks, etc. The police are certain, however, that the murder was done on the spot where the body was found, as all traces of blood, etc., point to this conclusion.

People resident in the houses which line both sides of Heathcote Rise have, of course, been questioned, but none of them can testify to having heard any disturbance. Dr. F. W. Billington of Holmdale, who acts as police surgeon to the Holmdale and Leewood district, examined the body at 11:30 P. M. last night. Dr. Billington gives it as his opinion that life had not then been extinct for more than two hours. The police are of the opinion that Lionel was killed on his return from the gymnasium whence, as all windows were locked, he had been unable to fetch the shoes and sweater. The police are completely puzzled by the absence of a motive for such a terrible crime.

Mr. and Mrs. Colby are extremely popular in their own circle and have no enemies. Lionel, too, was a very well liked boy. He had no enemies at school, and was a prominent and popular member of the local Boys' Club and also of the Holmdale troop of Sea Scouts. At present the police theory is that the crime was committed by a pervert or homicidal lunatic.

They have, of course, several clues which they are following up.

Mrs. Colby, Lionel's mother, is prostrate from shock, but I managed to secure an interview with Mr. George Colby, the father. He could give me no help, but stated that all he lived for now was to see the capture of the wretch who had robbed him of his only child.

GRAVE CONCERN IN HOLMDALE

Sir Montague Flushing, K. B. E., the prominent managing director of the Holmdale Company Limited, stated in an interview to-day that he was himself deeply and terribly shocked by the tragedy.

" 'How such a thing,' said Sir Montague, 'could take place in this happy little town of ours is utterly beyond my imagination!'

"Sir Montague added that he would be only too grateful if the London Press would give full publicity to his statement, 'that not only the citizens of Holmdale, but mothers and fathers throughout England could rest assured that the Holmdale Company (who are, of course, the proprietors of the whole Garden City) would do everything in their power to aid and assist the regular authorities in tracking down the author of the outrage.' "

3

That was in the *Evening Mercury* late afternoon edition. Similar writings were in the other evening papers. The station, usually deserted upon a Saturday afternoon, was besieged at the time of the paper-train's arrival by a crowd fully a third as big as that which upon weekdays left the six-thirty. Within four minutes of the arrival of the papers, the bookstall had not one left.

There was, in Holmdale to-day, only one topic of conversation. Holmdale was duly horrified. Holmdale was duly sympathetic. Holmdale was inevitably a town in which every third inhabitant was satisfied that, given the job, he could lay his hands upon the criminal in half the time which it would take the police. Holmdale was also, though it would have vilified you for making the allegation, very delightfully excited. It was not every day that Holmdale came into the public eye. Holmdale looked forward to Monday morning when, once more "up in town," it would be the centre of a hundred interested groups all asking, "I say, don't you live in that place where that boy's been killed?"

Something, in short, had happened in Holmdale. Holmdale was News. Holmdale was on the Front Page.

But Holmdale did not know that, on his evening round, a Holmdale postman was carrying in his bag three letters for which the London Press would have given the heads of any of their reporters. The first of these letters was delivered at the Hospice. The second at the White Cottage, Heathcote Rise, which was Holmdale's Police Station, and the third at the office of the *Clarion* in Claypits Road. In that order—because that was the way the postman went round—they were delivered, and in that order they were read.

Sir Montague Flushing, going through his evening's post, came suddenly across a yellow linen-paper envelope. He was a man who always speculated about a letter before he opened it, and this letter he turned that way and the other between his fingers. He did not know the paper. He did not know the backward-sloping writing. He had never seen ink so shinily black. He slipped an ivory paper-knife under the flap of the envelope. . . .

He found himself staring, with wide and startled eyes, at a single sheet of paper of the same texture and colour as the envelope. Upon this sheet was written, in the same ink and writing, but in larger characters:

My Reference ONE
R. I. P.
Lionel Frederick Colby,
died Friday, 23d November. . . .
THE BUTCHER.

CHAPTER THREE

The chief constable looked at Inspector Davis, then down again to his blotting pad where there lay, side by side, three quarto sheets of yellow paper, each bearing in its centre a few words written in a dead black and shining ink.

The chief constable cleared his throat; shifted uneasily in his chair.

"What do you think, Davis?" said the chief constable. "Hoax?"

Inspector Davis shrugged. "May be, sir, may be not. One can't tell with these things."

The chief constable thumped the desk with his fist so that the glass ink bottles rattled in their mahogany stand. He said:

"But, damn it, man, if it isn't a hoax, it's . . ."

"Exactly, sir." The inspector's voice and manner were unchanged. His cold blue eyes met the frowning, puzzled stare of his superior.

The chief constable picked up the centre sheet and read aloud to himself, for perhaps the twentieth time this morning:

"My Reference ONE
R. I. P.
Lionel Frederick Colby,
died Friday, 23d November. . . .
THE BUTCHER.

"Oh, *hell!*" said the chief constable, "I never did like that damn Garden City place."

Inspector Davis shrugged. "Hasn't been any trouble to us before, sir," he said.

"Certainly is now," said the chief constable. "So let's get down to business. I suppose you've tried to trace this paper."

Davis nodded. "It's what they call Basilica Linen Bank, sir. It's purchasable at any reputable stationer's. It's expensive, and it's only made in that yellow colour for Christmas gift boxes. The number of Christmas gift boxes of the yellow variety sold since the first Christmas display about three weeks ago is so large that we can't get any help that way."

The chief constable held up a hand. "One moment, Davis, one moment. Is this stuff on sale at the Holmdale shop? What do they call it?"

"The Market, sir," said Davis. "Yes, it is. But not the yellow variety. Therefore this paper was bought somewhere outside Holmdale."

The chief constable scratched his head. "Postmark?" he suggested without hope.

"The letters were postmarked 10:30 A. M., Holmdale."

"So they were posted actually in the place itself, on the morning after the crime was committed, and were delivered that same evening?"

"That, sir," said Inspector Davis, "is correct."

"And," said the chief constable, "we've no more idea of who killed this boy than the man in the moon!"

Inspector Davis shook his head. "No, sir. In fact, so far as we can see, the man in the moon's about the most likely person."

"I can't give you a warrant for *him*." The chief constable dropped his elbows on his desk and his face into his hands. He said after a moment:

"Damn it, Davis, we can't sit here *joking* about this!"

"No, sir," said Davis.

Once more the chief constable thumped the desk so that the ink jars rattled. "We've got to *do* something."

"Yes, sir," said Davis.

"What the hell," said the chief constable, *"are* we doing?"

For the first time Davis's face showed sign of embarrassment. He shuffled his feet. He cleared his throat.

"Of course, sir," said Davis, "we're making careful inquiries. . . ."

The chief constable exploded. "For God's sake, is it necessary to work that stuff off on me?"

Inspector Davis smiled, a faint, embarrassed smile. "There's nothing else to say. . . . If only we could find someone that could have any possible *reason* for wanting this boy out of the way. . . ."

"I know," said the chief constable wearily, "I know. Well, there's nothing more I can add, Davis. Carry on as best you can. Only, for God's sake, get a pair of handcuffs onto somebody before we have the whole countryside about our ears."

"Yes, sir," said Davis.

The telephone rang and the chief constable snatched at it.

"Who's this? . . . Oh, yes, Jeffson. . . . *What?* . . . Yes. . . . Go on, yes. . . . Where? What time? . . . Good God! All right, I'll send . . . Eh? What's that you say? . . . Just read that over again, will you. Slowly, while I write it down." He picked up a pencil; scribbled to the telephone's dictation upon his blotting pad; looked at what he had written; spoke again into the receiver: "All right, I've got that." His voice was no longer astonished, but weary, and with something of fear beneath its weariness. He spoke again: "Yes. . . . Yes. . . . I should think they would. Well, we'll do what we can as quick as we can. Ring off now, will you. Stay where you are, and I'll let you have a word within half an hour." He hung up the receiver and, with an abstracted air, lifted the telephone and placed it at the edge of his desk. He looked at Davis for so long and in such pregnant silence that at last Davis was forced to break it. He said:

"What was that, sir?"

"That," said the chief constable, "was Jeffson. You know Jeffson, I think. From Holmdale?"

"Yes, sir," said Davis.

"Jeffson," said the chief constable slowly, "was telephoning to tell me that at 9:15 this morning, a man called Walters, who's a milk roundsman in Holmdale, saw a small car—a Baby Austin—standing at the end of one of the roads. He would have taken no interest in this car except that as he passed and happened to glance down into it from his float, he saw what at first sight looked to him like a bundle of old clothes. He thought no more about it—for the moment." The chief constable's words were coming slower and slower. "But, Davis, he went back the way he had come, and as he got abreast of the Baby Austin, he looked down into it again. . . . And he saw that what he had thought was a bundle of old clothes was a bundle of new clothes . . . with something inside 'em. What was inside them, Davis, was a girl—a girl called Pamela Richards. . . ." The chief constable drew a deep breath.

"Pamela Richards," he said, "was dead. Pamela Richards had been killed in just the way Lionel Colby was killed. . . ."

Davis's lips, beneath his tight and tidy waxed moustache, pursed themselves. There came from them the ghost of a whistle.

The chief constable nodded. "Exactly, Davis. Only more so." The chief constable leaned forward, pointing the end of the penholder at the inspector. "*And*, Davis," he said, "almost at the moment when this milkman, Walters, was finding the body, three letters—letters like this"—here the chief constable tapped upon the centre of those three yellow sheets which lay upon his blotter—"letters like this were being read by Flushing, Jeffson, and the editor of the *Holmdale Clarion*—letters, Davis, which were unstamped, and which must have been delivered by hand during the night."

"Was that what you were scribbling down on your blotter?" Davis leaned forward in his chair.

"It was," said the chief constable. "I will read it to you. It said: *My Reference Two. R. I. P. Pamela Richards. Died Sunday, 25th November*. And it was signed . . ."

"The Butcher," said Davis.

2

"What's this? What's this?" said Percy Godly. "What's this? What's this?"

The boy with the red brassard of the *Holmdale Clarion* pushed forward the bundle of sheets which he held. "Special," said the boy. "Special extra. All about the Butcher." And that was in the official whine. "Blime, sir," said the boy, "ain't it torful!" And that was in the boy's own voice.

"How would I know?" said Percy Godly.

He pushed sixpence into the boy's hand and waved away the change and snatched one of the broadsheets. He leaned against the corner of one of the Market windows and looked down at his purchase. He saw, in staring headlines two inches deep:

WHO IS THE BUTCHER?
HOLMDALE PANIC-STRICKEN
IS OUR CITY TO BE ANOTHER DÜSSELDORF?
THE BUTCHER'S SECOND LETTER

PROMINENT LEADER OF HOLMDALE'S YOUNGER SET
DONE TO DEATH

WHAT IS BEHIND THESE MURDERS?

Editorial Office, Claypits Road.
This morning, at 9:15 A. M. Richard Henry Arthur Walters, a milkman in the employ of the Holmdale Market Limited, driving in the course of his rounds down New Approach, off Marrowbone Lane, saw a motor car—a small motor car of the "Baby" type—standing, apparently deserted, in the semi-circular sweep at the head of the Approach. As he passed, what Walters thought a peculiar bundle in the front seat of the car attracted his attention, and later, as he returned, passing the car once more, this bundle again attracted his attention. So much so that he halted his horse, got off the milk float, and investigated.

HORRIBLY MANGLED BODY
To Walter's surprise and horror, he found that what he had thought was a "bundle" was, in reality, the body of that well known and charming young member of Holmdale's "Upper Ten"—Miss Pamela Richards—the daughter of Mr. and Mrs. Arthur Richards, Sunview, Tall Elms Road. Walters discovered immediately that Miss Richards was not only dead, but that she had been dead for a considerable time. The injuries which had led to her death were almost identical with those which led to the death of that poor lad Lionel Colby, whose mother, the *Clarion* learns with regret, is likely to become dangerously ill with brain fever, brought about by her grief.

POLICE ACTIVITY

Official inquiries into the circumstances of Miss Richards's
death have elicited the following facts:

(1)   That in the opinion of the police surgeon, Dr. Billing-
       ton, Miss Richards had been dead, when Walters found
       her, for at least eight hours.

(2)   That Miss Richards, on the preceding evening, had left
       the house of Mrs. Rudolph Sharp in Tall Elms Road,
       after a bridge party, at 12 midnight.

(3)   That Miss Richards, at Mrs. Rudolph Sharp's request,
       had spent some time in transferring to their various
       homes those of Mrs. Rudolph Sharp's guests who either
       had no motor cars or who had not brought their motor
       cars.

(4)   That the last known person to see Miss Richards alive
       was the last of Mrs. Sharp's guests that she carried
       home—Mr. Henry Warburton of 5, Oak Tree Grove.

(5)   That Miss Richards had upon the day before broken
       off an engagement of marriage.

(6)   That Miss Richards both throughout the evening and
       at 12:10, when she bade good-night to Mr. Warburton
       and his family, had seemed in the best of spirits and far
       from anticipating evil fortune.

(7)   That Miss Richards had, so far as her parents and
       immediate friends and acquaintances can vouchsafe, no
       enemy whatever in the world.

EX-FIANCÉ

It is rumoured that Miss Richards's ex-fiancé is a well
known figure in Holmdale, but that the engagement was
broken off by mutual rather than individual arrangement.

POLICE THEORIES OF THE CRIME

In a long interview which our special representative had this
morning with Inspector Davis of the County Constabulary,
who is in charge of this and the Colby case, we learn that
three letters signed, "The Butcher," were received this morning, referring to the death of Miss Richards. These letters,
except that the reference was two and the name—that of
Miss Richards—and the date were different, were identical
in other respects with the letters received after Lionel Colby's
death. Inspector Davis was very frank with our representative.
He pointed out that in this case of murder without apparent

motive, investigation must necessarily be slower at the start
than in the case where a motive or motives are immediately
visible. His considered theory of how the crime actually took
place is as follows:

Miss Richards—after taking Mr. Warburton home—was
proceeding towards her own domicile in Tall Elms Road, via
High Collings, Marrowbone Lane, and, as a short cut, New
Approach. At the corner of New Approach (at the spot where
the car was found this morning) it is the police theory that
she was hailed and stopped the car, when the murderer—leaning into the car upon some pretext such as asking the time
or the way—must have struck at her, killing her instantane-
ously, and fearfully mutilating her in the same way that Lionel
Colby was mutilated. There can be no doubt, fortunately, that
death was instantaneous and therefore practically painless.

Police inquiries have ascertained, Inspector Davis told us,
that at that time all the households of the occupied houses in
New Approach were abed. A small car of the type owned by
Miss Richards does not make much noise, and none of the
occupants of New Approach heard a sound. There are no
street lights in New Approach, and after the dastardly murder
had been committed, there was nothing to prevent the male-
factor from calmly and cold-bloodedly going quietly upon his
way.

BEREAVED FAMILY

The *Clarion* learns with deep regret that Mrs. Richards,
Miss Pamela Richards's mother, is critically ill, owing to the
terrible shock imposed by her daughter's untimely end. Mr.
Richards also was prostrate with shock. It is truly terrible
to think how these tragedies affect, not only their victims, but
also those whose loved and adored ones have been so suddenly, and as it were, by some all powerful demon, snatched
from them in such a diabolic and undetectable way.

Mr. Percy Godly, a little whiter than usual about his jowls,
which were so like gills, crunched the single-sheet *Clarion* special
into a hard ball; threw it viciously into the gutter; raised himself
from his leaning posture and walked, a thought unsteadily, away.
He passed in his walk the whole long green-painted front of the
Market, Holmdale's one shop, and, at this time every morning,
Holmdale's social centre.

A man stepped into Mr. Godly's path; a man who said:

"Hullo, Godly. I say, Godly old man, I *am* damn sorry. Dreadful business!"

Mr. Godly apparently did not hear this man. He sidestepped and walked on, his eyes fixed in a wide and clear stare. Mr. Godly faced, at the far end of the Market, a group of young matrons who stood with neat and busily wagging heads, and talked together at the top of their voices, the subject for once being, in every case, the same. From this group the youngest matron detached herself and rushed towards Mr. Godly with hand outstretched as if to clutch him by the arm. But, still staring with that glazed look before him, he twitched the arm away before the hand could descend upon it, and walked steadily on.

The young matron stared after him. *"Well!"* she said, and went back to her group. The heads of the group had turned to follow Mr. Godly's progress until, at the corner by Holmdale's Inn, the Wooden Shack, he disappeared from sight.

"Poor Percy!" said the youngest matron. "I don't care what you say! I think that when Pam broke off the engagement it hit him very hard."

"Poor Percy!" said the second youngest matron indignantly. "Poor *Percy,* indeed! Poor Pamela, *I* say! Poor darling Pam!"

"I say!" said another, with something in her voice which brought all heads round to her and stilled the chattering mouths. "I say! Have any of you thought about this? I've only just realized that I haven't. First that boy—that was awful—and then Pamela. They're dead! Do you understand? They've been *killed!* They've . . . they've . . . There's some inhuman thing going about that . . . that . . . ." She stopped. She caught her breath. Her eyes were wide. White teeth caught at her lower lip. She suddenly burst into a peal of sound bearing some resemblance to laughter, but having in it no mirth.

The youngest matron put her fingers to her ears. "Oh, don't!" she said.

The red brassarded boy came running up to the group. Twenty yards from them he began to chant. "Special! Special! Extra! *Clarion* Special! All about the Butcher!"

"How dreadful!" The eldest matron fumbled in her purse. "Here, boy. Give me one. How much?"

"Tuppence," said the boy.

He had, it appeared, six copies left. The youngest matron was left without one. The previous record circulation of the *Clarion* for

one week had, to-day with this special and unprecedented daily
edition, not only doubled, but trebled itself. Holmdale was excited
and more excited. But Holmdale was beginning to wonder whether
excitement was so desirable as forty-eight hours ago it had seemed.

3

The Holmdale Theatre is in the Broad Walk. Facing it across
the white, wide roadway and the railed-off stretch of turf and rose
trees is the red brick building which houses the offices of the Holmdale Company Limited.

At nine o'clock upon Monday, the 26th November—the evening of the day upon which Pamela Richards's body was discovered—there was being held, in the Board Room in these offices, a
special meeting of directors and others convened by Sir Montague
Flushing himself.

Round the long table in the Board Room sat nineteen persons:
Sir Montague, the six directors of the main Holmdale Company,
and the eight directors of the associated and subordinate companies. There were also present Major Robert Wemyss John, who
was honorary yet active captain of Holmdale's surprisingly efficient
fire brigade; the Hon. Ronald Heatherstone, who was private secretary to Lord Bayford, upon whose property half of Holmdale
was built; Colonel Grayling, head of the Holmdale Branch of the
County Special Voluntary Constabulary; Miss Finch to represent
the Press, and Arthur Steele, Sir Montague's private secretary, to
take notes of the proceedings.

The meeting had begun at seven-thirty. Now, an hour and a
half later, it was drawing to its close. Sir Montague was speaking,
and speaking, for once, without that pomposity which until to-day
all those gathered about the table had thought part of the real man.
He was saying:

". . . I take it, then, gentlemen, that we are fully in agreement
that as from to-morrow, unless by to-morrow night the police have
laid their hands upon this—this fiend, we'll take the steps we've
been discussing. . . . If you have got them down, Steele? . . .
Thank you. . . . I think I'll read over these points just to make
sure there's no misunderstanding. First, Colonel Grayling, if he
gets permission from the authorities, will have every road patrolled
by one or more special constables, in addition to the regular constables who will be so employed. Second, Captain John will pro-

vide additional patrolling help out of his volunteers. Third, you, Mr. Heatherstone, will obtain, if possible, Lord Bayford's permission to use some of his outdoor staff, such as gamekeepers, for patrolling the entrances to and exits from the city, so that all incomers and outgoers after dark may be interrogated. Fourth, Miss Finch will issue another special edition of the *Holmdale Clarion* tomorrow, in which it will be clearly stated that the Holmdale Company are prepared to pay a reward of £1000 for information leading to the capture of the—the—murderer. Are we all agreed upon that, gentlemen?"

Sir Montague seemed somehow less portly than usual, and certainly less sure of himself and his own greatness as he looked round the table. There was something not without pathos in the anxiously outthrust face; something almost pitiful in the man's pallor and uncertainty; something certainly admirable in his earnestness. There were murmurs of assent.

"You needn't worry about my end," said young Heatherstone heartily. "Bayford'll lend you all his men. If he doesn't, I'll send 'em along without asking him."

"I'll get a rush edition out before noon, if I can, Sir Montague," said Miss Finch, and rose and fumbled beneath her chair for the perpetual umbrella.

"I'll get permission for the Specials all right *and* enroll a devil of a lot more." This in a growl from Grayling.

"Thank you. Thank you," said Flushing. "Well, gentlemen, I'm sorry to have kept you so long." He glanced at his watch. "I see it's already well past a normal dinner time. . . ."

There was a general shuffling as chairs scraped back over the thick carpet and a sudden muddled hum of many small conversations as men struggled into their coats.

Steele threw open the double doors leading from the Board Room to the hallway. Thirty-eight feet clattered along the hall and so to the main doors and the flight of steps leading down to the pavement. The porter, expectant of tips, flung open the doors. The first rank shivered a little as the cold air struck their faces. The night was dark, but stars blazed in a black and moonless sky. The frost had held, and there was a chill wind from somewhere in the northeast. Light, broken into a hundred little shafts by the bodies of the small crowd, flooded out from the hall and stabbed fingers at the darkness. Twenty-five yards away, straight opposite, the red and yellow signs across the face of the theatre winked cheerfully, and a yellow rectangle of light poured through the glass doors of the portico.

Young Heatherstone tightened his muffler and turned up the collar of his ulster. He said to Grayling beside him:

"Looks pretty cheerful, what? Hardly as if there was a— *Jumping Gabriel,* what's up?" The sudden change in his tone from one of idle pleasantness to one of urgent and vehement wonder brought a dozen eyes to peer in the direction of his pointing arm. From out of the theatre's portico there had rushed suddenly a man in the theatre's green and gold and scarlet uniform; a man hatless and, to judge by his manner, distraught; a man who, arrived upon the pavement, put to his lips a whistle whose shriek throbbed across the cold, dark air.

"What the devil!" said Heatherstone, and was gone, crossing the roadway in four strides. He took the railings to the grass in a leap and arrived by the side of the man who whistled before any of his companions had moved a foot. The first few of them to cross the road and the grass saw him, after urgent and gesticulating talk with the commissionaire, disappear at a run into the portico. The commissionaire, turning suddenly, made off to his right at a long, loping run.

Grayling was the first to reach the theatre after Heatherstone. He pushed open the heavy swing door which still vibrated with Heatherstone's entry. In the vestibule he found a white-faced and gaping crowd. From this he singled out a face—a face whiter even than those which surrounded it, but a face beneath the cap of green lace worn as part of their uniform by the women who served in the theatre. A man of sixty-five, Grayling, but a man who knew what he wanted and how to get it. He cut the girl out from the swelling crowd and barked at her:

"Where? What is it?"

The girl gasped something, pointing. He dropped her arm. He jumped for the arch upon his right which framed the stairs leading up to the circle and balcony. Despite his years and weight, he went up the stairs three at a time and came to the first-floor vestibule with its tea lounge and chocolate counter. The tall figure of Heatherstone was leaning his hands on the front of the chocolate counter, peering over it. He found Grayling beside him, and pointed.

"Look!" said Heatherstone.

In the uncarpeted semi-circle of floor between the blank back of the counter and the shelves, gaudy with sweatmeat boxes, there lay, like a crumpled life-size doll, the body of a young woman. Her face was pressed to the floor. Her arms were doubled beneath her. Her legs were ungainly asprawl in a position impossible to life. . . .

And on her back, between slight shoulders and waist, there lay a square yellow piece of paper.

And out from the paper, staring up at Grayling's eyes, printed in black ink, were four words:

WITH THE BUTCHER'S COMPLIMENTS

CHAPTER FOUR

Superintendent Arnold Pike of the Criminal Investigation Department was talking with his immediate chief. Pike was saying:

"Very well, sir, but you realize that I shall have to drop the Brandon business?"

Lucas shrugged. "Of course you will. But Broxburn can take that on. Anybody could do that, Pike, but this Holmdale job *isn't* anybody's meat."

"If you asked my opinion, sir," Pike said, with a wry smile, "I'd tell you the Holmdale job may not be *do*able!"

"Oh, rubbish!" said Lucas. "Take two or three men and get off as quick as you like. Get down there by lunch time."

Pike sighed. "Very well, sir."

"And for God's sake," said Lucas, "catch this lunatic or whatever it is before we get questions in the House. If only these county police would ask us in at once instead of waiting until they've made a mess of everything, life might be easier."

Pike nodded. "By jing, sir," he said, "I echo that wish!" He turned to the door; then checked. "By the way, sir," he said, "heard anything of Colonel Gethryn? How he is, I mean, sir?"

Lucas grinned and shook his head. "No. Beyond the fact that he's going to be in bed for another three weeks with that leg, nothing." He smiled at Pike with some slyness. "Why? Want help already?"

Pike laughed. "I'm not proud, sir, you know. I was just wondering whether, if he wasn't doing anything, he might like to come down."

"Well, he can't," said Lucas and laughed again. "And, anyhow, it's not his line, and you know it. This isn't a job for a man so much as a job for an organization. When you can't find a motive—in fact, when there *isn't* a motive, you're dealing with some form or other of lust-killing; and to pick a lust-killer—who may be, on the surface, a most ordinary, respectable citizen—out of a crowd of six thousand citizens isn't a job which can be done by deduction. It's got to be done by massed police work, cleverly directed. . . . You get along, Pike, and don't forget to show the world how the Düsseldorf business *ought* to have been handled."

2

Three rooms in the Holmdale Company's offices had been placed at the disposal of the police. In the largest of these, at three o'clock in the afternoon of his first day there, Pike sat in talk with the chief constable of the county and County Inspectors Davis and Farrow. There was, to begin with, constraint. The chief constable had overruled his subordinates and asked the aid of Scotland Yard. But his subordinates were not, as perhaps was natural, pleased with the decision. They were, officially, ready both to help and to take their orders from Scotland Yard. Unofficially, they were anxious to show that left alone, as in their own opinions they ought to have been, they could probably have done the job more quickly, more neatly, and with greater efficiency.

The chief constable, burly, red-faced, and even at this time genial, sat at the head of the table. Upon his left, side by side, each as stiffly erect as his fellow, both in plain clothes, sat Inspectors Davis and Farrow. Davis was tall and lean, with a sergeant major's blue eye and waxed moustache. His face was hard and wooden and always, if he had any feelings, a mask for those feelings. Farrow was tall and thick, with the shoulders and round head of a pugilist. His face, unlike Davis's, was a battleground for his inner emotions. At the moment he frankly scowled. His hot, reddish-brown eye regarded the trimly lounging figure of Superintendent Pike, who faced him across the table, with belligerent disfavour.

Pike had been in similar situations not once but a hundred times. He had his own methods. He was neither truculent nor chummy. He was very pleasant. His brown, lantern-shaped face smiled impartially at the other three.

They were talking of what had happened and of what might happen and of what steps should be taken to prevent such happenings. They dealt, with Davis as spokesman, with the Colby murder and came to the conclusion that everything up to this stage which could have been done had been done. They dealt, then, with the truculent Farrow as spokesman, with the murder of Pamela Richards, and came to the same conclusion. They dealt, now with the chief constable as main spokesman, and both inspectors as chorus, with the murder of Amy Adams, the waitress at the Holmdale Theatre chocolate counter. And here Pike found more to say after the others had finished.

"This girl Adams . . ." said Pike. "There's one or two points about her case. You're sure to have noticed, gentlemen, that this case is different from the other two at almost every point. First, while the others are killed by a wound in the stomach, which is ripped up—all untidy as you might say—Amy Adams is killed by a single thrust through the stomach which isn't anything but tidy. Second, third, and fourth, while Lionel Colby and Pamela Richards are killed at night and in the dark and in the open, this Adams girl is killed in the evening and in a well lighted public place and under a roof. Fifth, that while the first two had no—well, trade mark of the murderer's on 'em when they were found, Amy Adams did. Seventh, that while Lionel Colby and Pamela Richards had parents at least in comfortable enough circumstances, the Adamses are really poor folk living in a small cottage with the father actually out of work and on the dole."

Pike sat back in his chair and looked, with his brown, bright eyes, at the chief constable.

The chief constable pondered, stabbing at the blotting pad before him with a tortured pen nib. He raised his eyes at last to look at his two henchmen. "Thought of that?" he said.

Davis nodded. "Of course, sir," he said, "we've seen all that." His voice was, as usual, a flat monotone, but there was in it also a rasping of bitter and elephantine irony. "We couldn't help ourselves but see all that. It was us, you see, who did all the work and found out these facts."

"What I asked," said the chief constable mildly, "was whether you'd *thought* about it?" He looked now at Farrow.

Farrow could not, as had Davis, keep his eyes off Pike as he answered.

"Thought about it!" Farrow exploded. "Thought about it!" And then, with sudden realization of his company: "Beg your pardon, sir, I'm sure. But if we haven't been thinking, and thinking hard, about the whole bl—— about the whole business for these past seventy-two hours and more, I'd like to know what we *have* been doing."

"Yes. Yes." The chief constable was soothing. "Yes. Quite; quite!" He turned to Pike and said: "And what was *your* thought, Superintendent, when you put this 'difference' point to us?"

Pike shook his head. A faint smile twisted his wide mouth. He said:

"Nothing. . . . I'll have to explain myself a bit, sir. It's always been my way not to think at the beginning of a job. I've found it pays me very well. I just turn myself—or try to turn myself—into a machine for recording facts without theorizing. I don't worry about whys and hows and whats and its. I just try to collect facts whether they appear to have any bearing on the case or not. Then, suddenly, when I've been digging round long enough and hard enough, I maybe dig up something which seems to click in my mind and become a good starting-off place for a think. . . . I hope you follow what I mean, sir."

"*Chacun,*" said the chief constable with a most un-Gallic accent, "*à son goût.* I gather then, Superintendent, that you had no particular reason for drawing our attention to the differences which exist between the circumstances of Colby's and Pamela Richards's murders and Amy Adams's murder?"

Pike smiled at the chief constable. "That's right, sir. No particular reason except that, as the cleverest man I know is always saying, in this sort of job, if one collects oddities one sometimes gets somewhere."

Inspector Davis coughed, breaking the little silence which had followed Pike's speech.

"It seems to me," said Davis, "that we might get down to brass tacks; might get down, that is, to deciding what steps we're going to take to prevent any *more* of these murders. . . ."

Farrow grunted assent. "Ah, that's right! That's right, sir! And I'd like to add, what steps 're we going to take to ensure that we catch this blasted lunatic." He turned to his colleague. "There's only one way, Davis, to make *sure* of stopping these murders and that's to catch the man that's doing 'em."

"What," put in Pike mildly, "*are* the arrangements so far?"

The faces of Davis and Farrow, which had been turned each towards the other, turned now towards the interloper. The interloper remained unmoved. He was not smiling any longer, but his lantern face was placid, like a child's. The chief constable felt strain in the air. He hurried in with his stubby oar. He said quickly:

"What are we doing? I'll tell you, Superintendent." He fumbled among the papers stacked to one side of the blotting pad before him and produced at last some pinned together foolscap sheets. "Here's a copy of the present arrangements. I'll just go through them in brief for you and then let you have the papers."

"Thank you, sir." Pike's tone was diplomatically grateful.

The chief constable cleared his throat. "First," he said, "as from four o'clock this afternoon, every main thoroughfare and every secondary thoroughfare in this place will be patrolled by regular police drafted in from other areas of the county. The patrols will be in pairs and will be on throughout the night, coming off duty an hour after dawn. These patrols will be supplemented in regard to the secondary thoroughfares by volunteer patrols, composed of special constables, under the control of Colonel Grayling, who acts under my directions, and other volunteers under the control of the Holmdale Company, who also hold themselves at my directions. Further volunteers will be posted to cover the various cul-de-sacs, squares, keeps, and other non-thoroughfare ways. Further, as from five o'clock this afternoon, specially authorized guards (they will all be enrolled to-morrow as special constables to give them further powers) will be posted at all the entrances and exits of Holmdale. These men are being supplied, Superintendent, by the courtesy of Lord Bayford. An elaborate code of signals, in the case of any discoveries being made or any assistance being required, has been evolved. You will find full details of the whole scheme in the papers. Further, a reward of one thousand pounds has been offered by the Holmdale Company for information leading to the arrest of the murderer. . . . What's that, Superintendent?"

Pike shook his head. "Nothing, sir, nothing. I was only thinking what trouble you're going to have. I'm not sure that I believe in these advertised rewards."

"We couldn't," said the chief constable, "stop the Holmdale Company from offering the reward or the *Holmdale Clarion* from publishing the offer. And also, Superintendent, I'm not sure that the course isn't justified."

Pike shrugged. "P'raps you're right, sir!"

"It seems to me," said the chief constable, folding up the fools-cap sheets and handing them across the table, "that this lunatic who calls himself the Butcher will be hard put to it to try another of his games without getting caught. Eh? What? Don't you agree?"

Once more Pike's wide mouth twisted into a little smile: a smile doubting but by no means offensive. "Couldn't say, sir," said Pike. "I'm afraid I must stick to my own way. And that, as I've told you, is not to let myself form opinions in the early stages. I'm sure I hope you're right, though. The arrangements seem fairly complete. The danger is, of course, that they'll frighten this Butcher into stopping his games. And then what'll happen?"

The chief constable stared. "I'm afraid I don't quite follow you."

"What'll happen," said Pike, "is that nothing will happen, and then, when after a month or six months, or a year or six years, when all supervision is removed—when all your arrangements that is, are, so to speak, cancelled—well, then, this butcher gentleman might just start his games all over again."

The chief constable frowned. "Something in that, I suppose." He looked hard at Pike. "Meaning, Superintendent, that that's what you think *is* going to happen."

Pike shook his head. "I'm not thinking, as I told you, sir. . . . There's no doubt that it's what *may* happen. All we can hope is that it won't."

Inspector Davis muttered beneath his breath.

The chief constable turned upon him irritably. "What is it, Davis? What is it? Speak up, man!"

Davis flushed. "I was going to say, sir, that in my opinion we didn't ought to be talking about *hoping*. We ought to be talking about *doing*."

Superintendent Pike smiled at Inspector Davis. "I'm not at all sure," said Pike, "that Inspector Davis isn't right." He turned his head to look once more at the chief constable. "After all, you gentlemen know this place and what can be done with it. I've only just got here and want to look round before I say anything. . . ."

CHAPTER FIVE

Parallel with the long platforms of Holmdale station, upon the other side of the railway line, runs, for two hundred yards, the thousand-windowed, green-and-white-painted back of the Breakfast Barlies Factory. At the southern end of the building there shoot into the sky, sudden and massive, the four great grain elevators. These terrific towers are considered, by many of Holmdale's citizens, to be the one blot upon Holmdale's beauty. Others find them the strongest claim to beauty which Holmdale has—their grouping; their proportion; their smooth, sleek, immutable strength.

They stood now, these towers, a black mass against the blood-shot sky of a winter sunset. The thousand-and-one windows of the factory sprang from blackness into golden life. Behind them the work went on. Good honest grain, ton upon ton of it, was being beaten and thrashed, roasted and split, drenched and besugared until, behind the gleaming windows at the northern end of the building, its final and tasteless distortions were packed by white-clad females into blue-and-white cardboard boxes, bearing in letters of red and gold, the words *Breakfast Barlies*. Under the splendid insignia was a picture of the factory, the grain towers omitted. Under the picture were the words: *"Breakfast Barlies beat the band; with cream and sugar they are grand. Dad likes them, so does little Pete; no meal without them is complete."*

There were seven hundred and seventeen day workers in the factory. They were all well paid, well tended, and worked under conditions almost painfully hygienic. They started work at 8 A. M., and they finished work at 5 P. M. Save upon most unusual occasions, and then only when armed with an official permit, no worker was ever seen to leave the factory before the proper time. But it was only ten minutes past four when Albert Calvin Rogers came up the stairs from the belt room whistling, with hands in his overall pockets and cap over one ear.

Albert Rogers was a competent electrician hating electricity. Albert Rogers was a brilliant player of Association Football, loving the game with a devouring love. And in a pocket of the trousers beneath his overalls there lay a letter signed "Yours faithfully, F. T. Lovelace." This letter had come by the previous morning's post and had been in the pocket or his hand ever since. Thirty-six hours and more he had had it; but it had taken every minute of those hours and all the assurances of the many to whom the letter had been shown, to convince him that the letter was fact and no imagining.

But now he did believe it. Hence the small scene, most dramatic, which had taken place in the belt room ten minutes before. He had, as most workers, often mentally dramatized the visionary occasion upon which he would tell his immediate superior what he thought of him, but never—not, at least, until just now—had it occurred to him that such an occasion would ever befall him in reality.

Yet it had. And down there was Masters, the foreman, with a flea in his ear and the other ear beginning already to thicken. And here was he, an hour before knocking-off time, coming up, by the forbidden stairs, a free and melodious man.

Sergeant Stelch, the commissionaire, came out of his cubbyhole in resplendent wrath. In all the five-year history of Breakfast Barlies, Stelch had never before seen any one of the belt-room staff come up the directors' stairs nor heard an electrician whistle. The sight of the one added, in the same person, to the sound of the other, had at first amazed Sergeant Stelch and then infuriated him.

"Oy!" bellowed Sergeant Stelch.

Albert Rogers halted. He turned, and his wide smile added fuel to the other's wrath. "If you speak a little louder," said Albert Rogers, "a fellow might be able to 'ear you."

Sergeant Stelch advanced. The fine tips of his waved moustache seemed to reach forward, bristling.

Albert Rogers stood his ground.

"It's you, is it?" said Sergeant Stelch, his mouth not more than six inches from Albert Rogers's nose.

"Right," said Albert Rogers, "the very first time, my dear 'Olmes. Your methods are astonishing."

"None o' that now!" said Sergeant Stelch. "You know very well that no one of you blokes ain't allowed up these stairs nor in this 'all. You know the rules and regulations of this firm just as well as I do."

The smile of Albert Rogers grew wider. "If you're thinkin' of

me bein' in trouble," he said, "you've got it wrong. It's Breakfast
Barlies who's in trouble. I just 'anded in my resignation!"

Still whistling, still with his hands in his pockets, he walked out
of the main doors of the great building and down the sweep of the
white steps. He had never been that way before; had never, in fact,
wanted to. It was a much longer way than the way he and his
associates generally used. But to-night he used it, savouring every
step. He turned left at the end of the steps and walked along the
neatly gravelled, white-bordered driveway to the great gates across
the top of which showed in letters of blue and white light: "THE
BIRTHPLACE OF BREAKFAST BARLIES." Presently, as he came out
under this arch and spat reflectively behind him, his mind became
really busy not with the past but with the future. To-day was Friday, and the letter had said next Monday morning at nine o'clock.
And this meant that as from nine o'clock upon this unbelievable
Monday Albert Calvin Rogers would be a fully fledged and com-
paratively highly remunerated member of the Woolwich United
Association Football Club.

Halfway over the new iron bridge spanning the railway line he
halted. His fingers groped for the letter and found reassurance in
its comforting but by this time greasy crackle. There it was in black
and white. . . .

Albert Rogers went on a little faster. By now it would be nearing
five, and at five he could suitably crown this day by turning into
the public bar of the Wooden Shack. So down the slope of the
bridge he went, and turned sharp to his right and went behind the
lounge and dining room of the Shack, and so round to the back
where are the billiard saloons and public bar. The doors were open
and the lights ablaze. Already, although this was only a moment
past five, there were three customers and of these three, one—Frank
Howard—was a friend.

"Love us!" said Mr. Howard. "Look who's 'ere. Wattle, Bert?"

"With you," said Albert Rogers, "nothing. You'll drink with me
and so will everybody else. This is my lucky day." He turned to the
barman. "Stick 'em up, Ted."

The hand of Mr. Howard descended upon his friend's shoulder.
"You don't bloody well mean to say," said Mr. Howard in tones
of great astonishment, "that that bloody tale Wally was telling me
about you bloody well being a bloody footballer is bloody well
true?"

"Frank," said Albert Rogers, "it bloody is!"

"Kor!" said Mr. Howard.

"On Monday next," said Albert Rogers, ". . . but 'ere, read for yerself." He pulled out from his pocket the letter, unfolded it, and drew from its envelope the precious bethumbed sheet.

Mr. Howard read. "Well, well, well!" said Mr. Howard. "'Ere, 'ave another."

Albert Rogers had another; and then, when more friends came in, yet several more. Albert Rogers, who had a good head but not great capacity for bulk, switched from bitter to whisky. By half-past six he was in a condition which he himself, even at the time, described as three parts lit. He was, however, much in love with Mary Fillimore and had an appointment with Mary Fillimore for six thirty-five at a spot distant by fifteen minutes' walk.

"Enough's enough," said Albert Rogers, "I'm off."

"No," said a voice behind him—a new voice for this evening. "Not till you've had one on me, Bert."

Albert Rogers turned. "Blimey!" he said, "if it isn't old Todd." He swayed a little on his feet and held out a ready hand.

Mr. Edward Bultivle, chief compositor at the Lakeside Press, gripped the proffered hand, shook it warmly, and within two minutes placed firmly within it a glass containing yet more whisky. Mr. Bultivle then raised his own glass. "Here," said Mr. Bultivle, "is to the most promising Outside Right in League Football!"

"'Ear, 'ear!" said Mr. Howard.

And "'Ear, 'ear!" came hearty chorus.

"How the hic," said Albert Rogers, "did you know anyhic about it, Todd?"

"Off the next edition of the *Clarion,* of course," said Mr. Bultivle. "'Aven't I spent the whole flamin' day settin' the darn thing up? And didn't Tom Pearce where you lodge drop word into the *Clarion* office this mornin'? Of course he did, and of course Miss Finch put somethink in, and a nice bit it is, I can tell you, Bert! 'Ave another?"

"I will," said Albert Rogers firmly, "do nothink of the such. I . . . I'm goinc. I . . . I've got a 'pointment. What's time?"

Mr. Bultivle consulted a large watch. "The time," said Mr. Bultivle largely, "is twenty-three and three-quarters of a minute to seven. You're late already, boy. Stay and 'ave another."

But Albert Rogers had gone.

Albert Rogers was willing his unruly but magnificent legs to carry his thirteen stone of well proportioned bone and muscle fast, and as straight as might possibly be, up the length of Market Road; thus to Forest Rise, and so, eventually, to the hedged-in blackness of Links Lane. Halfway up Forest Rise he broke into a staggering run. He knew what Mary was when she was kept waiting. It wasn't that she was cross with him or gave him the rough edge of her tongue or anything like that. It was just that she was hurt, and it wasn't as though she made a fuss about it like some sorts would. It was just that she was disappointed-like at the waste of time and couldn't help showing it however much she tried.

Albert Rogers, running uphill on legs which although steadier were still unruly, once more cursed himself for a fool. At the top of Forest Rise and the steep downward slope which joins this house-flanked thoroughfare with the rurality of Links Lane, he slowed down to a walk. No good charging, on these legs, down a steep and dark and stony road.

He found himself blowing hard, a thing he hadn't done after a little run like that for perhaps four years. . . . He despised himself. . . . He got to the foot of the hill just by the little white stile into Crosbies Wood. . . . He passed the stile. . . . He was walking on the right-hand side of the road, and so he went by not more than a few feet from the stile. He thought that he saw, dimly through the dark, a figure leaning against the rail to one side of the stile, but he was not certain until, from just behind him, there came a voice. It said:

"I wonder whether you could help me."

Albert Rogers turned, swaying a little with the movement.

Albert Rogers started to say, "I beg your pardon . . ." But he got no further than the "beg."

Something very cold hurt him. . . . No, it wasn't cold, it was fire.

A little stifled cry, like the squeak of a small injured animal, came from his mouth. He doubled, his hands clasped vainly to his stomach. His knees crumpled beneath him. He felt light, light . . .

2

They had lodged Pike in Fourtrees Road, in No. 12. This was, for Holmdale and Fourtrees Road, a large house, having five bed-rooms, a sun parlour and something over quarter of an acre of garden. The owner, a spinster of fifty healthy years, was Miss Honoria Marable. Miss Marable was a prosperously retired sea-side boarding-house proprietress who, after thirty years of lodgers, was still weirdly unable to live happily without being constantly surrounded by these animals. No. 12 was Miss Marable's ambition brought about by Miss Marable's self. No. 12 was, necessarily upon a small scale, everything that boarding houses should be but so very seldom are.

Pike was given the large bedroom in the front of the house, a much windowed, cheerful room. Upon the evening of his first day in Holmdale, just after the evening meal, he sat up in his room looking out, through the glass of the bay window, at the dark, clear night. There was no moon, but the sky was encrusted with stars, and there was that strange translucency to the darkness which sometimes comes upon a winter's night.

It had been cold all day and now was colder. But there had been a fire—and a good one—in the room since early morning and Pike, seeing that the air was already misted with his tobacco smoke, threw open a pane of the bay window. Keen, sweet-smelling air rushed in. He knelt upon the window seat, took his pipe from his mouth and leaned out, taking deep breaths.

He could see dimly the black shapes of smaller houses upon the other side of the road and, a hundred yards or so to his left, a yellow splash of light where the street lamp stood, outside the small white cottage which was the house of Sergeant Jeffson of the County Constabulary and, therefore, also Holmdale's police head-quarters.

He put the pipe back into his mouth again, leaned his forearms comfortably on the sill, and waited until the measured, regular footfalls which he had heard when first he opened the window should pass beneath him.

They drew near and nearer, two men walking together, with slow and unvarying pace, upon the pavement upon his side of the road. He leaned out and peered downwards, straining his eyes. In a moment he levered himself back, satisfied. A patrol—and a patrol of regular constables. He had just been able to distinguish their helmets. The patrol went by at the same pace. The sound of their walking grew fainter and fainter and died away altogether as they breasted the small rise and went down the hill towards the end of Fourtrees Road and the semicircular sweep of Fourtrees Avenue which was one end of their beat.

Pike tapped the ashes out of his pipe against the window sill, sat back on his heels, and reached out a hand to pull the window shut.

But he did not close it. The sound of more footsteps came to his ears. These were not measured, regular footsteps. They were hurrying, stumbling footsteps; one person's. Pike threw the window wide and leaned out, listening. The footsteps were coming from the east end of Marrowbone Lane, and not the west, as had the patrol. They came tripping and stumbling along until they were exactly opposite him. Craning out of the window he could hear laboured, gasping breathing—a wild sound. Whether it was made by a man or woman he could not tell. But the whole sound-picture was strange enough to make him cross the room in a leap, fling open the door, go downstairs in four bounds, wrench open the front door, run down the path and vault the gate. . . .

Pike could run. Pike knew that he was gaining over a yard with every stride. But his running stopped within a hundred yards. The pursued halted under the street lamp opposite Jeffson's cottage, fumbled with Jeffson's gate and charged, reeling a little in his stride, up to Jeffson's front door. Pike slowed down to a walk, reached the gate himself and stood by it, waiting unobtrusive.

The street lamp showed him the small green door and the figure which was knocking on it; a tall, lean stooping figure which supported itself with its free hand against the doorpost. Its shoulders were bent and heaved to shuddering breaths. It had no hat, and a mop of white hair tossed with its movements.

The door was opened by Jeffson himself. Pike heard his deep growl and then a high-pitched, wavering voice in answer.

Pike pushed open the gate. He arrived at the door just as Jeffson waved his visitor inside.

"Just a moment," said Pike.

Jeffson opened the door again. "Oh, it's you, sir," he said. He heaved a sigh of relief. "Glad you've come, I must say." He jerked a thumb over his shoulder towards the dark recesses of the passage. "That there, that's . . ." Jeffson never finished his sentence. His visitor's voice came again from just behind him.

"Quick," it said, "quick! We can't stand here wasting time. Quick! quick!"

Pike and Jeffson looked at each other. Pike nodded. They stepped across the threshold, and Jeffson closed the door.

There was a room on the right of the passageway which was half parlour and half rural police office. A flood of hard light from a yellow-shaded electric lamp showed Pike a slippered and coatless Jeffson, burlier even than in his uniform, and gave him a clearer view of Jeffson's visitor; the clerical clothes, the ravaged face and the blue eyes which blazed out of it.

"This," said Jeffson awkwardly, "is the Reverend Rockwall." He turned to the cleric. "Mr. Rockwall, this is—" he hesitated, looking at Pike and receiving a nod, went on—"this is Superintendent Pike of Scotland Yard, who's down here about——"

"Yes, yes!" Rockwall seemed now to have mastered his voice. It was still high pitched and strained, but the note of hysteria had gone.

"Yes," he said again, "yes. But there has been another death . . . in Links Lane. . . . I was walking down there. I was going home. I tripped over something in the road. It—it——" He put up long, lean hands and covered his face.

Pike pushed forward a chair. "You'd best sit down, sir," said Pike.

Rockwall sank into the chair. He mopped at his forehead, which glistened with great beads of sweat. "I'm sorry," he said. "I'm sorry. . . . What I stumbled against was the body of a man. I could—I could tell that he was dead. He had—he had—there was a wound in his stomach." He shuddered and looked at his right hand. On the ball of the thumb was a dark, drying stain. Pike said quietly:

"How long ago was this, sir? Don't worry to tell us any more. Just answer my questions, if you would be so good."

"It seems," said Rockwall, "hours! But it can't be. I came here. . . . I ran . . . all the way. I don't know how long it took me."

Jeffson looked at Pike's raised eyebrows, then, calculatingly, at his other visitor. "Call it a quarter of an hour to twenty minutes," said Jeffson.

Pike said to Rockwall, "Did you see anybody else on your way? After you had found the body and were coming here?"

The white head was shaken. "No. Not a soul. All the way I was looking for someone. I felt that I should never get here."

Pike's hands were deep in his pockets, and his eyes were fixed upon the shining toe-caps of his boots. He rocked a little from heel to toe. He said:

"Get in touch with the patrol stations. Tell 'em to pull in everybody from now on. Get ready yourself. I'm going to get the car. Bring a man with a bicycle. I'll be back in four minutes. Mr. Rockwall, you will please stay here and then accompany us."

3

Two bright streams of white light—one stream from the headlights of the police Crossley, the other from the headlights of the

Holmdale Cottage Hospital Ambulance—flooded the narrow hedge-lined summit of Links Lane. Where the two floods intersected in a theatrical pool of whiteness a group of men stood looking down at something which lay upon the road.

Pike came suddenly into the centre flood of light. He said:

"Not a trace. There's a hard frost and even if there wasn't, this surface wouldn't take any prints. . . . There's nothing. Nothing at all. . . . Jeffson, you'd better tell the ambulance men to take this away." He nodded at the blanket-covered shape which so short a time ago had been Albert Rogers. "The only thing we've got to be thankful for at the moment is that we know who he was."

For a moment Jeffson stood motionless, looking down.

"Poor kid," said Jeffson. And then, lifting his head sharply, turned and strode off and became brusquely official with the ambulance men.

Pike moved nearer to the cleric and looked at him. Pike said: "You're *sure,* sir, that the body hasn't been moved since you saw it?"

Rockwall shrugged thin shoulders helplessly. "So far as I can tell, Superintendent, the poor fellow hasn't been moved. . . . But you must understand—you must understand that I—I—I was over-wrought—when I——"

"Quite, sir, quite. I just wanted to make sure. . . . Jeffson!"

"Yes." Jeffson came trotting up, moving his bulk lightly.

"Did you say something about this lad having a girl friend?"

Jeffson nodded. "Yes. That's right. Mary Fillimore it is. In service. Parlourmaid at Mrs. Sharp's in Tall Elms."

The ambulance men came shuffling with a stretcher. They set the stretcher down. They stooped and lifted the shell of Albert Rogers and bore it away.

Pike went on as if there had been no interruption. "Happen to know where they used to meet? Here?"

Jeffson shook his head. "Couldn't say. We could wake the girl. Shall we? Or get her in the morning?"

Pike considered this. "In the morning," he said.

Jeffson, tilting his helmet forward over his eyes, scratched the back of his head. "What's to do now, then?"

"Get back." Pike was curt. "Get back and see if the patrols have pulled anyone in. What's the time?"

Rockwall answered this. He pulled out a watch, bent to the lights of the Crossley and said: "Fifteen minutes to eleven." He seemed calm now, and in the thin face the blue eyes too were calm.

The hand that held the watch did not tremble, and the voice, though high pitched still, was steady.

"Thanks," said Pike. "Now we'll be going. Jeffson, send that bicycle man of yours the round of the patrols."

"I wonder," said Rockwall, "whether you would let me ride in your motor car as far at least as the beginning of Marrowbone Lane. This . . . this . . ."

"Of course, sir." Pike was quietly genial, in contrast to his recent curtness. "Come along."

There was a sudden roar as the engine of the ambulance started, and then a swinging of its light beams. It backed, turned, and then, with a soft purring in place of its roar, was gone. Against the hedge Jeffson spoke with a dim shape standing by a glittering bicycle.

Pike led Rockwall to the car, settled him in the front seat, and himself slid behind the wheel. Jeffson came running and climbed into the back. More swinging of lights. More backing and turning. Another, deeper purr as the Crossley went. . . .

Links Lane was once more black and empty and silent.

4

The hands of the clock on Jeffson's mantelpiece stood at five minutes to midnight. The little room was crowded. Behind the plain deal table, which seemed to be the end of parlour and the beginning of office, Pike sat in a chair with arms and Jeffson on one without arms. Huddled on the parlour settee was the Reverend Lucius Charles Augustus Rockwall. By the door, upright, uncomfortable and excited, nursing an awkward helmet upon more awkward knees, sat Police Constable George Birch.

Pike was speaking to Rockwall. He was saying:

". . . I think that's all. No, there's one other thing. If you wouldn't mind telling me, sir, purely, of course, as a matter of form, what the business was which had taken you to the neighbourhood of Links Lane?"

"Certainly. Certainly." Rockwall sat upright. "I had been to visit a sick parishioner of mine, who lives in the farm cottages at the top of Links Lane just within my cure——"

"Who's that, sir?" Jeffson put in. "Joe Starr?"

The white head was shaken. "No. Sarah Queen. You know her,

Sergeant? Of course you do! Poor old dame! I'm afraid she won't last another week."

"What time, sir," said Pike, "did you get to this woman's cottage?"

The heavy lids were lifted from the strange blue eyes. "I really couldn't say, Superintendent."

Pike was looking down at the pencil in his hands. He spoke without raising his eyes. He said: "Surely, sir, you could give us some idea."

From Rockwall's mouth there came a queer sound, presumably a laugh. "I daresay," said Rockwall, "that I could. . . . Let me think. . . . I left my house immediately after my evening meal. . . . I should say, Superintendent, that was at somewhere between seven and half past. I remember that I did not want to go out, but I had promised old Sarah that I would. I walked straight——"

"Just one moment, sir!" Pike's interruption was suave, but interruption nevertheless. "Did you walk to the cottage by the same way you came back? Through Links Lane, that is?"

Rockwall shook his head. "I did not, Superintendent. I took the short cut over the golf course, halfway up Tall Elms Road."

"But you came back," said Pike mildly, "by the longer road?"

Rockwall nodded. For a moment only the top of the white head was presented to Pike's eyes. "I came back," said Rockwall, "by the longer road . . . as you say. . . . The reason, Superintendent, was that it was so dark to-night that I had a great deal of trouble walking over the golf course. . . ." His thin lips curved into a self-deprecatory smile. "As a matter of fact, I twice measured my length upon it, tripping first over a wire fence which I altogether failed to see and secondly stumbling down over the edge of one of the greens. I really thought it safer, after leaving old Sarah, to walk back by the road. . . . Thank God that I did. Otherwise . . ."

"Otherwise what, sir?" said Pike.

Rockwall stared. There was an instant's silence. "Otherwise . . ." he said, "otherwise . . . Why, Superintendent? I am afraid I do not follow you. If I had not chosen to go back by Links Lane, I should not have . . . I should not have . . . made my terrible discovery, and if I had not . . . the . . . the . . . it might have been lying there still, uncared for and untended."

"Yes," said Pike. "Yes. I see, sir. . . . And we know from what you've already told us that it was somewhere about twenty minutes past nine when you made the discovery."

A film of vagueness seemed to have come over Rockwall's lined face, and his eyes were dull. He waved a thin, long-fingered hand. "As you say, Superintendent. As you say."

"Now the walk across the golf course, I should say, would take you . . ." Pike looked at Jeffson.

Jeffson twitched burly shoulders. "Say half an hour." He looked at Rockwall. "Do you agree, sir?"

Once more the thin hand was waved. "Yes. Yes. I should think you are right. I have never timed the walk. Yes. I should say half an hour. Quite half an hour. A full half hour."

Pike ceased to play with his pencil. "So that you would have arrived at the cottage of this Sarah Queen at about eight o'clock and, as I see it, left at a quarter-past nine. A longish visit, wasn't it, sir?"

Rockwall closed his eyes. "Why, yes. But that poor old woman, she's like all the rest of them . . . she was afraid." He raised his head from his hands and the lids from his eyes. He stared hard at Pike. "She was afraid, Superintendent, of death. . . . I gave her what comfort I could."

"Quite, sir. Quite." Pike looked at Jeffson again. "I don't think we need keep Mr. Rockwall any longer. Unless, Jeffson, there's anything you'd like to——"

Jeffson shook his head. "No, sir. No."

Pike rose and came out from behind the table. Rockwall rose to meet him. For a moment they looked at each other.

"I will be going on my way, then," Rockwall said. "If there is anything further I can do—any small assistance which may lie within my power—I hope you will call on me."

Pike nodded. "Thank you, sir. We'll do that. We are, of course, much indebted to you for acting so promptly and properly."

Jeffson opened the door. Police Constable George Birch sprang to his feet and stood out of the way. There was a moment's silence. Tall and bent, Rockwall stood in the centre of the little room. His eyes were darting glances here and there about the furniture.

"Lookin' for something, sir?" Jeffson said.

"Eh?" said Rockwall, suddenly raising his eyes. "Oh, thank you, Sergeant. Thank you. It was . . . I was looking for my hat."

"Hat, sir?" said Jeffson and began, too, to look.

Pike interposed. "When you came, sir, you had no hat with you," he said quietly.

"Eh?" Rockwall stared. "Oh, yes . . . yes . . . yes. It must have been lost in my haste. Thank you. Thank you. Good-night!"

He went through the door and into the passage, in which there was now a light. At a nod from his sergeant, Constable Birch followed along the passage and opened the front door.

Inside the room Pike and Jeffson, looking at each other in silence, heard the click of the door shutting and then slow, weary footsteps on the frozen path.

CHAPTER SIX

Pike looked at his watch. The hands stood at half an hour after midnight. He said:

"About time we were hearing from the patrols, isn't it?"

Jeffson crossed the room with heavy tread to the corner where the official telephone stood. He picked up the receiver and asked for a number. Pike walked over to the window, edged his way behind a parlour table, and stood looking out into the dark, cold night. He drummed with his finger tips upon the glass. Behind him in the warm, brightly lighted little room Constable Birch was striving to master a November cough, and Jeffson was holding a muttered conversation with his telephone. Pike went on staring into the darkness. He did not turn until, with the click of a replaced receiver, Jeffson spoke once more in his normal voice.

"They got three," said Jeffson.

Pike wheeled, nearly knocking over the little table. "Where are they?"

"One down at the police hut by the station and two on the way here now. What shall I do, sir? Tell 'em to get the one from the hut up here as well?"

Pike nodded. Once more silence fell. Constable Birch mastered his cough. Jeffson sat upon the edge of the official table and swung massive legs. Pike turned again to the window.

It seemed nearly as many hours, but it was actually ten minutes, before there came the sound of footsteps upon the road outside. Jeffson nodded at Constable Birch, who, putting on his helmet, left the room. They heard his heavy tread in the passage and then, simultaneously with the sound of the front door opening, the click of the gate latch and a tramping upon the path.

Pike and Jeffson waited. There entered to them three special constables and two others. The senior of the special constables reported. He was a small and stout and excited man. Jeffson handled him well and got rid of him and his two henchmen with admirable speed. The two prisoners were left standing in the middle of the room. Again Jeffson and Pike sat behind the official table, and again Constable Birch sat by the door nursing his helmet.

The prisoners were a tall and dishevelled young man, not quite steady on his feet—Percy Godly—and a small, untidy, nervous yet truculent person in a black felt hat, enormous horn-rimmed spectacles, and a hairy suit.

Godly, swaying gently, rather as a young sapling sways in a light breeze, seemed content to sway. The other man, seemed to be restraining speech, and hot speech, with the greatest difficulty.

"Sergeant Jeffson!" Pike was smoothly official. "Do you know these men?"

Jeffson nodded. "That's young Mr. Godly," said Jeffson, "the other gentleman—I'm afraid I don't know his name—is something to do with the film business."

"My name," said the small man in horn-rimmed spectacles, using a voice surprisingly deep and phenomenally fierce, "is Spring, Wilfred Spring. And I'd like to know what the hell——"

"Half a minute, sir, half a minute!" said Jeffson.

Pike smiled a pleasant smile.

"Sit down, Mr. Spring," he said. "Constable, give Mr. Spring a chair."

Spring exploded. Beneath the shadowing spectacles his dark, clever face seemed to grow thinner and darker.

"I don't want your damn chairs," he said. "All I want to know is what the hell——"

"Excuse me, sir!" Pike was smooth. "You've said that before. If you wait a moment I'll tell you. Are you resident in Holmdale?"

Spring controlled himself with a visible effort.

"Yes," he said, "14, Collingwood Road."

"And this other gentleman?" Pike looked at Jeffson.

"Mr. Godly," Jeffson said, "lives with his father, Mr. Emanuel Godly, just outside the city at Links Corner."

"Qui' ri'!" said Mr. Godly affably. "Absolooly ri'!" He smiled largely upon the room as he swayed.

Constable Birch, displaying initiative, brought a chair from a

corner and thrust it neatly against Mr. Godly's legs from behind
and so had him neatly seated.

"Good!" said Mr. Godly.

"Look here!" burst out Spring. "I mean to say, damn it all!"

"One moment, sir." Pike's tone was noticeably curter. "At nine-
thirty this evening the body of another murdered person was discovered within the bounds of this town. Acting upon my instructions, delivered at about half-past eleven, the police detained
everyone found within the town out-of-doors. I am naturally sorry
to cause inconvenience, but I am sure you will agree with me that
some such step as I took was absolutely essential in the interests
of the public."

Spring glared. The horn-rimmed spectacles slipped a little on his
nose. He thrust them back into position with an impatient hand.

"But, good God!" he said, "you don't suspect me!"

"Don't go so fast, sir. Naturally, I don't suspect anybody. And
yet, to do my duty, I suspect everybody. It is possible, you know,
to do both."

Pike looked hard at his indignant prisoner. The gaze of his brown
eyes met and held the gaze of the other brown eyes behind the
spectacles.

"I am sure," said Pike, "that you will agree with me, Mr. Spring,
that personal inconvenience must be borne in these strange circumstances. . . . May I suggest that you sit down?"

"But, blast it, tell me . . . Oh, *all* right!" Mr. Spring sat down
so hard upon the chair which Constable Birch pushed forward
that he almost rebounded from it.

"Carefoo!" said Mr. Godly, raising an admonishing finger.

"Jeffson," said Pike, "where did that special report that Mr.
Spring was taken in?"

"Junction of Market Road and Collingwood Road. According
to the report Mr. Spring was coming up Market Road from
Chaser's Bridge—that's the bridge over the railway, sir—and he just
got to the corner of Collingwood Road when the patrol stopped
him. Just after twelve, it was."

"The bastards!" said Spring. "Grabbed hold of me as if I was a
criminal." He glared at Pike. "God alive, man! Can't you hurry?
I want to go home. I've just done a hard day's work—a harder day's
work, I expect, than you've ever done in your life. I've been on
the go ever since half-past four this morning, and I'm tired, damn
tired! So would you damn well be! I've been on my feet the whole
day. I'm directing a film in which we're using half the blasted Air

Force, and as their own officers don't seem to be able to tell the men what to do, I had to do it for them! Always the same story!"

"Quite!" said Pike. "I'll try and see that you get back to your house as quickly as I can, Mr. Spring. I'm afraid, however, that I shall first have to worry you with some questions. I can assure you, sir, that the more readily and more concisely you answer these questions, so to speak, the quicker you'll be off home. . . . Now then, Jeffson, please take notes of the questions and Mr. Spring's answers."

"Right, sir," Jeffson said. "Ready when you are."

"Now, Mr. Spring, would you please tell me what you were doing when found by the patrol."

"Walking home."

"Where from?"

"Garage."

"What garage is that, Mr. Spring?"

"Damn it, don't let's waste time! There's only one garage in the place." Spring twitched about in his chair as if he would like to jump off it and wave frantic arms and legs. His spectacles kept slipping and the thrusts with which he jammed them back into place grew more and more savage.

Jeffson chipped in. He said to Pike:

"That's quite right, sir. There's only one public garage in Holmdale. It's down by Chaser's Bridge."

"Thanks," Pike nodded. "Now, Mr. Spring, what were you doing at the garage?"

"What the bloody hell d'you think I was doing at the garage? I was putting my car away, of course. I keep my car there. It's too big to go into the garage at the house. Besides, our other car's always there!"

"I see. And am I to understand that you had come straight into Holmdale from outside and gone straight to the garage to put your car away and were walking directly home?"

"You are."

"Where had you been outside Holmdale, Mr. Spring?"

"You must forgive me for saying so—I'm afraid I don't know who you are—but it does seem to take you a very long time to get an idea into your head. . . . I'd been working. I told you that. All day. And I've got to work all day to-morrow, and I should be very, very much obliged if I could go home. If you're looking for this lunatic who calls himself the Butcher, it's not me, although I'm not at all sure I'm not beginning to sympathize with him."

Pike smiled at that. "All right, sir. But we can't help being slow, you know. We've got to be careful. I'm afraid I'm still not clear on this point. Where, exactly, do you work?"

The tight and somehow fish-like mouth of Mr. Spring opened in amazement. He shut it again with a decisive click so loud as to betray the origin of his splendid teeth.

"Good God!" he said, and then: "Sorry! I'm a film director. I'm at present working outside Holmdale at the Empire Studios in Enswood. You may have heard of the picture. It's called *Death in the Sky*. I've got half the Air Force out on the job——"

"Yes. Yes. And you finished work at the Empire Studios, Mr. Spring, at what time?"

"I don't clock off, but I should say that when I finally got away it must have been about . . . let me see . . . I came home at a steady eighty, and it's about seventeen miles from Enswood. . . . You can say I left Enswood at between twenty and ten to twelve, getting to the garage at about twelve and getting hauled in by your busybodies at just after midnight. I was going home, and, I might tell you, looking forward to a whisky and soda and some food."

Pike nodded. "I see. Was there anyone in the garage, Mr. Spring, when you put the car away? Any night porter or anything?"

Spring was silent for a moment. Behind the horn-rimmed spectacles his hot brown eyes were veiled under heavy lids. He said:

"Can't remember. . . . Let me see. . . . No, don't think I saw anyone. I've got a special private lock-up there. All I did was just to ram the bus inside, lock the door, and start off for home."

"I see. Did you happen to notice whether you passed anyone, Mr. Spring, between your entrance to Holmdale from the main road and your arrival at the garage?"

"Couldn't say." Spring shrugged. The black felt hat which had been balanced on the back of his chair fell to the ground with a soft plop. "I wasn't looking, of course."

"I shay," said Mr. Godly, "I shay!"

"Did anyone, Mr. Spring," said Pike, "happen to see you leave the studios at Enswood? I suppose there's a gatekeeper there or someone?"

"I shay," said Mr. Godly indignantly, "the chap's dropped hish hat. Hatsh on the floor. Shomeone might have the deshenshy pick it up."

"Yes, there's a gatekeeper," Spring said. He paused a moment. "Half a minute, though, he wasn't there to-night, I remember noticing, and the gates were open. I say, though——"

"Well, that doesn't matter, sir. There's sure to have been someone on your staff about when you left the studio building."

Spring laughed—an awkward little sound. "Funny thing, but I'm pretty certain there wasn't, now I come to think of it. I sent them all home about half an hour before I left myself. I was going with the others, and I suddenly remembered some notes I had to make for the morning. I went back to my room and jotted them down. . . . Now I come to think of it, I don't suppose there was a soul saw me from the time my assistant went till I was pulled in by your men."

"I shay, ol' chap," said Mr. Godly, "I shay, d'you know your hatsh on the floor?"

Again Spring laughed. He was staring hard at Pike. "Makes it a bit awkward, doesn't it? I mean the whole thing's perfectly absurd. . . ." His tone was noticeably milder.

Pike leaned near to Jeffson and said something to him in a voice so low that it did not carry to any other ears in the room.

Jeffson nodded. "Yes, they did, sir. Nothing."

Pike sat back in his chair again and once more looked at Spring.

"If shomeone," said Mr. Godly suddenly, "doeshn't pick that hat up, *I'm* going to. Can't shtant hatsh on the floor."

"I think," said Pike, "that if you'd like to get along home now, Mr. Spring, we could arrange it. No doubt we can get hold of you at any time if we want any further information."

Behind their shields of glass and tortoise shell Spring's eyes for a moment looked astonished. But he said, after a moment's pause: "Thanks. . . . Thanks. . . . Very good of you." He stood up—a short, chunky figure. He stooped and picked up the black felt hat.

"Thank God!" said Mr. Godly. "Can't shtand sheeing hatsh on floor."

Constable Birch opened the door. With a jerky, bouncing walk, Spring went to it. He paused on the threshold, half turned, and flung a "Good-night" over his shoulder.

There was a murmur in answer, and he was gone.

Pike said to Jeffson, "Sure they went over him?"

"The special assured me of that, sir. It's written down in these notes here. They went through all his pockets. There's nowhere he could be carrying a weapon." Jeffson's jaw suddenly dropped. "Unless . . ."

"Exactly," Pike said. "Tell you what: Send this man down to the garage now, to go over every inch of that car. He'll have to do it without a warrant, but he should be able to, if he's sensible."

"The best man I've got," Jeffson said.

The round, childlike face of Constable Birch warmed to a rich red flood of colour.

"And now," said Pike, "what about *this?*" He was looking at Mr. Godly.

Mr. Godly was by this time fast asleep. His head lolled so that his left cheek lay cosily upon his left shoulder. His mouth was wide open. He looked like a stupid, happy child.

Jeffson got up, took two heavy strides, and stood over the sleeper. Jeffson's finger and thumb clamped themselves upon Mr. Godly's right ear and twisted.

"Wow!" said Mr. Godly, awake.

Jeffson went back to his chair.

"Mr. Godly," said Pike. His tone was very different from that which he had used to Wilfred Spring. "Mr. Godly, pull yourself together. I want you to answer a few simple questions. Do you understand?"

"No," said Mr. Godly. "Not one little bit."

Jeffson coughed. He said to Pike:

"He's three parts canned all his time and now he's right under, if you follow me."

Pike's mouth twitched to a half smile. He was saying, "All right, keep him here till he can talk," when the telephone rang. Jeffson strode to it and plucked off the receiver.

"Hallo!" he said. "Yes, Jeffson speaking. . . . I was just going to ring you. . . . Where is 'e? . . . What d'you say? Well, it doesn't matter a damn who 'e is, 'e ought to have been up here by this time, even if 'e was the Archangel Gabriel. . . . Eh! what's that? I can't hear you. . . . And who the hell told you to do that? Oh! . . . *All right!*"

Jeffson slammed back the receiver onto its hook with a jar that might have broken it. He turned a frowning face to Pike.

He said, "That third man was a doctor. Dr. Reade. Practises 'ere. They were just bringin' him up 'ere when they get stopped by Colonel Grayling——"

"And who," said Pike, "is Colonel Grayling?"

"Head of our branch of specials. Colonel Grayling knows Dr. Reade very well, like we all do. Well, Colonel Grayling tells the patrol—who, very unfortunatelike, were specials and not our men —it's sheer foolishness to arrest Dr. Reade and that you won't want to see 'im. And then they go and loose him at once!"

Pike's brows met together in a harsh, deep-cut frown. "Where's this Reade live?" he said.

"Marrowbone Lane, sir. 172. Big house on the left at the Market Road end. Maybe you've seen it."

"Come on!" Pike said.

2

It was ten minutes past one when the blue police Crossley pulled up outside No. 172, Marrowbone Lane. Pike switched off lights and engine.

"This the place?" he said.

"That's right, sir. Empty or all asleep, by the looks of it."

They stood at the gate looking through the darkness at the dim bulk of a low-built, verandaed house.

Pike leaned his elbows on the gate. "Reade married?"

"Yes." Jeffson dropped his voice. "But Mrs. Reade's away. Been away for some months now. Besides Dr. Reade, there's a house-keeper and a maidservant. Oh! and, of course, there's the dispenser; but I don't think she sleeps in. She's a Holmdale girl—Marjorie Williams."

Pike put his hand to the latch of the gate, passed through, and went up the path. His boot soles rang out a brisk tattoo upon the frozen path. He made no effort to dull their sound. Jeffson followed. They came to the end of the path and three steps which brought them up to the veranda. They crossed the veranda and were at the door. There were two bells on it, one with "Night" written above it in bold letters of brass. There was also a heavy iron knocker wrought like a snake. Pike set his thumb on the bell marked "Night." From somewhere within the house came to their ears a steady peal. He took his thumb away. They waited. After two minutes' waiting, he once more pressed the bell. This time he held his thumb upon it. The pealing went on within, steady and insistent, but they could hear no other sound. Pike lowered his hand.

"Knock!" he said.

Jeffson knocked.

"Knock harder!" Pike said.

Jeffson knocked harder.

Pike pressed both bells. . . . And then a light shone out above their heads, and there came the sound of a window violently flung open and a voice which said:

"What the devil's all this row?"

Pike nudged Jeffson. Jeffson went back off the veranda and stood in the path looking upwards.

"I'm Sergeant Jeffson," he said. "I'm afraid we must trouble you to come downstairs and let us in."

There was a muttering from the window, its words indistinguishable. Jeffson came back up the steps onto the veranda and stood beside Pike at the doorway. They heard movement within the house and then footsteps descending the stairs and coming along the hallway towards them. Bolts were drawn and there was the clanging of a safety chain. The door opened, and the lantern above the door sprang into light.

"Dr. Reade?" said Pike. He was looking at a thickly built, broad-shouldered man in the middle thirties, with a white heavy-jowled face under wiry and crisply curling jet-black hair. The black brows were a straight bar across his face and from under them bright, almost black eyes darted flickering glances.

"That's me," said the man in the door. "What do *you* want?"

Pike put a foot across the threshold. For a moment it seemed that Reade was going to bar his entrance, but almost at once he drew back.

"Come in!" he said.

Behind Pike came Jeffson. Reade moved away from them. They could hear him near them, fumbling at the wall. There was the click of a switch and three wall lamps shed a soft gold glow over the hall. Pike looked about him. He said:

"Can we talk here, sir?"

Reade's eyes darted glances this way and that; everywhere except at the faces of his two visitors.

"No," he said. "Better come into my office." He led the way to a door in the right-hand wall, opened it, and stood while they passed through before him.

Jeffson, burly and blue-clad but helmetless, stood with his back to a fireplace in which there flickered an electric fire. Pike, in answer to unspoken invitation, sat in one of the red-leather armchairs. There was a small, square oaken table in the centre of the room, and upon the edge of this its owner sat himself. He looked from one of his visitors to the other, furtively almost.

"We understand, sir," said Pike, "that you were taken up by one of the patrols this evening at some time after midnight. Mistakenly and against my orders they released you immediately——"

"I'm not clear," said Reade, "exactly who you are." His deep voice was querulously angry.

"I am from Scotland Yard, sir," Pike said. "At the present moment, I am, as you might say, in charge of the police activities." His tone was bland. "I must inform you, sir, that at about nine-thirty this evening we were informed that another murder had taken place. Immediately I had verified this, I gave word to all the patrols that any persons found in the streets of this town should be held, pending investigation of their movements. Mistakenly and against my instructions, the patrol let you go. In these circumstances, Sergeant Jeffson and I came round to have a word with you and to ask you to explain to us where you had been this evening. This is a matter of form, of course, but one which must, in the interest of the whole community, be carried out."

"Yes. . . . Yes," Reade said. "Of course. . . . Yes, I see." He raised his head, flinging it back with a movement almost theatrically defiant. "I suppose you want to ask me a lot of questions. Isn't that the way you do it?"

Pike shrugged. "Well, sir, that's as you like. You can either make a statement on which we may want to ask you questions afterwards, or you can answer my questions as I put them to you without making any original statement at all."

Reade swallowed. "There's nothing to say, really. But I'll have a try . . . when I was stopped by the patrol, it was a few minutes after midnight. I was walking down Broad Walk, coming in this direction. I've been overworked lately and suffering from insomnia. To-night I went to bed just after dinner. I thought I *could* sleep to-night. I soon knew sleep was impossible unless I took drastic measures. So I went out for a walk. I daresay it was foolish of me and may seem incredible to you, but my own state of mind had made me forget all about this—this Butcher business. I just went out as I would've done at any normal time in the same circumstances. I walked straight up Marrowbone Lane, round the Poultry Farm, and back down Runborough Lane, across the Playing Fields, and into the top of Broad Walk like that. I was halfway down Broad Walk when I was stopped. . . . That's all!" He sat staring at Pike. The eyes, Pike thought, were covered with a hard, protective glaze through which a man could see nothing of feeling.

Pike pondered. "Tell me, sir," he said after a moment, "while you were on this walk, how many people did you see before you met the patrol?"

Reade shook his head. "None." His mouth shut, after the word, in a hard, lipless line.

"No one at all?"

"No one."

"And how long would you say your walk occupied, Dr. Reade?"

The broad shoulders lifted, dejectedly. "I can't give you any accurate estimation. All I can swear to is that I wasn't out for less than an hour or more than two."

There ensued a long silence. Jeffson, shifting from one foot to the other, looked first at the doctor's pallid defiance and then at the inscrutability of Pike. Jeffson knew what he would do, yet had a sinking suspicion that this would be wrong. A good man, Jeffson, and one knowing his own limitations. He waited for what should happen. When it came it was so unexpected an anticlimax that he let out a little gasp, instantly repressed.

For Pike got to his feet and said:

"Well, thank you very much, Dr. Reade. I'm sorry to have had to disturb you." He looked round for his hat, which lay upon a chair to the left of the door. He made for it. "We'll be getting along, Jeffson," he said.

Reade sprang to his feet. "Look here!" he said violently. "What I——" And then closed his mouth into a tight line.

Pike stooped to pick up his hat; turned with it in his hand. "Yes, sir?" He was suave.

"Nothing," said Reade. "Nothing!"

Pike set his fingers to the door handle but dropped them as if struck by a sudden thought. "I'm sorry," he said. "Just one more question. Is there anyone besides yourself, Dr. Reade, sleeping in the house?"

There was a little movement of Reade's bulk; a recoil. "Housekeeper," he said.

Pike raised his eyebrows. "No one else?"

"No." Reade shook his head.

Pike took his soft hat in both hands and began to knead the brim. He seemed diffidence itself. "I wonder," he said, "whether we might have a few words with your housekeeper?"

Reade seemed to have grown bigger. As he stood, he looked taller, burlier, more self-assured. "What the devil for?" he said.

"Verification," said Pike. "I'm sure you'll see, sir, that it may save you some unpleasantness, as you might say, and us, perhaps, some work, if we could get some nearer hint as to the time you left the house. . . ."

"Good God!" said Reade. "D'you want to wake the poor woman up? She was in bed and asleep before I went to bed."

"Mrs. Reade, sir," said Pike inconsequently, "is away, I understand?"

"Thank God," Reade said. He came round the corner of the table and stood to face Pike.

Pike laid his hat on the chair from which he had just taken it. "I think, sir," he said, "it would be best if we saw the housekeeper." He turned for an instant, and his eyes met Jeffson's.

It was to Jeffson's credit that he understood. He came forward from the fireplace. He said heavily, looking at Reade:

"Isn't there a maid, too?"

Reade glared. He said, answering Jeffson's question but looking at Pike:

"There *was* a maid. I discharged her last week. She was impertinent and unsatisfactory. My housekeeper's been looking for another girl but so far hasn't got one. Therefore the only person in the house besides myself to-night is Mrs. Flewin."

"I see, sir." Beneath the diffidence of Pike's tone had come a subtle hardness. "Now, what I think's best is that you take Sergeant Jeffson here and go and wake this Mrs. Flewin and tell her you would be much obliged if she would answer some questions which Sergeant Jeffson will put to her."

Reade stood motionless while the two policemen watched him. "Oh! *All* right!" he said at last. He swung himself off the table, passed Pike and went to the door. He set his hand to the doorknob and turned. "This way, Sergeant," he said, and Jeffson crossed like a silent and agile elephant to the door.

Pike, straining his ears to listen, heard the footsteps—Reade's quick and light, like a cat's; Jeffson's solid and ponderous—go down the hall, turn left, and begin the ascent of carpeted stairs.

When the sound of the footsteps had died away and been replaced, after a small bridge of silence, by a rat-tatting of knuckles against a door, Pike ceased to listen. He crossed the office and sat himself upon the table in the spot where Reade had been sitting. He pulled from a pocket an oilskin pouch and a new but pleasantly maturing pipe. He began to fill the pipe. The filling was complete and the pouch rolled up and once more put away when he heard, following a broken murmur of voices, feet coming down the stairs—three pairs of feet this time: two leather-clad and softly ringing, the other soft and slipshod. He slipped off the table and crossed with light steps to the door. He waited, leaning against the door jamb, so that without obtruding himself into the passage he could see the foot of the stairs.

He saw the little procession. Reade first, and then an elderly and many-angled female wrapped in a dressing gown of blue flannel, with curling pins clustered thick about her head. And lastly Jeffson, blue-clad and silver-buttoned, heavy and stolid. At the foot of the stairs the cortège halted opposite a door which Reade flung open. The woman passed in first, and then Jeffson, already fumbling in a breast pocket for pencil and notebook.

Pike drew back a little. Down the hall towards him Reade came with slow steps. By the time he got to his office, Pike was once more seated upon the table. He had the filled but unlighted pipe in his mouth and a box of matches in his hand.

"Mind if I smoke in here?" he said.

Reade shook his head. "No!" he said savagely. "You can do anything in here. . . . After all, you're the big noise, aren't you?"

"I try," Pike said with urbanity, "not to make one."

Reade flung himself into a chair. He, too, pulled out pipe and tobacco. While he fumbled for matches he said:

"Well, Inspector or whatever you are, any more questions?"

Pike smiled. "I don't think I have any. Not yet, anyhow."

Reade laughed; a humourless sound, and there was dragging silence in the room until Jeffson came back. He stood in the doorway, seeming to fill it. He looked at Pike and, in answer to Pike's raised eyebrows, shook his head.

Once more Reade let out the harsh, barking laugh.

Pike got to his feet. "I think, sir," he said, "that that'll be all. For to-night." He turned towards the door.

Reade sat where he was. "You'll forgive me," he said, "if I leave you to let yourselves out." There was a sneer in voice as well as words, but there was something else behind the sneer. As Jeffson said to Pike when the car started, its headlights cutting a white swath down the blackness of Marrowbone Lane:

"Seemed to me, sir, as if 'e was scared!"

CHAPTER SEVEN

The car had not gone a hundred yards before Pike halted it.

"What is it?" Jeffson said.

"Had an idea," said Pike. "Get taken like that sometimes. Know the postmaster?"

"Yes, sir. Name of Myers."

Pike grunted. "Hmm! Where's he live?"

"'Bout two hundred yards away," Jeffson's tone showed endeavour to conceal curiosity.

Pike started the car. "Show me," he said. "I want you to knock him up, shove him into some clothes, and bring him along. Can do?"

In the darkness Jeffson nodded. "I can, sir. Know 'im well."

The car went on.

"Whoa, sir!" said Jeffson.

The car stopped. There was a scraping shuffle as Jeffson got out. Pike switched off the car's lights and waited in the darkness.

Pike lost himself in thought, until sounds from outside the car brought him to himself with a start. He shivered a little as he realized the cold. He leaned over and opened the door.

"'Ere's Mr. Myers!" came Jeffson's voice. "In you get, Myers."

Behind Pike there came a scrambling and puffing, and then the sound of a body settling itself upon the back cushions. Jeffson climbed in beside Pike. Once more the headlights cut a swath through the night. The car moved off, and the driver said:

"What's the nearest way to the postoffice?"

"First left, second right, first left," came a high, eager voice from the back.

The car devoured the half mile in a couple of minutes; stopped with a squeal of brakes and a flurry of gravel.

"Out you get!" said Pike, and within a moment was peering at a thin and bespectacled person introduced by Jeffson as Mr. Myers, our postmaster.

"I don't know yet, Mr. Myers, what the superintendent wants. . . ."

"Easy!" Pike said. "Can we get in? Got a key, Mr. Myers?"

Mr. Myers had a key and, leading them round to the back of the small brick-tiled postoffice, used it.

The side door of the postoffice clicked behind them. They stood in darkness until at a touch of the postmaster's fingers lights sprang up all about them.

"This," said Mr. Myers, "is the Sorting Office." He peered at Pike with an avid curiosity. "Now, sir?"

Pike looked about him and saw two desks, walls bare save for almanacs and a clock, and three long trestle tables. The windows of the room—long, narrow windows—were barred and netted. "Sorting Office, eh?" said Pike. "Now, then, Mr. Myers, that nine o'clock collection. The nine o'clock is the last collection, isn't it?"

"Except," said Mr. Myers, "in the very outlyin' boxes like Arrowcourt, Forest Road, Two Tiddlers Corner over the Other Side, and such, the last collection is nine, Superintendent. With a final collection here at nine-thirty."

"Right!" said Pike. "When are letters cleared at this last collection sorted?"

"The succeeding day, Superintendent, at 5 A. M."

"I want to see 'em," said Pike.

"Cer-tainly, cer-tainly!" Mr. Myers bounded at a small door facing the one by which they had entered. It swung upwards and closed again, only to reopen a moment later to admit the back of Mr. Myers bent into the shape of a C. Mr. Myers was dragging with both hands and all his inconsiderable weight at a bulky mail sack. With Jeffson's help the sack was hoisted to one of the tables, tilted, and emptied of a cascade of envelopes and cards and little parcels. Pike, with eager fingers and a look of concentration which lent a sharp, knife-like appearance to his lean face, burrowed into the great scattered pile of paper.

"Hah!" he said suddenly, and straightened himself.

"God strike me dead!" said Jeffson. He was staring at what Pike was holding in his right hand. A square, yellowish envelope bearing a superscription in a backward-sloping script with jet-black, shining ink.

Pike, the envelope between his fingers, advanced upon Mr. Myers. "Any way of telling which box this came out of?"

Mr. Myers shook his head decisively. " 'Fraid not, Superintendent." His eyes on the envelope, he was pale.

Pike produced a penknife, laid the envelope down, and with

great care not to touch more of its surface than was necessary, carefully slit it open.

Delicately, he drew out the envelope's contents. Three sheets of paper this time. He opened the first. He read. Over his shoulders the other men read too. They saw:

My Reference THREE
R. I. P.
Amy Adams,
died Monday, 26th November . . .

THE BUTCHER.

Pike opened the second sheet. It read:

My Reference FOUR
R. I. P.
Albert Rogers
died Friday, 30th November . . .

THE BUTCHER.

Pike opened the third sheet. It read:

DEAR POLICE:

Enclosed please find my memos regarding those unfortunates, Amy Adams and Albert Rogers.

I really am so very sorry that I am late with my memo in regard to Amy Adams, but pressure of business (after all, you know, I have had a lot of staff work to do) has made it impossible for me to let you have this earlier.

I must now pass quickly on to the main point of this letter, which is to tell you to keep your spirits up. I quite realize how disheartening, to say the least, it must be for you never to know when and how and where and who I am going to strike next. I hate causing unnecessary pain to others and am, therefore, undertaking to give you warning wherever possible of any future little jobs which I may be contemplating. This will, don't you think? add quite a spice of excitement to our game.

Believe me, Police
Yours tolerantly,
THE BUTCHER.

CHAPTER EIGHT

(Extracts* from personal report to Assistant Commissioner C. I. D. by Detective Superintendent Arnold Pike. Dated Saturday, December 1, . . . Received Scotland Yard by special messenger 11:30 P. M. same day.)

Arrived Holmdale with Sergeants Blaine and Curtis at 2:30 P. M. on Wednesday the 28th ult. Was met by chief constable of county and Inspectors Davis and Farrow. Sent Blaine and Curtis to pick up what they could from local constabulary, under Sergeant Jeffson, and proceeded myself immediately to meeting with chief constable and two inspectors above mentioned. Relations between myself and inspectors at first strained. Usual resentment, though under control, fairly evident. Smoothed matters down and am now on good terms. Both inspectors capable men. C. C. content to leave real control to me. At meeting learnt of steps already taken to safeguard population against further outrage. Scheme (for an unavoidably hurried and patchwork measure) very good, but naturally merely protective. (I attach copy of the scheme with pencil notes in its margin showing the alterations and additions I have proposed and which have been carried out.)

THURSDAY, 29TH ULT.

Put in long day, with two conferences not worth reporting, and many hours reading mass of documentary evidence (all of it worthless) collected by police in regard to first three murders. During day was 'phoned for by local sergeant to go to station, as a man had just given himself up, stating that he was the Butcher. Sergeant in a state of excitement. Proceeded immediately to station. Found elderly man, in state of nervous collapse, who stated himself to be

* It should be noted that although these are extracts there are no germane points whatsoever omitted. The only omissions are of purely routine and, in this context, unnecessary detail. For instance, plans of patrol placing and details of the patrol scheme quoted by Pike as being attached to the document are among the omissions.

Edward William Marsh, a Holmdale resident. Failed to get any coherent statement from him, merely reiteration of "I did it. I did it. I am the Butcher." At once sent Curtis to Marsh's house, where, after inquiry of his sister who keeps house for him, it was found, beyond doubt, that upon all the occasions when the murders were being done, Marsh was in the house. He is a mild epileptic and, according to Dr. Reade, his medical adviser, a neurotic subject. Called doctor, who recommended removal to a nursing home. Since this "confession" there have been three more. Two from elderly women, and one from a garage mechanic known to be "simple." Have also had trouble with would-be detectives, vindictive gossips, and overimaginative persons. These troubles so acute and apparently so upsetting to the normal work of the local police that have put Curtis in sole charge of this side. Everyone properly investigated but must note that have very little faith in catching our man this way. Curtis doing invaluable work. Blaine on patrol organization. His report for last three days copied below.

PROGRESS

Naturally no actual progress except in regard to safety measures. I have, however, satisfied myself upon one or two points which should go some way towards eventual solution. In order to make these points more clear, I give table of murders. Would like to have this studied carefully before my conclusions are read.

CONCLUSIONS DRAWN FROM COMPARISON OF MURDERS

(1)   The expert opinion (see attached docs.) tends to prove that all wounds were caused by the same implement. All wounds are the same except in the case of Amy Adams, the girl killed in the theatre, where there was only the piercing and not the post-piercing rip. (This latter accounted for by need for extra caution on murderer's part owing to locus of murder.)

(2)   Every case a Butcher letter.

(3)   Implication must be that murderer is not only a resident in Holmdale, but one who has some intimate connection with Holmdale in all its class spheres. As proof of this we have:

(a)   Murderer's knowledge of who his victim is (in the case of Pamela Richards it is true that there were cards in a pocket which the murderer could have seen, but there were only initials on Lionel Colby's clothes. There were *no* identifying marks or papers upon Amy Adams, nor would the murderer have had time to look at them if there had been. And on Albert Rogers the only means of identification was a crumpled and torn envelope which had not been disturbed from his pocket and from which his name had been almost obliterated).

(b)   Silent delivery by hand, during the night, of the letters in the case of Pamela Richards (showing too, murderer's knowledge of Holmdale geography).

(c)   The very short time in which these letters must have been prepared (such a short time that it looks almost, in some cases, as though the murderer must have known beforehand whom he was going to murder).

(d)   (See separate conclusion No. 4 below, which applies separately but is also proof of this conclusion.)

(4)   That the Butcher chooses for his victims young persons of either sex

(a)   whose deaths come at a time when they are having a run of good fortune, and

(b)   who leave behind them persons, *resident in Holmdale,* to whom the deaths are more than usually painful.

Summarizing these points (at the risk of repetition) I submit, as a final conclusion, the following:

That these are a pervert's "lust murders" with a triple satisfaction in them for the murderer (i. e., the killing itself; the youth and happiness of the victim, and finally the observation of the distress caused by the killings), and that the murderer is a resident of Holmdale, who has business, or perhaps official opportunities of mixing with all classes of the community, *and therefore is certain to be found, not among the labouring classes or skilled workman class, but must belong to the clerical or governing class, probably the latter of these.*

Further reference yesterday's case of Albert Rogers. This is the first of the cases which has happened while I have been in charge. I accordingly submit précis of steps taken. Using fifty men in charge of Curtis and Blaine, had carried out, between 7:30 A. M. and 3:30 P. M. a house-to-house canvass. Each householder, or householder's representative, had submitted to him the following form of questionnaire.

(1)   Give particulars of all people staying in this house as from evening of November 25th to December 1st.

(2)   Were all these persons in the house last night?

(3)   If not, who was absent, during what times, and why?

TABLE A

Name	Age	Cause of Death	Type of Place	Time and Date	Social Standing	
Lionel Colby	11	Stomach pierced, then ripped	Populated road	Approx. 9:30 P. M., 23d Nov.	Clerical class	Only child. Brilliant at studies. Very athletic. Capt. school football team. Promising little boxer. Both parents devoted. Butcher letter received per post by Police, Holmdale Company chairman and editor Holmdale *Clarion*. Postmarked Holmdale, 10 A. M., Nov. 24th.
Pamela Richards	19	As above	In motorcar on semi-populated road	Between midnight, 25th Nov. and 5 A. M., 26th Nov.	Leisured class	Very popular. Beautiful. Parents devoted. Troublesome engagement broken off at girl's own wish. Happier engagement foreshadowed. Butcher letter received next morning, having been delivered by hand.
Amy Adams	17	Stomach pierced but not ripped	Theatre lounge	Between 9 and 9:30 P. M. 26th Nov.	Labouring class	Winner of County Beauty Contest, and therefore possible source of increased income to family. Butcher notice (see attached docs.) found on body. Butcher letter delivered with Albert Rogers' below.
Albert Rogers	21	Same as Colby and Richards above	Unpopulated road	Between 6:30 and 9 P. M., 30th Nov.	Skilled workman class	Ambition realized by recent engagement as professional footballer. No parents, but "walking out" with girl. Football engagement would have made marriage quickly possible. Butcher letter found in post early A. M. 1st December.

NOTE.—For steps taken by local police immediately following discovery of murders 1, 2, and 3, see documentary extracts attached. These need not be carefully considered, as they are nonproductive, though this is no fault of the police work, which seems to have been as efficient as can be expected. In regard to 4, Albert Rogers, this murder was done last night and the steps I have taken to deal with it are outlined below, but after my statement of conclusions to be drawn from above table.

(4)   If unable to state why, give present whereabouts of absent person.

These reports are now being checked, so far with no result. The questionnaire was easily filled in as regards individual houses, but as regards block of flats, and one guest house or hotel, results cannot be hoped to be so satisfactory. I do not anticipate a definite result from this questionnaire, but felt the step ought to be taken, particularly as, if it brings no suspicious movements to light at all other than those we know about already (see below), we shall have a basis for supposing that the Butcher is (i) *a householder, living alone,* or (ii) a householder who has the coöperation of his household (most unlikely) or (iii) *a resident in the flats or hotel.*

SUSPICIOUS PERSONS HELD BY AUTHORITIES

After my inspection of body at 11 P. M. three men were held by the authorities—W. Spring, P. Godly, and Dr. Reade. All are residents. For details of questioning, etc., please see Sergeant Jeffson's notes attached.

The murder was reported by the Rev. Rockwall. His movements were questioned, and a report of the questions and answers is also attached.

I have not detained any of these four men, though none of their stories can be called satisfactory. I have let them go, but am having them watched. I can do no good at the present stage by wholesale and indiscriminate arrests.

Further reports as to progress in the Rogers case will be submitted from time to time.

PROPOSALS

Subject to not receiving contrary instructions from you, I propose to put the two following schemes into operation at such time as I think fit.

(1)   To expend a certain sum, probably not in excess of £ 30, in having a concealed light fitted over the wall letter box at the main postoffice here. The letters posted into this box go straight down the shoot into the first sorting room. The proposed light will be controlled from the bottom of the shoot. As from the installation of the light, a man will be constantly on duty at the foot of the shoot, and as soon as he sees one of the yellow Butcher envelopes, he will press the switch. The light will then flash momentarily from the top of the box. There will be outside the postoffice, inconspicuously, three plainclothes men, who, on seeing the light,

will, by signal, close the single road which leads between the post-office and the Market. Anyone who has been observed to post a letter during the time immediately preceding the flashing of the light will then be held and questioned. I have chosen the main letter box for the obvious reasons that such a scheme could not be carried out at outlying pillar boxes, and also because I think it highly probable that the Butcher letters are all posted at the main box, this being more frequently used and therefore less liable to provide opportunity for observation. This scheme may have many weaknesses, but we must try everything in the circumstances. I submit that any constructive scheme is better than none. I should be glad of authority for the expenditure.

(2) To obtain similar paper and ink to those with which the Butcher writes his letters, have his disguised handwriting carefully imitated, and start a fake correspondence of my own, addressing the letters to the same three people (the editor of the *Holmdale Clarion,* the chairman of the Holmdale Company, and the sergeant of police) in the hope that I may thus force the Butcher into some slip. I do not propose taking this course at present, but submit it herewith for consideration and comment.

(NOTE.—The obvious objection to any schemes of the sort outlined above is that, to be a hundred per cent. efficient, such schemes should be carried out with the coöperation only of persons who are demonstrably not capable of being the Butcher. In the case of the fake letters this could be done, but I am afraid in the case of the letter-box suggestion, one or two Holmdale persons will *have* to be "in the know." I would, however, pick those with due regard to the improbability of their being in any way connected with the outrages.)

ARNOLD PIKE,
Superintendent.

2

(Additional report enclosed in same envelope as full report above. Dated 1st December, and time 5:30 P. M., marked "Confidential and Urgent.")

Further to my long report enclosed herewith of to-day, and in confirmation of telephone message just now—I have to report that at 4:45 P. M. this afternoon, Mrs. W. Reade, wife of Dr. Reade (one of the persons mentioned in the long report as being taken by the authorities last night) called at the police station and informed the sergeant in charge that, returning unexpectedly from a long holiday, she had found that Dr. Reade's dispenser, a Miss Marjorie Williams, had left the house on the afternoon of yesterday (Friday, the 30th), and had not since returned. The housekeeper, Mrs. Flewin (see also statements attached to long report) had heard Miss Williams in an agitated voice answering the telephone at about half-past two in the afternoon and had then seen her rush out of the house, pulling on her coat as she ran, and holding a hat in her hand. She (Mrs. Flewin) had been in her room upstairs at the time. She had told Mrs. Reade that she had assumed at the time that Miss Williams had thought her away from the house, as it was her afternoon off. Dr. Reade had been out at the time. He had returned just before dinner at about seven o'clock, and then acted as set out in attached report.

On interviewing Mrs. Reade myself, I soon discovered that she is jealous of her husband and Miss Williams. It seems to have been some rumour that there was a liaison between these two which had brought her back on this unexpected visit to her home. I asked her why she thought it necessary to come to the police because Miss Williams had gone out and failed to return. She replied that Miss Williams, though a Holmdale resident, lived alone, was an orphan, and had no one to look after her, and that this curious behaviour seemed to her (Mrs. Reade) especially in view of the recent outrages, a matter in which the police should be informed. I tried to gather from the lady what Dr. Reade's attitude would be towards her action in coming to the police. She stated that she had not yet seen her husband, but thought that he would be annoyed. This did not, however, deter her from endeavouring to do her duty. I am trying to get in touch with the plainclothes man watching Dr. Reade, and if there is anything in his report which shows Dr. Reade's movements to have been at all suspicious, I shall use one of my special warrants and hold him for the time being.

ARNOLD PIKE.

P. S.—Dr. Reade has returned, and the plainclothes man D/O Harboard is now with me. He reports as follows:

"Reade left house 11 A. M. this morning and proceeded on (apparently) usual round of medical visits, returning own house 12:45 P. M. After lunch (2:00 P. M.) Reade again left house and got into car. I followed. For three hours he drove round and about

Holmdale (on outskirts) frequently stopping car and descending to enter copses and thickets. Owing to necessity of being unobserved could not get very close while he was thus away from car; from what I could see, however, he seemed to be watching for something in every instance. Behaviour very strange. Demeanour nervous, apprehensive, excited. Returned home 5:03 P. M."

Under these circumstances I am taking immediate steps to execute warrant so that Reade may be held pending further investigation.

There is, of course, nothing yet to connect Reade's strange behaviour with the outrages, but his unaccountable "walk" last night and unsatisfactory statements, added to his behaviour this afternoon, have made me decide that he must be held for the time being, at least. I shall charge him according to the formula you devised for emergency arrests during this case.

CHAPTER NINE

According to many, the chief among Holmdale's much advertised amenities is the fact that the bars of the Wooden Shack open every morning at ten. At one minute and thirty seconds past ten, Mr. Percy Godly leaned over the wooden counter of the saloon bar.

"George!" said Mr. Godly. "George!" He rapped upon the counter with a florin. "George! For God's sake, George, I'm waiting!"

George came at last. "Mornin', sir," said George. "Usual?"

Mr. Godly nodded, "But make it a double."

George busied himself with a large glass and many bottles. Mr. Godly, anxious to while away the time until the filled glass should be his, picked up a copy of the *Holmdale Clarion* which lay upon the bar counter. With unsteady fingers he flicked it open and began to read. . . .

"Jumping Gabriel!" said Mr. Godly. "What's all this?"

George set the glass, now nine tenths full, gently upon the counter before his customer. "What's all what, sir?" said George.

"All this," said Mr. Godly, and read aloud:

"PROMINENT HOLMDALE GIRL MISSING.
MYSTERY OF DOCTOR'S DISPENSER.
WHERE IS MARJORIE WILLIAMS?

"The *Clarion* learns with alarm and consternation that Miss Marjorie Williams, a popular figure in Holmdale circles, has mysteriously disappeared. As all her friends are aware, Miss Williams was the able assistant and dispenser of Dr. Reade, one of Holmdale's leading physicians.

"On the afternoon of Friday last, the 30th November, Miss Williams was seen to leave Dr. Reade's house—Dr. Reade being absent upon his afternoon rounds—in what appeared to be an extremely agitated condition. Before leaving the house, Miss Williams had been heard to answer a telephone call and appeared to be much agitated thereby. On leaving the house, Miss Williams was seen, as she ran down the path into Marrowbone Lane, to be struggling into her coat. She carried her hat in her hand. She was seen thus leaving the house and was seen again at the junction of Marrowbone Lane and Holmer Road. After that she seems to have vanished into thin air!

"Nothing has been heard of Miss Williams since. The *Clarion* are empowered to offer a substantial reward to anyone able to inform the police, either through the *Clarion* or direct, of any further movements of Miss Williams, either upon Friday the 30th November or subsequently—either upon the Saturday or Sunday."

Mr. Godly finished his reading with an air of triumphant, if somewhat weary, melodrama. "What d'you think of that, George!" said Mr. Godly, and reaching for his glass, emptied it at a gulp.

George closed one eye, very knowingly.

"Same again," said Mr. Godly, pushing his glass forward.

George once more busied himself with bottles.

"Marjorie Williams?" Mr. Godly was saying to himself. "Marjorie Williams? Damn funny thing, George, I thought I knew all the girls in Holmdale."

Again George set down the glass, this time filled only to seven eighths of its capacity. "R!" said George darkly. "Tell you what you ain't done, sir. You ain't looked at the Stop Press. 'Ave a dekko at that!"

Mr. Godly, having half emptied the second glass, turned for the paper with fingers which already were a little steadier. Again Mr. Godly read, this time silently. He saw:

LATEST

Prominent Medico Detained by Police

The *Clarion* are authoritatively informed that following police inquiries regarding the disappearance of Miss Marjorie Williams, Dr. Reade has been detained by the police upon a certain charge.

LATER

Upon being interviewed, Mrs. Reade, the wife of Dr. Reade, stated emphatically that she was convinced of her husband's innocence of anything to do with Miss Williams' disappearance. "My husband," said Mrs. Reade, "is not that sort of man. I am sure that this dark mystery will shortly be cleared up and that those responsible for my husband's detention will be brought rapidly to book."

Mr. Godly pursed his loose-seeming lips and breathed out a small, thin whistle.

"What," said Mr. Godly, "d'you know about that, George?"

George shrugged his shoulders; a shrug which spoke volumes but which implied that what George did not know about anything which George might be asked was not worth knowing.

2

They were talking about it everywhere. In the Market; in the Wood Cutter—the Wooden Shack's only rival; in the factories; at the Golf Club; at the corners of the streets; in back gardens; in drawing rooms and lounges and parlours.

"I tell 'ee," George Farmer was saying in the public bar of the Wood Cutter, "my girl Francie, she bin an' seen 'um. She war goin' home, along about six last evenin', when a girt stubby sort of a feller joomped out of 'edge like. Girt face 'e 'ad on 'im, Francie said, like some sort of a goberlin."

"But this 'ere," said Ted Lorry, tapping the *Clarion*, "did say summat about a Dr. Reade."

George Farmer shook his head. George Farmer spat ruminatively into a far corner of the bar. "Carn't 'elp what paper says. This 'ere what joomped out of 'edge like on my Francie was a girt, stubby sort of a goberlin sort-of-a-chap."

3

Mr. Colby was on holiday. That is to say, he was at home and not at his office. Following his terrible loss, Mr. Colby had been granted by his office a month's leave of absence. He had wanted to take Mrs. Colby away from Holmdale for this month. But women, as Mr. Colby, in those happy days which seemed so far behind him, had often said, "were kittle cattle," and Mrs. Colby strangely preferred to stay in Holmdale and in their little house. Mr. Colby acceded to her wish, but had a private wish of his own that soon she would ask him, "Take me away." Personally he found that every corner of every street in Holmdale; that every square inch of every room in his house; that every sound and sight and smell in this neighbourhood reminded him of Lionel, and his one wish nowadays seemed to be to attain a state where thinking of Lionel was, if not impossible, at least infrequent. For to think of Lionel was, to Mr. Colby, most acutely painful. The thought of Lionel seemed to grip him with a cold bony hand which clamped its fingers about his insides.

Mr. Colby sat apathetic in his parlour. Beside him, upon the arm of his comfortable chair—the chair upon whose arm Lionel had so frequently been reprimanded for bouncing—there lay one of the now almost daily special editions of the *Holmdale Clarion*. Mr. Colby, sucking at an empty pipe, kept looking at this paper. He supposed that he wanted to read it, but although once or twice his mind had bidden his hands to take hold of this paper and bring it properly within his field of vision, so far his hands had refused to obey. . . .

Odd! thought Mr. Colby. He'd found this sort of thing happening more than once during the last week. And it seemed to be getting worse. This, he thought, would never do. . . . He made a great effort. A frown, deeper even than the perpetual frown which had come since Lionel's death, creased his brow. . . . The hands obeyed. They moved and took up the paper and opened it and held the centre page so that his eyes could properly read it. . . .

Mr. Colby read. For a few moments what his eyes were reading was not communicated to his brain. He went on staring at the same few lines of large-lettered print. As, however, his eyes did not move from these few lines, gradually their meaning sank into his mind.

Mr. Colby shot to his feet. Clutching the paper in a shaking hand, he blundered towards the door and ran out into the passage crying:

"Mother! *Mother!*"

Mrs. Colby's uncertain answer came faintly to him down the narrow stairs. Up them Mr. Colby blundered, falling and picking himself up without knowing he had fallen.

He blundered into the bedroom. Mrs. Colby was sitting huddled on the edge of the bed. During these past few days her plump comeliness seemed to have sagged, so that now she was, as it were, withered behind her shell. Her shoulders drooped. Her hair was lank and wispy. Under her eyes were two black half moons, and the eyes themselves had a glittering, permanent-seeming glaze.

"Mother!" said Mr. Colby, blundering to the bed and somehow seating himself beside his wife. He held out the paper.

Mrs. Colby turned dull eyes upon it. . . . She stared. She shut her eyes; then opened them wide.

"I don't believe it!" said Mrs. Colby.

Mr. Colby's fingers opened, and the paper fluttered down to the floor.

"My *God!*" said Mr. Colby. "My God! Don't believe it! Don't believe it! What d'you mean: Don't believe it!" He pointed a shaking hand down at the *Clarion,* making little stabbing movements with a stubby forefinger. "It says so in the paper," said Mr. Colby.

"I don't care," Mrs. Colby said dully. "I don't care. I don't believe it."

Mr. Colby sprang up from the bed, a wild, quaint little figure with, just for this instant, a certain power and dignity about it.

"If I had that man here!" said Mr. Colby.

Mrs. Colby shook her head wearily. "I don't care," she said. "I don't believe it."

Mr. Colby raged. *"Don't believe it!"* he mimicked savagely. "What d'you mean with your 'don't believe it'! . . . Can't you see it there, in the paper? Can't you see he's been arrested? Don't they know he's the Butcher? . . . My God!" said Mr. Colby. "If there was any justice in this heaven-forsaken world, they'd have him burnt to death." Suddenly, the force which had been in him went away. He was like a lighted candle, suddenly snuffed by ruthless finger and thumb. He fell on his knees by the bed. His head lolled awkwardly on Mrs. Colby's knees. Sobs shook him. Mrs. Colby put an absent-minded hand to his head and passed its fingers through his hair.

Over his head her lips still shaped the words: "I don't believe it!" And suddenly she said aloud, in a new, strange voice:

"It wasn't him. He's . . . human. . . . What killed Lionel wasn't human. . . ."

Upon her knees Mr. Colby's round, untidy head rolled like a child's.

4

"My dear," said Mrs. Lightfoot, "you can't *imagine* what I felt like! To think that man was here only last Tuesday, putting a swab down Ted's throat! And all the time he might have been murdering us all without anyone to stop him!"

"I know, Lucy," Mrs. Stirling nodded her head so hard that she bumped her chin on the top rail of the dividing fence. "I always did think there was something about him."

Mrs. Lightfoot pegged her husband's woollen drawers to the line with vicious thrusts. "That white face he's got, and that black hair . . ."

"I know! And those sort of wild-like eyes!" Mrs. Lightfoot shuddered, covering her face with her hands.

5

"Stands to reason!" Bilby thumped the work bench. "Stands to reason, you don't get a feller like that, a feller as'll stay up all night same as 'e did with my Jack, lookin' after a sick kid—you don't get a feller like that goin' round stickin' daggers into innercent people's stummicks. Stands to reason!"

"Stands to reason my arse!" said Bilby's mate. "Here's this dispenserer of 'is, vanished like. And there 'e is, wandering about the same night young Bert Rogers is done in! . . . Course 'e's the Butcher. All I wisht is they'd let the guy out and let a few o' the boys get at 'im. It'd do more good, that would, than 'angin'!"

The voice of the foreman chipped in on the conversation. In the foreman's hand was a copy of the same edition of the *Clarion* as that which lay upon the bench between Bilby and his argumentative mate.

"You," said the foreman's voice, "can say what you qualified-well like. This 'ere doctor may 'ave done away with this 'ere sus-pencer, but what I *can* tell you is this: this 'ere doctor is *not* the 'Olmdale Butcher. And I'll tell you for why: this 'ere doctor ain't the 'Olmdale Butcher 'cos 'e don't look no more like the 'Olmdale Butcher than your foot, Bilby, looks like the Queen's!" The fore-man came near to Bilby. He bent until his face was opposite Bilby's and prodded Bilby in the chest with a bony forefinger which felt like the end of a spanner. The foreman sank his voice until it be-came a sinister and rasping whisper.

"The 'Olmdale Butcher, Bilby," said the foreman, "'*as bin seen.*"

"Coo!" said Bilby.

"Yes," said the foreman. "Seen by a reliable witness—my brother-in-law. I dunno whether you knows my brother-in-law, but 'e works at Breakfast Barlies': 'is name's Leslie Todd—'e mar-ried my sister out o' pity, and now 'e's the one to be pitied. Well, Leslie, 'e was comin' 'ome the day before yesterday, acrost the fields between Breakfast Barlies' and Attwater Road. 'E's just goin' 'ome whistlin' merry like to keep 'is spirits up, just on account of all the talk on account o' this 'ere Butcher, when 'e sees somethink *and* 'ears somethink which, I might tell you, sends 'is spirits down with a bump. Somethink seems to pop out from the ground 'afore 'im, somethink which 'e sees as 'e approaches is an old man, a very, very tall old man with a very, very long beard, and this old man, 'e 'as waving white 'air, Bilby, and in 'is right hand, Bilby, 'e's got a gleamin' knife—and this old man 'e lets out a 'owl, and it makes one spring toward Les——"

"*Coo!*" said Mr. Bilby again.

"Well," said the foreman, still in his dreadful whisper, "may you say so! Leslie, 'e gives one shriek-like, and then 'e's orf, an' 'e don't stop, I might tell you, till 'e gets 'ome. 'E 'asn't got over it yet. 'E wakes up in the night a-shiverin' and a-sweatin' and a-cryin' out that the Butcher's arter 'im. 'E says 'e'll 'ear them poundin' feet comin' arter 'im in 'is sleep for the rest of 'is natural. . . . Well, and what's the matter with *you*, me lad?" This last sentence, in his natural and ireful voice, the foreman addressed to Bilby's mate.

"I was only wonderin'," said the mate, "why the 'ell your ruddy brother-in-lor don't go and report 'is blood-curdlin' narrative to the p'lice?"

"My brother-in-law," said the foreman with slow wrath, "is no

B.F. 'E did report the 'ole 'orrible incident *exackly* like it occurred!"

"Coo!" said Mr. Bilby.

6

"My dear fellow!" said Mr. Runciman. "My *dear* fellow! You don't mean to tell me seriously that dear old Reade has been *arrested!*"

"My dear Runciman," retorted Mr. Calvin, "I think you heard me. If you didn't hear me, I can only suggest the application of slightly more soap and water."

"Well," said Mr. Runciman, "I'm damned!"

Mr. Calvin smiled. "Very possibly, Runciman; in fact, I should say, inevitably. But there it is. It appears that Reade has been taken up under suspicion of being the Butcher."

Mr. Piggott-Smith put in his word. "Can't understand," he said, "haow on earth a decent chep lake Reade kems under suspicion lake this."

Mr. Piggott-Smith subsided under the combined glares of Runciman and Calvin. Piggott-Smith was a retired Something-or-Other while Runciman was chairman of the Holmdale United Laundries Limited, and Calvin a director of the Holmdale Electricity Supply Company Limited. Runciman and Calvin detested each other but were as one in determination to blot out Piggott-Smith and all his kind.

"The whole thing is nonsense," said Runciman. "Blasted rot, my dear fellow! What I mean: a decent chap like Reade, the sort of a chap who's always good for a hand of bridge and that sort of thing; the sort of chap one has to dinner and all that; well—you know what I mean, Calvin—that sort of a chap—he can't possibly be this Butcher."

"I see no valid reason," said Calvin, "why anyone shouldn't be the Butcher. For all you know, Runciman, I might be. For all I know, you might be: in fact, looking at you, I'm not at all sure that you're not."

Runciman laughed, an annoying sound. "As a matter of fact, my dear Calvin," he said, "you are, as usual, quite utterly wrong. What I want to know is this: why don't the police *do* something? For all I can see, they might just as well not be here at all. . . . Now if they'd only get someone with a *business* head to help them get some *method*. . . ."

7

All the foregoing conversations took place upon the morning of Tuesday, December 4th. At half-past three in the afternoon of that day, a busy time at the Market and also at the postoffice, which faced the most southerly door of the Market, four men—four unobtrusively loitering men—became, on a sudden, no longer loiterers and no longer unobtrusive. The eyes of one of them, as he loitered, had been fixed on a spot just above the wall-slit letter box of the postoffice, and he had seen there a red light flash. He ran forward from the far side of the road, putting a whistle to his lips and blowing three short, sharp blasts.

He was Detective-Sergeant Curtis, C. I. D., who was Pike's right hand; his three companions were plainclothes men from County Constabulary headquarters.

To watch the four of them work was like watching sheepdog trials. From a scattered total of some thirty people on the short street, each picked his quarry; such quarry being, of course, a person or persons who within the past few moments had been seen depositing letters in the box. Curtis had two; the others one apiece —and the five were neatly shepherded into the postoffice and the postmaster's room. . . .

Here they were left to face another of Pike's men, Detective Officer Blaine. Younger than Curtis, and smoother, Blaine was already a past master at handling this sort of situation. Even as he started to speak, he was cataloguing the five and their emotions in his mind: one matronly housewife (resentment, curiosity); one unmarried girl, not quite so attractive as she thought she was (fear, excitement); one middle-aged man (controlled, unreadable); one elderly man (outraged citizen); one fifteen-year-old boy (wide-eyed wonder).

Blaine gave his little speech: it was regrettable that the ladies and gentlemen had to be inconvenienced. But as members of the community their assistance was required by the police. A simple routine had been devised, and if they would coöperate fully, there should be no need to detain them very long. . . .

They were quiet enough for the moment, and he began to take their names: Mrs. Arthur Hitchin; Miss Eunice Doulton; Mr. Israel Gompertz; Mr. Danvers Crawley—

The wide-eyed boy, breathing heavily, was just saying, "—George

Lancelot Evans. I work at the Market—" when Blaine heard a car pull up outside. He glanced out of the window and saw Pike.

He said to the five, "Excuse me a moment," and went quickly out of the room, closing the door carefully behind him.

He found Pike just inside the entrance. With Pike was Curtis, who was in the act of handing over to his Superintendent a square, yellow envelope . . .

Pike ripped it open, and pulled out the two yellow sheets it contained. Curtis at one shoulder, Blaine at the other, he unfolded the sheets. And read:

DEAR POLICE:

You will remember that in my last letter I promised to let you know of any future jobs I intended to carry out. Now please don't get excited. This is not, exactly, the first of my "warning" letters, as I shall call them, but it is a line to let you know of a job of mine which has been completed without your knowing anything about it, and over which, I gather from our local broadsheet, you have made a grave or comical error. You have arrested Dr. Reade, and although you have given no reason for his arrest, it is clear to me, at least, that this has to do with the disappearance of his dispenser (dispenser of what?) Marjorie Williams.

Marjorie Williams was an experiment of mine in a new technique. I must say that the whole job has given me the very greatest satisfaction. I am far from vindictive, however, and would not wish poor Dr. Reade to languish in prison much longer. I will therefore tell you where you may find the body of Marjorie Williams.

If you will go out of Holmdale and along the bypass road, travelling southwards, until you come—just before the Batley crossroads—to four new bungalows which are not yet inhabited and will go to the third of these, you will find that the door of the cupboard under the stairs is not quite shut. I am afraid one of her feet *would* get in the way.

Good-bye, Police, for the present, and please let poor Dr. Reade out of jail.

Yours in sportsmanship,
THE BUTCHER.

Curtis muttered something under his breath, and Pike said, "H'mmm." Handling them with care, he stowed sheets and envelope in an inner pocket; and then, rubbing at his chin, pondered in silence.

Apparently coming to a decision, he started toward the door of the postmaster's room; then suddenly checked and swung round on Blaine. He said to Blaine:

"You carry on in there; I'm going out to that bungalow with Curtis. You know what to do?"

"Yessir." Blaine was crisp. "Tell 'em they were seen posting letters. Ask 'em for names and addresses on said letters. Verify these with the postmaster." He drew a breath. "And see what we get."

Pike nodded. "Right. And don't let *any* of them go till I get back. Not under any circumstances, Blaine!"

He turned to Curtis. "Collect a couple of uniformed men," he said. "And let's get started." He pushed out of the swinging doors and went to the car.

8

The four bungalows on the bypass road were bright in the slanting winter sunshine; four little gaily painted boxes of red brick and white stucco.

Less than fifteen minutes after he had left the postoffice, Pike was opening the unlocked front door of the third—to find immediately that the Butcher had kept (as was apparently the Butcher's way) strictly to the truth. . . .

Directly facing Pike as he entered, straight across the little hallway, was a cupboard. And the door of the cupboard stood slightly ajar. . . .

When Curtis came into the bungalow a moment later, it was to find the cupboard door wide, and his Superintendent kneeling beside what was left of Marjorie Williams.

9

When Pike pushed open the door of the postoffice, he had been away from it for forty-five minutes.

He found a harassed-looking Blaine waiting for him on the threshold; and, outside the closed door of the postmaster's room, a constable in uniform.

He looked at Blaine, and Blaine shook his head. Blaine said: "Nothing doing, sir." He scowled. "The bastard's been too clever for us by half!"

"How?" Pike was grim.

"One of those five in there"—Blaine jerked a thumb—"is a boy that works in the Market. In the Market they've got what they call a courtesy post box; customers can post letters while they're shopping. Part of the boy's job's to clear the box out and post the letters over here—"

"And that's what he did just now, eh?" Pike was impatient. "How many?"

"I make it twenty-two, sir. He doesn't remember noticing any yellow envelope. But that doesn't mean anything, even though the others all check out. Because—"

Pike cut him short. "Because we're left with the weak point of the whole scheme, you mean?"

"Yes, sir. All the Butcher would have to have done is post something else besides the yellow letter."

"I know," said Pike. "I know." He pointed to the postmaster's room, from behind the door of which had just come a booming, angry voice. "So he just might be in there, mightn't he? Any ideas?"

Blaine shook his head. "I don't know, sir. I'd say not, on the whole. There's one real quiet one—Gompertz . . . Wish you'd take a look yourself, sir."

"Sounds as if I'd better," said Pike as the angry voice swelled louder.

He strode past the man in uniform and opened the door. . . .

He was met by the full and resounding fury of Mr. Danvers Crawley, eyes blazing, face a startling turkey-red under his mane of white hair. Mr. Crawley, it seemed, knew his rights and liked to bellow about them. Mr. Crawley had a cousin in the Home Office; high up in the Home Office! And through his cousin Mr. Crawley could, and most definitely would, make trouble for whatever jumped-up jackanapes from Scotland Yard was responsible for this outrage of holding Mr. Crawley, pent up and deprived of his sacred liberties, for hour upon hour of this lovely afternoon! What were things coming to, Mr. Crawley demanded to know. Since when, in this land of the free, could any upstart of a so-called policeman assume to himself the privileges of a dictator? By what right—

It was at this point that Pike let out a bellow himself. It was an order for silence, and it so far exceeded in volume Mr. Crawley's own efforts that Mr. Crawley was shocked into obedience.

"Now see here," said Pike, with normal volume but steely tone. "I'll give you a choice. Either you leave here, now, with the thanks of the police for having assisted them in their inquiries, the way a proper subject should; *or* you leave here, now, in the charge of a constable, who will take you to the County jail. . . . It would be very simple for me," he added mendaciously, "to charge you with obstruction."

Mr. Crawley left, standing not at all upon the order of his going. And Pike, with considerable relief, became his pleasant self again as he spoke with the four remaining letter-posters.

He had no trouble with them. Mrs. Hitchin was disgruntled; but it turned out that her disgruntlement was caused by having had to endure, for three quarters of an hour, the proximity of Mr. Crawley. Miss Doulton was charming and wished she could *really* help. George Lancelot Evans asked plaintively that someone in authority should certify to the truth of the story he would have to tell to account for his absence from work; then beamed when assured that this would certainly be done. And Mr. Gompertz, with two words and a smile which didn't seem to reach his dark eyes, was civility itself.

Pike watched them go. They had been no trouble; but they had been no satisfaction either. Not of any kind. He wondered about Mr. Gompertz, and then wondered if he wasn't a fool for wondering. . . .

He suddenly felt very tired. He had a strange, ineluctable feeling that someone, somewhere, was laughing at him. He could almost hear the laughter.

CHAPTER TEN

After the finding of Marjorie Williams, the nerves of Holmdale were tautened to so tense a pitch that the two blank days which followed were almost unbearable. By as early as Wednesday night, in fact, public morale had reached a point where, paradoxically enough, some new horror would have meant relief from tension.

With the release of Dr. Reade, and the knowledge that the Butcher was still unknown and at large, Holmdale was beside itself. And of all the feelings and emotions which worked upon the town and its inhabitants, suspicion was paramount. Many men suspected their neighbours; some men (as Pike's early report had shown) even suspected themselves; and all men, very naturally, instantly suspected anyone whom they did not recognize at first glance.

Witness the case of William Richards, who, upon being accosted by a stranger who asked him for a match, committed sudden mayhem upon the stranger, and was still committing it when stopped by a police patrol, who revealed that the stranger was in fact no stranger at all but a man whom, in normal times and circumstance, Mr. Richards would have known by sight as a cashier at the Market. . . .

There were, of course, many other kinds of manifestation of Holmdale's state of mind, not all of them bred by suspicion. There were futile spyings by citizens upon other citizens. There were indignation meetings, of church groups and social clubs and like associations. There were ludicrous (and sometimes vicious) reports to the police by Mrs. This concerning the allegedly mysterious doings of Mr. That.

And above all there were letters to the press; letters not only to the *Holmdale Clarion,* but to big London papers such as the *Mercury,* the *Planet,* and the *Looking Glass;* letters signed "Ratepayer," "Indignant," "Victim," and, of course, "Pro Bono Publico."

The number of these effusions which were given space (in addition to the headlines and editorials) was some measure of the horrified interest the whole country was taking in the Butcher and his macabre activities. It was a swelling, clamorous interest, which rapidly reached such a pitch that, upon December 5, in the House of Commons, the Home Secretary was forced to answer more Parliamentary questions on this single subject than he usually answered, upon all subjects, in a week. . . .

But despite all the furor, the basic business of living went on unchanged, in Holmdale as well as the outer world. The weather was good, and out of clear skies there shone, alternately, gay winter sunshine and bright silver moonlight; so it must have been a sort of communal mass-imagination which made Holmdale feel that over it there loomed a black and lowering cloud. . . .

2

Upon the morning of that same Thursday, Superintendent Arnold Pike of the Criminal Investigation Department sat in Miss Marable's "lounge" at No. 12, Fourtrees Road and played chuffers with Millicent Brade.

Millicent Brade was three years old and was the daughter of Mrs. Augustus Brade. Millicent Brade's father was in India, building, as Millicent had frequently explained to Superintendent Pike, a very long road for chuffers to run along.

Chuffers, with the rules laid down by Millicent, was an exacting game requiring, upon the part of the coöpted, vivid imagination, steel muscles, inexhaustible patience, and a certain capacity for imitating the grosser noises connected with railway life.

It seemed that all these qualifications, in full measure, were possessed by Arnold Pike. From his lips there escaped a hissing, for all the world like the hissing of the Flying Scotsman. His arms worked like pistons. And every now and then a brazen voice burst from him, declaiming the names of imaginary stations upon an imaginary line . . .

When Molly Brade, who was Millicent's mother, came quietly in, Superintendent Pike had momentarily exchanged the rôle of a fast express for that of the long, highly arched tunnel through which the fast express must pass. He marvelled at Millicent's knowledge of railways and how railways function. He perhaps discounted the fact that of her three years of life Millicent had spent something like a quarter in railway carriages.

"Millicent!" said her mother. "Millicent! You're being a nuisance."

The tunnel disintegrated and became, in a gymnastic flash, a man in a quiet blue suit and very shiny boots; a man whose lean brown face was darker than usual by reason of its sudden flush.

Millicent, too, rose to her feet, but much more slowly. She was a disgruntled train, as any train might be disgruntled at finding its tunnel suddenly taken away from around it. She regarded Pike with indignation.

Molly Brade smiled upon the untunnelled Pike and said:

"It *is* good of you!"

Pike fidgeted. He put his hands in his pockets and took them out again. He looked at his boots and then up at the ceiling. He said:

"If you'll let me contradict you, Mrs. Brade, it isn't at all." He looked down at the still frowning Millicent. "It's a pleasure, as you might say. And I *mean* that." He looked everywhere but at Molly Brade's smiling blue eyes.

"All the same," Molly said, "it *is* good of you. Especially when you must be so busy; so—so rather terribly busy."

There came from Pike's mouth a short, hard laugh. "Busy!" he said, and laughed again. "Busy! I wish I was, Mrs. Brade. I almost wish I was so busy I didn't have time to play with this very charming young lady. . . . *Busy!* If you ask me, Mrs. Brade, I ought to be busy, but I can't *be* busy." Now he was looking straight into Molly Brade's eyes, and now the flush of embarrassment had gone, and the frown, which had been absent during the game of chuffers, had returned in full measure. He said, after a long pause:

"I've always said—give me something to do and I'll get on with it. . . . But I take that back now, as you might say. Right back! . . . If you knew . . ."

"But I do know or at least I can guess." There was sympathy in the blue eyes; sympathy at which a tired and harassed and self-doubting man might warm himself.

Pike looked at his watch. "All the same, Mrs. Brade," he said, "thanks very much for reminding me. I must get along now. . . . The least I can do is to put in an appearance." He stooped down and kissed Millicent. He bowed stiffly—a curious, jerky little bow from the middle of his back—to Millicent's mother. He left the room with long, quick strides. The door shut softly but decisively behind him, and presently Molly Brade heard the opening and shutting of the front door.

She dropped upon her knees beside her daughter. She said: "Have a good game, darling?"

Millicent nodded gravely. "Nice man," said Millicent. "Good chuffer!"

3

As he drew abreast of the lamp-post, and the small green gate leading up to Jeffson's white cottage, Pike's heart sank, for outside the gate, drawn up to the curb, was a big green old-fashioned

Daimler saloon which he knew belonged to the chief constable.
The chief constable alone could be handled so that he was very
little trouble, but with each aide that he brought with him, his capacity for being a nuisance was increased quite disproportionately.
And heaven knew how many the green Daimler would hold and
this morning had held. Pike opened the gate, walked up the little
path, pushed open the front door, which was ajar, and so went into
the little room upon the right, which, with every succeeding day,
grew less like parlour and more like police station. The chief constable was there, and with him were Davis and Farrow. The chief
constable sat behind Jeffson's official table while Jeffson himself
sat, massive and properly silent, upon a chair to one side. There
was no decline in the chief constable's plumpness, but there was in
his colour; he was pasty to-day, and with new lines etched upon his
comfortable face. Davis was unchanged; the lean type of sergeant
major. Farrow, the burly, seemed to Pike's quick eye to be a little
more stupid and a little less aggressive.

As Pike entered, he became aware that the hum of talk which
he had heard as he walked up the path and through the door had
died down to an expectant, yet somehow minatory silence.

There were greetings all round: curt greetings just sufficiently
civil. Pike, at the chief constable's invitation, sat himself upon a
chair to face the chief constable. Davis and Farrow, who, Pike
was sure, had been sitting before his advent, now stood stiffly behind the chief constable, one at his left shoulder, the other at his
right. The greetings over, the chief constable looked at Pike.

"Well?" said the chief constable.

Pike's face was a studious blank. "If you mean, sir," he said,
"is there anything to report, I'm afraid the answer's in the
negative."

The chief constable tapped with his finger-tips upon the edge of
Jeffson's table. He said:

"What I would like to know, Superintendent, is what we are
doing."

Pike shrugged. He was finding it difficult this morning to keep
his temper. He said:

"You know, I think, sir, all that we are doing. I've taken no
steps at all other than those you suggested. Except, of course, the
letter box—which didn't come off. . . ."

There was a stifled sound from Farrow and its echo from Davis.
Once more the chief constable hit the table. "D'you mean to

tell me, Superintendent, that we've got to go on . . . go on . . . *letting* this—lunatic . . . have his way with us?"

Pike swallowed. He said, after a longer pause than his first:

"I'm afraid that's what it means, sir. . . . At the moment."

The chief constable looked at Pike. The chief constable in the next instant proved himself a shrewder man than most would have expected. He said:

"I think you've got something up your sleeve, Superintendent. If you have, I think we ought to know about it. I must say I don't like the idea that you're not taking us fully into your confidence."

Pike, momentarily, was taken aback. He said at last:

"I'm sorry, sir, I'm sure. If you feel that there's anything wrong about the way I'm handling this matter . . ."

"It isn't that. . . ." The chief constable, at this direct riposte, seemed uncomfortable. "All I meant was . . . Well the fact is, I've had one or two suggestions made to me, Superintendent, and I think I'd better give them to you right away."

Pike crossed one leg over the other. He looked hard at the chief constable. "Please do so, by all means. If anyone's got any notion whatsoever about dealing with this matter; if anyone can give us any sort of workable suggestion, then I'm all attention."

The chief constable coughed and cast a glance, over his right shoulder at Farrow. The chief constable said:

"For one thing, Superintendent, it has been suggested to me that, whatever the cost, we ought to double the patrols."

"Getting the men, sir," Pike said, "from where?"

The chief constable swelled out his cheeks and exhaled with a puffing sound.

"My dear fellah!" said the chief constable. "My dear fellah! You surely must know of all the offers of volunteers we've had since this business began! And now I come to think of it, I know you know. The last time we met we were talking about it. . . . And now Jeffson tells me the number of offers he's had in the past forty-eight hours has almost doubled the total previous offers—" The chief constable stopped abruptly. He glared.

For Pike had shaken his head. And Pike was saying:

"I'm beginning to think we ought not to have any patrols at all. . . ."

There was a snort from Inspector Farrow, and this time a quite audible snigger from Inspector Davis.

The chief constable wisely went on as if there had been no sound from behind him. He said:

"That sounds damned nonsense to me! Doesn't seem to be any sense in it, damn it!" He scowled.

Pike discovered within himself a desire to rise from his chair, to seize the large inkpot which stood just before the chief constable, and to empty it over the chief constable's bald head. But he said, with iron calm:

"If you'll allow me, sir, I'll explain. The reason why I don't think we ought to add to our patrols; the reason why, sometimes, I even think we should have no patrols at all, is that we might be supplying the Butcher with some beautiful, free-for-nothing camouflage to work under. After all, he *is* someone—probably a resident—who knows Holmdale upside down and sideways and backwards and through and through. So if we start putting Special's armlets on every able-bodied man in Holmdale—well, we're just playing into his hands; offering him the very shelter he needs!"

The chief constable's eyes were wide. There was no sound or movement from the men behind him.

"Offering him the very shelter he needs," Pike repeated. "*If* we're not doing that already!" The last six words fell into the silence like lumps of pig-iron into a pond; the rippling circles they set up were almost palpable.

The chief constable twisted uneasily in his chair. He said, slowly:

"I see what you mean, Superintendent. . . . But aren't you going rather far? I mean to say, damn it! *I* don't live in Holmdale, but I know Holmdale. You might almost be saying that you don't know *I'm* all right!"

"If you will forgive me, sir," Pike said with firmness, "that's exactly what I am saying."

"Eh!" said the chief constable sharply, and Farrow made a movement, repressed by Davis's fingers on his arm.

"Don't misunderstand me, sir," Pike said. "What I'm saying is this: the only thing I do know about this Butcher is that he can't be me or any of the men I've brought down with me. But, so far as we're concerned, there isn't a single person in and about this place who mightn't be him. Hope you follow me, sir. You've got to remember this man's that most dangerous sort of lunatic—the sort of a lunatic who doesn't *show* as a lunatic, as you might say. . . . He's the sort of man you meet and I meet every day—we probably *are* meeting him every day. He's the sort of man that when we find out who he is we shall all, maybe, get the shock of our lives!"

For a long moment there was no sound in the small room.

But at last the chief constable, clearing his throat, spoke awkwardly. "Your point's well taken, Superintendent," he said, sounding somehow shy. "So I'll tell you the only other suggestion is one Inspector Davis here has made. Inspector Davis suggested to me last night that it might do a good deal for public safety if we could manage somehow or other to establish a curfew. . . . What d'you think about that?"

This time Pike did not pause before he answered: "I have thought about it, sir. I must say I'm against it."

"Against it!" said the chief constable in astonishment. "Damn it, man! I thought it was good. With no one on the streets, how could this madman operate?"

Pike nodded. "I know, sir. But if we make everything so safe for everybody that the Butcher *cannot* operate, what he'll do is to lie low, *or* move on somewhere else. I don't think he'll do the latter, but I'm pretty certain he'll do the former. He's cute, this gentleman. And what should we do, and where would Holmdale be, if he did lie low? Right, as you might say, in the soup! You can't keep up this expense we're incurring every day indefinitely. What would happen would be that after about a month with no Butcher stuff, all the extra police would be taken out and all protections would have to be removed. Then, after a nice fortnight's holiday at Blackpool or somewhere, the Butcher would start his tricks again, and we should have to start our tricks again. With no good done to anyone by the work we're putting in now. . . . No, sir, it won't do. We've got to be like the scientists in this game. If necessary, sir, we've got to let one or two or three more people run the risk of meeting the Butcher—that's the way we're going to catch him. If we make them all safe from the Butcher *before* we know any more about him, then . . ."

He broke off. He shrugged. It was an eloquent shrug.

There was another silence in the small room.

It was broken not by anyone within the room, but by the sound of heavy footsteps on the flagged path of Jeffson's front garden. The chief constable—he did it with the air of a man welcoming any diversion, however small—turned in his chair and peered out of the window, craning his head to see between Mrs. Jeffson's lace curtains.

"Postman," he said, in some disgust.

Pike looked up sharply. "Postman, d'you say?" He was out of the room in a flash. . . .

He came back with a letter in his hand, and one glimpse of the envelope brought the chief constable out of his chair and round the table in a rush, with Farrow and Davis close behind him, craning over his shoulders.

Pike said, heavily:

"When you said 'postman,' I knew that there was something up." He was looking at the chief constable. "I know the posts here by heart. There isn't one at this time . . . But the postmaster's had orders to send any of *these* up at once. . . ."

"Open it, man!" said the chief constable. "For God's sake, open it!"

Pike opened it. Using only the tips of his thumb and forefinger, he pulled from the envelope a single sheet of square yellow paper. He read the note once to himself, slowly and deliberately. And then he read it aloud:

"DEAR POLICE:

"In accordance with my promise, I hereby inform you that I intend to do another of my little jobs upon Friday, December 7th—and that, Police, is *to-morrow*. Or it will be by the time you read this letter.

"Yours pityingly,
"THE BUTCHER.

"P. S.—I don't know which one of you police will read this, but if it isn't Superintendent Arnold Pike of Scotland Yard, I hope that whoever it is will convey to Superintendent Arnold Pike of Scotland Yard my respects and kindest and warmest regards. I should like to suggest to Superintendent Arnold Pike of Scotland Yard that he take some early opportunity of altering his sphere in life. He is not cut out for a detective! But then, who is?"

CHAPTER ELEVEN

They were still in Jeffson's room, which now was shrouded in a blue mist of tobacco smoke. It was an hour since the arrival of the postman with this last epistle of the Butcher's. The hour had been spent in discussion, never very amicable, of what steps should be taken to make utterly certain that the Butcher would be prevented from carrying out his threat.

Pike had taken very little part in the talk, but the chief constable —mercifully for Pike, who was thinking his own thoughts—had been disagreeing with his subordinates; more, the subordinates had been disagreeing among themselves. The chief constable was in favour of an immediate and police-enforced order that all persons resident in Holmdale should be forced to remain in their houses from seven o'clock, or earlier, upon the following night. Davis agreed with him, but went even further. Davis suggested, and kept on reiterating his suggestion, that the confinement to houses should start much earlier, say at four o'clock in the afternoon, so far as the residents actually in Holmdale at that time were concerned. In regard to those persons resident in Holmdale, but not having returned to Holmdale from their business or pleasure by that time, he suggested that these should be held up at their points of entrance to Holmdale—whether these were the railway or the roads—interrogated, and escorted in groups to their homes.

Farrow, surprisingly, held a very different view, Farrow, Pike was astounded to note, seemed a sudden convert to Pike's way of thinking, for, while he disagreed, he kept sending his eyes towards the yellow splash upon the table which was the Butcher's letter. Farrow, since the arrival of this last letter, had been a different person. He was now a man, perhaps not of vivid intelligence, but a man of sound if slow commonsense. Farrow, not looking at Pike, stoutly opposed this rigid curfew measure. He said, gazing at the chief constable:

"It won't do, sir. It won't do at all! We've got heaven knows who among the specials and the fire brigade and even the regulars.

If we make a curfew and shut everybody else up, we're just giving the chap—if he *should* turn out to be this here Butcher—an extra chance, a double-plated chance!"

Davis shook his head. So, a moment later, did Davis's admiring mentor, the chief constable.

"You're wrong, Farrow," said the chief constable, "quite wrong. If, as you suggest, and as I believe the Superintendent here suggested before you, the Butcher is one of the specials or someone like that, and we *do* have the curfew, *then,* if there was another crime, we should know, shouldn't we, where to look for the murderer? And that would be something, eh, Davis?" The chief constable turned round to look, with some pride in his own lucid reasoning, at Inspector Davis.

Davis nodded emphatically. The chief constable glared triumphantly at Superintendent Arnold Pike.

"Eh?" said the chief constable. "Eh? What about that? Eh?"

Pike, who had been listening to all this with one half of his alert mind, shook his head.

"I'm sorry, sir," said Pike, "I can't agree. I am most strongly with Inspector Farrow. . . ."

"Eh?" said the chief constable. "What's that? What's that?"

"I don't," said Pike, very clearly, "agree with you and Inspector Davis. I agree with Inspector Farrow. . . . You are quite wrong, sir, in supposing that, if we had your curfew to-morrow night, and there *was* a murder, we should necessarily know that we had to look among the patrols for our murderer. We should know nothing of the sort. . . . This Butcher, sir, is a clever devil. He has proved that not once but twenty times, and if he's so clever, well—he might be someone nothing to do with the patrols, and still get out and do his job. Then you'd be barking up the wrong tree, and he'd be somewhere else, laughing at you."

Another silence, broken at last by the chief constable. He growled:

"That's two for curfew and two against; me and Davis against you and Farrow." His glance at Pike was compound of deference to the institution which Pike represented and personal hostility to the man himself, while his look at Inspector Farrow was just plainly irate.

Farrow coloured; coughed to hide embarrassment; shifted his great weight uneasily from foot to foot.

Pike was unmoved. He merely nodded.

"Quite so," he said. "Mine and Inspector Farrow's opinion

against yours and Inspector Davis's." There was nothing in his words to startle the chief constable, and yet, somehow, the chief constable was startled. He stared a moment, grew red in the face, and said at last:

"You seem very decided, Superintendent."

Pike said, "I am, sir. . . . Completely."

Another pause. . . . But in keeping silence, as in other things, Pike was more than a match for the chief constable, and it was the chief constable who spoke first.

"Very well, Superintendent," he said, in a voice thick with mingled emotions. "What do you suggest?"

Pike pondered. "Just yet, sir, I don't know. Maybe nothing. We mustn't fall into the error of thinking *only* about this latest threat. And that's the way, if I may say so, you seem to be heading."

The chief constable shifted in his chair, which creaked loudly. He had opened his mouth to speak when there came the sound of brisk tapping footsteps on the path outside, and then a brisker rat-tat-tat on Jeffson's knocker.

Jeffson himself went to the door, to return in a moment to face the chief constable. "It's Miss Finch, sir. Editor of the *'Olmdale Clarion*. She wants a word with you, sir. She wouldn't take no for an answer, sir."

The chief constable, after an automatic glare, seemed to welcome this diversion. The briskness with which he welcomed it seemed to suggest that he was out of his depth and that any floating log which came along within his reach was certainly to be snatched at. He said:

"Show her in! Show her in!"

Jeffson went back to the door and opened it; and there entered to the company, Miss Finch.

Miss Finch's appearance was, as usual, severe but extremely well tailored. She nodded to Jeffson as she passed into the room. She bowed, very slightly, to the chief constable. She gave to Superintendent Arnold Pike, whom she had met at one of the many meetings of the Holmdale Company which had taken place since his advent, a fleeting but wide and delightful smile. Miss Finch, knowing what was what, managed somehow to address her words ostensibly to the chief constable while conveying the impression that Pike's ears were the ones for which she really spoke.

She said: "I hope you'll forgive me, Sir Geoffrey, for crashing in like this, but to tell you the truth, a letter has just come to me at the office which I felt I ought to bring up to the police as soon as possible." The gravity and tenseness of Miss Finch's face relaxed for a moment into a smile which made her seem considerably younger. The chief constable rose to his feet. He was gallant. He had a penchant for women just of Miss Finch's type: pleasant-faced, well-cared-for, sophisticated women who knew how to dress well without flummery; witty, self-reliant, perhaps rather "managing" women, who looked as if they might, quite easily, manage Sir Geoffrey. And Miss Finch, in particular, had very fine and very lustrous dark-brown eyes.

The chief constable came forward. He took a chair from the hands of Jeffson and set it for Miss Finch. He took from her hands her bag, and the umbrella from which, so folk in Holmdale would tell you, she was never separated. Having put his burdens down upon one of the parlour chairs, the chief constable returned to his visitor. He answered her as if her words had only just been spoken. He said:

"Of course I don't mind, Miss Finch, of course. . . . We're here to do what we can. You've frequently helped us in the past, and we're here to help you as far as is in our power. . . ." He was pompous.

Miss Finch, a busy woman, cut across the flow. She said briskly:

"Had to come and see you. Because just now a boy from the postoffice slipped down to my office, and gave me this." Miss Finch produced from a side pocket in her admirable tweed coat a square yellow envelope covered with backward-sloping and angular and very black writing. . . .

The chief constable's eyes started out under his prawn-like eyebrows. For a moment he stared, dumbfounded, at the envelope in Miss Finch's fingers. Collecting himself, he stretched out a hand to receive it, but he never did receive it. A hand came from somewhere and suavely took it before his fingers had closed upon it. This other hand was Pike's. And Pike said:

"Excuse me, sir. . . . I'd like to add this to my collection. If I may, sir, I'll open it."

It appeared that he took the chief constable's assent for granted, for before the chief constable could speak he had borne the letter to the table and, treating it as gingerly as he always treated these epistles, had taken out his pocket knife and gently slit its flap. . . .

Inside the envelope was a replica of that letter which still lay, now slightly askew, like a yellow blot upon Jeffson's table. . . .

"But how on earth," said the chief constable to Miss Finch a little later, "did you get it at this time in the morning? We had ours up here; but then the Superintendent here had arranged for a special delivery. . . ."

Miss Finch interrupted the chief constable. She smiled, and the smile took the edge from any discourtesy. She said:

"I'm sorry, Sir Geoffrey, but you're asking me to give away trade secrets. However, seeing that it's you who ask—and seeing the—the —rather awful gravity of the whole thing, I'll tell you. I'm afraid that I've been guilty of—shall we say *finagling*. With the result that, like you, I get immediate delivery of any of these—these awful letters . . . When I got this, just now, I just *had* to bring it straight here."

"Of course, of course," said the chief constable. He smiled brightly upon Miss Finch and added: "I can only say that I thank you very much for your public-spirited action in leaving your work and coming up here personally to deliver this. You couldn't know that we had already received our version." Duty holding its own against the opportunity for gallantry, he started to rise, making it clear that, however grateful he was to Miss Finch, he now expected her to depart.

Miss Finch, however, seemed of a different mind. She said:

"I was wondering, Sir Geoffrey, whether I could have a little consultation with you about whether this letter could be used by my paper. . . . I quite see that in some circumstances it might be dangerous or against the public welfare to print it, but if in any way it would help the police investigation if I did give it prominent publicity—why, then, I'd be only too glad to do so." Here Miss Finch paused a moment and laughed, a friendly little laugh which made the chief constable smile warmly at her. But he never got out his reply, for Pike's voice cut smoothly in:

"May I suggest, sir, that we aren't yet sufficiently advanced in our plans to know whether it would help us to give publicity to this letter or not? In the circumstances the best thing we can do, both from our own point of view and this lady's, is to promise to let her know within a couple of hours whether she can use this or not?"

The chief constable started, stared for a moment. He said, after that moment: "Yes—er—yes. . . . Yes. . . . Yes. . . . Quite." He turned to his visitor. "I think, Miss Finch," he said, "that the Superintendent here is right. We're just having an er—er—a meeting. We've got to take some further steps. Until we've decided what they should be, we'd better leave your knowledge in abeyance, if you don't mind."

Miss Finch rose to her feet. She was brisk and business-like. She said brightly that she quite understood. . . . At the doorway she turned round and added that she hoped that they would not forget to "give the *Clarion* a call." They must not forget that while the Press, in a horrible business like this, would do anything within reason, or perhaps beyond reasonable bounds, to help the police, the Press must nevertheless live, and that therefore the Press expected a tit-for-tat. In other words, if the police could not eventually see their way to letting her publish this latest effusion of the Butcher's, would the police give her something else? She was very keen to get a special edition out to-morrow. It was not so much that the special editions were desired by the *Clarion,* to whom they gave a vast deal of extra work, as that the public were so eager to have first-hand and locally originated news. . . .

The chief constable, escorting Miss Finch to the door, promised that when there was anything that the police could "give" to Miss Finch and the *Clarion,* he would see that they did so. He went back, uplifted by the fascinating smile which the *Clarion* had given him, to sterner work.

He found Inspector Davis sullenly gazing out of the window, while, their heads together, Pike and Farrow—this sudden strange alliance—talked in undertones. Then Pike turned away. Without a word he went to a corner and from one of Mrs. Jeffson's many occasional tables picked up his hat.

He said, "If you'll forgive me, sir, I'll be getting along."

"Eh?" said the chief constable sharply. "What's that?"

"If you'll forgive me, sir," Pike repeated firmly, "I'll be getting along."

"Eh?" said the chief constable again. "What's that? Getting along. . . . What for? Damn it, man, we haven't finished."

But Pike was adamant. "I'm afraid you'll have to excuse me, sir," he said. "I've got what you might call a small idea. I'm going to see whether it's workable before I tell you about it. Don't go thinking it's anything big, because it isn't. But it might help. . . . Where will you be this evening, sir?"

"Here," said the chief constable fiercely. "Here."

"Very well, sir," said Pike and was gone.

The chief constable glared at the closed door. "How that fellah" —he spoke ostensibly beneath his breath but actually with considerable volume—"ever got where he is at the Yard, *I* can't think."

From beneath his waxed moustache Inspector Davis emitted a coughing sound.

Farrow, very glum, said nothing.

2

Arnold Pike was not a man who needlessly omitted meals. His experience had taught him, sometimes painfully, that to go without food and drink when food and drink may properly be had is to impair a man's ability. And so the first thing he did was to call at the garage next to Miss Marable's and take out the blue police Crossley. He then lunched well but quickly at the Wooden Shack, and within forty-five minutes was driving over Chaser's Bridge.

The offices of the Holmdale Electricity Supply Company lie three hundred yards south of Chaser's Bridge upon the left-hand side of the road. At ten minutes to three, after a wait of seven or eight minutes, Pike was shown into the manager's room.

Mr. Calvin, though curt and a thought sardonic-seeming, was nevertheless brisk enough and obliging.

"Anything we can do," said Mr. Calvin, "of course we will do. I think we've told the police that already."

"You have. And, needless to say, we are grateful." Pike was curt and business-like too, though of an equal politeness. He put to Mr. Calvin certain questions. Mr. Calvin, having made calculations upon a scribbling pad and once consulted with a subordinate, gave answer in the affirmative.

"We can do it," said Mr. Calvin, and shut his mouth like a trap. "What we'd like to know, and as soon as possible, is whether you want us to do it or not, Superintendent. You'll understand that we need a little time for preparation, and we shall need more time than we would normally if you want it done . . . well . . ."—Mr. Calvin shrugged—"quietly."

Pike said: "I'll let you know, if not this evening, before ten-thirty to-morrow morning."

Mr. Calvin nodded. "In case you do want it," he said, "I'll get the stuff down from our Lewisham depot right away. That won't hurt, and I don't suppose the charge'll hurt the government or whoever it is."

Again Pike nodded. "That's right." He rose to go. He shook hands with Mr. Calvin, who, it seemed to him, was one of the few really decisive persons he had met since his arrival in Holmdale.

Outside, the blue Crossley was waiting, and the Crossley's nose was headed away from Holmdale's outskirts.

Pike was suddenly seized with a wish, an imperative wish, to be alone.

He felt that curious, *overfull* feeling about the head which comes to a man when his subconscious has developed a thought and tries to compel that thought out of itself and into the conscious mind before it is really ready to deliver. He knew that if he went back to the Jeffsons and Davises and chief constables, the only effect their society would have upon him would be to thrust this half-born idea still further back into intangibility. He felt there was a chance, if he were to get away for an unstrained, uninterrupted two hours, he might, from the recesses of that inner mind, pull out whatever idea it had developed.

He got into the car and shut the door behind him. He sat motionless for a full three minutes; then started the engine, and drove slowly off, heading for the open country. . . .

3

The two hours' worth of freedom had no effect. And it was a grim and preoccupied Pike who returned to Holmdale, and put the Crossley back into its garage in Fourtrees Road. He shut the garage, and hesitated upon the pavement. He looked first to his right at the garden and pleasantly curtained windows of No. 12. He looked then to his left and across the road, where the lamp outside Jeffson's cottage showed a pale, sickly radiance. He chose, his sense of duty driving him to Jeffson's cottage. He walked there with long quick strides and pushed open the door, which was ajar, and within a moment was inside what once had been Mrs. Jeffson's parlour.

Jeffson was there and so were Davis and Farrow, but that was all.

Pike realized with a start that he should have known by the absence of the green Daimler that the chief constable was no longer there. It showed him, this little lack in observation, how preoccupied he was. He stood in the doorway and looked at its occupants through the smoke. Jeffson rose clumsily. Davis nodded with a curt nod, but Farrow—the one-time inimical Farrow—came toward him with a greeting.

"The chief," Farrow said, "left a message for you. He had to get back. Would you tell me, or Davis, what it was you were going to tell him, and we'll report when we get back. We'll be leaving in about twenty minutes. He's sending a car back for us." He was un-smiling, and yet Pike warmed to him.

"I've been," Pike said, "to the Electricity Company. I asked Calvin, the manager, whether he could arrange to supply power for searchlights for to-morrow night, and as many nights as we might want them."

"Eh!" said Farrow. And suddenly his broad heavy face was illuminated by a grin. "That's a good one!" he said. "Here, Davis."

"Calvin," said Pike, "told me it could be arranged if we wanted it. Must say I haven't quite made up my mind, though. Anyhow, they'll be ready if we want 'em."

"How many?" said Farrow.

"Twelve doubles. That's to say, twenty-four lights altogether, in pairs, one pair at each important road junction or wherever we want 'em. Only, we've got to tell Calvin the wiring points at least four hours before they're needed."

Farrow still smiled. "That'll knock the old Butch," said Farrow, like a large schoolboy. "If he don't want to operate down the lighted ways, the fact the lights are there'll make him shy of the dark ways close to! That's good, Super."

Pike shook his head. "It's not good. It's just a sop, as you might say. But you've got it wrong, Inspector. My idea was not to have the lights all blazing away *all* the time. My idea was to have 'em switch on and off, sort of irregularly, so no one would know when they *were* going on. . . ."

Farrow slapped fist against palm. "And that's a better one!" said Farrow. "All right, Super, I'll tell the chief as soon as we get back." He added, *sotto voce:* "Not that it'll matter whether I tell him or not. . . . I'll tell you something: he's dead feared of you."

"That," said Pike, turning to go, "is just as well."

He went. He turned sharp left out of Jeffson's cottage gate and then, crossing the road, came to Number 12. He went in, and in the hall met Molly Brade with Millicent.

Millicent made a rush at him. Millicent had a lot to tell him. First, she had seen the Flying Scotsman roar through Holmdale station that morning. Second, she had bought a new toy chuffer. Third, she had evolved a new game which, she seemed sure, could only properly be played with his participation.

Molly Brade intervened. She said, in the tone of one who means exactly the opposite: "You're being a nuisance again, Millicent."

Millicent ignored her mother. Millicent looked up at Pike, her blue eyes fixed meltingly upon his brown ones.

"Play chuffers?" she said.

Pike, shyly but firmly turning down the half-hearted remonstrances of Millicent's mother, went, tealess, to play chuffers. He liked playing chuffers for the pleasure that the game brought to Millicent and to himself. Furthermore, the playing of chuffers brought with it much possibility of subsequent talk with Millicent's mother. . .

CHAPTER TWELVE

There was another meeting in Jeffson's cottage at half-past ten upon the next morning. Which, of course, was the morning of Friday, the morning of the day during which the Butcher had stated that he would "do another job."

It occurred to Pike, as he walked from Miss Marable's to the police cottage, to wonder whether the Butcher, if he could not, by killing someone before midnight, fulfil his promise to the police, might be so maniacally disgruntled as to kill himself. Pike both feared not and hoped not—an awkward state of mind.

This morning the chief constable again was not in Jeffson's room, but Farrow and Davis were. And with Farrow and Davis, who had obviously spent much of last night with pen and paper, Pike went over the arrangements for the day.

He approved a scheme for tightening the patrol supervision, and approved also the suggestion that the patrols should begin to function, not at 4:30 P. M. when the darkness was almost complete, but as early as 3:15, when the first signs of dusk would begin to evince themselves. He approved also the rearrangement of the patrol groups and control. . . . In short, he approved everything that had been done since the previous afternoon by Davis and Farrow. Farrow, having now got over his first reluctance to show his *volte-face* in regard to the Superintendent's merits, frankly beamed. Even Davis, though the points of his waxed moustache still showed tendency to bristle, was more affable than before.

"And now," said Farrow. "What about these searchlights, Super?"

Pike looked at him—and shrugged. "I've been thinking about these searchlights most of the night. In a way, I want to have 'em put on. In a way, I'd rather they weren't put on——"

"I know," said Farrow, interrupting. "You're thinking, Super, that these searchlights, like the patrols and what not, are all what you might call 'preventative' measures——"

"Exactly." Superintendent Pike smiled at Inspector Farrow. "That's just what they are, Farrow, and preventive measures are just, really, what I don't want. . . . But, all the same, I believe that when the next hour's up I shall ring Calvin and tell him I want the lights. . . . You know what's the matter with Englishmen, don't you? They're too blame soft-hearted. If we were sensible, if we were Germans or Frenchmen, we'd have the *real* humanity to let one or two more people die so we could stop this business once and for all. . . . But will we do it? You know we won't!"

He looked at Farrow and shook his head gloomily. He turned to leave, and Davis said, "Hey, where you going?"

Pike swung round on his heel, a very quick movement. Something in the way in which he looked at Inspector Davis made Inspector Davis almost visibly shrink. There was a long pause.

"For a nice little walk," said Pike, and was gone.

This time he turned right-handed out of Jeffson's cottage gate, walked down the length of Fourtrees Road, round the sweep of Fourtrees Crescent, down the hill by the Laurels Nursing Home, then left down the steeper hill into Dale Road. In Dale Road he hesitated; almost turned left to walk out of Holmdale altogether and down to Billsford; changed his mind and turned right and walked up Dale Road towards the centre of Holmdale.

He walked slowly. His hands were thrust into his pockets, and his chin rested on his tie. His eyes were on the ground, and his thoughts only just sufficiently with him to permit of his walking safely.

He came at last to the end of Dale Road and automatically turned right into Market Road. From the junction of Market Road and Dale Road to the Market itself is perhaps a quarter of a mile. At his ordinary pace Pike would have covered this in something under five minutes. At his pace to-day he took ten.

He was walking on the right-hand side of the road—the side, that is, upon which the Market itself lies. He would have passed the Market, not knowing that he had passed it, if it had not been for Mr. Percy Godly.

The time was past eleven o'clock, and Mr. Godly was on his way from the Wooden Shack to the Carters, which lies at the top of Burrowbad Hill on the Main Road. Mr. Godly having what he would have called, "taken a good load aboard" at the Wooden Shack, was none too steady in his walking.

Pike and Mr. Godly met, chest to chest, outside the first of the Market's swing doors. Mr. Godly reeled, staggered, clutched at a lamp post, and finally fell. Pike picked him up and dusted him off and looked rather hard at him.

Mr. Godly, waving a white hand, said indistinctly:

"Absolooly charmed! Very rare one meets genelum! Only too d'lighted to've been . . . to've been . . . to've been . . ." Mr. Godly gave up.

Pike propped him against the lamp post and left him. He put his hands back into his pockets and resumed his thoughtful walk. He passed along to the end of the easterly façade of the Market.

He would, no doubt, have crossed over the road, which runs between the Market and the postoffice, and passed down the rest of Market Road to Chaser's Bridge had not a large and puffing and gravel-filled lorry obstructed his way.

Taking the line of least resistance, Pike swung to his right, keeping upon the pavement, and thus was walking along the southern frontage of the Market. He passed three quarters of the length of this frontage and came abreast of the small sudden archway from which come at odd times the Market's messenger boys; the archway which divides the Market proper from the offices of the Market's organizers and also the hairdressing departments. Unconsciously Pike raised his head to look into this archway, for he was accustomed to see here, when he passed—as upon a few occasions he had at this time—the silver-gray and royal-blue perambulator of Miss Millicent Brade.

There again was the perambulator. Pike, alert now, looked round for Molly Brade. She was not in sight nor, at this moment, was anyone else. He crossed to the perambulator. He felt that perhaps a little light conversation about chuffers would do him good— and there was always the possibility that while one was talking to Millicent, Millicent's mother would return. But he was disappointed. For, instead of being wide eyed in her carriage, looking out with those large blue eyes across the fields at the just visible railway line, Millicent Brade was fast asleep.

She had upon her dark head a cap of blue velvet cunningly edged with fur. Over her was a white woollen coverlet across which there solemnly tramped a procession of blue elephants. One arm lay outside the coverlet, and from the sleeve of the fur-cuffed coat there peeped a hand from which the glove had slipped. It was very cold this morning, and the hand looked blue. Pike, gazing at his small and sleeping friend from the end of her carriage, noticed this hand. He came round to the side of the carriage and gently lifted it.

And then, as suddenly as if it had burnt him, he dropped it. From where he stood now, he could see something which he had not seen before. Behind the pram, huddled against the wall and hidden hitherto by the pram itself and also by a small buttress-like projection of the concrete of the wall, lay the body of a woman.

Pike knew who it was even before, with ashen face, he knelt beside it. . . .

Millicent Brade slept peacefully on. Just below her lay her mother. Her mother was dead.

For a moment a blackness descended upon Pike's world, and there was a roaring in his ears. . . .

CHAPTER THIRTEEN

The grandfather clock on the landing of No. 12, Fourtrees Road was striking noon as Pike came out of the room in which, with Miss Marable, Millicent Brade was supervising the traffic control of a brand-new and complicated railway system. Pike—how, he never quite knew—had not only succeeded in removing Millicent from that passageway without waking her, but also had convinced her that her mother had had suddenly to go upon a chuffer journey. For the time being, Millicent was busy and serene and happy.

There was a man waiting for Pike downstairs. It was Curtis who, having meant to speak so soon as he saw his chief, was stricken for a moment into silence by the sight of his chief's face. Curtis said:

"It's all right, sir, we've got him. Found him at the Carters up on Burrowbad Hill. He's very drunk; leastways, he's acting very drunk. Dunno which myself. . . ."

"Get a doctor!" Pike's words came out like small, keen bullets.

"Got one, sir," said Curtis. "First thing I did. Dr. Seneschal. With him now——"

"What's he say?"

"Didn't wait, sir." Curtis was gathering something of Pike's urgency. "Came to report. Blaine went down to the Market with Jeffson and four men. Farrow and Davis are there, too. They're following your instructions and letting the catch out one by one and searching 'em." Curtis shrugged. "But, somehow, I don't fancy they'll get anything."

But Pike for a long moment said nothing; then suddenly:

"What's that row outside?"

Curtis seemed startled. He had just heard the noise himself.

In two strides Pike was at the door. But even before he had flung it open, he knew what the noise was coming from.

It was coming from people; partly from their movements, but mainly from their voices. Or, rather, from their *voice*. Because there were enough of them—perhaps thirty, perhaps forty—to make them into a mob, with fused emotions and a single gabbling mouth.

They surged on the pavement, and around the Crossley. They poured through the little gate and up the pathway toward the door. They brandished things above their heads—walking-sticks, umbrellas, cricket-stumps.

Curtis at his shoulder, Pike stood where he was and surveyed them. The mob-voice changed from snarl to shout. The shouting was high pitched, and Pike saw that more than half the vanguard —more than half the whole crowd, in fact—were women. He heard himself speaking, and his tone was the tone of that young police constable Arnold Pike who, twenty years before, had "moved along" his first street crowd somewhere in Rotherhithe.

"Now then," he said, "what's all this?"

From the leaders, one woman rushed at him. Her fingers were hooked like claws, and her face was distorted, mouthing. The claws reached for his face, but he caught one wrist and twisted it behind her; held her, doubled over.

She screamed, and the mob-voice echoed the scream. A man came charging through the front rank of women; a big fellow, wielding a heavy, shillelagh-like stick. He was going to swing it at Pike's head; but Curtis, with a fist like the knee of an ox, caught him squarely on the point of the chin and he staggered backwards, crashing down into the greenness of Miss Marable's neat box hedge.

"Now *then!*" said Curtis. "Now then! Any more for any more?"

Apparently there were not. The mob-shout turned to an uneasy mutter, and through it came the voice of the woman Pike was holding. She was screaming still, but now words were audible—

"*Police!* . . . Call yourselves police! . . . Letting this devil walk around free! . . . Murdering—*murdering—*"

Pike twisted the wrist he was holding, almost savagely. The woman screamed again, but this time wordlessly, on a higher note.

In sympathy, the mob-voice swelled again. But only for a moment; because Curtis moved forward.

"All right," said Curtis. "All right! Stop your shouting. Speak one at a time if you got anything to say." He bunched the ox-like fist again. "Or step right up if there's any more for any more."

Again there were no takers forthcoming. Pike looked at Curtis. "Put this woman in the car," he said. "She's under arrest." He spoke loudly, into a sudden silence. "Charges are obstructing the police in the execution of their duty, and acting in a manner likely to cause a breach of the peace. Also assault. And no bail, Curtis. She's better inside."

"Yessir," said Curtis smartly. He took the woman from Pike, noticing as he did so that the man he had hit was now on hands and knees by the box hedge, vomiting.

Apparently, others had noticed it too. Because, by a curious process of mass metamorphosis, the mob was a mob no longer but merely a collection of shamefaced and frightened and everyday persons.

A man started the exodus, backing through the gate and shambling off. The others followed like drifting sheep—and Pike and Curtis marched their prisoner down a clear pathway to the car. She tried to hang back, but Curtis drew her irresistibly on. He bundled her into the rear seat and sat beside her, slamming the door. She seemed to have shriveled. She sobbed, and tears ran down her cheeks. She looked now what in fact she was, a terrified and bewildered woman.

Without a glance at his prisoner, Pike slid in behind the wheel and started the engine. He turned left into Marrowbone Lane and drove slowly along it. He had just passed Collingwood Road, when, without warning, he pulled into the curb and stopped. He turned and spoke to Curtis behind him. "Let her get out," he said. Curtis, reaching across the woman, opened the door.

"Out you get!" said Curtis, jerking his thumb at the way to freedom.

The woman stared at him vacantly. Her face still worked, and unshed tears stood in her eyes.

"Out you get!" said Curtis again.

But still she made no movement. Pike turned in his seat. He said, quietly:

"You don't want to go to prison, do you? If you don't, get out. I don't know your name; I haven't seen you before; so I can't come for you later—*if* you go now."

Then she went. Standing on the edge of the pavement she looked at Pike and said something. They never knew what it was, for Curtis's slamming of the door drowned her words. She was left standing on the pavement staring after them as they drove away.

2

When they reached it, all the doors of the Market were closed. And all around the Market was a thin, ever swelling crowd which, having sensed drama from afar, was flocking to gaze with wildly speculating eyes at the blank white walls and now shrouded windows.

There are five entrances to the Market, and outside each of these was a uniformed constable. Patrolling the right-angled two sides of public frontage of the Market were two uniformed sergeants, and these, every now and then, paused in their patrolling and bade the encroaching crowd to "move on there."

The policeman guarding the central entrance saluted as Pike came up with Curtis, pushed open the swing doors and found Inspector Farrow. At the sight of Pike, his frowning, heavy face took on a look of pleased relief. He touched his cap.

"Any results?" said Pike.

Farrow shook his head. "Not yet."

"How you working it?" Pike was crisp.

Farrow consulted the back of an envelope upon which were pencilled notes. He said:

"There were a hundred and fifty-three customers in here when you had the doors closed; fifty-one assistants and eleven on the manager's staff, including the general manager himself, Mr. Cuthbert Mellon. Blaine's split the whole lot into two batches. One batch is in the café with a couple of uniformed men watching 'em.

The other batch is in the Hairdressing, with the same. Blaine got a couple of sisters from the hospital for searching the women, and two of my sergeants are doing the men. As they're done they're giving their names and getting passed out through the back way. . . . All right, sir?"

Pike nodded. "Very good. How many've they run through?"

"I was round there a minute ago, sir, and they'd done seventy-one, they told me."

"Any trouble?"

Farrow shrugged. "Some of 'em were a bit upset like. Some a bit scared. No real *trouble*. Shall I take you across there, sir? They're searching 'em in the manager's suite."

Pike nodded. He fell into step beside Farrow, and they started to walk, Curtis following like a solid ghost, through the echoing building, threading their way between its now tenantless, well stocked counters.

"Right through there, sir." Farrow pointed to a door, at the far side of the department labelled "Refined Footwear," which bore upon it in red and black letters "Private—General Manager."

Pike strode on; he edged his way behind the shoe counter, and, reaching the door marked "Private," flung it open onto one of those dramatic coincidences which happen so far more often in real life than the drama critics would admit.

Between two large and blue-clad policemen there stood, his arms upraised, a small and dark and, for the nonce at least, furtive-looking little man. One of the uniformed figures was still probing in pockets upon the small figure's right-hand side. But the other—Jeffson—who had, obviously, been probing upon the left, had suddenly straightened itself with an air almost comically blent of shock and triumph. . . .

And in his right hand Jeffson held something aloft.

Pike leapt forward. He snatched at Jeffson's find. . . .

He found himself staring at a square yellow envelope. It was unsealed and empty. But, as if ready and waiting for an enclosure, it was already addressed, in a curiously backward-sloping hand and in thick, shining black ink:

> *The Chief Constable,*
> *C/o Sergeant Jeffson,*
> *13 Fourtrees Road,*
> *Holmdale.*

3

The small and furtive man from whose pocket Jeffson had extracted this envelope was Wilfred Spring.

The two sergeants fell back. Pike looked at the envelope; twisted it this way and that between his fingers. And then he looked at Spring. He said:

"Well, what've you got to say?" His tone showed nothing of the pulsing excitement inside him.

"What have I got to *say!*" Spring, now that the opportunity for speech had been vouchsafed, shed much of his furtiveness. With his own words he seemed to swell. It was as if, with each of his sentences, he became more and more convinced that Wilfred Spring, being a person of importance, should not be thus mishandled by a parcel of policemen. . . .

"What have I got to *say!*" said Wilfred Spring and proceeded to say it. There was a great deal of it. It appeared that Mr. Spring had no notion whatsoever of how the strangely qualified envelope had found its way into his peculiarly perverted pocket. Mr. Spring thought it was carnally obvious it must have been planted there. Did the misbegotten police really imagine that Wilfred Spring, one of the best known—if not the best known—director in England (or anywhere else, for that matter) should be considered as having either the time or inclination to go about murdering people.

"Good God, man!" said Mr. Spring, now fully himself again. "What the hell do you take me for?"

Pike looked at him in silence. Pike's face showed nothing of his thoughts, which were mixed, to say the least. He said at last:

"We'll have to detain you, Mr. Spring. For the time being at least."

4

It was three o'clock when, outside the white-fronted cottage-police station, Wilfred Spring entered the police car and was driven away to the county jail. There were left, crowded into Jeffson's room, the chief constable, his satellites Farrow and Davis, Detective Officers Curtis and Blaine, and Superintendent Arnold Pike.

"*I* think," said the chief constable, "that's our man." He looked first at Farrow, then at Davis. He disregarded Curtis and Blaine and looked last at Pike.

Pike shook his head. "I'm sorry, sir, I can't agree. If I may put it bluntly, I think you made a mistake in holding him. Especially in view of the statements from his wife and that Market assistant."

Tempers were on edge this afternoon, and the chief constable exploded. "Blast it, man, a fellah of your experience ought to know a wife's evidence isn't admissible—"

Pike interrupted. "I beg your pardon, sir, but we aren't in court yet. Believe me, you're going to find that Wilfred Spring was demonstrably inside the Market when"—there was the slightest check here in Pike's even voice—"when Mrs. Brade was killed. And that absolves him of being the Butcher . . . Unless there's more than one killer, which is so improbable I won't even think about it."

There was an uncomfortable silence, broken at last by the chief constable. He said, to no one in particular:

"God damn it! God damn and blast it all!"

He reached for the telephone.

5

It was five o'clock, an hour after Wilfred Spring had been released, that a mass meeting of Holmdale citizens, rapidly and indeed spontaneously convened, took place on the wide tree-lined grass plot opposite the northern aspect of the Market.

A wild meeting this, and as foreign to Holmdale and its ways as had been the demonstration outside Miss Marable's house.

There was much talk—and even some singing. There were wild, fierce speeches against the police and their lack of training, method, initiative and morality. There were, throughout the speeches, roared "Hear-hears." There was a motion put to the meeting by the most impassioned speaker—a part-time political orator—and carried unanimously, to the effect that the citizens of Holmdale should take the law into their own hands. What, quite, they were going to do with the law when they had it, was left in the thinnest of thin air. . . .

But everyone was much moved. They were all, for the moment, fire-eating, fire-breathing hard cases. They were all, for the moment, ardent disciples of Judge Lynch. They were for somebody's blood; preferably, of course, the Butcher's, but if the Butcher's were not available, then for the blood of those responsible for this terrible delay in bringing the Butcher to book.

Arms were brandished. Voices grew hoarse. Eyes were fierce. Some of the more youthful components of the crowd—it must have numbered three hundred at least—procured from somewhere fuel for a bonfire which soon was sending shooting tongues of red and yellow flame twenty feet into the air. . . .

On the outskirts of the crowd Dr. Reade stopped his Chevrolet two-seater and listened to the crowd's uproar with a sardonic smile on his heavy face.

The Reverend Rockwall passed by quickly, shaking his head and muttering to himself.

Safely at home, Mr. Wilfred Spring was turning over in his mind the possibilities of a great publicity campaign to be linked up with a suit for false arrest.

In a cell in the county jail Mr. Percy Godly was thinking, with tears in his eyes, of the cruel devil in blue who so smoothly and so often refused his bribes and prayers and pleadings for "just one little one."

In the centre of the crowd stood Miss Ursula Finch, her umbrella clamped firmly beneath her left arm, her keen mind taking mental shorthand notes for a more startling issue of the *Clarion* than even she had ever conceived.

In the front ranks of the crowd Mary Fillimore, her usually soft blue eyes hard and staring, found suddenly that she had no more voice left with which to shout.

In the centre of the crowd Mr. Colby turned with excited gratification to his neighbour, saying: "Thank God! Thank God! . . . High time more sensible men took matters into their own hands."

Upon the first-floor balcony of his pleasant house, the Hospice, stood Sir Montague Flushing, looking out with troubled face and frightened eyes at the leaping flames of the bonfire.

"What a terrible, dreadful business this all is!" thought Mrs. Rudolph Sharp, as she tried to extricate herself from the fringes of the crowd. . . .

It was nearly seven when Farrow and Davis appeared, the former in charge of the squad of uniformed police, the latter bringing with him the Batley fire brigade. . . .

By seven-fifteen, there was no more crowd. There were only the sodden ashes of the bonfire—and, in many Holmdale houses, persons whose spirits, as well as their raiment, had been thoroughly dampened. . . .

6

It was much later, at an hour when most of Holmdale was either in bed or getting ready to go there, that Pike sat in his bedroom in Fourtrees Road and thought about Wilfred Spring. He was regretting that he had not been able to prevent the chief constable from incarcerating Wilfred Spring, even temporarily. He did not object, upon humanitarian grounds, to Mr. Wilfred Spring's incarceration, because he thought that incarceration would do Mr. Wilfred Spring a great deal of good, but he did object to the odium which must necessarily fall onto the police from the pens and mouths of press and public. The Butcher still at large, and a drunkard and a film director in jail. What a pair, press and public would say alike, to pick upon! Could there be any two more unlikely to be this homicidal pervert than a man whose ambition was to crowd into himself as many drinks in a day as was possible, and a man whose ambition in life was to produce as many flickering ghosts as possible? The one would be too busy with his alcohol; the other too busy with his ghosts. The one would be able to satisfy in his fuddled brain any latent impulse to horrid violence, and the other equally able to do so (as indeed he seemed to have done) with his puppets. A drunkard, Pike thought . . . and a film director. . . .

"I wonder," Pike thought, "what sort of job that is . . . a film director's. Must feel like a sort of god half the time. Funny things, pictures. Some people like 'em, others don't. Some would walk forty miles to see Lilian This and Percy That in *Love's Ashes*. Others shuddered at the very name of Lilian or Percy. . . . Great invention, though . . . Think of slow motion, for instance. Why, with a slow motion camera you could tell what a man did even if he didn't know he'd done it himself . . . And how useful it ought to be in the future—though it was doubtful whether anyone could put it to this use—in teaching history. By jing, if they took films of all the historic happenings—or happenings likely to be historic—which took place, and did 'em from now on, why, the kids in about a hundred years' time would know more about us than we knew about ourselves. . . ."

Yes, odd things, films! Very useful in all sorts of ways—all sorts of ways—they'd even been useful to scientists. . . . No reason really why they shouldn't be useful to the police. . . .

"*Good Lord Almighty!*" said Pike aloud.

He leapt up and backwards from the window seat as if a bullet had narrowly missed him. He made one stride of it to the door and five strides of it across the landing—past the door behind which slept Millicent Brade, too tired by a transcendental game of chuffers to be kept awake wondering at her mummy's strange departure. He went down the stairs in two silent leaps.

He slammed the front door behind him. He ran up to Marrowbone Lane, and all the way to the house where Curtis was billeted. There was a light in an upper window, and at this window he threw a handful of gravel plucked from the garden path. By chance the lighted window was Curtis's own, and it was Curtis who leaned out gruffly demanding: "What the hell?"

"Pike here," said Curtis's superintendent. "Come down! Urgent!"

Curtis came down. Into the narrow passage Pike pushed his way. "Where can we talk?" he said.

Curtis ushered him into a sitting-room and snapped on a light. Pike said:

"You're going to get the car and drive up to London, to the Yard. While you're en route, I'll be on the phone, fixing everything. You're not going to get much sleep, because when you've collected what they'll have waiting for you, you're coming right back here. What you're going to collect, in our car and maybe a couple of others, is thirteen cinema cameras *and* men who know how to use 'em. You won't come straight back here; you'll go to Batley, to the Royal George. I'll be waiting for you there, from 2:30 A. M. on. Then we'll start smuggling 'em into Holmdale, a little at a time. And please the Lord I'll find hiding places for 'em." He watched Curtis struggling with curiosity. "Got all that?" he snapped.

Curtis repeated his orders briskly. And then surrendered. "What's the stunt, sir?" he said.

Pike smiled; the sort of smile Curtis had not seen from him all the time they had been in this place.

"I want thirteen cameras, and thirteen operators, because there are thirteen pillar boxes in this god-forsaken imitation suburb. Don't you see, Curtis, that the Butcher's bound to write to us again? And don't you see, Curtis, that if, as from to-morrow, there's a secret twenty feet of film taken of every person that posts a letter everywhere, we'll be able at least to narrow down our field after we've got the next letter? And p'raps more than that. P'raps a lot more!"

A wide replica of his chief's smile appeared upon Curtis's face, but only to fade almost as soon as it had come. Curtis shook his head. "I'm afraid, I don't see it. I thought I did for a minute, but even if we did get pictures of everyone who posts letters on a day when this 'ere Butcher posts a letter, I don't see how we're that much better off, as you make out, because——"

Pike cut across this speech. "Don't be a fool! Even if you didn't know it, you must've realized that by this time I've got an arrangement with the postmaster that the postmen making each collection from the boxes put each box's lot into separate small bags so that instead of the letters being mixed up together, we'll know, after every collection, which letters have come out of which box."

Curtis raised thick brows. "I didn't know that, sir," he said.

Pike snapped at him. "Well, you ought to've guessed. The only thing that can go wrong with this is, if it's the postmaster or one of the postmen who's the Butcher—then we're pipped. But it's a good move. It's an idea. It's the best idea I've had since I've been down here."

CHAPTER FOURTEEN

At seven-thirty the next morning, which was that of Saturday, December 8th, the telephone in Miss Marable's hall rang shrill and impatient. It went on, at first intermittently and then without break, until—still rather sleepy eyed, the elder of Miss Marable's two "dailies" stopped its ringing with her "'Ullo!"

The telephone was curt and official, and, to Janet, a thought alarming. It was, it said, speaking for the chief constable and wished to talk with Mr. Pike. Janet, stammering but ultimately clear, stated that she would call Mr. Pike.

But she did not call Mr. Pike because Mr. Pike was not there. Mr. Pike's bed had been slept in, but Mr. Pike must have risen and gone out very, very early, because she had entered the house at six forty-five, and she knew that, between then and now, no one had so much as moved within the house.

All this Janet, still stammering a little, eventually told the telephone. . . .

Pike came in at a quarter to eleven pleased indeed with his morning's work. It had been a tough job to do in the time, with the necessity for secrecy making it the more difficult. But it had been done and well done. . . . He went upstairs for a belated shave, whistling beneath his breath. And then he passed the door behind which Millicent Brade, this morning a little querulous, was eating her breakfast, and the whistling ceased . . .

But he was all the more pleased with the morning's work, for this seemed to him the first really powerful move against this powerful devil. . . .

2

"God Almighty!" said the chief constable. "Where in Satan's name have you *been,* Superintendent? We've been huntin' for you all over the blasted shop. What you been *at?*"

Pike sat down, facing the wrath across Jeffson's table. At the chief constable's shoulders were Farrow and Davis. In the background, Jeffson hovered.

"Sorry, Sir Geoffrey," said Pike smoothly. "I'd no intention of keeping you waiting."

"But where have you *been,* man?"

"I was out for a while, sir." Pike was gentle with the chief constable. "Then I had to get off a report to the Yard." He sat back. He made it placidly obvious that this was all he was going to say.

There was a silence, which stretched . . . And then, perhaps saving the chief constable from apoplexy, came sounds from outside the window.

They were followed by the sight of a young man hurrying up the path. He carried a big, official-looking manila envelope.

"He's from the postoffice," said Jeffson, and started for the door.

But Pike was before him. Pike vanished; to reappear a moment later with the young man's burden.

He slit it open and tipped its contents out onto the table. Three square yellow envelopes fell so that they lay fully exposed to the glaring eyes of the chief constable and his two satellites, three square yellow envelopes upon which were addresses written with a peculiarly backward-sloping hand and in a curiously black and shining ink.

"God Almighty!" said the chief constable.

There was a little hissing intake of breath from Farrow and a nervous grunt from Davis. They bent over the envelopes. The first was addressed to The Chief Constable of the County, c/o Police Station, Holmdale. The second was addressed to Sir Montague Flushing, The Hospice, Holmdale, and the third was addressed to Miss Ursula Finch, Editor of the *Holmdale Clarion,* Claypits Road, Holmdale. . . .

The contents of the three envelopes were identical. Each contained three single sheets of yellow notepaper. In each case, upon the first of these sheets, there appeared the following letter, differing only in its line of greeting:

> I must confess that I am regarding your efforts with a great deal of amusement. You have not got very far, have you? I don't think it is for want of trying, but I must say, without in any way intending to give offense, that I consider that it *is* for want of brains.
>
> I am afraid the message by this little note of mine is going to cause you more trouble than ever, but it really cannot be helped!
>
> I am writing to tell you that I propose to take a little—and I hope you will agree well earned—holiday. In other words, I am not going to carry out any further removals for quite a little while. When I really feel like it, of course, and when the time is propitious, I shall start again. You can hardly expect me to be so magnanimous as to give up altogether, can you?
>
> I hope this will not put you in a very awkward position though I fear it may.
>
> > Very cordially yours,
> > THE BUTCHER.
>
> P. S.—I am so sorry that I have hitherto omitted to send you my little reference notes—which I hope will be useful for your files—in regard to the late Marjorie Williams and Molly Brade. I now repair this omission and enclose them herewith.

The first enclosure was as follows:

My Reference FIVE.
R. I. P.
Marjorie Williams,
Died Friday, 30th November, . . .

THE BUTCHER.

And the second:

My Reference SIX
R. I. P.
Molly Brade,
Died Friday, 7th December, . . .

THE BUTCHER.

3

The sheets of yellow paper still lay open before the chief constable, but now, for the first time since they had been put there, the chief constable was not looking at them. Instead he was looking, twisting round in his chair, at the door which had just slammed behind Superintendent Arnold Pike.

The chief constable straightened himself. He looked from one of of his subordinates to the other. He said, in a tone curiously blent of bewilderment and indignation:

"Where's he *gone?*"

Farrow, frowning, was silent. Davis sniffed one of his most expressive sniffs.

4

"Yes," said the postmaster. "They were taken from the box in Inniless Road by the second collection." He looked eagerly at Superintendent Pike, who faced him across the table. "As you said, Superintendent, I didn't say anything to anybody, and as I sorted the things myself I don't suppose there's anybody knows. *And* I didn't—bearing in mind your instructions, Superintendent— give that information in the covering note."

Pike cut him short. "Quite right. Quite right." He got suddenly to his feet, pushing back his chair with a squeaking sound across the postmaster's floor. He leaned his palms on the table and, looking down at the postmaster with eyes which seemed to bore through the postmaster's head, he said, speaking slowly and deliberately, in great contrast to his previous curtness: "You know, Mr. Myers, you are carrying a great responsibility."

The postmaster shifted uneasily in his chair. "I realize that, Superintendent," he said nervously, "I realize that, I assure you. . . ." He laughed a small, restrained and yet almost hysterical laugh. "But how do *you* know, Superintendent, that I'm not the Butcher himself?"

Pike's mouth twitched to a smile. "I know that," he said, "because I've taken the trouble to find out, Mr. Myers, that on the occasions of these killings, you were conducting yourself ordinarily and properly somewhere else."

"Been doing things thoroughly, haven't you?" said the postmaster, and laughed the nervous laugh again.

Pike regarded him somberly. "Now, Mr. Myers, you've been helping the police very considerably; would you like to help still more?"

Mr. Myers swelled with importance. "Only too glad!" he said.

5

Within five hours Mr. Myers, astonished and thrilled, was sitting in the long barnlike tea room of the Royal George in Batley. The time had gone fast for Mr. Myers. He had been whirled here and there in a closed car driven at a speed which he knew was illegal and felt was dangerous. He had been first to No. 19, Inniless Road and from the car had watched the curious and stealthy emergence from No. 19—which was an empty house!—of a man carrying a square, black, and apparently very heavy box. This man had joined the party in the car, seating himself beside the Superintendent, who was driving. The car had then hurtled Mr. Myers and the rest of the party out of Holmdale by Dale Road and along the Main Road, by way of the new by-pass, to Batley.

Mr. Myers kept his eyes and ears open and, as befitted his new rôle of assistant to Scotland Yard, his mouth shut. Mr. Myers, arrived at the Royal George, witnessed a curious transformation. Superintendent Pike seemed to be no longer Superintendent Pike. His very speech and gait—almost, if he had not known this to be impossible, Mr. Myers would have said his clothes also—had changed. He was now, it seemed, a Mr. Fortescue, and Mr. Fortescue was a gentleman who had something to do with the film industry; something which he appeared to wish to keep a very close trade secret; something about which the Royal George had been partially taken into confidence. . . . And the men who composed the rest of the party—the strange man who had emerged from the house in Inniless Road and the two men who, at first, were called Curtis and Blaine by Superintendent Pike and now were called Ashbridge and Barney by Mr. Fortescue—all now seemed to have changed not only their labels but their deportment. . . .

Mr. Myers's head had begun to reel. But now, seated uncomfortably upon an upright wooden chair, gazing through the dark at a sheet upon which moving pictures were being shown, Mr. Myers began to recover a belief in the world's sanity. For Mr. Myers was looking at the Inniless Road pillar box. . . . The pictures were in jerky pieces and in a way were all the same. . . . They showed persons; persons whom, as one of the oldest inhabitants of Holmdale, Mr. Myers knew not only by sight but by name, walking up to the Inniless Road pillar box and dropping letters and packages into its maw. . . .

The pictures were shown through once in silence, and then Mr. Fortescue—only now Mr. Myers discovered with a shock that it was Superintendent Pike again—now Superintendent Pike came close to Mr. Myers's chair and spoke into Mr. Myers's ear.

"We're going to show the films again," said Superintendent Pike. "I want you to tell me, if you can, who the people you see on this screen may be. . . ."

CHAPTER FIFTEEN

(Confidential memorandum by Superintendent Arnold Pike, C. I. D. to Assistant Commissioner E. Lucas, C. B., etc., C. I. D., dated Monday, December 10, . . .)

Have not sent you any word since Friday, but have now to

report that a scheme which I worked out on Friday has already been justified with results which I *think* may get us somewhere.

On Friday morning, as you were officially notified, there was another Butcher outrage, a Mrs. Brade being murdered in broad daylight outside the big shop here. On Friday evening I thought of the above-mentioned scheme which, in brief, was as follows:

In anticipation of the Butcher letter which, it seemed fairly certain, would follow this crime or precede the next, to take cinematographic pictures of all persons posting letters at all boxes. Result hoped for (as you already know, the post collections are made so that it can be told what box a letter came out of) to narrow down the field of inquiry by concentrating upon all people posting letters during the time the Butcher letter must have been posted. (N. B. I thought it highly improbable that the Butcher would repeat the trick of slipping in his letter with those of someone else, as he did in the Market once before. He is too clever to do this, and therefore, I reasoned, would be most likely to post his next epistle himself.)

I should at once inform you that as soon as I thought of the cinematograph scheme I made the decision not to inform *anyone* down here in regard to it. I told Curtis and Blaine, of course, but I instructed them not to mention the matter. I have even kept the chief constable in the dark. I am sure you will appreciate that the situation here, as far as I am concerned, was one of complete ignorance. Anyone—*anyone at all*—might be the Butcher. As my previous report showed, it was even more likely that the Butcher should be one with whom I come into frequent contact than one of the more ordinary residents.

I hope you will approve of my secrecy. If I am to continue working on this case, I do hope that this will be preserved. I am determined from now on to keep this secrecy even in regard to any other steps which I may take.

Am glad to report that the cinematograph scheme had immediate and satisfactory result. On Saturday morning, while I was at a meeting with the chief constable and others, the postmaster sent up three identical Butcher letters which had been found in the second collection. I got away from the meeting as soon as I could and immediately went to interview the postmaster (see note at foot of this letter). He informed me that the letters had been found in the Inniless Road pillar box. I cautioned him to keep quiet and immediately proceeded to Inniless Road (see separate report to follow as to how the cinematograph men were posted), took the film from the operator there and sent it by Curtis into Batley for private development. Later I collected the postmaster (Myers), Curtis, and Blaine, together with the Inniless Road operator, his camera, and a projector, and proceeded to Batley to a room for which I had arranged—under an alias—in which we could show the film. When the film was ready we ran it through, and Myers was able, fortunately, to tell us who each of the twelve persons posting letters between the eight o'clock collection and ten o'clock collection was.

You will appreciate that one of these twelve persons *must have posted the Butcher letters,* and that, therefore, one of these twelve persons is, in all probability (see argument above), the Butcher himself. In other words, *we have reduced our "suspect list" from approximately five thousand to twelve.*

I give a table in which I have set out the names of the twelve persons, their particulars, etc., and, most important, three columns showing, first, whether they could properly account for the letters posted, second, whether subsequent inquiries proved them to have really indubitable alibis for the times of all the Butcher murders, and third, the reason they posted their letters in the Inniless Road pillar box:

The first question arising out of this table is, of course, the ability of *all* the twelve persons to account for the letters posted (i. e., to state to whom the letters were addressed and what the letters contained). The fact that they were all able to account for the letters did not worry me. I expected it, because—as I foreshadowed in my last report—I thought the Butcher, when posting a letter (in a disguised handwriting and on special paper, etc.), would be clever enough to post at the same time—in case he was asked—a genuine letter written on his paper in his own handwriting.

The next question is the large one of narrowing the field of twelve "possibles." I did this by examining the answers which I have classified under the sixth heading in the table. Analysis of the entries under this heading shows four entirely satisfactory persons—Claud Nickells, Mrs. Tildesley-Marshall, Mrs. Wills, and Philip Matthews; two partially satisfactory persons—Emily Potts and James Stelch; two persons whose statements have not yet been checked (but who, I should add, seem to be almost certainly speaking the truth), Muriel Rowland and Harry Fornby; and four persons whose statements are unsatisfactory in themselves, or un-

Name	Address	Age	Occupation	Whether Able to Account for Letters Posted	Alibis for Times of Outrages	Reason for Posting in Inniless Road Pillar Box
Claud Nickells	30, Inniless Rd.	40	Clerk	Yes	Satisfactory	House by pillar box
Mrs. Tildesley-Marshall	14, Prester Ave.	37	Married woman	Yes	As above	On way to the Market
Emily Potts	The Laurels Nursing Home, Minters Ave.	29	Nursing sister	Yes	Partly satisfactory. Two dates unsupported by evidence	On way to case
James Stelch	3, Inniless Rd.	50	Commissionaire at Breakfast Barlies, Ltd.	Yes	Satisfactory as to three dates. Others unsupported by evidence	On way to work
Ursula Finch	Flat over Clarion offices, Claypits Rd.	35	Proprietor and editor, Holmdale Clarion	Yes	Unable to give witnessed statements as on all occasions alone in Clarion office	Returning to office after seeking interview with Miss Marable re Mrs. Brade
Muriel Rowland	2, Fourtrees Rd.	19	Stenographer	Yes	Statements being checked	On way to station
Sir Montague Flushing	The Hospice	56	Chairman to Holmdale Co.	Yes	Statements vague and unsatisfactory. Uncheckable	Passing in car
Harry Fornby	3, Batley Croft, Batley	30	Bricklayer	Yes	Impossible to check statements yet. Not resident in Holmdale	Opposite work
Sydney Jeffson	Police Station	45	Sergeant of Police	Yes	No witnessed statements. On duty alone	Passing on round
Mrs. Roger Wills	14, Inniless Rd.	27	Married woman	Yes	Satisfactory	Nearest post box
Philip Matthews	4, The New Approach	14	Schoolboy	Yes	Satisfactory	On way to school
L. C. A. Rockwall	Vicarage, Church Rd.	61	Anglican minister	Yes	None actually, although many near times vouched for	Taking constitutional

checkable, or both—Ursula Finch, Montague Flushing, Sydney Jeffson, and Rockwall.

Nickells, Tildesley-Marshall, Wills, and Matthews I am accordingly leaving out of consideration. Their statements have been carefully checked, and there is no doubt that they could not have been, upon any of the occasions, anywhere near the scenes of the outrages.

In regard to the next two classes of partially cleared and checkable but unchecked—Potts and Stelch, Rowland and Fornby—I am having these people kept under surveillance until such times as their statements are completely checked up or not. For this purpose I shall use some of the extra men for whom I applied to you over the telephone yesterday and whom I met at Batley this morning. (I have sent D. O. Handley back, as I am afraid he is not quite the type for the job, being too noticeably a police officer. I should like to get Richards if I can.)

In regard to the last class—Finch, Flushing, Jeffson, and Rockwall—I have put these under special watch, which I hope will be carried out skilfully enough for them not to notice it. There is, of course, the fact that the Butcher, who *must* be one of these twelve, and, in my opinion, one of these last four, must be aware, by reason of the questioning, etc., that we are getting close to him. But any danger which this might have led to of the Butcher "drawing in his horns" is neutralized by the fact that he had already decided to do this, *vide* his last letter, copy of which was sent to you the day before yesterday.

I also propose to have carried out, as soon as practicable, a search of the houses of the four in the last class. In order to do this, if possible, without the knowledge of the persons, I am proposing to hold interviews with these persons, either at my rooms here or at the police station, in which I shall probably apologize for any inconvenience which the recent questioning, etc., may have caused them. I hope that such interviews, if I carry them out properly, will serve the double purpose of keeping the suspect away while the search of his house is being carried out and also lull him (for one of them, in my opinion, in all probability is the Butcher) into a false sense of security and possibly decoy him into making a step which would enable us to arrest him.

Following the unfortunate arrests of Reade, Spring, and Godly, all of whom had to be released, I am bearing in mind your instructions that no other arrests shall be made until there is ample evidence or unless the safety of the public seems to call for it urgently.

I hope progress is satisfactory: I consider it so myself. I have every hope that we are at last nearing some definite conclusion. I hope, also, that my policy of keeping from everyone down here, including the local police, all the recent steps I have taken (as reported above), and any future steps whatsoever until the arrest of the Butcher, will be approved and respected, and that anyone from headquarters will not let even the chief constable have any inkling. (Some justification for this policy will be found on looking at the list of the four main suspects.)

From now I will send you memoranda daily, of course telephoning any urgent or important developments.

(*Signed*) ARNOLD PIKE.

P. S.—In regard to the postmaster, Myers, whom I had, over the pillar-box scheme, to take into my confidence, I should report that I have persuaded Myers to remain out of Holmdale until such time as I recall him. He is at present staying in rooms which I found for him in Penders Cross, a little village outside Batley. I have taken the responsibility of informing him that his expenses will be paid and also that some adequate honorarium will be paid to him at the end of the business. He seems trustworthy (of course, before I took him into my confidence I found out that he had adequate alibis for all the outrage dates), but I didn't want him going back, after seeing the films, to Holmdale, and possibly being unable to keep what he knows to himself.

A. P.

CHAPTER SIXTEEN

Mr. Egbert Lucas was speaking on the telephone to Superintendent Arnold Pike.

". . . You said something last night, when we spoke, about it being all right to ring you on this line. D'you mean I can say anything?"

"Yes, sir."

"How's that?"

"Myers, sir—the postmaster. I made an arrangement with him for a special line here. Good job you rang up when you did. I was just going out. . . . Anything wrong, sir?"

"Don't sound so anxious, man! No. We're very pleased with you. You ought to've heard the commissioner this morning. . . . No, there's nothing special. As a matter of fact, we're getting so worked up that we keep expecting you to make an arrest at any minute. . . ."

" 'Fraid you'll be disappointed, sir."

"Eh? What's that? What's wrong now?"

"Nothing exactly wrong, sir, except the result of the last of the searches—Rockwall's house and Flushing's. Flushing's was very difficult, but Blaine and Curtis managed it between them very well, with Stallard tricking the servant out of the way and me talking to Sir Montague in the Station. . . ."

"Are you trying to tell me, Pike, that you didn't find anything anywhere?"

"That's it, I'm afraid, sir. Not a thing that shouldn't be there. And nothing that would fit in with what the doctors say the weapon must be like. And no Butcher paper. No ink. Nothing!"

"That shake your faith at all, Pike? In your own scheme, I mean."

"No, sir. It's only made me all the more determined——"

"Look here, Pike, what's your own private thought about this? Which one of the four are you betting on? Jeffson?"

"Well . . . If you don't mind, sir, I'm not going to commit myself at this stage. Not even in my own mind, as you might say."

"Very cautious, Pike. But what are you going to *do* now? Seems to be a bit of a deadlock. There's the Butcher having notified you he's going to rest, and there's you with four suspects you can't narrow down. . . . It's the devil of a job!"

"I've got an idea, sir. Had it just before you rang up, as a matter of fact. I was just going out to see whether I couldn't do something about it."

"Good man! What is it?"

"I'd rather not say, sir, in case I don't carry it out."

"All right, Pike. All right. Good-night, and good luck."

"Good-night, sir, and thank you."

2

The chief constable was astonished. Across his own study table he looked with bewilderment at Superintendent Pike.

"I don't understand!" said the chief constable. "I don't understand at all! . . . Damn it, I don't understand!"

Pike was apologetic. "I'm sorry, sir; perhaps you'll tell me what's troubling you?"

"Good God!" the chief constable exploded. "Good God, Pike! When the damn thing was at its height, when people were being slit up right and left and I and my men suggested this curfew, you put your foot on it. *Now,* when there's nothing doing and the damn lunatic's told us there's going to be nothing doing for a bit, you come here and calmly say that you agree at last to the curfew suggestion. Blast it, man, it's not sense!"

Pike was still apologetic, but none the less firm. "Let's say I think everything's *too* quiet, sir. And the Butcher may be tricking us again . . . Let's say I've come round to the opinion that a curfew is what we want."

The chief constable, slightly mollified by the deferential tone, was still bewildered.

"I don't see how I can *now,*" said the chief constable. "When the thing was at its height I could've enforced *any* measure. Now it's all eased off and they're all relaxed instead of tense, well, a thing like that'll take a bit of enforcing. They'll all be wanting to go to the pictures and out to the pub and that sort of thing every evening. Don't see how we *can* do it, Superintendent. Damned if I do! And I'm not sure that we ought to!"

"I don't mean, sir," Pike explained, "that we ought to make the curfew compulsory. What I meant was that I'd like you to issue a police request, as you might say, asking people 'in view of certain knowledge which has come into the hands of the police'—or something like that—asking people to help by not going out at all after, say, eight o'clock at night. . . ."

The chief constable hummed. The chief constable hawed. But at last, under Pike's urbane persistence, he gave way.

3

The "voluntary curfew" had been in operation for two nights. And so it was that Curtis, driving much too fast through the thick white mist which shrouded the Main Road, was stopped at the junction of the Main Road with the Dale Road entrance to Holmdale.

He pulled up with a whining of brakes. The white mist eddied in smoky whorls, and, rubbing the window with his sleeve, he looked out. He saw the outline of a uniformed constable who held a bull's-eye light. He lowered the window and produced his C. I. D. card.

The constable, peering, looked first at this, and then, carefully, at its presenter. . . . The constable fell back, raising a hand to his helmet.

"Beg pardon," said the constable, "we're gettin' very 'ot, specially now the fogs're beginnin'."

Curtis nodded and slipped the car into gear and was off down Dale Road.

Ten minutes later—the fog in the valley of Holmdale was so dense that it took ten minutes to cover a distance usually killed in two—he pulled the car up outside No. 12, Fourtrees Road.

Pike himself opened the door. He seemed tense, on edge. He pulled Curtis into the house and barked at him, "Did you get it?"

Curtis nodded. He stood in the light, blinking. His eyes smarted, and the fog still tickled his throat. "Yes," he said at last. "Think he's made a good job of it, too."

By a blazing fire in Miss Marable's best front room, they bent over a table and examined part of what Curtis had brought from London—a square sheet of yellow paper upon which there were many lines of writing; Peculiar writing in peculiar ink.

Pike grunted; raised his head; bent again to his examination. "Not bad!" he said. "Not bad at all!" He took from his pocket a wallet, and from the wallet another sheet, neatly folded, of the same coloured paper—the first Butcher letter. He unfolded it and smoothed it out with careful hands and laid it beside the sheet on the table.

"It's good!" said Pike at last. . . . "Who did you get to do it? Brodski or Maxwell?"

"In the end," said Curtis, "Foxy did it."

"Are the others as good as this?" said Pike. "And the envelopes?"

"Every bit," said Curtis. "No difference between 'em. . . . And I saw Mr. Lucas, sir, and he said to tell you that he thought your draft was very good. He only altered a couple of words."

Pike grunted. "Yes, I saw that. He's right. Just read it out, Curtis, and let's listen to it. . . ."

4

The telephone in Miss Marable's hall rang shrilly. Miss Marable went to it herself and within a moment was running up the stairs.

Miss Marable knocked at Pike's door and, most unusually walked in without awaiting answer.

Pike was in his favourite position on the window seat. He turned and got to his feet. "Good-morning," he said.

"Oh, Mr. Pike!" said Miss Marable. "They've just telephoned from the police station. It was the chief constable himself speaking." Miss Marable was breathless. "He sounded very urgent. Would you go round at once, please. He said that three times." Miss Marable was a little pinker than usual in the cheeks. "He said that three times," she repeated, "and then rang off."

Miss Marable departed and Pike smiled to himself: a smile which was, at first, merely a twitching of the corners of his mouth, but which, by the time he was descending Miss Marable's stairs, was almost a grin.

But there was no smile, nor hint of a smile, on his lean face as he went in to the room which, for weeks which seemed to Mrs. Jeffson as many years, had been no use as a parlour at all.

The chief constable was there, and Davis and Farrow were there and, of course, Jeffson. They all, even Jeffson, were crowded round the table. So intent were they that Pike stood there for fully a minute before anyone noticed his presence. It was the chief constable who saw him first.

"*There* you are!" said the chief constable. He seemed changed. His heavy face was sagging, and had lost its colour. The pouches under his eyes were like black bruises. His voice, which trembled like his hands, seemed to be hiding fear under irritability. "Look at this, Superintendent. Look at *this!*"

Pike came nearer to the table, halted suddenly, and stared. "Another Butcher letter!" he said.

Farrow, without a word, picked up the yellow sheet by its corner; held it so that Pike could read. Pike read, half aloud:

"DEAR POLICE:

"I regret to say that I find this life of inactivity quite insupportable. You may or may not be glad to hear this. I fancy that you will be both. You will be sorry because you will doubt your ability to prevent my activities and glad because you will not be kept in this dreadful suspense.

"In order to make things pleasantly easy for you I hereby announce my intention of carrying out the seventh of my— shall we call them removals?—to-morrow (Monday, the 17th December).

"I am afraid that last time I gave you warning my sense of humour got the better of me, and knowing that you would be expecting me to carry out my work at night, I carried it out in broad daylight, thus completely confounding you.

"This time, however, I will descend to no such mean tricks, and I hereby give you full warning that the times between which my work will be executed ('executed' is rather good, don't you think?) will be 7 and 10 P. M.

"As usual I have sent copies of this letter to dear Sir Montague and to the *Holmdale Clarion*.

"Tolerantly yours,
"THE BUTCHER.

"P. S.—I find myself in an extraordinarily kind mood to-day. I cannot bear to think of you poor police trying, in despair, to cover the whole of Holmdale for three hours on Monday night. So, in addition to telling you the date and time, I will tell you, approximately, the place. The job will be done between the junction of Market Road and Forest Road at the northwestern end, and the Wooden Shack at the southern end. Don't worry about your curfew. Nothing like that is going to stop me!

"THE BUTCHER."

"Well!" said Pike. "I'll be *jiggered!*"

He thought for one horrid instant that he had been guilty of overacting. But he looked round at the faces of the other men and found in them no suspicion. . . .

CHAPTER SEVENTEEN

Monday was a clear day of bright, hard, frosty sunshine. But with evening there came, with that frequent paradox of English climate, a drop in temperature. As early as four o'clock the mists began to gather again. By five, all Holmdale was shrouded in a fleecy blanket of white fog. By six o'clock, even in the brilliantly lighted patch before the Market, it was difficult for a man to see more than ten yards ahead of him; by seven o'clock he could not see more than five.

At a quarter-past seven at the junction of Collingwood Road with Market Road, Blaine, walking at a pace inconsistent with the visibility, ran into a living organism as solid as himself.

"*Uh!*" Blaine grunted; then reached out a hand to grope; but even as he reached out his hand, another hand clutched his shoulder.

Detective Officers Frank Blaine and George Curtis recognized each other.

"Christ!" said Blaine, "I thought you were the Butcher."

Curtis laughed. They fell into step. They proceeded down Collingwood Road and turned, crossing the road until they were on the grass plot facing the northerly façade of the Market. The fog was very thick here; so thick that barely could a man see his own hand at arm's length. They halted.

"About here, was it?" said Curtis.

"Anywhere along this side," said Blaine. He craned his head forward between his square shoulders and stared at the blurry blobs of light which were the lamps before the Market. "That's what he wrote, wasn't it? . . . The bloody bastard!" he added viciously.

Through the fog, brushing aside its white billows with black bulk, Curtis moved closer. His hand closed its fingers upon Blaine's arm. He said, quietly:

"Time you were told, boy."

"Get out!" said Blaine, incredulous. "Why, I was in the station

just after A. P.'d left, and Jeffson showed it to me. I've seen too
many of those Butcher letters not to know one when I see it."

Curtis's fingers tapped emphasis on Blaine's shoulder. "That
letter, I tell you," he said, "was written by Foxy Maxwell. I was
there while he did it yesterday. If I'd seen you since I'd 've told you.
A. P. said it was all right if I did."

"Well, I'll be——" Blaine said what he would be. And, when he
had recovered from the first shock of astonishment, asked almost
querulously:

"But *why?*"

"My boy," said Curtis, "A. P.'s good. You and me know that.
But this is the best he's ever done. He's got these what he calls
'possibles' down to four: the old parson, Monty Flushing, Miss
Finch of the *Clarion,* and—and"—here Curtis dropped his voice
still lower—"you know who!"

"You mean Jeffson?" Blaine's voice was a whisper.

Curtis coughed. "Blast this fog!" he said. "Yes, that's right! Well,
that's something, isn't it? We started with five or six thousand suspects, and we've got down to four. There's not many men at the
Yard could've done *that* in the time. In fact, no one could except
A. P. . . ."

"Yes. Yes." Blaine was impatient. "But what about the letter?
What's the idea?"

"Can't you see?" Curtis was all bland superiority. "A. P. knew
this letter'd be seen by all of 'em except Rockwall—and he'll get to
hear of it. Now, one of those four's the Butcher, isn't he?"

"Not *is,*" said Blaine the cautious. "*May* be!"

"Well, I say *is,*" said Curtis. "But I'll take your point. So I'll say
one of those four's most likely the Butcher, isn't he?"

"Yes," said Blaine. "So?"

"So all those four've heard about this new Butcher letter and
mostly seen it. So the one that *is* the Butcher, what does *he* think,
now he finds some other bloke's been writin' Butcher letters and
braggin' Butcher brags?"

"We-ell," said Blaine. "I suppose he'll be sort of puzzled and
jealous. All at the same time."

Curtis was approving. "Almost A. P.'s own words!" he said.

Blaine was still working it out. "So A. P. calculates this fake
letter might draw the Butcher out in the open, eh? Because he'll
be bound to try and see who it is trying to step into his shoes. That
the way of it?"

"Certainly is." Curtis gestured into the fog. "Anyone comes along this road here—'specially if it's one of the four—well, we'll be ninety-nine and three-quarters per cent. sure who the Butcher is. And that, me boy, won't do us any harm!"

"That it won't!" Blaine said. "You're right; A. P.'s really on the target, isn't he?"

"Mind you," said Curtis, "whoever comes along—*if* 'e comes along—is going to be all ready with a bloody good excuse for bein' where he is—"

Blaine nodded. "That's right. So ten to one we can't nab him then and there. But we'll *know* ... ." A fit of coughing cut him short as the fog pierced his throat. It was thicker now, swirling round them in dense eddies, pressing close about them like a wet and gray and impalpable blanket.

"Getting cold," Curtis growled. "Let's walk."

They paced up and down, up and down, two large looming shapes in the white darkness. Every now and then they stopped to listen; then resumed their walk. The warmth came back to their feet and, in some degree, to their bodies, but the fog did not lift. It got into their eyes and made them smart; it got into their noses and made them feel as if they were breathing wool; it got down their lungs until they coughed.

And every now and then Blaine would ask Curtis, or Curtis would ask Blaine: "What's the time?"

And this went on until, with the last asking, Blaine said: "Nine-fifteen. I wonder——"

"S'sh!" said Curtis and gripped his arm with iron fingers.

They stood motionless. Not a sound came to them. Blaine shifted uneasily, but Curtis's fingers tightened their clamp; held him quiet.

"Listen!" said Curtis.

At first muffled by the deadening curtain of fog, but rapidly growing until it was living and human and recognizable, there came the sound of rapid, crisp footsteps.

Blaine started forward.

"*Wait!*" Curtis whispered. "A. P.'s there. Over the other side. Wait!"

They waited. As the footsteps seemed to draw abreast of them, beating their way into the extra whiteness made by the Market lamps, they heard other footsteps, coming out of nothing: footsteps which their ears recognized immediately.

The first set of footsteps ceased abruptly. The second ceased also. . . .

"Come on!" said Blaine.

They guided themselves off the grass and onto the road and crossed the road where the fog was thinned by the lamps. As they drew near they heard Pike's voice, and another. They drew nearer, on tiptoe. The voices were cast in pleasant tones. But they knew. They were closer now, and not only their ears but their eyes told them that one of the speakers was indeed Arnold Pike. But they were looking at the other. . . .

2

At half-past eleven that night, Curtis and Blaine sat, each upon the edge of his chair, in Miss Marable's lounge. Pike, his back to the crackling fire, surveyed them. He said, looking at Blaine:

"So Curtis put you wise, did he?"

Blaine nodded. "Yes, sir."

There was a moment's silence, then Pike spoke again. He said, looking at Curtis this time:

"You saw?"

Curtis grunted affirmation. He looked at his chief with some anxiety. Pike's face seemed longer and leaner, and the lines of his frown looked as if they had been cut into his forehead with a chisel.

It was Blaine who broke the silence.

"What's going to happen, sir?" he said. "What can we do?"

Pike shrugged. For the second time during this case he used an oath. "I'm damned," he said, "if I know! I hope I shall to-morrow. You two get off and carry on with your ordinary duties, saying *nothing to anyone*. If I'm not here to-morrow, it means I'm up in town. Good-night, now!"

They went; and Pike was left staring at Miss Marable's fire. Presently, he dropped into a chair, put his elbows on his knees and his chin into his cupped hands. . . .

3

The next day Pike did go to London. In Holmdale, Curtis and Blaine, carrying on with stolid faces their entirely unnecessary duties, awaited him.

They did not see him until half-past six that evening, which was the evening of Tuesday, the 18th December. And when they did see him it was to receive news which flabbergasted them.

"*Leaving,* sir?" said Blaine. "Without laying a finger on that . . ."

Pike nodded. "We're going, to-morrow morning. I'll see the chief constable to-night. I'll also see you two again to-night."

Curtis and Blaine looked at him. They were used to his moods and varying expressions. But they could read nothing from the long, blank face he turned on them.

"Isn't there *any* way we can make the arrest?" Blaine knew the answer, but the question had burst from him out of sheer frustration.

"On what we have now?" Pike was mournful. "You know there isn't. We've searched the house, haven't we? And all the belongings. And found nothing. Nothing! And then some more nothing. We've got no finger-prints, no evidence—nothing at all except in our own knowledge. . . . How *can* we make an arrest? We'd be the laughing stock of the country in five minutes!"

4

"Well," said the chief constable, "in a way I'm very sorry. In a way I can see what he means." He tapped the official letter at the foot of which Pike, pretending not to look, could see Lucas's signature. "I mean I can see Scotland Yard's point of view. And I must say, Superintendent, that, after your valuable advice—er—er—" the chief constable got into difficulties here and finished up with a weak "and all that. I do feel that my own men can carry on. So perhaps it's all for the best."

The chief constable rose, extending a podgy hand which trembled. Pike shook it without warmth. He also shook hands, displaying less warmth still, with Davis. He turned and clasped the hamlike fist of Inspector Farrow and gave this a hearty enough shake. He nodded to Jefferson, made a curious little ducking nod to the chief constable, and was gone.

Outside the Crossley waited. In it were Curtis and Blaine. Pike climbed into the car, and they drove away.

They circled the town, and many saw them go.

That was at noon on Wednesday, the 19th December. By one o'clock all Holmdale knew of their going. There were mutters in Holmdale. There were outcries in Holmdale against the leaving;

and also satisfaction in Holmdale on account of the leaving. Holmdale, as always since the beginning of its curse, was divided into many camps.

The chief constable, Farrow at one shoulder and Davis at the other, reread the letter signed by Egbert Lucas. In the corner Jeffson stood erect, awaiting instructions. The chief constable mouthed over to himself the letter's last paragraph:

". . . The Commissioner, therefore, desires me to state that he feels it unnecessary that Superintendent Pike and his subordinates should remain any longer in Holmdale. While the Commissioner is willing and anxious to offer all the help he can in the most tragic and unusual circumstances, he is unable, owing to the scarcity of officers and men, to allow Superintendent Pike and his subordinates to remain with you indefinitely. Should any further developments or new turns to the situation arise, he will, of course, be only too glad to give you the benefit of any assistance which the Department might be able to provide. In the meanwhile, he hopes that you will agree to the withdrawal of his men.

"I am, sir,
"Your obedient servant,
"EGBERT LUCAS."

"And that," said the chief constable pettishly, "is that! I can't say Scotland Yard's gone up in my estimation. What've they done that we couldn't have done? Eh? Eh? . . ."

Farrow grunted. But Davis said:

"Nothing, sir, and not near as much, if you were to ask me. And I reckon we've got this Butcher under, anyway, sir."

The chief constable shook his head, but a pleased smile creased his mouth. "Well," said the chief constable. "He certainly didn't carry out the threat in his last letter, did he?"

"Nor," said Davis confidently, "he never will."

Farrow grunted.

CHAPTER EIGHTEEN

There was fog again upon the Wednesday and Thursday nights. But on Friday the wind changed and there was slashing rain and hail. The stones rattled on Holmdale's red roofs, and the gutters of Holmdale ran with turgid, black-brown water.

The storm started late in the afternoon, and continued into the night. So that, what with the weather and the general, continued observance of the "voluntary curfew," it seemed that, except for police and members of the special patrols, there could not conceivably be any human abroad within Holmdale's limits.

And yet, at around eleven o'clock, there most certainly was; an odd and pathetic and solitary wanderer.

A small person this, in a short and dirty garment of knitted wool which exposed lanky legs from ankle to mid-thigh. Over the garment was a short coat of threadbare black stuff, too big in the shoulders, and moth-eaten about its collar and cuffs. There were thin and almost soleless shoes on the small feet. She had no hat, and her hair, which was drawn back over her ears into two plaits with bedraggled tape bows at their ends, was saturated with the rain.

The water streamed down her face, and the occasional hailstones stung her. She was in Collingwood Road, slinking along like some furtive animal in the shadow of the hedge. Footsteps came towards her; heavy, martial footsteps of one of the chief constable's recently doubled patrols. She slunk into the shadow and crouched behind a gate. She shivered.

The footsteps went by, slow and ponderous and stately. The little figure crept out again from the gateway and onto the pavement. Once more it slunk furtively along. . . .

2

There was light in the offices of the *Holmdale Clarion* and also a light above, in the hall of the flat belonging to the *Holmdale Clarion's* editor.

Miss Finch had come downstairs, from flat to office. Miss Finch was writing a letter. The sheet upon which she was writing lay square upon her blotter. It was covered with writing. Miss Finch, suddenly discovering the need for more paper, rose and went to the corner of the room in which there stood, in their magnificent, specially presented, entirely free, bookcase, the forty-seven volumes of the American *Cyclopædia*. She took out the volume marked Par-Pork; opened it; laid it flat upon the top of the bookcase table, and ran her finger and thumb lightly over its edges until she found what she sought—some twenty-four pages whose outer edges adhered one to the other. Into the centre of the pocket made by these pages Miss Finch slid her left hand and brought it away bearing another sheet of the yellow notepaper. There was a glove upon her left hand.

She went back to the desk. She dipped a strangely nibbed pen into a small inkpot and settled herself once more to her task. She wrote:

> . . . and, therefore, I really do feel

But she got no further. Suddenly she raised her head. Her large and beautiful eyes narrowed to slits as she listened. Her neatly coifed head was cocked to one side like some small bird's. Miss Finch, with a smooth, hasty movement, hid the two sheets of her letter beneath the top sheet of her blotter. With another movement, just as smooth, the ink bottle went into the left-hand drawer of her desk. A key locked this drawer and was slipped into one of the pockets of Miss Finch's admirably cut tweed jacket.

The sound she had heard came again, a timid rapping upon the office door knocker. Miss Finch rose. She went through the open glass door marked "Editor" and into the passage. While she walked many expressions passed over her face, but when she opened the door it wore the smile which did so much towards enhancing her charm. She threw open the door and stood looking out into the wild darkness of driving, beating rain; then suddenly saw at her feet a small, huddled limpness, half sitting, half lying upon the bottom of the three steps which led from the door down to the pavement.

Miss Finch, reaching out a hand, snapped on the passage light. Its effulgence bathed the steps. . . .

"Well, my little dear," said Miss Finch, "what's the matter?"

She did not go down the steps, but she peered downwards. From the limp, woebegone bundle a small head was raised; a small head from which there stuck out, ridiculously, two little plaits of hair tied tightly at their ends with dirty tape. The face which looked up at Miss Finch was a white oval in the yellow light. Out from it stared dark eyes, black-rimmed with fatigue and terror.

"I'm afryde!" said a thin and trembling little voice. "Got lorst . . . and up there . . . and up there . . ."—a thin arm came out and made slight gestures—"up there, there was a man. 'E chysed me. . . . I'm afryde. Let me come in, lydy!"

"You poor little dear," said Miss Finch slowly. "Yes, come in. Come in." She stood on one side. The small figure heaved painfully to its feet and made gasping way up the steps and over the threshold.

"Coo!" said the thin voice. " 'Tain't 'alf luvly an' warm in 'ere." Thin fingers came out and clutched Miss Finch suddenly and fiercely by the arm. "Lydy, that man, 'e chysed me. 'E can't get in 'ere after me, can 'e?"

Miss Finch's hand came slowly out and patted the thin, sodden shoulder.

"Of course he can't, my dear. Of course he can't. Poor little thing, you're drenched through and through. Come in. Come in."

Miss Finch, still with hand holding and caressing the thin shoulder whose bones she could feel beneath the shabby and drenched cloth, propelled her visitor gently towards the open door of the editorial office. "There's a fire in here," said Miss Finch. "You can get warm, dear, and dry your clothes."

The waif, catching sight through the open door of the red glow of a large gas fire, dashed forward and crouched on the hearth, shivering now so that her teeth chattered in her head.

Miss Finch followed slowly. Miss Finch stood looking down at her visitor. There was a bright sheen, like unshed tears, over Miss Finch's eyes.

"Coo!" said the visitor. " 'Tain't 'arf lovely and warm in 'ere! 'Tain't 'alf bleedin' cold ahtside."

"My dear!" Miss Finch was shocked. "My *dear!*"

"Well, 'tis," said the visitor. "Perishin' cold and bloody awful wet!"

"Yes, dear," said Miss Finch with something like a break in her voice. She knelt down beside the woebegone figure and with gentle hands took off the sodden coat. She stood back while it dripped a little pool of black water onto the gray carpet. Her visitor crouched over the fire like a tragic monkey, holding out grime-stained hands to the glow.

Still holding the coat, Miss Finch spoke again. She seemed to have some difficulty with her voice. It was not the voice with which she had spoken when she had opened the outer door. It was a thicker voice, choked a little as if the words she spoke were too big for her mouth. She said:

"But what are you doing, dear? Out alone at this time of night! And what is your age? . . . How old are you, dear?"

"Firteen." The waif looked with a frightened movement over her shoulder and up at Miss Finch. She put up her hand as if to guard herself from a blow.

"I ain't done nuffink wrong. I got lorst, I told yer!"

"My dear," said Miss Finch and moved forward a little. The wet coat was brushing against her legs, but she didn't seem to notice it. "Of course you've done nothing wrong." She seemed suddenly to become aware of the wet coat. She hung it, with care, on the back of an office chair, and turned again to the fireplace, and stood looking down at her guest.

"Tell me," said Miss Finch, "how did you come to get lost? How is it that you, a child of thirteen, are wandering about like this? You don't live here in Holmdale, do you, dear?"

"Don't live anywheres," said the guest. "Farver's got a caravan, and we go rahnd to fairs, and when we stopped to 'ave a bit o' dinner this afternoon I finds a hystack. I lies dahn and goes to sleep, and when I wakes up Dad and Mum and the bleedin' caravan and Spot—he's my dog—well, the 'ole bleedin' lot's gorn, missus. Ever since, I been on me trotters tryin' to catch up wiv 'em. But it comes over reel dark, and then I sees this 'ere plyce and I means to knock at some door and arst for a doss or p'raps a bite o' grub. And then that gryte man 'e chyses me—Kor! 'e didn't 'arf frighten me. . . ."

"My poor little girl," said Miss Finch. "So you're only thirteen, and your daddy has a caravan, and he's gone away with the caravan, and you don't know where you are, and your daddy doesn't know where you are?"

"That's right, missus, that's right!" She sniffed; passed her hand across her eyes. "That's right. I dunno where I am, and Dad, 'e doesn't know where I am—not that 'e'd care so bleedin' much if 'e never saw me agyne."

"You mustn't say that," said Miss Finch in a new and somehow crisper voice. "You mustn't say that!" She smiled down at her visitor.

"I know what you'd like," said Miss Finch. "You would like a nice hot cup of cocoa with lots of nice milk and sugar in it and some bread and butter? Now, wouldn't you?"

"Not 'arf, I wouldn't!" said the visitor. "You jest show 'em to me, missus."

Miss Finch bustled out. "I will. I will." Her voice came back through the open door.

And then came the sound of her feet running up the carpeted stairs to her flat above.

The visitor cast a hunted glance about her. She looked at the door. She looked at the gaily curtained windows. She looked round at the stern though comfortable furniture. She stood in the centre of the room by Miss Finch's table and gazed up at the big skylight window in the roof. Nervously she played first with an inkpot, then with a pencil, and lastly with Miss Finch's ebony ruler with the ivory tips.

Upstairs, Miss Finch, her breath so laboured that her breasts seemed at times to be going to burst the silk blouse which covered them, stood before the bentwood hatstand in the passage of her little flat. . . .

Miss Finch went, half-pace by half-pace, towards the bentwood stand. Her hand, crooked like a claw, grasped the handle of her dumpy umbrella. . . .

Miss Finch sat upon the topmost step of the stairs and with her left hand silently removed her shoes. Miss Finch, levering herself to her feet with a thrust of the umbrella, began slowly and very, very quietly to descend the stairs . . .

Miss Finch reached the door of the editor's room. She halted just before she was within the sight of anyone inside it. She seemed to have difficulty with her breath. She moved the umbrella from the right hand to the left, her right hand hovering over the handle. She took two steps forward. Her face now was dead white; her eyes had a glassy, polished look, like sea-washed pebbles.

Now she was squarely in the doorway. Crouched by the fire was her visitor, staring with vacant, childlike eyes into the far corner, holding in her hands Miss Finch's ebony ruler, one of its ivory ends between her lips. Miss Finch's left hand, holding the dumpy umbrella, went behind her back. Miss Finch came brightly into the room. She spoke in a light, clear voice. She went near to her guest. She said:

"Your cocoa won't be a minute, dear. It's just on the boil. Stand up now, and let's see what we can do about your wet clothes."

The eyes of the waif fixed their gaze on her face. Slowly the small figure rose to its feet, gripping the ruler. "All right, missus," said her thin, high voice.

They stood facing each other . . . The waif backed. A little choked cry came from her. She took another step back, then two more; then more, in a stumbling run which fetched her up with a bang against the table of Miss Finch's assistant editor. Her eyes roved wildly this way and that—to the door; to the window; to the skylight above her head.

"What's the matter, dear?" said Miss Finch, coming forward slowly.

The eyes of the waif were wide and staring, and the waif's mouth opened, and a scream came from it.

Miss Finch came nearer. "What's the matter, dear?" she said again.

Again, with her eyes fixed upon Miss Finch, the waif screamed. Miss Finch's left hand came from behind her back. Her right hand clasped the handle of her dwarf umbrella. Her two hands came apart. . . . The umbrella, without the handle, fell to the floor with a soft clatter, but in Miss Finch's right hand there was a thin something which gleamed blue in the yellow light. . . .

Miss Finch drew in her breath with a little hissing sound. She moved her right hand.

Miss Finch's visitor raised, with a wild, ineffectual gesture, the ebony ruler.

Miss Finch laughed. . . .

With a sound which, in that small quiet room, was like the rending of heaven itself, the glass and frame of the skylight smashed inwards. From six feet above her, something dark and huge and heavy fell beside Miss Finch and clutched at her. . . .

Miss Finch rolled upon the floor. . . .

Outside there came another, different crash and the tinkling of more broken glass . . . and heavy running footsteps along the boarded passage.

The waif collapsed upon the table. The ebony ruler fell from her hands to the floor, hitting the gray carpet with a little thud. . . .

There was scuffling on the floor.

The doorway suddenly framed two men, so that, with the man who rolled upon the floor with Miss Finch, there were three men now here.

The two newcomers bent over the struggling heap, but before

they could put their hands on it, there was a click and a jingle, and Pike got to his feet. There was a long, bleeding scratch running down from the corner of his left eye to his jaw. His eyes were bright and fierce, but his mouth was wide in a smile of triumph.

On the Persian rug before the gas fire Miss Finch struggled, despite the handcuffs, to sit up. Her eyes seemed to have changed colour; they were wide and staring. Her mouth worked but no sound came from it. . . . Her face was no longer chalk white but duskily flushed.

Pike went forward. Behind him the two men moved close. Pike stooped. He tapped his prisoner on the shoulder. He murmured official words. . . .

The woman's face remained expressionless. . . . Her mouth went on working. . . .

Pike came to the end of his rigmarole and then, as he began to straighten himself, she flung back her head and spat into his face.

3

Two cars pulled up outside the headquarters of the county police in St. Raglands. The hands of the clock over the town hall stood at one forty-five. The passengers of the first car made a little procession which wound quickly through the swing doors. The uniformed sergeant saluted, and Pike smiled at him.

"Get my message to Sir Geoffrey?" he said.

The sergeant saluted again. "Yes, sir. He's in there waiting. If you'll follow me . . ." They followed him.

He threw open a door, and the procession filed in. There was the chief constable, and there, too, were Farrow, smiling all over his prize-fighter's face, and Davis, looking like a glum fox.

The chief constable came to Pike, holding out his hand.

Pike shook it.

"My God!" said the chief constable and could get out no more words. He looked over Pike's shoulder at those who had followed Pike. "But where is—where is she?" he said.

Pike looked round too. "In the second car there, with another of my men. She's not a pleasant sight."

The chief constable once more looked over Pike's shoulder. He saw Curtis, whom he knew, and Blaine, whom he knew, but in between Blaine and Curtis was a small and shivering waif.

The chief constable looked at Pike in bewilderment. "Who's this?" he said.

Pike's smile grew wider yet. He turned to the waif. He said:

"You must pardon me. May I introduce Sir Geoffrey Mainwaring, the chief constable of the county. . . . Sir Geoffrey, this is Miss Barbara Fairley. I don't know whether you go to the theatre much, Sir Geoffrey, but you're sure to have heard . . ."

The chief constable was staring until his eyes seemed in danger of leaving his head. "Not," he said, "not Dinah in *The Golden Cup?*"

"Quite right!" said the waif, and then, looking from one escort to the other. "For God's sake, has anybody got a whiskey and soda?"

THE RYNOX MURDER

EPILOGUE

George surveyed the Crickford's man and the package with pompous disapproval.

"Bringing a thing like that to the front!" said George. "Oughter know better. If you take your van down Tagger's Lane at the side there, you'll find our back entrance."

George may have been impressive; was, indeed, to a great many people. But the vanman was not impressed. He evidently cared little for George's bottle-green cloth and gilt braid; less for George's fiercely-waxed moustache, or George's chest, medals or no medals.

"This unprintable lot," said the vanman, " 'as got this 'ere obscene label on it. My job ain't to stand 'ere chewin' the unsavoury rag with any o' you scoutmasters! My job's to deliver. Are you or are you not medically goin' to take unclean delivery?"

The normal purple of George's cheeks slowly turned to a rich black. George could not speak.

"If you don't," said the vanman, "gory well 'urry, off we go with the lot." He stooped and looked at the label. "And it's addressed to one of your big noises—F. MacDowell Salisbury, *Ess*quire. President: Naval, Military & Cosmo—Cosmo—whatever the 'ell it is, Assurance. That's you, ain't it?"

He held out a grimy thin-leaved book, together with a quarter-inch stub of unpointed pencil. A dark thumb pointed to the foot of the open page.

"You signs," said the vanman, "along dotted line 'ere, *if* you can write. Otherwise you'd better put your mark and I'll write somethink against it for yer. 'Urry up now!"

It will always be matter for conjecture as to what George would have done at this stage had not at this moment the car of F. MacDowell Salisbury drawn up immediately behind the Crickford's van. This left George only one course. Quickly he signed. Quickly laid hold of the unwieldy package—two large and extremely heavy sacks formed this package; sacks tied together at their top. With considerable exertion of his great strength he managed to drag them up the two remaining steps and in through the swing doors of glittering glass and mahogany. Just as, puffing, he had rested them against a corner of the panelled wall, the president came up the steps. George got to the door just in time; held it open; touched his cap; strove to keep silent his laboured breathing.

" 'Morning, George!" said the president.

George touched his cap again. He could not speak yet. The president was in good humour. Instead of striding straightway down the marble-floored corridor to the lift, he halted, his head on one side. He surveyed George.

"George," he said, "you look hot."

"I am—fuf—sir!"

The president's eyes strayed to the unwieldy sacks. "Weight lifting, George?"

"Yessir. Just as you come, sir, I was telling the Crickford's man that he ought to 've took the lot round to the Lane entrance, but I saw it's for you, sir, so I brought it in this side."

"For me?" The president's tone and his eyebrows went up.

"Yessir, according to the label."

"Extraordinary thing!" The president walked over to the corner, bent down over the sacks and lifted the label. "Extraordinary thing!" he said again. He put a podgy white hand to the joined sacks and tried their weight. "Feels heavy," he said.

"Heavy, sir," said George, "it is!"

Again the president stooped to the label. Yes, it bore his name; also, in red ink and capital letters—staring capitals—the words:

EXTREMELY PRIVATE AND
CONFIDENTIAL
PERSONAL FOR MR. SALISBURY
ONLY

"Well, I'll be damned!" said the president. "Better get a couple of men and have it brought up to my office."

2

The president, with podgy white forefinger, pressed the third of the bell pushes upon his desk.

"Miss Winter," he said, to the bell's genie, "have they brought up those sacks?"

"The sacks have just come, Mr. Salisbury."

"Right! Just give the fellows a bob each out of the Petty Cash, and then I'll come out. Most extraordinary looking thing, isn't it, Miss Winter?"

"Yes, Mr. Salisbury."

Miss Winter, very severe, very neat, most efficient, went back to the outer office. The president, walking slowly after her, saw her distribution of largesse; saw the porters touching clean hats with dirty forefingers; saw the door close behind them; went out into Miss Winter's room.

Very untidily heaped in its very tidy centre were the sacks. Miss Winter was bending down, reading the label.

"Got a knife?" said the president.

Miss Winter had a knife. Miss Winter always had everything.

"Just see," said the president, "whether you can cut the string."

Miss Winter could cut the string and did. The sacks fell apart. The president stirred one with his toe. The contents were hard yet yielding.

"I can't make it out!" said the president.

"Shall I open a sack?" said Miss Winter. A very practical woman.

"Yes, yes. Let's have a look."

Once more Miss Winter stooped; once more the penknife came into play as it ripped the stout thread which kept the mouth of the sack closed. Miss Winter inserted a hand. . . .

"Good God!" said the president.

He took two short steps and stood at Miss Winter's shoulder. Upright again, she was holding between her hands a thick elastic-bound wad of one-pound Bank of England notes.

"Good God!" said the president again.

He bent himself over the mouth of the open sack and thrust in his own arm. His hand came away with yet another package. . . .

He let the sack lie flat upon the floor, bent over it, caught it a little way down from its top and shook. Other packets fell from it upon the floor. . . .

He looked into the sack. . . .

There could be no doubt! The sack—it looked like a hundred-weight-and-a-half corn sack—was filled, crammed, with bundles of one-pound Bank of England notes. They were not new, these notes. The bundles did not bear that solid, block-like appearance of unused paper money, but, although neat, were creased, and numbered—as Miss Winter at once was to find—in anything but series.

"Good *God!*" said the president. Himself, with Miss Winter's knife, he cut the threads which bound the mouth of the other sack. And this second sack was as its brother. If, indeed, there was any difference, it was that this second sack held still more bundles than the first. The president stood in the middle of the floor. Round his feet there lay, grotesque and untidy, little disordered heaps of money.

The president looked at Miss Winter. Miss Winter looked at the president.

"I suppose," said the president, "that I *am* at the office, Miss Winter? I'm not by any chance at home, in bed, and fast asleep?"

Miss Winter did not smile. "You certainly are at the office, Mr. Salisbury."

"And would you mind telling me, Miss Winter, what these things are that I'm treading on?"

"Certainly, Mr. Salisbury. Bundles of one-pound notes, not very clean, I'm afraid."

"I'm going back to my room to sit down," said the president. "If you wouldn't mind coming in again in a few minutes, Miss Winter, and telling me all over again what there is in those sacks, I should be very much obliged. Also you might empty the sacks and find out if there is anything else in them except—except—well, except bundles of one-pound notes!"

"Very well, Mr. Salisbury. And would it not be as well, perhaps, if I also ring up Crickford's and see whether I can ascertain who is the sender of this—er—of this—er——" Even Miss Winter for once was at a loss for words.

"Do! Do!" said the president. "And don't forget: Come in and tell me all about it all over again!"

"Very well, Mr. Salisbury."

3

"If," said F. MacDowell Salisbury to his friend Thurston Mitchell, who was also vice president of the Naval, Military & Cosmopolitan Assurance Corporation, "you can beat that, I shall be much surprised."

Mr. Mitchell could not beat it. He said so. "If I hadn't," said

Mr. Mitchell, "seen the damn stuff with my own eyes I wouldn't believe you now, Salisbury. . . . What did Crickford's say when Winter got on to them?"

"Crickford's," said Mr. Salisbury, "agreed to make inquiries of their branches. They did. This package was delivered yesterday evening at their Balham receiving office. The customer, who did not give his name, paid the proper rate for delivery, asked when that delivery would be made, and—" Mr. Salisbury shrugged his plump shoulders despairingly—"just went."

"What did he look like?"

"According to what Crickford's managing director told me on the phone, the clerk said that the sender was a 'tall, foreign-looking gentleman.' Little beard, broken English, rather exaggerated clothes—that sort of thing. Came in a car."

"Car, did he?" said Mr. Mitchell. "Now, did they . . ."

Mr. Salisbury shook his head sadly. "Mitchell, they did not. They couldn't tell me whether that car was blue or green, open or closed, English or American. They couldn't tell anything. After all, poor devils, why should they?"

Mr. Thurston Mitchell paced the presidential room with his hands in his pockets, his shoulders hunched, and a frown drawing his eyebrows together into a rigid bar across his high-bridged nose. He said:

"And there wasn't anything, Salisbury? Nothing in those sacks except money?"

"Nothing," said the president. "Nothing, Mitchell, of any description—except one grain of corn which I have here upon my desk. I thought I'd better keep it as a souvenir."

"Well, I'm damned!" said the vice president.

"Quite," said the president. "Yes, Miss Winter, what is it?"

Miss Winter came to the presidential desk. There was about her a certain excitement, intensely restrained, but discernible nevertheless. She bore, rather in the manner of an inexperienced but imaginative recruit carrying a bomb, a small, oblong brown-paper parcel. She placed it upon the presidential table. She said:

"This has just come, Mr. Salisbury. By registered post. I thought I'd better let you have it at once because—well, because I fancy that the printing on it is the same as the printing on the sack label."

The president stared. The vice president came to his shoulder and did the same thing.

"By jove!" said the president. "It is! Here, Mitchell, you open it. *You* haven't had a thrill to-day."

The vice president, having borrowed Miss Winter's penknife, cut the parcel string, unwrapped three separate coverings of brown paper, and found at last a stout, small, deal box. It had a sliding lid like a child's pencil-box. The vice president slid away the lid. He looked, and put the box down before the president. He said:

"Look here, Salisbury, if any more of this goes on, I shall go and see a doctor. Look at that!"

Mr. Salisbury looked at that. What he saw was a sheet of white paper, and in the centre of the sheet of white paper a new half-penny. . . .

"Don't look like that, Salisbury," said the vice president. "You can't want any *more* money!"

The president removed the halfpenny and the sheet of paper. "I've got it!" he said, "whether I want it or not!"

Underneath the sheet of paper were, in three lines of little round stacks, forty-six new pennies. They were counted, with a composure really terrific, by Miss Winter. And underneath them was another piece of plain white paper. But this piece of plain white paper bore in its centre, neatly printed with a thick pen and in thick black ink:

*THIS IS THE BALANCE. THANK
YOU VERY MUCH!*

Total: £287,499 3s. 10½d.

(Two hundred and eighty-seven thousand, four hundred and ninety-nine pounds, three shillings and tenpence halfpenny.)

N. B. Not for personal use. For the coffers of the Naval, Military & Cosmopolitan Assurance Corporation.

The president looked at the vice president. Both looked at Miss Winter.

"Miss Winter," said the president, "would you be so very kind as to leave the room? I'm sure that in one moment Mr. Mitchell will say something which it would be better for you not to hear."

BOOK ONE

CHAPTER ONE

Thursday, 28th March: 9 A. M. *to 12 noon.*

Entwhistle, the Fordfield postman, pushed his bicycle up the steep hill into Little Ockleton. The sack upon his back was heavy and grew heavier. The March sun, even at half-past eight this morning, seemed to carry the heat of July. Entwhistle stopped, puffed and mopped his head. He thought, as he thought every morning, that something ought to be done by the authorities about this hill. He pushed on again and at last was able to mount.

It was so rarely that he had a letter for Pond Cottage that he was nearly a hundred yards past it when he remembered that not only did he have a letter for Pond Cottage but that he had an unstamped letter for Pond Cottage. That meant collecting postage from Pond Cottage's occupier. The extra hundred yards which he had given himself was alleviated by the thought that at last—if indeed Mr. Marsh were at home—he would see Mr. Marsh and talk to Mr. Marsh. He had heard so many stories about Mr. Marsh and never had occasion to add one of his own to the many, that the prospect was almost pleasing. He dismounted, rested his bicycle against the little green paling, and went through the gate and up the untidy, overgrown flagged path.

Mr. Marsh, it seemed, was at home. In any event, the leaded windows of the room upstairs stood wide.

Entwhistle knocked with his knuckles upon the door. . . . No reply. He fumbled in his satchel until he found the offending, stampless letter. . . . He knocked again. Again no answer came. Perhaps after all he was not going to see and talk with the exciting Mr. Marsh. Still, one more knock couldn't do any harm! He gave it and this time an answer did come—from above his head. An answer in a deep guttural voice which seemed to have a curious and foreign and throaty trouble with its r's.

"Put the bloodstained letters down!" said the voice. "Leave 'em on the step. I'll fetch 'em."

Entwhistle bent back, tilting his head until from under the peak of his hat he could see peering down at him from that open window the dark-spectacled, dark-complexioned, and somehow uncomfortable face of Mr. Marsh. Mr. Marsh's gray moustache and little pointed gray beard seemed, as Entwhistle had so often heard they did, to bristle with fury.

He coughed, clearing his throat. "Carn' do that, sir," he said. "Letter 'ere without a stamp. I'll 'ave to trouble you for the postage, sir."

"What the hell are you talking about? Put the damn letters down, I say, and get your ugly face out of here. Standing there! Put the letters down and be off."

Very savage, the voice was.

Entwhistle began to experience a doubt as to whether it would be quite as amusing to see and talk to Mr. Marsh as he had supposed. But he stuck to his guns.

"Carn' do that, sir. Letter 'ere unstamped. 'Ave to trouble you for postage, sir."

"*Dios!*" said the voice at the window, or some sound like that. The window shut with a slam. Involuntarily Entwhistle took a backward step. He half expected, so violent had been the sound, to have a pane of glass upon his hat. He stood back a little from the doorstep. He could hear quite distinctly steps coming down the creaking staircase, and then the door was flung open. In the doorway stood a tall, bulky figure wrapped in a shabby brown dressing gown. Its feet were in shabbier slippers of red leather. The hair was black, streaked with gray. The moustache and little beard were almost white. The tinted glasses staring straight into Entwhistle's Nordic and bewildered eyes frightened Entwhistle. They gave to Entwhistle, though he could not have expressed this, a curious uneasy feeling that perhaps behind them there were no eyes at all.

"Where's this damn letter? Come on, man, come on! Don't keep me standing about here all day. It's cold!" The bulk of Mr. Marsh shivered inside his dressing gown. He thrust out an imperious hand.

Into this hand Entwhistle put the letter. It was twitched from his fingers.

"I'll 'ave to trouble you for postage, I'm afraid, sir."

Mr. Marsh made a noise in his throat; a savage animal noise. So fierce a noise it was that Entwhistle backed involuntarily two steps. But he stayed there. He stuck to his guns. He was, as he was overfond of saying, a man who knoo his dooty.

Mr. Marsh was staring down at the envelope in his hands. A frown just showed above the tinted spectacles. White teeth below them glared out in a snarl and Mr. Marsh emitted a string of violent sounding and most unpleasing words. He put his thumb, as Entwhistle watched, under the flap of the envelope and with a savage jerk freed its contents, a single sheet of typewritten paper. Mr. Marsh read.

"F. X. Benedik," growled Mr. Marsh. And then another word. This time an English word which Entwhistle omitted when telling of the adventure to Mrs. Entwhistle.

"I'll 'ave," began Entwhistle bravely, "to trouble you for——" There was a flurry within the door. It slammed. The violence of the slamming detached from the lintel a large flake of rotting timber which fell at Entwhistle's feet.

Entwhistle pushed the postman's hat forward on to the bridge of his snub nose. The stumpy fingers of his right hand scratched his back hair. What, he wondered, was he to do now? It did not occur to him to knock again at the door. Mr. Marsh might be good gossip, but Mr. Marsh was most obviously not the sort of man for a peace-loving postman to annoy. But there *was* the excess fee and when he got to Fordfield he would have to account for that. . . .

He was still debating within his slow mind when something— some hard, small, ringing thing—hit the peak of his cap with sharp violence. He started. The cap, dislodged by his jerk, fell off; rolled to the path. Bewildered, he looked down at it; stopped ponderously to pick it up. There beside it, glinting against a mossy flag, was a florin. Still squatting, Entwhistle looked up. The upstairs window was open again. From it there glared out Mr. Marsh's face. "It was," said Entwhistle to Mrs. Entwhistle that evening, "like the face of a feen in 'uman shape. And," said Entwhistle, "'e was laughin'. To 'ear that laugh would make any man's blood run cold, *and* I don't care 'oo 'e was. Laughin' 'e was; laughin' fit to burst hisself. What did I do? Well, I picks up the two bob and me hat and I says as dignified like as I can, 'You'll be requirin' your change, sir.' Just like that I said it, just to show him I wasn't 'avin' no nonsense. What does 'e say? When he's finished laughin' a few minutes later, he says: 'You can keep the something change, and swallow it!' Funny sort of voice he's got— a *violent* sort of voice. That's what he says—'You keep the some-thing change, and you something well know what you can something well do with it.' What did I say? Well, I says, still calm and collected like, 'D'you know, sir, throwin' money like that, you might 'ave 'it me in the face,' and then 'e says, 'Bloody bad luck I didn't!' just like that: 'Bloody bad luck I didn't! You something off now or I'll chuck something a bit 'eavier.' "

Thus the indignant Entwhistle to his wife. Thus, later that same evening the histrionic Entwhistle in the bar of The Coach and Horses. Thus the important Entwhistle in the Fordfield Police Station three days later.

2

James Wilberforce Burgess Junior was spinning a whip-top with no mean skill upon the cement path outside Ockleton Station booking office.

James Wilberforce Burgess Senior, Ockleton's stationmaster, porter and level-crossing operator, watched for a moment with fatherly pride and then turned away to enter the hutch which was his booking office. He came out of the hutch a moment later a good deal faster than he had gone in. A sudden howl from James Wilberforce Junior had torn wailing way through the sunny morning.

James Wilberforce Junior was huddled against the wall, one hand at his ear and the other rubbing at his eyes. His top and his whip lay at his feet. Just within the doorless entrance was "that there Mr. Marsh."

The Ockleton Burgesses, for many generations, have not been renowned for physical courage. Some fathers—however big, however sinister-seeming, the assaulter of their innocent child—would have struck first and spoken afterward. Burgess did not strike at all. He said a great deal, though, and this was listened to, with an exaggerated and ironic courtesy, by "that there Mr. Marsh." Standing there in the shadow, the odd, pointed black hat tilted forward upon his head; the dark glasses making pits in his face instead of eyes; his white teeth gleaming when he smiled his savage, humourless, and twisted smile, he seemed to Burgess, no less than previously to Entwhistle, "a feen in 'uman shape." He cut presently across the whiningly indignant outburst of outraged fatherhood. He said:

"Cut it out! Cut it right out! I want a ticket for London." His deep, somehow foreign voice boomed round the tiny brick box.

"Throwin' your weight about!" said James Wilberforce Burgess Senior. "Strikin' defenceless children! Don't you know it's dangerous to 'it a child on the yeerole?"

Mr. Marsh took a step forward. Mr. Burgess took three steps backwards. Mr. Marsh pointed to the door of the ticket hutch. Mr. Marsh said, and Mr. Burgess swore afterward that his teeth did not part when he said it:

"Back in the kennel, you! And give me a ticket for London."

Here Mr. Marsh, Burgess reported, put his hand into his pocket and pulled out half-a-crown which, with a half-turn of his body, he threw to the still snivelling James Wilberforce Junior.

"There," he said, "that'll buy him a new ear!"

"All very well, sir," said Burgess, now speaking through the pigeonhole, "walking about, striking defenceless children . . ."

Into the pigeonhole Mr. Marsh thrust his dark face. "Give me a fair turn," said Mr. Burgess afterwards. "Sort of as if the devil was looking at you through a 'ole."

Mr. Marsh received his ticket. Mr. Marsh was presently borne away by the nine-ten Slow Up from Ockleton. He had bought a day-return ticket.

Upon the Ockleton platform that night, there waited for Mr. Marsh's return not only James Wilberforce Burgess Senior, but James Wilberforce Burgess Senior's sister's husband, one Arthur Widgery. This was a big and beery person whose only joy in life, after beer, was performing the series of actions which he invariably described as "drawin' off of 'im and pastin' 'im one alongside the jaw!"

But Mr. Marsh did not take advantage of the return half of his ticket.

3

Mr. Basil Musgrove, who had charge of the booking office of the Royal Theatre, was this morning presenting an even more than usually bored exterior to the world. Last night Mr. Musgrove had been out with a set of persons to whom he was usually wont to refer as the boys. Consequently Mr. Musgrove, underneath his patent leather hair, had a head which was red hot and bumping.

Mr. Musgrove said into the telephone: "No, meddam. We do not book any seats at all under three shillings!"

Mr. Musgrove said, to a feminine face peering in through his pigeonhole: "No, meddam, we have no stalls whatsoever for this evening's performance. I am sorry."

Mr. Musgrove, when the face had vanished, put his head upon his hand and wished that the boys would not, quite so consistently, be boys. Mr. Musgrove's heavy lids dropped over his eyes. Mr. Musgrove slept.

Mr. Musgrove was awakened most rudely. Something cold and sharp and painful kept rapping itself against the end of his nose. Mr. Musgrove put up feeble hands to brush this annoyance away, but, instead of being brushed away, its rappings grew more frequent and so discomfortable that Mr. Musgrove's eyes were forced to open. With their opening the world came back with a rush, and Mr. Musgrove saw what it was that had awakened him. It was the ferrule of an ebony walking stick, hovering barely half an inch from the end of his nose. Behind the stick he saw a pair of dark, blank eyes set in a face which, he told some of those boys the next night, was just like Old Nick looking at you. . . .

Mr. Musgrove drew back with a start. His chair tilted underneath him, and only barely did he escape a fall.

The walking stick was withdrawn. The window now was filled with this devil's head under the strange pointed black hat; there were dark glasses; a little gray block of beard; a white, twisted inimical smile.

"Er—" said Mr. Musgrove—"er—er—I beg—er——"

The stranger said a word. And then: "Three stalls to-morrow night?"

"No, no!" said Mr. Musgrove. "No, no, no!" He strove to collect his scattered wits. "No, sir. No. We are entirely full for both the matinée and the evening performance to-day."

The face seemed to come nearer. Almost it was through the pigeonhole. Mr. Musgrove recoiled; once more felt his chair rock beneath him.

"I didn't ask about to-day." The harsh voice seemed to find trouble with English r's, though none with English idiom. "I asked about *to-morrow!*"

"Oh. Er—I'm sorry," Mr. Musgrove babbled. "I'm sorry. I'm afraid I didn't catch what——"

"Have you or have you not three stalls for to-morrow night's performance?"

"To-morrow, sir, to-morrow?" said Mr. Musgrove. "Three stalls, sir, three stalls. Would you like them in the middle, sir, at the back, or, in the front at the side . . . I have a nice trio in H——"

"I don't care," said the voice, "where the hell the damn seats are! All I want is three stalls. Give 'em to me and tell me how much they are so that I can get away from your face. It's not a pleasant face, I should say, at the best of times. This morning it's an indecency."

Mr. Musgrove flushed to the top of his maculate forehead. The tips of his ears became a dark purple colour. As he said to the boys that evening, "D'you know, you chaps, if it had been any other sort of a man, well, I'd have been out of that office and set about him in half a second. You know me! But as it was, well, believe me or believe me not, I just couldn't move. I was rooted! All I could do was to give him his three seats and take his money. You see some odd customers in my job, but I've never seen such an odd one as that before, *and* I don't want to see another ever. Horrible old bloke! Sort of nasty, sinister way to him, and what with that beard and those dark glasses and that limp—he sort of seemed to drag his left leg after him and yet go pretty fast—he was a horrible sort of chap! I'm going to look out for him to-morrow night and see what sort of company he's got. . . . Thanks, Ted; mine's a port and lemon. Cheerioski!"

CHAPTER TWO

Thursday, 28th March: 12:30 P. M. *to 3:30* P. M.

The offices of Rynox (Unlimited) are in New Bond Street. A piece of unnecessary information this, since all the world knows it, but it serves to get this sequence started.

Up the white marble steps of Rynox House—Rynox themselves use only one floor in the tall, narrow, rather beautiful building—there walked, at twelve-thirty in the early afternoon of this Thursday, Francis Xavier Benedik—"F. X." to his many friends and few but virulent enemies.

The doorkeeper, a thin, embittered person graced with the name of Butterflute, smiled. The effort seemed—as F. X. had once indeed remarked—to sprain the poor man's face. But smile he did. Everybody smiled at F. X.—except those few but very bitter enemies. F. X. paused upon the top step.

"'Morning, Sam," he said.

"Good-morning, sir," said Butterflute.

"How's the sciatica?"

"Something chronic, sir."

"That's a bad job. How's the family?"

"Not too well, sir," said Butterflute. "Wife's confined again; *I* dunno 'ow she does it! My boy got three weeks yesterday, for D. and D. in charge of a motorcar, and me daughter—well, sir——"

F. X. was grave and sympathetic, also determined. "Damned hard luck, Butterflute. Damned hard! Anything you want, just let me know, will you?"

Butterflute touched his cap. "Yes, sir. I will that, sir. Thank you, sir."

F. X. went on and through the main doors and so along the corridor to the lift: a tall, burly but trim, free-striding figure which might have been from the back that of an athletic man of thirty. It was only when you saw his face that you realized that F. X. was a hard-living, hard-working, hard case of fifty-five. You realized that, and you were quite wrong. Wrong about the age, anyhow, for this day was the sixty-seventh birthday of Francis Xavier Benedik. But whatever your guess, whoever you were—unless indeed you were one of those very few but very violent enemies—you loved F. X. on sight. He was so very much the man that all the other men who looked at him would have liked to be. He had obviously so much behind him of all those things of which, to be a man, a man must have had experience.

"'Morning, sir!" said Fred. Fred was the lift boy. In direct contrast to Butterflute, Fred did not smile. You see, Fred otherwise always smiled, but Fred felt, as did everyone, that one must do something different for F. X. So instead of smiling Fred looked grave and portentous.

"'Morning, Frederick! Lovely day!"

"It is that, Mr. Benedik, sir. Beautiful day."

The lift purred softly and swiftly upward. Frantic would-be passengers on the first, second, and third floors were passed with a cool contempt.

The lift stopped. For other passengers Fred was wont to jerk the vehicle, being the possessor of rather a misguided sense of humour, but for F. X. Fred stopped it as a lift should be stopped; smoothly, gently, imperceptibly.

At the gates F. X. paused. He said over his shoulder:

"You look out for that girl, Fred."

From between Fred's stiffly upstanding cherry-coloured collar and Fred's black-peaked cherry-coloured cap, Fred's face shone like a four o'clock winter sun.

"Beg pardon, sir?" said Fred.

"The neat little thing on the first floor, Fred. Between you and me, you might tell her that their Inquiries door wants a coat of paint, will you? . . . She's all right, Fred, but you want to watch that sort with black eyes and gold hair."

The winter sun took on an even deeper shade.

"Oh, Fred!" said F. X.

The lift shot downward at the maximum of its speed.

Past the big main doors upon this top floor—the big doors with their cunningly blazoned sign:

RYNOX

S. H. RICKWORTH   ANTHONY X. BENEDIK

F. X. BENEDIK

went F. X., with his long, free stride which seemed somehow out of place in a city. Past these and past the next small door bearing the sign:

RYNOX

Inquiries Here

and so to one of modest and unmarked mahogany. The handle of this door turned in his fingers. He went in, shutting it behind him.

" 'Morning, Miss Pagan. 'Morning, Harris." Thus F. X., hanging up his light gray, somehow dashing-looking hat.

"Good-morning, Mr. Benedik," said Miss Pagan. Her sad blond beauty was illumined by one of her rare smiles.

" 'Morning, sir," said Harris.

"Mr. Rickworth in, Miss Pagan?"

"Yes, Mr. Benedik. I think he's in your room. He said he wanted to see you particularly before you started work."

"Mr. Anthony here?"

"Not yet, Mr. Benedik. Mr. Anthony wired from Liverpool that he was coming in on the twelve-fifty; would you wait lunch for him?"

F. X. crossed the room, stood with his fingers upon the baize door which separated this outer office of his from the corridor leading to the partners' rooms.

"Anything else, Miss Pagan?" he said. "I don't want you to come in with the letters just yet. Wait until I've seen Mr. Rickworth."

"Very well, Mr. Benedik." Another of Miss Pagan's rare and sadly beautiful smiles. "No, nothing else except Mr. Marsh."

A frown marred the sunniness of the senior partner's tanned face. "Marsh," he said. His voice grated on the ear. "Has he been bothering you?"

Miss Pagan shrugged elegant shoulders. "Well, not bothering, Mr. Benedik, but he's rung up twice this morning, the second time only five minutes before you got here. He seems to want you very urgently. And he seems very angry."

"Ever see him," growled F. X., "when he didn't?"

Miss Pagan shrugged again. "I've only seen him once, Mr. Benedik. I must say, though, on the telephone he always does sound angry."

"Angrier than his letters?" said F. X.

"That," said Miss Pagan, "would be impossible. . . . Anyhow, he said would you please telephone him as soon as you got here."

F. X. raised his eyebrows. "Number?" he said.

"I asked him for the number, Mr. Benedik, and he wouldn't give it." Miss Pagan's eyebrows suggested that Mr. Benedik should know by this time what Mr. Marsh was like. "All he'd say was, 'the Kensington number.'"

F. X. laughed, a snorting contemptuous laugh. "That's like the fool!" he said. "All right, I'll get on to him. I'll see Mr. Rickworth now. I'll ring when I want you, Miss Pagan."

"Very well, Mr. Benedik."

2

"But good gracious me!" said Rickworth. "My dear Benedik, I daresay that I have not your push, your ability to handle big things courageously, but I do know, and I think you know too, that I'm a man with a certain amount of business knowledge, and what I say, Benedik——"

F. X., whose gravity throughout this interview had amounted to more than sadness, suddenly grinned. The whole man, with that flash of white teeth, shed twenty hard-fought years. He said:

"Sam, my boy, when you clasp your hands like that over that pot-belly of yours and start calling me Benedik, I can't help it, but I want to kick your bottom. You know, Sam, the trouble with you is that you've got the ability of a card-sharp, the tastes of an emasculated Nero, and the conscience of an Anabaptist minister. You're a mess, Sam, an awful mess, but you're not a bad fellow as long as you don't hold your belly and call me Benedik, and—" momentarily the smile faded—"and as long as you don't try to teach F. X. Benedik his job. Good Lord, man, don't you think that I know what state the business is in? You seem to forget, as a matter of fact, that I *made* the damn business. I know how deep we are in it, but I know, too, how high we're going to soar out of it after this waiting business is over, so for God's sake stop moaning. If you want to get out, get out! Go for a holiday or something. Go and hold your belly in a cinema. Don't come here and try to make that fat face of yours all long. I can't stand it, and I won't!"

Samuel Harvey Rickworth laughed, but it was a laugh that had in it an undercurrent of fear.

"My dear F. X.," he said, "I'm not being what I suppose you'd call 'a wet sock.' I'm merely trying to show you the sensible point of view. Rynox gave up practically all their other interests for the Paramata Synthetic Rubber Company. You did it. You backed your own judgment, and we, very naturally, followed you. But even at the time—at the beginning, I mean—I freely confess I got nervous. I thought to myself, can he pull it off? . . . What's the matter? . . ."

F. X. had sunk into an armchair of deep and yielding leather. His long legs were thrust stiffly out before him. A large white silk handkerchief covered his face. His hands were folded over his chest in the manner of a sleeping Crusader. From under the handkerchief his voice came hollow:

"Nothing's the matter. Go on, Samuel, go on!"

Again Rickworth laughed. "It's all very well," he said, "but I will finish. It's my opinion, F. X., and I'm not joking, that you have done what you'd call 'bitten off more than you can chew.' Look at us, overdrawn here, overdrawn there; creditors beginning to get uneasy, and what are we waiting for? Orders that may come but equally may not, and—and—" his fat, well-to-do voice grew suddenly sharp—"and, F. X., Rynox is unlimited! You would have it, and it is, and whereas I might not say all this if we were a limited company, as a partner in an unlimited company I must say all this."

The handkerchief flew a foot into the air as F. X. let out his pent breath. Suddenly he hoisted his bulky length from the chair, took two steps, and clapped a lean brown hand—which to Samuel

Harvey Rickworth felt like the end of a steel crane—upon Samuel Harvey Rickworth's shoulder.

"Sam," said F. X., "you are, without doubt, a barrel-gutted old fathead! Now, for God's sake, go out, buy yourself a drink, and come back more cheerful. I've got enough troubles without seeing those podgy hands of yours clasping that obscenity you call a stomach. What you wear those buff waistcoats for, I can't make out! They only accentuate it. What you want, Sam, is a bit more of your daughter's spirit. If I were to tell Peter what you've been saying this morning——"

"I say, F. X., you wouldn't do that, would you?"

F. X. put back his head and laughed. "By God, Sam! I believe I've got you!" he said. "I haven't tried it before, but I'll try it now. If I have any more of this S O S stuff, I'll tell Peter, that's what I'll do! And then she'll tell Tony, and then you'll get it hot all round. Now, buzz off, you old blight!"

Rickworth went, but the door was only just closed behind him when it opened again. It admitted only his round pink-and-white face, timid under the ivory sheen of his baldness.

"I say, F. X.," said the face, "you won't really tell Peter, will you? I mean, damn it, business is business. . . ."

The latest edition of the Directory of Directors smote the door with all its half hundredweight of matter one tenth of a second after Samuel Harvey Rickworth had closed it.

F. X. reached out for the telephone; picked it up; lay back in the chair with the receiver at his ear and the body of the instrument cuddled closely against his chest. Like many men who have lived at least half their lives in very different places from City offices, he always spoke very loudly over the telephone. "Kensington," he shouted, "four-double-nine-nine-oh. . . . Is that Kensington four-double-nine-nine-oh? . . ." His voice was thunderous. "Can I speak to Mr. Marsh? . . . Eh? . . . What's that? . . . Mr. *Marsh,* I said. M for Marjorie, A for Artaxerxes, R for rotten, S for sausage, H for How-d'ye-do. . . . Marsh. . . . Oh, right. I'll hold on."

He reached out a long arm, the receiver still at its end, and pressed that one of the buttons on his desk which would bring Miss Pagan. When Miss Pagan came he was talking again. He was saying:

"Well, certainly, we've got to get this matter settled. I can't make you see reason by writing, so I suppose we'd better meet. Now I'm very busy. I suggest we should meet some evening, as soon as you like. Not to-night. I've got a dinner party. To-morrow night, say. Just a moment, I'll ask my secretary. . . . All right, keep your shirt in! Keep your shirt in! Keep letting it hang out like that and you'll be arrested for exhibitionism."

He looked up from the telephone, clasping the mouthpiece firmly to his waistcoat.

"Miss Pagan," he said, "got my book?"

"Yes, Mr. Benedik." Miss Pagan's tone was faintly injured. Of course she had his book.

"Am I doing anything to-morrow night?"

"There's nothing in *this* book, Mr. Benedik."

"Well, I don't know of anything," said Benedik; then into the telephone: "Marsh, still there? . . . Look here, Marsh, I'm free to-morrow night. Come along to my house and see me, will you? And I want to assure you that we're going to settle. You worry the life out of me, and you worry the life out of my people, and we're all sick to death of you! Understand what I'm talking about? I'm going to *settle!* Are you free to-morrow night? . . . Right, ten o'clock suit you? . . . Right. Well, come to my place. . . . What's that? . . . You know damn well where I live. Oh, well, perhaps you're right, perhaps I never told you; thought you might come round worrying the servants or something. Four William Pitt Street, West one. . . . No, Mayfair. . . . Yes, come through the market if you're coming from the Piccadilly side. Four. That's right. . . . Right, ten o'clock to-morrow night. Good-bye!"

He replaced the receiver with a savage little click; set the telephone down upon his desk with a bang. "And," he said looking at it, "God blast you!" He looked up at Miss Pagan. "Shove that down, will you? Ten P. M., house—for to-morrow this is, you understand—10 P. M., house, Marsh. And put it in big red capital letters. And I'd like to tell you this, Miss Pagan, that if ever that—" he drew a deep breath—"if ever that person—I can't say more in front of a gently nurtured English girl—if ever he puts his wart-hog's nose in this office after to-morrow night, you have my instructions to crown him with the heaviest thing you can lay your hands on. And if he rings up, ring off. . . . Mr. Anthony back yet?"

"Not yet, Mr. Benedik. Shall I ask him to come and see you as soon as he gets in?"

"Please," said F. X. "And now you might bring me that last lot of reports from Lisbon. . . . And please ask Mr. Woolrich to come along and see me."

The Lisbon reports had been brought and read and digested

before Woolrich came. Twice F. X., now alone, had looked at his watch before there came a soft tapping upon the door and round its edge Woolrich's sleek fair head.

F. X. looked up. He said:

"Enter secretary and treasurer with shamefaced look. And you'd better hurry, too."

Woolrich came in.

"I'm awfully sorry, sir," he said. "Afraid I missed my train this morning. I'd been down to the country."

F. X. looked at him. F. X., after one frosty instant, smiled. "You're always," he said, "going down to the country. You know, Woolrich, you ought to be careful of that country. I'm not sure it's doing you much good. In fact, if you weren't such a damned good man I should have a great deal more to say about it. . . . Sit down!"

Woolrich moved over to the big chair at the far side of the desk. He was a tall and broad-shouldered and exquisitely dressed person of an age which was hard to determine. He might have been anything between 25 and 40. Actually he was 36. His tan was as deep almost as F. X.'s own, and his ash-blond hair was bleached by the sun and open air—but under the startlingly blue eyes were dark and lately almost permanent half-moons.

"Look here, Woolrich!" F. X. leaned forward. "I've just been looking over this last lot of reports from Lisbon. I expect you've read 'em."

Woolrich nodded. "I think," he said, "I could say 'em over by heart."

"You mean," said F. X., "you know you could. . . . Well, there's only one thing that worries me, and that's Montana. You know and I know that Montana's not on the level—unless it pays him to be. And is it paying him?"

Woolrich nodded. He said, with emphasis:

"It is. If he went over to real rubber he'd never get the money. There aren't any flies on Montana. You know that, sir, and he must realize that if he started any double-crossing he might do well for a bit but in the long run he'd get ditched. I've thought it all out."

"That," said F. X., "is my opinion too. . . . All right, we'll leave it there. Now . . ."

They plunged into many and intricate details of business. They did, in ten minutes, so used were they to each other, so much pleasure did each mind take in the other's, as much work as most other couples in London, standing in the same relation, would have spent two hours and more upon.

F. X. rose and stretched himself. His big body seemed suddenly to tower. He said:

"Well, that's that! Anything else, Woolrich?"

Woolrich pondered a moment. His blue eyes narrowed as he thought and one corner of his well-cut, clean-shaven mouth twitched to a little constricted grin of concentration. At one corner of his mouth there showed a gleam of teeth as white as F. X.'s own. He pulled out a small notebook; flipped over its pages.

"Nothing to-day, sir."

"You don't want to go down to the country this afternoon?" F. X. looked at him.

A dark flush darkened Woolrich's tan. He shook the blond head. "No, sir." He stood up. "If there's nothing else I'll go and have a bite of lunch. Busy afternoon after what we've done."

F. X. nodded. "No, there's nothing else."

Woolrich walked to the door. With his fingers on its handle he turned. He said:

"By the way, sir, I hear that fellow Marsh has been ringing up——"

"Oh, him!" said F. X. "That was before you came in. . . . All right, don't blush. I meant to tell you, I've made an appointment with Marsh to-morrow night. I'm going to meet him after all, and I'm going to settle with him."

Woolrich came away from the door, back into the centre of the room.

"Good Lord, sir!" he said. "You don't mean to say you're going to——"

F. X. shook his head. "No, no, no! Woolrich, I'm not wringing wet—you know that. No, I'm going to tell Mr. Marsh that if he likes to take a little douceur he can buzz off; if he doesn't like to take it, he can buzz off just the same. I'm fed up with him. . . . And if after to-morrow he ever rings up or shoves his face in here again, you can have him buzzed off with my love. Anyhow, we don't want things like that blocking up the place."

Woolrich paused on his journey to the door. He said:

"I've never seen him, sir, and I don't want to. But from what you said I should imagine you're right."

"I am!" said F. X. with feeling. "Anthony here yet?"

"I'll send him along, sir," said Woolrich and was gone.

3

Francis Xavier Benedik and Anthony Xavier Benedik stood
expectant just within the main doors of the Alsace Restaurant.
They were waiting for Petronella Rickworth, who infinitely preferred to be called Peter. Peter was Samuel Harvey Rickworth's
daughter and did not look it. She was also—or perhaps primarily
—the future wife of Anthony Xavier Benedik. She was very, very
easy to look at. Her engagement to Tony Benedik had broken, at
least temporarily, more hearts than any feminine decision in London for the past six months.

Peter was always late. Tony looked at F. X. "Another little
drink?" he said.

"That'll be three," said his father.

"Right-ho, if you say so!"

They drank standing, their eyes fixed upon the revolving doors
through which presently Peter would come. Standing there, utterly
unconscious of their surroundings, glasses in hands, they were a
couple which brought the gaze of many eyes to bear upon them.
Exactly of a height, exactly of a breadth, with the same rather
prominent-jawed, imperious-nosed, hard-bitten good looks, the
same deep, wide shoulders and narrow horseman's hips, they
were a walking, talking proof that heredity is not an old wife's
tale. What lineage, God knows, for F. X. himself could scarcely
tell you whence he came, but wherever this was, it and his own
life had stamped their stamp upon the man, and this stamp
was upon the son. They did not, these two, behave like father and
son. They were more like elder and younger brother—much more.
In only one particular was their aspect different. In the dress of F. X.
was a careless, easy mixture of opulent cloth and "I-like-a-loose-
fit-blast-it-what-do-clothes-matter?" carelessness. In the dress of
Tony was a superb and apparently utterly unconscious elegance.

The revolving doors revolved—and Peter was coming toward
them with her hands outstretched.

"My dears," she said, "do not—do not say all those things which
are trembling on your tongues and shooting darts of fire from your
too amazingly similar pairs of eyes! I'm sorry! I'm sorry! And I'm
sorry! How's that?"

"Very well," said F. X. "In fact, Peter, I think you're too well-
mannered. After all, you know, any couple of men ought to be

only too damn glad for you to lunch with them at all, let alone worry if you're a few minutes late."

"Few minutes!" said Tony. "Few minutes! If you do this, my girl, after we're married, you'll only do it once. At least, only once a month."

Peter's golden eyes stared at him. "Once a month? Why only once a month? Why not once a week?"

"The effects, of the beatings," said Tony, "will last three weeks, five days and seven hours exactly. We've got a table. Shall we go in, F. X.?"

"If," said his father, "the lady wills."

The lady did will, and presently they sat, a trio to draw all eyes, over a meal which was probably the best of its kind in all London.

It was over coffee that F. X. said:

"Peter, I want to talk to you about your family."

Peter laughed. "Family, sir?" said Peter. "It's the first I know about it!"

"I mean," said F. X., "the other way round, backwards. Your father."

"Oh, *Daddy!*" said Peter. "What's he been doing? You don't mean to tell me that cross-eyed one in the Palazzo chorus has been getting Daddy into trouble, do you?"

"Your father," said F. X., "said nothing to me about cross-eyed Palazzo's. Nothing at all. He wouldn't. He might think I'd take a fancy to them. I'm worried about your father"—his smile was gone now—"because your father is getting worried about Rynox."

"What abysmal cheek!" said Peter. "Worried about Rynox! I'll scald his fat little ears! . . . Or shouldn't I?"

She leaned her elbows on the table and looked into the eyes of F. X.

"Have a cigar, Tony?" said F. X. "All right, Peter, I'm going to shoot in a minute. There's a maître d'hôtel with long pitchers just behind. Have a cigar, Tony, go on? . . . Look here, Peter, I don't know whether Tony's told you. Being Tony he probably has, but Rynox is on about the stickiest patch of country we've ever struck. The position exactly is this—that *if* we can keep going for another six months, we shall be rolling along on top of the world, and right on top of the world. If we can't keep going for six months, we shall be rolling along somewhere in Lambeth gutter. Now, I'm not joking, Peter. I'm talking dead straight. Rynox is mine. I mean, I started it, and I don't believe, for business purposes, in limited companies. A limited company means limited credit, and I like my credit hot, strong and unbounded. Hence the unlimited condition of Rynox. But, Peter, do you know what an unlimited company means? It means that if the company fails, all the creditors can come down upon not only the company, but upon all the individual partners in the company. That is, upon me first, then Tony, and then your father. They can take not only the chairs and desks and pictures and carpets out of the office, but the tables and pianos and bath taps out of your house!"

"Yes, sir," said Peter. "Yes, I knew that."

A good lie; she hadn't known that. Both men knew that she hadn't known that. Both men if possible loved Peter more than they had five minutes ago.

"Your father," said F. X., "being a shrewd but timid Leadenhall Street business man, has frankly got the wind up. I keep soothing him down but I'd like you to help. I'd like you really to soothe him right down." He turned to his son. "Tony, has Sam said anything to you lately?"

"Sam," said Tony, "thinks that if a man is under fifty he ought still to be playing with rattles. Sam doesn't understand me, I don't understand Sam. How on earth Peter ever managed to be—sorry, old thing! Anyway, in answer to your question, F. X. Benedik, Sam has *not* said anything to me. I think he has to Woolrich, though."

F. X. laughed. "If he said anything against Rynox to Woolrich, I know what he'd get! That boy's keener on his job than anybody so fond of trips into the country's any right to be. Rynox is graven on his liver."

Tony moved the glasses from before him; leaned across the table; said in a different tone:

"Look, Dad, we're going to pull this off, aren't we? Because if you think it's too much for you—but of course you don't!"

"I don't think anything," said F. X. "I know, boy. I know. By the way, did you see that friend of yours? Young Scott-Bushington?"

Tony's lip curled. "I saw him all right. Cold feet though. Nothing doing, F. X."

F. X. grinned. "Don't look so solemn, boy. That's all right. Look here, Peter," he turned to the woman who was going to be his son's wife, "I don't know how much Tony tells you, but I'd tell you everything and then some. What Rynox wants, Peter, is a hundred and seventy-five thousand pounds."

"That *all?*" said Peter.

F. X. smiled. "It sounds a lot of money, my dear, but in this sort of business it's, well, just nothing. You know what Rynox is doing, don't you, Peter? Rynox has practically chucked all its other interests into the fire to break the Paramata Synthetic Rubber Company."

Peter nodded. "Oh yes, I know that. Tony does tell me things."

"I expect," said F. X., "that he does. And if I may say so, quite right too. Well, the Paramata Synthetic Rubber Company's going —not west, but big. We've got the plant, we've got the stock, we've got the orders—some of them. We've got four big orders, Peter, hanging fire. They're coming along all right; they're German, three of them. But we've got to last out until they do come and then a bit, see? And that's what your father's worried about. He thinks we can't hang on, and I tell him we can. I tell him we've damn well got to! So you get at him, Peter, and tell him so too." He turned to his son. "Tony!"

"Sir?"

"Paris for you, my lad. I want you to go and see Menier. If we don't recall that Valenciennes loan within the next six months we ought to be shot. I'd like it within a month. Just see what you can do, will you?"

Tony drew patterns upon the cloth with the haft of his fork. "Right! Yes, I know Menier pretty well. We're rather pally, as a matter of fact. When do you want me to go?"

"Better take the five o'clock plane. That gets you there in time for a full day to-morrow and Saturday and as much of Sunday as you'd like. Come back Monday morning. . . ." F. X. looked at his son for a long moment. "Stick at it, Tony. And by the way . . ."

Tony cocked an unobtrusive ear. He knew F. X.'s "by-the-ways. . . ." They generally concealed a major point.

"By the way," said F. X., "while you're with Menier you might sound him. That Caporal group of his might put up fifty thousand. You could tell him six months and 10 per cent, if you like. Anyway, try."

Tony nodded.

At that moment the faces of father and son were so alike in every line that they might have been, not elder and younger brothers, but twins. Peter looked at the watch upon her wrist. "My dears," she said, "I must go. What about you? Or doesn't Rynox do any work in the afternoon?"

F. X. stood up. "They do. We've been chewing the rag here a bit too long. Come on."

They went on. Outside, father and son put Peter into a taxi; watched while it purred out of Alsace Court and into the Strand.

F. X. turned to his son. "Going back to the office, boy?"

Tony nodded. "And you?"

F. X. shook his head. "Not this afternoon. I'm going away to think."

Tony waved a stick—they were halfway up the court by this time—at a taxi with its flag up. "You have this?" he said, "or me?"

"You," said F. X. "I'm walking."

The cab came to a standstill abreast of them. Tony put a foot upon its running board and fingers to the handle of its door. "Rynox House," he said to the driver.

His father looked at him.

Tony opened the taxi door. He said over his shoulder:

"See you on Monday, then." He made to enter the cab.

"Tony!" said his father.

"Hullo!" Tony turned round; saw his father's outstretched hand; raised his eyebrows. "Good Lord!" he said, but he took the hand. They shook; a firm grip, each as strong as the other.

"Do your best," said his father, "with Menier."

Tony nodded; leapt into the cab; slammed the door. The cab churned away. Out of the window Tony looked. "So long, F. X.," he said.

"Good-bye!" said F. X., and raised his hand in salute.

CHAPTER THREE

Friday, 29th March: 9 A. M. *to 10* A. M.

F. X. sat at breakfast. Through the big French windows of his dining room in William Pitt Street the spring sun blazed, turning the comfortable but rather sombre room into a chamber of temporary glory. F. X., so to speak, read the *Morning Mercury* with one hand and with the other conversed with his man, Prout.

Prout was a short, stiff little man. There was a legend about Prout—started probably by F. X. himself—to the effect that he had nineteen hairs and that twelve of these were upon the right side of his parting and seven upon the other. He was clean-shaven —very shaven and very, very clean. He was also very quiet. There was another legend—this one having its birth with Tony—to the effect that Prout really was a "foreigner" only knowing three words of English: "Very good, sir." Prout, who had been with F. X. now for seven years—ever since Rynox had been founded—adored F. X. In a lesser, quieter way he was fond of Tony. For Peter he would have gone through nearly as much, if not quite, as for F. X. himself.

"If you, Prout," said F. X., "were Lord Otterburn, and you owned the daily paper with the largest net sale (don't forget net, Prout, there's always a lot of holes in a net), what would you do?"

Prout put a cover upon the dish of kidneys. "Nothing, sir," said Prout.

F. X. looked at him. "And a very good answer too. Don't know what it is about you, Prout, but you always say the right thing with the most delightfully innocent air of not knowing you've said it."

"Yes, sir. . . ." said Prout. "Excuse me, sir, but Mrs. Fairburn wanted me to ask you whether you could see her for a moment before you leave for the office."

F. X. nodded. "Certainly, certainly." He looked at his watch. "You'd better tell her to come in now, hadn't you? I shall be off in a few minutes."

"Very good, sir," said Prout and left the room so silently, so unobtrusively that the moment he was gone F. X. wondered, as he always wondered on these occasions, whether Prout had really ever been with him at all.

The door opened again. Mrs. Fairburn came in. Mrs. Fairburn was F. X.'s housekeeper. She, too, had been with F. X. for seven years. She, too, strictly within her very strict notions of right and wrong, would have done anything for F. X. She was, as Tony frequently said, almost too good to be true. Her hair, quite black despite her fifty-odd years, was scraped from her forehead and piled high upon the back of her head. She wore black satin. And always when she walked it rustled with a most alarming rustling. About her severely corseted waist was a belt, and inevitably from this belt there dangled a bunch of keys.

"Good-morning!" said F. X. "Lovely morning, Mrs. Fairburn!"

"Good-morning, Mr. Baynedik. Truly a delaiteful day. It makes one feel really as if spring were drawing on."

F. X. nodded. "Yes, doesn't it? Well, what's the trouble, Mrs. Fairburn?"

The thin lips of Mrs. Fairburn parted in one of her rare smiles. "No *trouble,* Mr. Baynedik. Nothing of the sort. Only rather an extraordinary thing has happened." She produced from some recess in the black-clad angularity of her presence, an envelope; advanced with this toward the table. "Mr. Baynedik," she said, "this letter came by a district maysenger boy last night when you were out. It is, as you see, addressed to the Housekeeper and Staff. Seeing this address, Mr. Baynedik, Ay opened the letter and inside Ay found three orchestra fauteuils for the Royal Theatre for to-morrow night's performance. It is a piece which is apparently entitled *The Sixth Wife of Monsieur Paradoux.* . . . Rather, I must say, an astonishing title, Mr. Baynedik."

F. X. struggled with a smile. "Certainly. Certainly. Damn silly names some of these people call their damn silly plays. Well, what about it, Mrs. Fairburn? Do you want to go?"

"Ay did think, Mr. Baynedik, that perhaps we would like to go, as these seats have been presented to us so kindly, albeit so mysteriously."

F. X. frowned. *"We'd* like to go. . . . Oh, I see. You want to take the rest of the staff, Mrs. Fairburn? Yes, take them by all means. Do you all good, I'm sure. And you can keep an eye on them and see that they don't get into mischief. Wonder who's sending you theatre tickets?"

"Ay cannot," said Mrs. Fairburn, "understand the gift mayself, Mr. Baynedik. But Ay believe there is a saying to the effect that one should not look at the mouth of a horse that has been given to one. Ay must confess that Ay could never see the meaning of this saying but Ay have no doubt it is an apposite one."

F. X. buried himself behind his paper. "Yes. Go, by all means. It's very good of you, I'm sure, to chaperon the other two."

"Thank you, Mr. Baynedik. Ay am sure that both Ay and the gairls are most grateful. Perhaps if you would not mind just casting your eye over these tickets to ensure that we are not being made the victims of some cruel hoax. . . ."

F. X. stretched out from behind the paper. "Let's have a look."

With deliberation Mrs. Fairburn drew from her envelope three yellow slips.

F. X. took them and looked at them and grunted. "Seem quite all right. I shouldn't worry about where they came from. As you say, a gift horse and all that. I expect it's some new advertising stunt or other. Get up to anything, these people nowadays." He thrust the tickets back upon their owner. "Yes. Do all go. With Mr. Anthony in Paris, you needn't worry about dinner. Just leave me something cold." He waved aside thanks. "And you might tell Prout I want him, will you?"

Mrs. Fairburn rustled out; to be replaced almost immediately by the silent Prout. F. X. looked at him.

"Well, Prout," he said, "Mrs. Fairburn and the gairls are going out to-night. Very giddy! You'll have to look after me by yourself."

"Yes, sir," said Prout. "Very good, sir. At what time would you like to dine, sir?"

F. X. considered. "Seven-thirty," he said at last.

He looked up at Prout's wooden visage and smiled. "Don't worry, Prout. You'll get away in plenty of time."

Prout was silent, but into his demeanour there crept the very faintest tinge of discomfort.

F. X. grinned at him. "All right, man. Why shouldn't you go to The Foxhound? Damn good pub. . . . I'll dine at seven-thirty, then."

"Thank you, sir. Very good, sir. Shall I get the car, sir?"

"No. I'll walk to the office. Lovely day." He stood up and folded his paper and threw it onto the breakfast table.

Prout opened the door and followed his master into the hall; gave him his hat, gloves, and stick.

F. X. stepped out into the sunshine.

CHAPTER FOUR

Friday, 29th March: 11:30 A. M. *to 12 noon*

Mr. Selsinger's gun shop in Vigo Street is very dark and very low and very old, but it is—so many people will tell you—the only place in the world in which to buy a gun. So, anyhow, thought Peter (christened Petronella) Rickworth. Into the old dark shop, whose walls are lined with wood and steel, Peter brought, at half-past eleven that morning, some of the sunshine which blazed upon all the rest of London.

Mr. Selsinger himself, short and dapper and white bearded, came forward to serve her. Peter smiled at him. Mr. Selsinger, notoriously the most wooden-faced man between Bond and Regent streets, smiled back.

"'Morning," said Peter. She looked vaguely around her. "I want," said Peter, "to buy a gun."

"Quite," said Mr. Selsinger.

"A gun," said Peter again vaguely. And then, with a little burst of confidence which made Mr. Selsinger her slave for at least so long as she should be within his shop: "As a matter of fact, it's a present for my fiancé, and d'you know, I tried and tried to think of something that he wanted, and then my future father-in-law put me up to this. I expect you know him—Mr. Benedik."

"Mr. F. X. Benedik." Mr. Selsinger smiled again; this time the smile of the prosperous tradesman welcoming the friend of an excellent customer. "Certainly, madam. Mr. F. X. Benedik has been a customer and a very good customer of mine for a number of years." Now Mr. Selsinger put behind him, with one wave of his slim white hand, the delights of social intercourse. "May I ask," said Mr. Selsinger, "what sort of firearm you are requiring?"

Peter, who had never used one, was vaguer yet. She said: "I know nothing about guns, but I think it's a sporting gun I want. In fact, I know it is. Mr. F. X. Benedik did tell me. He said . . . I've forgotten, d'you know."

Mr. Selsinger became helpful. He asked questions; many questions. At last he went to the rack labelled "Three" and took from it a dully gleaming affair of blue steel and polished wood. "If I might suggest it, madam, I think this is what you want. There is no better shotgun, if I may say so, in the world to-day."

"It looks lovely!" said Peter, refraining from holding out the hands into which Mr. Selsinger so obviously wished to place his pet. "I suppose it's a most frightful price?"

Mr. Selsinger made a negative movement with his head. He also said something, but what the words were Peter did not hear. They were drowned by the storming entrance of another customer.

The low door swung open and crashed back—with a bang which ought to have and just did not break its plate glass against a show case. The bell, which the opening of the door set going, pealed angrily. A shuffling followed. Mr. Selsinger stared. His white beard twitched with something very much like anger. Peter turned a head which strove not to seem too much interested.

The newcomer was a tall and somehow menacing figure. One didn't, Peter thought, notice his clothes, but one couldn't miss his hat. A black hat, perched forward right over his face and its dark glasses. A soft black hat with a high crown pinched into a point. Beneath the dark glasses the gray moustaches and the little tuft of imperial seemed, not funny, as many moustaches and beards seem funny, but extraordinarily—and, thought Peter as she turned away, rather frighteningly *important*. As he walked this man seemed to drag his left leg behind him. It did not bend, this leg, and it was carried so that its foot was broadside on to his progress. The inner side of the shoe, at each stride, scraped along the polished boarded floor with a little hissing squeak most distressing to the ear.

Mr. Selsinger, with a murmured word of apology to Peter, went to the counter and leaned over it and touched a bell behind it. A little bell pealed musically somewhere in dim hinter regions. Mr. Selsinger then turned back, ignoring the newcomer, and began once more to expatiate upon the beauties of the gun now laid across the counter.

"It is, I can assure you, madam, a gun which any gentleman would very, very much appreciate, and it is the sort of gun, madam, which one need not be—if I may put it this way—ashamed of giving to a gentleman. However good a shot that gentleman may be, in fact, the better shot that gentleman may be the more strongly will he appreciate a gun like this. I have no hesitation, madam——"

What Mr. Selsinger had no hesitation about was never to reach Peter's ears. There came suddenly from behind her a roar. The newcomer was impatient.

"God blast it!" roared a raucous and somehow un-English voice, "God sear and wither it! Am I going to get served or am I not?"

Mr. Selsinger's neat little face for one shocking instant was suffused with a lively glow. And then, with his return to decent, orderly pallor, came his superbly controlled voice.

"I am afraid," said Mr. Selsinger, facing the blank-eyed stare of the stranger, "that I, myself, am attending to this lady. I have rung the bell, as you doubtless heard. One of my assistants will very shortly attend to you."

The stranger took four scraping steps and now stood so close to Mr. Selsinger that he almost touched him.

"No!" said the stranger, and he spoke through his teeth, which were very white teeth. "I don't want any of your damned assistants. What I want is a gun! Do you sell guns or don't you? Do you sell guns? Sell me a gun and be bloody quick about it! Twopenny ha'-penny little tradesman. Can't understand what's the matter with this bloody city!"

There came from the back of the shop a young and hitherto confident salesman. Towards him Mr. Selsinger waved a white hand.

"Mr. Hopkins," said Mr. Selsinger, "perhaps you would attend to this gentleman. He wishes—er—to make a purchase."

The stranger exploded. "Wishes to make a purchase, you little nincompoop! You sawn-off little abortion!"

Mr. Selsinger once more went pink from his eyes down to the edge of his neat white beard.

"You will pardon me, sir," said Mr. Selsinger stiffly, "but your language . . ." One of Mr. Selsinger's hands indicated in the most gentlemanly manner possible the presence of a lady. The stranger, stooping down from his height, thrust out his face until the dark glasses seemed to Mr. Selsinger to be less than an inch from his own trim pince-nez.

"*Mierda!*" said the stranger, still without opening those startlingly white teeth, "I come into your damn shop, and I wait about, and then you send me a little poopstick like your boy friend Hopkins here. I want a *gun,* man!"

Disconcertingly, the stranger put back his head and laughed; a neighing mirthless sound which was described afterward by Mr. Selsinger as "positively blood-curdling."

"Guns," said the stranger, "guns! Bloody little white maggots like you and your boy friend here selling guns!"

"Hopkins," said Mr. Selsinger, trembling with a mixture of rage and fear. "Hopkins, will you please step into the street and see whether you can catch the eye of the constable."

There was a clatter as the stranger's stick dropped to the wooden floor. For one triumphant moment Mr. Selsinger thought that he had conquered, but alas! the stranger was only laughing. The stranger was in a paroxysm. "For God's sake," he said, "will you sell me a gun?"

It was at this point that Hopkins, a youth by no means so devoid of sense, took matters into his own hands.

"Excuse me, sir," said Hopkins briskly, "what sort of a gun is it you're wanting?"

The tinted glasses of the stranger seemed to look him up and down.

"Heavens!" said the stranger, "it speaks! . . . I want a nice big forty-five Colt with a rough grip, if you've got it. Or possibly one of those heavy German automatics."

"If you will follow me, sir," said Hopkins then, and led the way to the far end of the shop while Mr. Selsinger, palms outspread on a level with his shoulders, turned to Peter.

"I cannot tell you, madam," began Mr. Selsinger, "how deeply I regret . . . It is not often that in a quiet neighbourhood like this we——"

Peter cut him short. "Really," she said, "it's quite all right. Please don't worry. And I'll have this gun. It's a beauty, I'm sure."

Her voice, perhaps from a strongly repressed desire to laugh, was both louder and higher pitched than usual. She said:

"I'll tell Mr. Benedik how very kind you've——"

Once more an interruption. From where he stood beside Mr. Hopkins, poring over a case of automatics and revolvers, the stranger swung round. "Benedik!" he said. His voice was a harsh roar. "*Benedik!*" he said and laughed again. And if his laugh before had been a sound unpleasing, now it was ten times more so.

Even Peter—that most matter-of-fact and courageous young woman—felt the blood ebbing from her face.

Mr. Selsinger fluttered helpless hands.

But it was all over very soon. Back to the case of pistols the stranger swung, the stiff left leg seeming to trail behind its fellow on the turn. He pointed down to the case. "I'll have that one," he said.

Peter pulled herself together. "If you would send the gun, then, to this address." She gave a card into Mr. Selsinger's trembling hands.

"Yes, madam. Certainly, madam. A pleasure."

Peter, with one glance behind her, went out into the sunlit street. As the door closed behind her she was aware of relief.

CHAPTER FIVE

Friday, 29th March: 7:30 P. M. to 10:20 P. M.

F. X. came to the end of his dinner; took a cigar from the box held out to him by Prout; put it to the flame held out to him by Prout.

"Good work," he said to Prout. "Very fair meal."

"Thank you, sir," said Prout. "Will you take coffee here or in the library?"

"In the library, I think," said F. X. "Just trot it along there as quick as you can, will you? I've got to run down to South Kensington to see Mr. Rickworth."

The coffee was drunk by eight-fifteen, and by eight-twenty F. X. was at the hall door.

"Taxi, sir?" said Prout, and from some secret recess on his person produced a large whistle. He ran down the steps into the road; blew three times heartily; returned.

"See here, Prout," said F. X. standing on the topmost step. "I'll be back as soon as I can, but there's some one coming to see me at ten. On business. A man named Marsh. If he should arrive before I get back, just put him in the study, and see he has everything he wants. Then, as I said, you can slip off to The Foxhound. Because if I am late, it won't be more than a couple of minutes."

"I see, sir," said Prout. "Thank you, sir."

"Right!" said F. X. He went down the steps as a taxi drew up at the curb. "Good-night, Prout, in case I don't see you again."

2

In the saloon bar of The Lion and Flower, which stands at the corner of Lansborough Mews in Knightsbridge, Mrs. Welbee (port and lemon) and Mrs. Edwards (gin and pep) sipped at their drinks and conversed with the portly landlord, Horace Bliss.

"Very quiet in 'ere to-night, Mr. Bliss," said Mrs. Welbee.

Mrs. Edwards nodded in agreement. "That's hups," she said. "Oh, pardon me!"

Bliss rubbed his hands together. "Oh, I don't know, Mrs. Welbee. Never very busy this time of the evening. I've no doubt you'll see a little company before long. Either some of the old faces or some new ones. . . ."

"Personhups'ly," said Mrs. Edwards from her chair, "I must say, Mr. Bliss, that I prefers the old comhupsrades, if you know what I mean. I like to see the old—hups—faces."

"Well, well, Mrs. Edwards, each man to his taste, as the French say."

"Them French," said Mrs. Welbee doubtfully, "they'd say any-think!" She looked toward the door. "Ow, Gawd save us! Wot's this?"

"HUPS!" said Mrs. Edwards.

The newcomer was a tall and burly man. His left leg was stiff and seemed to trail behind him as he walked. Dark glasses hid his eyes, and his head was out-thrust as if striving for better sight. Upon his head was a strange black hat, high and pointed. He had gray, fierce moustaches and a little block of gray beard. As he walked up to the bar, he muttered ceaselessly to himself, and with each muttering came a flash of white teeth in the dark face.

He rapped upon the bar with a coin. "Brandy!" he said in a queer, hoarse voice, and when the astounded Bliss gave no imme-diate response, repeated the word in a snarling bellow, *"Brandy!"*

Bliss's rosy cheeks grew pale. There was, he decided, something uncommon nasty-seeming about this customer. He turned to his shelf, took down from it a bottle and a glass. "And 'ow much brandy would you be wanting, sir?"

"Fill it up!" said the hoarse voice.

"Beg pardon?" said Bliss.

Once more that forward movement of the head. Once more the hissing, deliberate repetition:

"Fill it up, I said!"

Mr. Bliss filled it up. He kept hold of the glass with his right hand. He said:

"That'll be five shillings."

The stranger plunged his hand into his trousers pocket; threw down upon the bar a handful of silver. Some of the coins rolled to fall near the feet of Mrs. Edwards. Wheezing, she bent to pick them up. The stranger, his back to her, took no notice. He raised the glass, looked at the light through it, put it to his lips and with one twist of his wrist sent the three-quarter tumblerful down his throat. Bliss watched him with goggle eyes.

He set the glass down; he turned. Mrs. Edwards was still grovelling. She had in her palm now two half-crowns, a shilling, and a sixpence. There was more, it seemed, to come. The stranger made for the door. The shoe on the foot of the lame leg hissed raspingly over the floor.

Bliss came to life. Just as the stranger's hand was on the door, Bliss realized what Mrs. Edwards was doing.

"HI!" called Bliss, "just a minute, sir!" His tone was sharp and eager and the stranger whipped round with an agility amazing in one of his condition; whipped round, at the same time flashing his right hand toward his hip pocket.

"What's that?" It was more a snarl than a voice.

"All right, sir. All right!" Bliss backed away until a sharp crack on the back of his head told him he could back no farther. "If you like to drop money about and then not claim it, that's your funeral. And what are you doing with your hand in that pocket, anyway?"

"Ha!" The stranger laughed; a sound, as Mrs. Edwards was to say later, "enough to freeze the hupsmarrow in a body's bones."

The stranger laughed again, and took his hand from his hip pocket. He turned his glance—that blank, black glance—upon the two women in the corner. Mrs. Welbee clutched at Mrs. Edwards. "Ow, my Gawd!" said Mrs. Welbee under her breath. "Ow, hups!" said Mrs. Edwards.

"That money," said the stranger, "you can keep. If you drink with that money, the drink will probably choke you."

He swung back again to face the petrified Bliss. He said, "You! Can you direct me—I am a stranger to London—" they noticed here for the second time what trouble he had with his r's. He seemed to say them right down in his throat—"can you direct me to William Pitt Street, Mayfair?"

Bliss shook his head. He stammered, "D-don't know the neighbour'ood. Don't know the neighbour'ood."

"Bloody parrot!" said the stranger.

He turned away. His lame leg trailing, he made for the door. There was a little, eddying draught as it swung closed behind him.

3

F. X. stood before the fire in Rickworth's study. He shook his head. "No, Sam, no!" he said. "I won't stay. In the first place I haven't changed; in the second place I don't feel much like a party to-night."

"Oh, be a man, F. X.! Might just as well. Be a man!"

"Sammie," said F. X., "the picture of you telling someone to be a man is almost more than I can bear. No, I'm going, old son. Just that little chat to straighten up the Carruthers-Blackstone matter was all I wanted. No, I won't have another drink, and no, no, no, I won't come to your party."

"Shall I tell Jevons to get you a taxi, F. X.?"

"Sam, you can keep your taxi. I'm going to walk—a lovely night like this. No, I'm going to walk quietly home, and when I get home I'm going to have my interview with Mr. Marsh."

Rickworth looked puzzled. "Marsh?" he said. "Marsh?—Oh, isn't he the fellow who's always writing you letters and ringing you up and all that sort of thing? I got him on the 'phone the other day. Wouldn't seem to take no for an answer."

F. X. nodded. "When you say nuisance, Sam, you understate the case. That fellow's a swarm of locusts. He's a public blight." He began to move toward the door. Rickworth came with him.

"What's he after, exactly?" he said. "This man Marsh, I mean?"

F. X. laughed; a laugh with, in it, perhaps, a little less than his usual humour. He said:

"What's he after? Didn't I ever tell you, Sam?"

"Good Lord!" said Rickworth. "I remember. Yes, he's the man that thinks he was the inventor of the Paramata recipe. Knew you in South America or something."

"That's the boy!" said F. X. "Still, he's been pestering me for the last year now. I'm going to settle with him to-night."

Rickworth looked shocked. "You're not going to pay him any money!"

F. X. grinned. "Pay him hell! As a matter of fact, I'm going to offer him twenty-five pounds or a kick-out. I think he'll take the twenty-five quid. He's one of those hard cases with a soft-boiled inside. Well, I must push along, Sam. Good-night."

Rickworth saw him to the door. "Sure I can't get you a taxi?" he called after him on the steps.

On the pavement F. X. paused. "Not on your life," he said. "I'm walking."

"Good-night, then!" said Rickworth.

"So long, Sam!" said F. X., and raised his stick in salute.

4

Prout, sitting comfortably astraddle behind the *Evening News* in the library's biggest chair, shot suddenly to his feet. An indignant frown creased his usually expressionless face. What I mean, thought Prout, it's all very well to *knock;* it's all very well to *ring*. . . .

Before he had got halfway down the hall to answer this knocking and ringing, it came again, and if the first knocking and ringing had been excessive, it had been as nothing to this second assault.

Prout broke into a run. Really, he couldn't have this! He put his fingers to the door handle and remembered, as he did so, that this was probably Mr. Marsh. . . .

If it was Mr. Marsh, thought Prout, all he could say was that Mr. Marsh was a very odd and a very nasty, dangerous-looking sort of customer. What with them dark spectacles and that little bit of beard and that funny black hat, to say nothing of the way that leg of his seemed to trail round after him as if it didn't belong somehow . . . Well! . . .

"Good-evening, sir!" said Prout.

"Marsh," said a harsh grating voice. "My name's Marsh. Benedik in?"

"Mr. Benedik," said Prout, "is out, sir. For the moment only. Mr. Benedik left word, sir, that if you was to come by any mischance before he got back that I was to ask you to step inside and make yourself comfortable while you were waiting. He will not, in any case, keep you waiting more than a very few minutes."

A sound which Prout could only liken to the growl of a dog was his reply. Prout led the way through the hall and then down the passage to the study. After him, trailing the lame leg with a little scraping sound upon the carpet, came the visitor. He still kept on his pointed black hat. Prout stood aside. The visitor passed in. To the visitor's back Prout said:

"Is there anything I could get you, sir? . . ."

"All you can do for me," said the visitor without turning, "is to take yourself off out of it. It's Benedik I want."

"If you would care, sir," said Prout with considerable dignity, "for a whisky-and-soda, you will find syphon, decanter, and glasses on the table there."

The face of the visitor turned round to peer at him. The voice of the visitor said:

"I may wear dark glasses but I'm not blind."

"Very good, sir," said Prout and withdrew. He shut the door.

For a few minutes he dallied, awaiting his master's return, and then, knowing his master and remembering his master's instructions, he donned his cap, put pipe and tobacco into his pockets, and set out for The Foxhound and its saloon bar. The front door of No. 4, William Pitt Street closed softly behind him.

CHAPTER SIX

Friday, 29th March: 10:30 P. M. *to 12 midnight*

As every soldier carries a Field-Marshal's baton in his knapsack, so may every police constable be said to tote a potential Superintendent's truncheon. Some police constables, realizing this, do nothing about it; some do far too much. But there are a few—and from among them the future Superintendents are likely to come—who neither miss opportunity nor try to manufacture it.

Of this kind was Constable BL413, Ernest Henry Lawrence. Lawrence's beat lay across Mayfair from India Court on the west to William Pitt Street on the east. At 10:20 P. M. exactly Lawrence was halfway between the two extremes of his beat. That is to say, he was in the centre of Shepherds' Market. He had been on duty for an hour, and during that hour nothing at all had happened. Lawrence was thinking to himself, now for a quiet night, and then Lawrence suddenly stiffened. He had heard sounds which he knew—he was a man of quick ear and ready intelligence—to be pistol shots. And not one pistol shot, but a fusillade of pistol shots. . . .

Lawrence began to run. Despite his uniform, which he had often thought must have been specially designed to prevent quick movement, he made very creditable pace. He had only memory to guide him, for after that outburst silence had fallen again upon the neighbourhood. He came out of Goss Street into William Pitt

Street which runs across it at right-angles. At the junction he stopped. His ear and memory combined could tell him no more. But Lawrence was in luck. There came to his ear the sound of running feet. He wheeled round to face the runner. It was, perhaps fortunately for the runner, a man whom he knew. It was, in fact, Arthur Wiggin, the potman of The Foxhound.

"Hi!" said Arthur Wiggin as soon as he saw the uniform. "Hi!" He came pelting up. He peered for a moment. "It's you, Harry, is it? Thank God! Hear that bloody barrage just now?"

Lawrence nodded. "I did. What d'ye know?"

"Number four," said Arthur Wiggin. "Number four, boy! That's where it come from. Up this way!" They began to run side by side. As they ran:

"See anything?" asked Lawrence.

"Nary thing. Heard plenty, though! There you are, boy, that's the 'ouse. What you goin' to do?"

"You'll see! Now, you assist the Law! You go up to the front door and kick up hell's delight until somebody answers. I'm going round the back."

Lawrence put his hand to the locked iron gate which leads down between Nos. 4 and 5 to the communal garden at the back; put his hand upon the gate and vaulted it—helmet, dragging coat, lumbering boots, and all. He knew the lay of these houses, did Lawrence. In a moment he had reached the back door of No. 4; had smashed his fist through the pantry window, unlatched it, and was halfway in. As he scrambled, sucking at a bleeding fist, across the darkness of a scullery between the kitchen door and the pantry, he heard the beginnings of Arthur Wiggin's assault upon the front.

Lawrence found switches and pressed them. The basement was flooded with light. He tore up the basement stairs.

"Hi!" yelled Lawrence. "Hi! Anyone about? Hi, there!"

Only the echoes of his own voice came back to him. The house was quiet; dead quiet. Lawrence went more slowly. He slipped out his truncheon, wrapping its thongs about his fingers in the approved style. He came out at the top of the servants' stairs. "Hi!" he yelled again.

Once more, only echo.

Lawrence did not smoke. He had therefore a keen nose. There came to his nostrils the acrid tang of gunpowder. It was drifting toward him from a little passage on his left. He switched on a light and ran down the passage. There was one door at the end, shut but not locked. He opened the door and went through it, arm and truncheon guarding his head; one never knew. . . .

There was only one person in the room, and that a dead man. He lay with his body face downward across the sill of the one open window. The sill supported him just below his breastbone. His legs sagged hideously. His left arm was out of the window; his right hung down inside the room, in its tightly clenched fingers a revolver . . .

There was a telephone upon the big writing table. Lawrence used it, reporting to his station. Having reported, he went back to the body and stood looking down at it; all that was left of F. X. Benedik.

"Tck-tck!" said Lawrence, shaking his head and clicking his tongue against the roof of his mouth.

Mr. Benedik had been shot through the head. The bullet had entered—it must have been fired at close range, thought Lawrence —just over the right eye. It had come out just behind the left ear.

"Tck-tck!" said Lawrence again. He stood by the writing table. He took off his helmet and laid it down. His eyes searched the room. They saw, in two of the walls, the marks of bullets—seven in all. The holes upon the eastern wall seemed bigger than the holes upon the western wall. Lawrence's eye left the bullet holes; travelled about the room. Suddenly they widened. On a chair, drawn up in front of the fire, lay a man's hat; a black hat of a peculiar shape; a soft black felt hat with a soft crown pinched up high into a point. Gingerly, using the brass fire tongs to do it, Lawrence picked up the hat. Inside the brim in ink was written "B. MARSH." He put the hat back where he had found it; replaced the tongs.

He went back to the body, knelt down, and looked at the revolver so tightly clasped in the dead hand. He knew a little of firearms, enough to guess that this was the gun which had made the smaller bullet holes.

Lawrence spoke to himself. "Reg'lar duel," he said. "That's what it was!" He shook his head sadly as he climbed to his feet. F. X. had been, as he was with everybody, popular with Lawrence. . . .

BOOK TWO

CHAPTER SEVEN

(Telegram from Petronella Rickworth to Anthony X. Benedik. Handed in at 1 A. M. Saturday, 30th March.)

BENEDIK HOTEL POMPADOUR BOULEVARD MARAT PARIS RETURN IMMEDIATELY GRAVE NEWS F. X. PLEASE COME   PETER

2

(Letter from Magnay's Bank, Limited, to Messrs. Rynox, dated 30th March.)

DEAR SIRS:

I am to express the deep and sincere regret of my directors and myself at the tragic demise of Mr. F. X. Benedik.

I have, I fear, also to state, in regard to the A and B accounts of your firm, that it is unfortunately impossible for me to allow any further drawings until these accounts are placed upon a sounder basis.

With respect to the C account, this, as you know, (*vide* my letter of the 27th instant) has been closed as regards any further drawings.

So soon, of course, as one or more of the accounts is placed upon a credit basis, we shall be only too glad, not only to permit drawings upon that account, but to consider the possibility of re-opening accommodation upon the other accounts.

In the meantime, however, I fear that my directors will not countenance any applications for further accommodation, that already granted to your firm being considerably in excess of the usual.

Yours faithfully,
ALBERT PERCIVAL HERRING.
Manager.

3

(*Letter from the Midland & Capital Bank, Limited, Lombard Street, to Messrs. Rynox, dated 30th March.*)

DEAR SIRS:

I have the painful duty of expressing the very sincere regrets of my directors and myself at the tragic and untimely end of Mr. F. X. Benedik.

I have also to state, on the explicit instructions of my directors, that it is unfortunately impossible for the bank to allow any further increase in the overdraft with which your firm is at present being accommodated.

The directors hope that they will see, within a few days, the substantial reduction which was personally promised—by Mr. F. X. Benedik himself—a few days ago.

Yours faithfully,
MAURICE HIPLAM.
Manager.

4

(*Letter from the Arcade & General Finance Corporation to Messrs. Rynox, dated 30th March.*)

DEAR SIRS:

We note that the last interest payment on our loan (B4124) to you on the 27th February last is still unpaid.

We would ask you to make immediate steps to meet this. Failing your satisfactory reply within this week, we shall—though we are, in the present painful circumstances, most reluctant to adopt such a course—be compelled to place the matter in other hands.

Yours faithfully,
DOUGLAS IAN MACFARLANE.
Director.

5

*(Departmental Report by Detective Inspector F. Wellesley, C. I. D.,
1st April.)* *

SUBJECT F. X. Benedik, deceased.

PLACE 4, William Pitt Street, W. 1.

TIME Approx. 10:30 P. M.

Proceeded to William Pitt Street as above, on Superintendent
Fox's instructions, at midnight on Friday, the 29th ult. Found
there, Police Sergeant (BL342) Humphreys and Police Constable (BL413) Lawrence. Copy of Sergeant Humphreys' report
is attached at A together with a copy of

PLANS ATTACHED Constable Lawrence's Preliminary Report (A1).
Attached at B is a plan of the study at No. 4, William Pitt Street
and at B1 the ground-floor plan of the house and garden.

POSITION OF BODY The body of deceased had not been moved when
I arrived. It was lying face downward across the sill of the window (marked X on Plan B). The head and shoulders were out
of the window, and also the left arm. The right arm was hanging
down inside the room; in the hand a small six-chambered .32
Colt revolver. From this revolver four shots had been fired.

CAUSE OF DEATH Deceased had been shot through the head, bullet
entering above the right eyebrow and coming out behind the left
ear, at short range, bullet inflicting this wound being from a
Luger automatic pistol. Deceased had obviously been shot, at
very close range, from just outside the window as he leaned
out. Bullet was found embedded in the western wall of the
study midway between the end of the fireplace and the junction of the western and northern walls (marked A). This bullet
has been submitted to Professor High, who gives it as his considered opinion that it is undoubtedly the one which caused
death.

BULLETS FOUND IN ROOM Other bullets (nine in all, were found in
the room. Three of these were from the Colt revolver in the dead
man's hand and six from the Luger pistol. The six Luger bullets
(this is excluding, of course, the one which caused death) were

---

* It is not necessary to give copies of all the purely routine and merely
repetitive reports, etc., attached to D. I. Wellesley's report. The plans, however, as being of use to the reader are given.

embedded in the eastern wall of the study, where it forms a party wall to the passage leading from the hall. The three bullets from the Colt were found grouped together in the angle made by the junction of the western and northern walls.

LUGER AUTOMATIC PISTOL I found a 9 mm. Luger automatic, recently fired and with its magazine empty, in the shrubbery which lies on the far side of the path from the house (see Z on Plan B). The markings on the Luger bullets found (including that which caused death) showed that they came from this pistol.

Inquiries show that the weapon was purchased from Selsinger & Co., Vigo Street, W. 1, on the morning of Friday the 29th ult.

COLT REVOLVER The Colt revolver found in deceased's hand was known by the household to have been in his possession for many years.

HAT In a chair (see Y on Plan B) was found a black hat of the "sombrero" variety. Inside the band is written "B. Marsh."

SUMMARY OF STATEMENTS TAKEN *P. C. (BL413) Lawrence* heard several shots while on beat, and running up William Pitt Street met:

ARTHUR WIGGIN, Potman at Foxhound Public House.

Wiggin was returning from an errand and walking out of William Pitt Street when he heard the shots and guessed, from their direction, that they were proceeding from No. 4.

WILLIAM PROUT, manservant to deceased.

Prout stated that deceased dined at 7:30 P. M. on Friday and then went out, stating destination to be house of Samuel Rickworth of No. 18, Consort Gardens, South Kensington.

Deceased, Prout states, left instructions to the effect that a Mr. Marsh was going to call at about 10 P. M. and that if he (deceased) was not back when Marsh called, Marsh was to be admitted and left in the study. Prout states also that deceased gave him permission to go out so soon as Marsh should have been admitted, as he (deceased) would not be more than a few minutes after Marsh.

Prout states that at 10:10 he admitted a man who stated his name was Marsh. He wore the hat subsequently found in the study.

Prout's description of Marsh is: Tall, heavy build, gray moustache and imperial beard, dark glasses, peculiar limp with left leg which he seemed "to drag after him." P. can't say as to clothes except that it is definite that the clothes were not evening dress but a "dark suit." States Marsh's manner violent and hectoring.

Five minutes after admitting Marsh, Prout left the house and proceeded to The Foxhound P. H. in Shepherds' Market. Remained there, throughout the time of the shooting and in the presence of many witnesses, until he heard the news from Wiggin and returned to 4, William Pitt Street to find Sergeant Humphreys in charge.

ELSA VICTORIA FAIRBURN (*widow*), housekeeper to deceased.

Fairburn, accompanied by the other two female servants (see below), left the house at 7:30 P. M. to proceed to the Royal Theatre for the evening performance. Returned home with aforesaid companions at 11:20.

Fairburn states that upon Thursday evening the 28th ult., a letter was brought to the house by a District Messenger Boy, this being addressed to "Housekeeper and Staff, 4, William Pitt Street." She opened it and found that it contained three back stall seats for Friday evening's performance at the Royal Theatre. Nothing else was in the envelope. Across the corner of the tickets, Fairburn states (and this evidence is corroborated by the other two servants), was written in pencil in printed characters "Compliments." Fairburn states (corroborated by Prout) that she told deceased on Friday morning, the 29th ult., of this incident and received his permission to go to the theatre, taking the servants. She has no idea at all of where the tickets could have come from. She also states that she mentioned the "mysterious origin" of the present to deceased, and he, too, was mystified but thought "it was part of a publicity campaign."

Fairburn had been housekeeper to deceased for seven years.

SARAH JUBILEE BRIGGS, cook to deceased.

Corroborates evidence of Fairburn.

Briggs had been in the employ of deceased for two years.

VIOLET DORIS EMMELINE WATSON, house-parlourmaid to deceased.

Corroborates as above. Watson had been in deceased's service for eighteen months.

SAMUEL HARVEY RICKWORTH, partner in deceased's business, Rynox.

States that at approx. 9 o'clock on Friday evening, the 29th ult., deceased called to see him on a business point. They discussed the point and deceased, refusing to join a party which was going on at that time in Mr. Rickworth's house, left, stating he must get home as he was expecting a visitor, such visitor being a man named Marsh.

Questioned as to his knowledge of Marsh, Mr. Rickworth states that he had not personally come into contact with Marsh. He knew, however, that Marsh was a one-time acquaintance of Mr. Benedik's, from South America. Mr. Rickworth had frequently heard deceased speak of Marsh who, deceased stated, was a madman who imagined himself the real inventor of the new synthetic rubber process (Paramata Synthetic Rubber Co.) which has lately been the main concern of the firm Rynox.

Mr. Rickworth further stated that Marsh was always writing letters to deceased both at his home and his office and frequently telephoning for appointments. Upon one occasion Marsh visited the office of Rynox without an appointment and created a disturbance. None of the partners was in and eventually deceased's secretary, Christabel Pagan, had to have Marsh threatened with ejection by commissionaires.

Mr. Rickworth further stated that after telling him of Marsh's intended visit to his house that night deceased added some words to this effect: "For the last two or three years he's been worrying my life out. I'm going to settle with him." Deceased, Mr. Rickworth states, then added that he intended to make Marsh an offer of a small payment for the sake of getting rid of him: if Marsh did not take the payment, then matters would have to take the ordinary course.

Questioned further, Mr. Rickworth stated that deceased had never so much as hinted at the possibility of personal violence from Marsh.

CHRISTABEL PAGAN, secretary to deceased.

States that she knew of the appointment at 10 P. M. at William Pitt Street with Marsh as she heard deceased making this over the telephone. Marsh had twice already rung up that morning. Corroborates evidence about Marsh's letters, telephone calls, and visit. States that deceased never seemed more than very much annoyed over Marsh's pestering; certainly never gave any hint that Marsh might be dangerous.

Showed to me file of letters (two specimens attached at C 1 & 2)—(whole file available if necessary) from Marsh. The address on all letters except four in the file is: Pond Cottage, Little Ockleton, Surrey (see later statement by George Hillman). The other four bear no address.

Miss Pagan's description of Marsh's appearance tallies with that given above by Prout. She also states that his manner was "frightening"; he had a curious inflection to his voice and used guttural r's; he walked with a dragging limp of left leg.

BASIL WOOLRICH, secretary and treasurer to Rynox.

States he heard deceased once or twice make mention of a man, Marsh, who was pestering him. Had also heard some mention of the incident (see above) when Marsh called at the office. Had never thought much about this matter. Could not help further.

LESLIE MUSGROVE, Box Office Clerk, Royal Theatre.

States that on the morning of Thursday the 28th ult., sold three stalls (J. 15, 16, & 17)—the numbers sent to Fairburn and staff at No. 4, William Pitt Street (see above) to what he describes as a "queer character." No name was given, of course, during the transaction. Musgrove's description of the purchaser of the tickets tallies exactly with the description above. States the man was "very rough mannered and had a domineering way of talking. Rather foreign looking. Used a lot of bad language."

EMANUEL BUTTERS, manager Crofton Street branch District Messenger Service.

States that at 12:15 P. M. on Thursday last, the 28th ult., he was given a letter addressed to "Housekeeper and Staff, No. 4, William Pitt Street," and was asked to have this letter delivered between 6:30 P. M. and 6:45 P. M. Instructions were most explicit. According to Butters (corroborated by two boys) this letter was handed in by "a big man with a limp. Very excitable and violent in his ways." His further description tallies with that given above. Butters also states that the man made quite a scene until he was definitely promised that the letter should be delivered exactly within the times he mentioned.

CHARLES BYRON SELSINGER, gunsmith.

States that at approximately 11:40 A. M. on Friday last, the 29th ult., a strange customer came into his Vigo Street shop and purchased a Luger automatic pistol. (This pistol he subsequently identified as the pistol found in the shrubbery outside the window of the study at No. 4, William Pitt Street.)

Selsinger states that the customer who made this purchase was eccentric and violent in his ways. Among other offences, he used foul language in front of a lady client. At one time, he (Selsinger) asked his assistant to fetch a constable but withdrew this command on the purchase being completed. Selsinger's description of the purchaser of the Luger agrees in detail with that given by other witnesses of Marsh. States that he was most offensive in speech and most alarming in behaviour. Walked with a sinister and peculiar dragging limp. States also that the name of the lady customer in the shop at the time was Miss Rickworth. (This is a peculiar coincidence.)

FRANK ALBERT HOPKINS, assistant to Selsinger.

Corroborates Selsinger's evidence down to last detail.

PETRONELLA RICKWORTH, daughter of Samuel Rickworth, partner in Rynox, Ltd.

Corroborates evidence of Selsinger and Hopkins and adds that she thought the man not only dangerous but insane.

GEORGE HILLMAN, of Pond End Farm, Great Ockleton.

States that a Boswell Marsh rented Pond Cottage, Little Ockleton, from him on a year's lease, the transaction taking place on the 3d September last. States knew nothing personally of his tenant except what he saw of him at the interview. Describes him as a "big, queer-like, foreign sort." When asked, agreed with the description of Marsh given above. States also that he received several minor complaints but being an easy-going sort of chap, had never taken these up, not living in Little Ockleton and rarely going there. Knew nothing else. States that he had no reference from Marsh and didn't consider this necessary as the whole amount for the yearly tenancy was paid by Marsh at the time the lease was signed. It was not paid by check but in notes.

GENERAL OPINION OF MARSH—LITTLE OCKLETON DISTRICT

Bears out all previous evidence to show that Marsh was eccentric in behaviour as well as appearance. Cordially detested by all villagers. Varied tales of threatened violence toward men and children.

SARAH CHIGWELL, charwoman employed by Mr. Marsh.

States she was never frightened of Mr. Marsh. Also states that, except to pay her and give her instructions, he never spoke to her. Also states (statement corroborated by various as above) that Marsh did not use Pond Cottage more than a few days in each month. Nearly always his visits were over week-ends although on more than a few occasions he came down for a night in midweek. Description of Marsh tallies with all those above. In further description of Marsh without a hat, states that his hair was "black with a lot of gray about it." Could not state colour of eyes as never saw Marsh without spectacles.

ANTHONY XAVIER BENEDIK, son of deceased.

States he was in Paris from Friday evening last the 28th ult., until Monday morning at 2 A. M. when recalled by his fiancée, Miss Peter Rickworth (see above). States had heard his father frequently mention Marsh but had never paid any serious attention to the possibility of Marsh's being dangerous. Knew nothing of Marsh and had never seen him. Had once spoken to him over the telephone. No further help possible.

(This concludes the testimony of all the persons interviewed to this stage.)

(SUMMARY) BOSWELL MARSH, having, by correspondence and telephonic and personal message extending over the last six months, expressed the opinion that he had been unfairly treated by deceased, obtained on Friday the 29th ult., an interview with deceased. He and deceased were alone in the house. The interview commenced at approximately 10:15 P. M. At approximately 10:30 P. M. P. C. (BL413) Lawrence heard a repeated succession of shots from the neighbourhood of William Pitt Street and, upon investigation, made the discovery of deceased's body. In the room was a hat which bore Marsh's name and was habitually worn by Marsh. In the shrubbery across the path immediately beneath the open window of the room was a Luger pistol purchased that morning by a person answering exactly to the description of Marsh.

The house was empty because the manservant, as usual, had been given permission to go out between ten and eleven; because Mr. Anthony X. Benedik, son of deceased, was in Paris; and because the housekeeper and two female servants had gone to the theatre, the tickets for the theatre having been presented to them anonymously, the anonymous buyer being a person whose description tallies exactly with that of Marsh.

Marsh, as the evidence collected will show, bore, or thought he bore, a definite and bitter grudge against deceased.

Deceased was lying half in and half out of the window. In his right hand was his own revolver from which four shots had been fired. Deceased had been shot through the head by a bullet from the automatic pistol bought that morning by the man whose description tallies with Marsh's.

Documentary evidence—specimen letters attached and also ex-

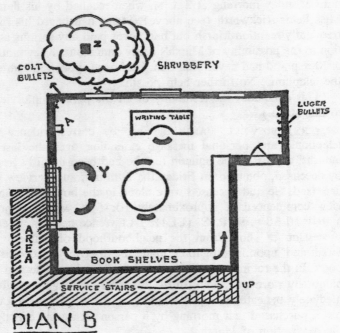

PLAN B

Study of NO 4 William Pitt Street

X — Position of body.

A — Position of bullet which caused death.

Y — Chair in which Sombrero hat was found.

Z — Point where Luger pistol was found.

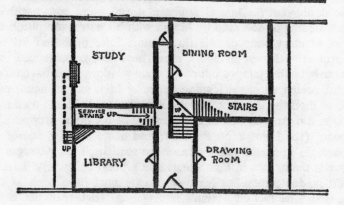

PLAN BI
GROUND FLOOR PLAN OF
NO 4 William Pitt Street.

tracts, attached at D, from deceased's diary—shows that Marsh imagined himself (rightly or wrongly) to be a victim of sharp practice on the part of deceased. (*N. B.* It will be noted that this documentary evidence of Marsh's ill-will begins many years ago —see extracts from deceased's diary referring to interviews and correspondence with Marsh. See also specimens of recent letters from Marsh. These begin, as will be seen, when Marsh arrived in England six months ago.)

CONCLUDED that deceased was shot by Boswell Marsh at the end of the interview commencing at approximately 10:15 P. M. on the night of Friday, March 29, such shooting being the result of an interview at which Marsh sought to obtain redress for imaginary or real grievance against deceased. There seems no doubt that the interview began stormily and ended with the threatening of deceased by Marsh with his automatic pistol. Deceased must, atop of this threatening, have produced his own revolver; whereupon shots must have been exchanged, and Marsh, having jumped out of the open window, must have turned and, seeing deceased leaning out after him, gun in hand, must have fired the last shot, which killed deceased. Marsh then must have run straight across the gardens, in his flight dropping the pistol (see Point Z on Plan B), and made exit by one of the passages upon the other side of the gardens, i. e., passages between the houses in Fox Street. The ground being very hard, he left no footprints, but his way of exit must have been as suggested. The fact of Marsh's having been frightened out before actually killing deceased is borne out to my mind by the finding of his hat within the room. If he had gone after killing deceased, he would not have left his hat as testimony against himself.

ACTION Every effort is being made to trace the present whereabouts of Marsh. Warrant for Marsh's arrest has been made out and is being held pending discovery.

F. WELLESLEY, D. I.

6

(*Letter from Messrs. Rynox to Magnay's Bank, Limited, dated 1st April.*)

DEAR SIRS:

In reply to yours of the 30th ultimo, I have to express the gratitude of my directors for your kind expressions of condolence concerning the tragic end of our senior partner, Mr. Francis X. Benedik.

I have to inform you with respect to the remainder of your letter under reply that by the end of this week the firm will be placing upon a credit basis both the A and B accounts, paying £12,750 into the A account and £17,312 17s. 3d. into the B account.

Yours faithfully,
for Rynox,
BASIL WOOLRICH,
Secretary & Treasurer.

7

(Letter from Messrs. Rynox to Midland & Capital Bank, Limited, Lombard Street, dated 1st April.)

DEAR SIRS:

In reply to yours of the 30th ultimo, I have to express the gratitude of my directors for the expressions of condolence concerning the tragic end of our senior partner, Mr. F. X. Benedik.

I have to inform you with respect to the remainder of your letter under reply that by the end of this week the reduction of our overdraft promised by Mr. F. X. Benedik (£7,000) will be made.

When this sum has been paid into the account I shall be glad if you will favour me with an interview at your earliest convenience.

Yours faithfully,
for Rynox,
BASIL WOOLRICH,
Secretary & Treasurer.

8

(Letter from Messrs. Rynox to the Arcade & General Financing Corporation, dated 1st April.)

DEAR SIRS:

Your letter of the 30th ultimo: I send you herewith this firm's check, dated for the 7th instant, for £279 13s. 11d. being the last interest payment on our loan (B.4124).

Yours faithfully,
for Rynox,
BASIL WOOLRICH,
Secretary & Treasurer.

9

(Letter from Basil Woolrich to Hugh Gleason, dated 1st April.)
Private and confidential.
DEAR GLEASON:

Don't worry about Rynox. It's all right. Our accounts not only with your firm but with our brokers and others will be settled within a short period—ten days at the outside.

I'd be much obliged and so would A. X. Benedik if you would do what you can to counteract the rumours which are going round about the firm's insolvency. I think you would find it would be not only to your own but to everybody's advantage if you could work along these lines for us.

Perhaps you could meet me for lunch to-morrow at the usual place.

Yours sincerely,
BASIL WOOLRICH.

10

(Memorandum from Anthony Xavier Benedik to Basil Woolrich, marked Confidential, dated 1st April.)

Hope you have written Banks, Arcade, & Gleason as arranged. Rickworth fixed. He won't trouble us just yet awhile. When he comes back he may be more reasonable. Destroy this.

11

(Letter from Naval, Military & Cosmopolitan Assurance Corporation to Anthony Xavier Benedik, dated 1st April.)

DEAR SIR:
Policy No. HI.32. Francis Xavier Benedik, deceased.

We have to acknowledge receipt of your letter of to-day's date containing claim for payment of £277,777 the amount for which Francis Xavier Benedik, deceased, was insured with this corporation.

The matter is receiving the attention of the president himself, and you will hear from us within a short while. We trust that you will appreciate that the unusual and very tragic circumstances of Mr. F. X. Benedik's death, coupled with the unusually large sum assured, put the matter outside mere routine.

I am, sir,
Yours faithfully,
for Naval, Military & Cosmopolitan
Assurance Corporation,
E. THURSTON MITCHELL,
Vice-President.

12

(*Letter from Rynox to Grey Friars Trust, Limited, dated 2d April.*)

DEAR SIRS:

In reply to your letters of the 28th, 29th, and 30th ultimo, and your telephone messages of yesterday, I have to inform you that I have now discussed the situation with Mr. Anthony X. Benedik.

Mr. Rickworth, to whom your letter is addressed, is at present in the country suffering from a nervous breakdown brought on by the terrible shock of the news of Mr. F. X. Benedik's tragic end.

Mr. Anthony Benedik, on behalf of the firm, empowers me to state that the balance of our debt to you (£3,254) over our joint deal in the matter of Rampole's Limited, will be paid to you within the next few days.

Mr. Anthony X. Benedik also wishes me to state that if necessary he will meet you over this matter. He is, however, very busy and trusts that this letter will serve the same purpose as an interview. The latest date for payment would be ten days from to-day, but in all probability the payment will be made some little time before that.

Yours faithfully,
for Rynox,
BASIL WOOLRICH,
Secretary & Treasurer.

13

(Letter from Fielder, Puckeridge, Fielder & Fielder, Enquiry Agents, to Naval, Military & Cosmopolitan Assurance Corporation, dated 2d April.)

DEAR SIRS:

Policy No. HI.32. Francis Xavier Benedik, deceased.

Further in re yours 30th ultimo. Our agents have now covered whole field of inquiry. Attached is our report plus résumé of police report kindly lent by Scotland Yard. From this you will see that there is no doubt as to cause of death, deceased having been undoubtedly shot by Boswell Marsh. Police now searching for Marsh but so far unsuccessfully. Think they must get him within a day or two.

Considered opinion: Claim lies; Corporation liable for full amount of policy, £277,777. For Fielder, Puckeridge, Fielder & Fielder,

A. K. MIMRAM.

14

(Letter from Petronella Rickworth to Anthony Xavier Benedik, dated 3d April.)

DARLING:

I hope you are having my medals struck. In regard to ribbons for same, please consult yours faithfully as I don't trust your eye.

I know you didn't think I could do it, but I've done it. I am, you know, rather an extraordinary young woman. As soon as I got your note on Monday I tackled Samuel, going to the office to do it. I'm sorry to say that I found him in a most deplorable condition of pure funk. To tell you the truth, Tony, I hadn't quite believed you until the sight and sound of him made me realize that it was true. If I'd been a creditor of Rynox I'd have tried to get whatever it is they do—petition filed, isn't it?—just after one glimpse of him.

It was very funny really. When I walked in he tried to shoo me out like a hen shooing its young. But I wasn't to be shoon. As a matter of fact, I went into the room and locked the door. And then I told him what you told me on Sunday night. I pointed out to him that you and Woolrich were quite undoubtedly the stuff. I told him that, equally undoubtedly, he wasn't. I told him that no Rickworth should ever show such blue toes. I told him that if he'd only come away from that office and give it a chance under you and Woolrich, the whole thing would come so straight that in a very little while he'd be even more opulent than he had been. I asked him what he thought, F. X. . . . Oh, Tony darling, isn't it dreadful? He was so utterly dear!

To go back to Samivel, however, I told him this, I told him that, and I told him several sorts of the other. All to no purpose. All he could say, when I kept ramming your name and your excellence and your F. X.-ishness down his throat—all he could say was that *he was surprised that after what had happened you could give your mind to the office!!!!!!!*

I'm afraid that finished me, or perhaps I should say glad. Anyway, I suddenly became the complete Cassandra, or whoever the lady was who was always very clever. I pretended to crack. I pretended to give way to parental and superior knowledge. I said that of course he must know best, now I came to think about it. I was very, very sad. I was very, very unhappy. I was very, very frightened. I left the office and went home.

When he came back in the evening—I suppose you and Woolrich managed to keep him from doing anything too utterly silly during the day—when he came back I was absolutely prostrate. I was having a real, double-barrelled, super A quality nervous breakdown. I couldn't stand London—no, not for one minute longer could I stand London. I wept and shuddered and started at little noises. Most convincing performance. It brought out all the man in Samuel. Asked what had best be done for her, the maiden replied, "Take me, Father, to the country! Take me away from—all this!"

Samuel, driving the Sunbeam himself (poor old fellow, the maiden couldn't bear the thought of anyone else being in the car except her father) took me away from all that. We went to where we are now. You know my best time, Tony—an hour and ten minutes. Samuel took two and a half! Ye gods! it was terrible. The nervous breakdown was almost genuine at the end. We hurtled through the night at well under twenty. Every time a rabbit looked out of a hedge we stopped. Every time a lorry pulled out across us we went on!!

But we got here—I think the time was about 3:75 G. M.—and we went to bed, having found, to Samuel's horror and my apparent dismay, that Kate wasn't there as she should have been but paying a visit to that mother of hers who will never die. (Please note, dear sir, that Kate's absence was due to the machiavellianism—is that spelt right?—of our Miss Rickworth who, by telephone, presented Kate with a holiday.)

Now, as for the rest of the story, let me tell it from another angle. Read what our special correspondent has to say:

STRANGE MYSTERY IN SURREY WEEK-END COTTAGE
Prominent Business Man Loses Understandings

Our frightfully special correspondent writes:

MR. SAMUEL RICKWORTH, a prominent director of RYNOX, is held a prisoner in his charming and palatial country residence on Hindhead. Mr. Rickworth, the best of fathers, although pressed and hedged about by the cares of business, had driven his daughter, that well-known and extraordinarily beautiful young leader of Hammersmith society, down to the country on the previous night.

On arriving at his country residence (chming view, 45 mins. stn., Co's water; c; unusual offices); Mr. Rickworth was horrified to find that the whole of the extensive staff had absented themselves without leave. He therefore took over the duties of housekeeper, cook, and nurse and tenderly put Miss Petronella Rickworth to bed. Then, exhausted, he himself retired.

On waking next morning at approximately 10:30 A. M. Mr. Rickworth leapt from his bed, intending to attire himself and then to see to Miss Petronella's wants, obtain attention for her, and proceed immediately, driving his high-powered car, back to London and work.

Imagine Mr. Rickworth's dismay when he found that not only had the trousers of the clothes he had been wearing the night before disappeared, but that also there was not, so far as he could find, another pair of these far from decorative but almost essential garments in the house.

In panic and a dressing gown Mr. Rickworth hurried along the numerous and softly carpeted passages to the room of Miss Petronella Rickworth. Miss Petronella Rickworth seemed a good deal improved in health. She could not, however, throw any light at all on the mystery of the missing leg wear.

Later. Mr. Rickworth still without trousers.

Later still. Mr. Rickworth, for fear of sciatica, sitting up in bed swearing, and reading *Pilgrim's Progress.*

Later than ever. Mr. Rickworth, with Napoleonic flash of insight, decides to telephone for trousers, but is horrified to find that the telephone is cut off.

Too late. Mr. Rickworth, having conducted a hunger strike for some time in protest at Miss Petronella's most unfilial refusal to do anything about trousers, breaks down and descends to the charming dining room with its outlook over the Surrey hills in order to eat the by no means despicable meal prepared by Miss Petronella's own fair hands.

Seriously, darling, after twelve hours of this I began to get the wind up. After all, one never knows what a parent will do if driven far enough. But, thank the Lord, it's all come out all right. He really is, when he can get over himself, rather an old dear. He's given me his parole that he won't go back to London until told. And I have given him back one pair of trousers. I have, however, cut a piece out of the seat so that he can't go out of doors.

If you can, do come down and see me. Don't come in, in case he has a suspicion—most unjust, I'm sure, Mr. Benedik—that the scheme has been anything to do with you. Just pull up in the lane outside and hoot about four times.

Do come if you can, dear, I'm longing to see you. If you were any one but you, I should say I hope you don't think the rather idiotic tone of this letter shows that I'm not feeling for you and for myself. As you're you, I'm not going to trouble to say it.

Bless you!
PETER.

15

(*Extract dated 4th April from official shorthand record of Coroner's inquest held on the body of Francis Xavier Benedik. Coroner, Dr. Ongle. Extract is from Dr. Ongle's summing up, but also contains the jury's verdict.*)

. . . And so, gentlemen, I think you will not find any other course open to you than to fix upon this man, Boswell Marsh, as the person directly responsible for the shooting of the deceased. You have listened to the chain of evidence, which proves that Marsh was a man of violent and unpleasant nature, imagining himself wronged by the deceased. You have seen, too, documentary evidence supporting this. You have seen and read the very full diary left by the deceased covering the last twenty years of his life, and from that have gathered that, right from their first acquaintance in South America, Marsh and the deceased were at loggerheads. You have had it conclusively proved to you that Marsh visited the house in William Pitt Street on the night of deceased's death and that the pistol found, dropped by Marsh in his flight, had been purchased by Marsh that morning. You will have seen, from the evidence, the subterfuge employed by Marsh to ensure that the housekeeper and two female servants should be absent from the house that night, and you will assume that Marsh had sufficient knowledge of the ways of that house to know that the manservant, too, would be absent at the time of the arranged appointment.

These are just a few points which come to me as after-thoughts. I do not think, gentlemen, that there is anything else which I need say. You will now please consider and confer if necessary, and then let me have your verdict. . . .

Mr. Coroner, I have consulted with the jury and I find that there is no need for us to retire. Our verdict is that death was due to wilful murder, at the hands of Boswell Marsh.

16

(Letter from Naval, Military & Cosmopolitan Assurance Corporation to Anthony Xavier Benedik, dated 7th April.)

DEAR SIR:

Policy No. HI.32. Francis Xavier Benedik, deceased.

Further to our previous communication and also to the interview which our president had with you yesterday, I have pleasure in enclosing herewith the corporation's check for £277,777. (Two hundred and seventy-seven thousand, seven hundred and seventy-seven pounds.)

I am, sir,
Yours faithfully,
MARADICK FOWLER,
Treasurer.

17

(Memorandum from Chief Commissioner of Police, Major General the Earl of Stynge, K.C.B., D.S.O., M.V.O., C.I.E., etc., to Superintendent Shanter, dated 19th April.)

BENEDIK

I note your report on this case. It is highly unsatisfactory. The preliminary investigations seem to have been conducted with intelligence, but the work of the department after the preliminaries seems puerile.

Benedik was shot on the 29th of last month. Three weeks have elapsed. There is no doubt whatsoever that the murderer was Boswell Marsh, and Marsh has not been taken. Why? A man of such distinctive appearance cannot easily hide himself. The ports have been watched, and all his usual places of resort, and yet you have not got him.

I expect to hear of his arrest within the next ten days.

STYNGE.

18

(Memoranda covering period April 29 to May 31.)

From CHIEF COMMISSIONER *to* SUPERINTENDENT SHANTER.
BOSWELL MARSH

Please report.—STYNGE.

From SUPERINTENDENT SHANTER *to* CHIEF COMMISSIONER.
BOSWELL MARSH

Regret have no further progress to report.

T. SHANTER, *Supt.*

From CHIEF COMMISSIONER *to* SUPERINTENDENT SHANTER.
BOSWELL MARSH

Ref. my memorandum of last week. Please report.—STYNGE.

From SUPERINTENDENT SHANTER *to* CHIEF COMMISSIONER.
BOSWELL MARSH

Much regret department has no further information yet to hand in regard to the above.—T. SHANTER, *Supt.*

From CHIEF COMMISSIONER *to* SUPERINTENDENT SHANTER.
BOSWELL MARSH
Reference previous correspondence and our meeting of Tuesday, have new steps produced any information regarding whereabouts of Marsh? STYNGE.

From SUPERINTENDENT SHANTER *to* CHIEF COMMISSIONER.
BOSWELL MARSH
Much regret new steps produced so far nothing further re above.
T. SHANTER, *Supt.*

19

(Extract from Minutes of Chief Commissioner's weekly meeting with superintendents, Scotland Yard, dated July 2.)

17634. DECIDED that Standing Item No. 4—Boswell Marsh—shall in future be deleted from the agenda, no further progress or information having come to hand. Matter to be raised at every sixth meeting.

BOOK THREE

CHAPTER EIGHT

1st October: 1:30 to 2:30 P. M.

The restaurant of Monsieur Isidor Laplanche is in Dover Street. Its small and neat exterior gives to the unsuspecting client who tries it for the first time no indication either of the excellence of Monsieur Laplanche's food, wines and cooking, nor of the preposterous charges made by Monsieur Laplanche.

Peter Rickworth had never happened before this day to enter the Restaurant Pyrenees. But she did so now, to find Tony waiting for her; and with Tony, her father—a Samuel Rickworth even pinker, even plumper, even more prosperous-seeming than when we last saw him.

Tony looked at his watch.

"Hullo, Parent!" said Peter. "If you will wear waistcoats like that I don't think you ought to put chains across them. . . . It's absolutely useless, Tony, to do that tongue-clicking, watch-gazing stuff at me."

"I know," said Tony, "I know. But I always shall. Have a drink?"

They had one, and Peter approved. She also approved of the lunch, and it wasn't until it was over that she looked at her escorts over her coffee cup and said suddenly:

"Well, chaps—how's business?"

"Business," said Tony, "is big. Or just about to be."

"My dear boy!" Samuel Rickworth was aghast. "Just about to be, you say! It *is!* It *is!*"

"Nothing," said Tony, "to what it's going to be. It's going to be so BIG in about another three months that what it is now will look like two penn'orth of cold gin by comparison."

"Give me another cigarette," Peter said. And then, "Are you serious?"

Tony looked at her. He nodded. "Stone cold serious." He looked at her father. "This morning," he said slowly, "we heard from Hamburg and Brisbane. Both cables confirmed the orders."

Samuel Rickworth stared. "God bless my soul!" he said at last. "You don't mean it, my boy!"

"I never," said Tony, "say anything I don't mean."

"Except," said Peter, "when you mean to."

"God *bless* my soul!" said Samuel Rickworth again.

Peter was still studying her betrothed. She said:

"And will Hamburg and Brisbane make you so busy that you won't have time to remember that we're supposed to be getting married at the end of next month?"

"I shouldn't think so," said Tony. "I tell you what, I'll ask Woolrich if he'll give me leave."

Peter's eyes blazed. "As much as mention that man's name to me, young Benedik, and I'll——"

"Now, now!" said her father. "What's the matter with Woolrich, anyhow? I must admit that when Tony wanted to make him a partner I wasn't altogether in favour of it. But since he's been one, I must say I've had an even higher opinion of his capabilities than I had before."

"I do not like thee, Doctor Fell," said Peter. "And nor do you, Tony."

Tony shrugged. "Whether I like him or not doesn't matter two hoots. He's too fond of slipping off to the country, but then he always was. I remember the Guv'nor used to pull his leg about it. And if F. X. stood for a man taking a day's holiday every now and then without asking, well, you can bet that man's a good man. And Woolrich is good. That Brisbane show's entirely his."

"Wool me no more riches," said Peter. "I don't like him, I don't like him, I don't like him. If you grasp my meaning, I don't like him. The conversation having thus been tactfully changed, I will ask you, Xavier, exactly why Brisbane and Hamburg make such a tremendous difference?"

Tony looked at her. His gray eyes softened and he said:

"All right, I'll tell you. It's not only because they're big orders in themselves, but because of what they'll lead to. Rynox is straight now, and has been for quite a while. It's even been making money —all out of Paramata—but, Peter, the money it *has* been making is going to look like little Leonard's post office savings book. . . . Yes, absolutely! I mean it." He knocked the ash off his cigar and got to his feet, a big man but lightly moving.

Peter looked up at him. "Going?" she said.

He leaned on the table and looked down at her, giving a slight and sidelong glance at Samuel Rickworth. "Yes," he said. "Rynox never sleeps. Come with me; you'll be able to see your friend Woolrich."

"Sometimes," Peter said, "I almost dislike you. . . . Good-bye, darling."

CHAPTER NINE

2nd October: 12 P. M. *to 5* P. M.

To Basil Woolrich, sitting in the room at the top of Rynox House which used to be that of F. X., came the clerk Harris.

"Excuse me, sir," said Harris.

Woolrich looked up. In these last months of hard work much of the tan had faded from his face. A deep frown had carved permanent lines between his brows, and the corners of the well-cut mouth were perpetually downdrawn.

"Excuse me, sir," said Harris again, "but there's a a-a person in the outer office . . . And—well, to tell the truth, sir, we can't get rid of him. Says he's got very important business with the firm. But he won't state what it is, and he won't make an appointment. He refuses to talk to anyone except yourself or Mr. Benedik."

Woolrich frowned. "What's his name?" he said.

Harris produced a card. He laid it upon the blotter of the junior partner, who picked it up and examined it. A cheap affair, recently printed, which bore no address; no club; nothing save the three words: "Captain Inigo James."

Woolrich looked at Harris. Woolrich said:

"What's he look like?"

His head on one side, Harris considered a moment.

"A tough lot, sir," he said, after a pause, "very tough. Looks like he'd just come back from some tropical country, sir. And there he is, sitting in a chair between Miss Pagan's desk and mine, looking as if it would take a charge of dynamite to shift him." Harris grew eloquent. "Like some sort of heathen idol, sir. He's sitting there; not saying anything; not *doing* anything. Just sitting there staring across the room, and every time we say anything to him he just repeats: 'I want to see Mr. Benedik, and if Mr. Benedik's not here I want to see another partner.'"

Woolrich stood up and stretched. He walked over to the window, and stood for a moment looking out.

"All right," he said. "Show him in, Harris."

Harris stared, started to say something; then muttered apology in his throat and was gone.

Woolrich went slowly back to his desk and picked up the card and looked at it. He threw it down and seated himself, and was lighting a cigarette when there was a rap on the door.

"Captain James, sir," said Harris.

Woolrich rose. A tall and easily graceful figure, even taller than F. X. or Anthony. His face wore the wooden mask with which the English business man will meet any caller the nature of whose call is unannounced.

Harris, leaving himself upon the outer side, shut the door with a soft click. The newcomer crossed the room toward Woolrich. He was a short and thick and extraordinarily solid-seeming man. While his height could not have been an inch more than five-feet eight, his weight, and all good hard weight by the look of it, must have been considerably more than two hundred pounds. His gait was rolling. He was clean-shaven. His face, which was a square, mahogany-coloured slab, had eyes which seemed to be set almost midway down its length; very small eyes of a curious faded blue whose whites were streaked with crimson. He wore an old and faded suit, double-breasted, of a vaguely seafaring kind.

Woolrich looked at him.

"Good-afternoon," he said.

Captain James smiled, revealing a jagged and irregular set of tobacco-coloured teeth. With the smile there came a miasma of Holland's gin.

"I'm very pleased," said Captain James, "to make your acquaintance." His voice was just the sort of voice which Woolrich imagined would proceed from that mouth and body—a deep booming sound, somehow out of tune.

Woolrich pointed to a chair. "Sit down, won't you?"

"Sure," said Captain James. He sat, placing upon each knee, a square, short-fingered, powerful hand with a thatching of black hair.

Woolrich remained standing. He looked with disfavour—disfavour which he did not endeavour to conceal—upon his visitor. But his visitor went on smiling, and his visitor's eyes went on steadfastly holding Woolrich's gaze.

"If you wouldn't mind," said Woolrich, "stating your business as quickly and briefly as you can . . ."

The smile of Captain James disappeared.

"My business," said Captain James, "is with the other partner, Benedik."

Woolrich got to his feet. "In that case——" he said coldly.

"Now hold it!" said Captain James. "I am seeing you, Mr. Woolsack, because I want to make quite sure that I *do* see this Benedik. I want your assurance that I *will* see this Benedik."

"I fail to see"—Woolrich's tone was an insult in itself—"how I can ensure you an interview with Mr. Benedik if I don't know what your business is with Mr. Benedik."

"Now isn't that spoke pretty!" said Captain James in tones of admiration. "But I'm not here for that sort of stuff, Mr. Woolsack. I'm here on *business*. And very, very important business!" He leaned forward; raised his right hand from his right knee, and pointed a banana-sized forefinger. "See here, Mr. Woolsack," said Captain James, "this Rynox is a big concern, isn't it? This Rynox, from all they tell me, is going to be a lot bigger very soon. But suppose this Rynox, right now, was to get a nasty smack in the eye! How about that? Suppose a story was to start round about Rynox— a nasty story, Mr. Woolsack. How about that, eh? I'm just showing you how important my business is. . . . A nasty story . . ."

Woolrich rose. "If this is a sample of your business conversation, I think the sooner we put an end to it the better."

"Ve-ry smooth!" said Captain James. "But it doesn't go down with me. Not on your life it doesn't. And you can push all your pretty little buttons for all I care and bring in all your damn little clerks."

"If this," said Woolrich, "wasn't faintly humorous, it would be quite impossible."

"And if you," said Captain James, "would get it through your thick skull that I want to see Benedik and I'm *going* to see Benedik, we'd be a whole lot better off."

For a long moment, Woolrich looked at Captain James, liking what he saw less and less.

"All I can do," said Woolrich, "is to mention your visit to Mr. Benedik. Whether he sees you or not is his own affair. If you'd tell me something of your business I might be able to be more useful. As it is, I can't."

Captain James got to his feet, a process which looked as if it ought to take, by reason of his amazing solidity, much longer than it actually did.

"I'm much obliged to you, Mr. Woolsack," said Captain James. "I shall be more obliged to you when I've seen Benedik. My address, at the moment, is Croft's Hotel, Milady Street, Strand. Phone number—that's right, mister, write it down—phone number, Strand 12340. And don't forget, mister, that see him I've got to. Or else!"

Woolrich was pale. Woolrich was not used to this sort of thing. But Woolrich did his best. He said:

"I hardly think that tone will do you any good. If I might give you a warning, it certainly won't pay with Mr. Benedik himself."

Captain James smiled a smile which did not reach his bloodshot eyes . . .

2

Tony reached Rynox House at four-thirty that afternoon. To him came Miss Pagan.

"This," said Miss Pagan, laying down a sheet upon his table, "is from Mr. Woolrich, Mr. Benedik."

Tony looked up. "I was just going to have a talk with him."

Miss Pagan shook her head. "I'm afraid you can't do that, Mr. Benedik. Mr. Woolrich has gone."

"Eh?" said Tony sharply. *"Gone?"* He looked at his watch; then shrugged. He picked up the typewritten memorandum and read:

"A man called James (Captain James) called here this afternoon and could not be moved until he had seen me. Unpleasant customer. Would not tell me his business. Insisted on seeing you. He seems to think he can injure the firm in some way; seems to be threatening to do so if you don't see him. I would advise your doing so, therefore, as soon as you can. His address is Croft's Hotel, Strand, W. C. 1. Telephone number: Strand 12340.

"Sorry could not wait, but am going into the country this evening. Will be back, if possible, on Monday. Have left telephone number with clerk should you want me.

"B. WOOLRICH."

"And who the devil," said Tony, looking at Miss Pagan, "is Captain James?"

Miss Pagan shook her blond head. "I'm afraid I haven't any idea, Mr. Benedik. I can tell you, though, that when Mr. Woolrich says Captain James is unpleasant, he is understating the case. The man is a dangerous-looking person. He actually scared young Harris." Miss Pagan's shoulders moved in a little shudder. "Me too, if it comes to that."

"He did, eh?" Tony looked at her. "Well now, it seems to me that if the staff of Rynox needs scaring, someone in the firm ought to do it . . . So I think I will see Captain James. Yes, indeed. What's my first free time to-morrow?"

Miss Pagan consulted her notebook. "Unless you have fixed anything else, Mr. Benedik, eleven to eleven-thirty."

"Right," said Tony. "Ring up that number"—he tapped Woolrich's note—"and tell this staff-scarer I'll see him at eleven-fifteen. And I hope," he said, "that he'll try and scare me. Life, Miss Pagan, is too soft and easy. Ear-pullers welcome!"

"Certainly, Mr. Benedik. . . ." said Miss Pagan. "Have you anything to dictate?"

Tony had, and began it.

CHAPTER TEN

3d October: 11:30 A. M. *to 5:30* P. M.

Charles, who was small and had his torso longitudinally divided by brass buttons, opened the door of Tony's outer office. Charles piped:

" 'E's in the waitin' room, Miss Pygan."

Miss Pagan turned her blond head. "Thank you, Charles," said Miss Pagan.

From his table at the other side of the room Harris spoke. "Who's that?" he said.

Miss Pagan twitched an impatient shoulder. "Captain James."

"Oh, him!" said Harris, and then again, "Oh, is it!" His tone for these five monosyllables told more than the words themselves. It told of what George Ferdinand Harris, vice captain and treasurer of the Pimlico Road Cyclists' Club would like to do to Captain James if he, George Ferdinand Harris, could only get the chance.

Miss Pagan regarded George Ferdinand Harris with that beautiful and utterly impersonal stare which for the first six months of his acquaintance with it had almost reduced George Ferdinand Harris to gibbering idiocy.

"Why," said Miss Pagan, "don't you just drop into the waiting room? You might have time to teach him some manners."

But Harris was very busy. The tips of his ears showed a dark purple, most unbecoming.

Miss Pagan lifted the desk telephone at her side and spoke into it softly. . . .

At the other end of the telephone, Tony said:

"Have him sent along, please."

"Very well, Mr. Benedik." Miss Pagan hung up the telephone. Miss Pagan pressed a bell, and Charles came running. "Charles," said Miss Pagan, "will you take Captain James along to Mr. Benedik at once."

"Sure will," piped Charles, who was a devotee of American films. He paused at the door. "That is," he said, "if Mr. 'Arris don't want to." The door opened . . . and shut. Charles was no longer with them.

Miss Pagan laughed; Harris muttered under his breath; even the lobes of his ears were now dull purple.

Charles opened the door of Tony's room. "Capting James, sir," said Charles.

Tony had been standing by the window. He came forward as Captain James rolled into the room. He looked at Captain James. The small eyes of Captain James met, coolly, the hard gray stare.

Captain James held out a hand. "Real pleased," said Captain James, "to make your acquaintance."

Tony did not see the hand. Tony said:

"Sit down, will you?"

"I might," said Captain James, and sat.

The room was silent save for the subdued roar, hushed by height, of the traffic in New Bond Street.

"Well?" said Tony at last.

"Well well!" said Captain James. "And that's *three* holes in the ground. . . . See here, Mr. Benedik, am I to understand you've seen that partner of yours, what's his name?—Woolsack. Tall fellow, about your size, fair hair, bit fratefully haw-haw?—You seen him since I saw him?" Captain James crossed one short, thick column of a leg over the other. Captain James chewed ruminatively upon that mysterious object which always he seemed to carry in his left cheek. Captain James with his left eye, which seemed smaller and more piglike than its fellow, sent a roving glance over the floor.

"We don't keep them," Tony said. "Sorry."

"Eh?" said Captain James. "Keep what?"

"Spittoons," said Tony. "If you'd like to move your chair nearer to the window, however . . ."

Captain James smiled, showing the irregular fawn-coloured teeth. Not a nice smile. The small eyes glared up at Tony's.

"Getting fresh?" said Captain James.

Tony shook his head. "Always am," he said. "Same like the daisies."

"What are we?" said Captain James. "A cross-talk turn?"

Tony shrugged. He walked over from the window and sat, behind the big desk, facing his visitor. Clear gray eyes stared into bloodshot eyes of glazed and faded blue. Neither pair wavered.

"What's this?" said Captain James. "Hypnotism?"

"I understand from my partner," said Tony, "that you've got something of great importance to tell me. Something that you want money for, I suspect."

"Mr. Woolsack," said Captain James, "seems to have the right idea." He put one fur-backed hand to a pocket; brought it away bearing a soiled and greasy and crumpled envelope. "Just run your eye," said Captain James, "over that." He tossed it onto the desk.

Tony stared at this stain upon the virgin whiteness of his blotting pad; took from the envelope several sheets of irregularly folded, grayish coloured paper. With this in his hand he looked at Captain James.

Captain James was smiling, broadly this time.

"You want me to read this?" Tony said.

"You folks in this place," said Captain James, "certainly do seem to have the brains."

Tony turned his chair so that the light from the window fell comfortably over his shoulder. He unfolded the sheets. . . .

There was silence in the room for five minutes; ten; fifteen. . . .

At last Tony laid the papers, now neatly folded, face downward upon his table. Again he looked at Captain James.

"Well?" said Tony. His face was pale; there were lines carven into its leanness which had not been there half an hour before. The pupils of his gray eyes had contracted to black pinheads.

Under the stare Captain James lost his smile and shifted uneasily, uncrossing his legs.

"Do you expect," said Tony, "that I shall take any notice of this?"

"I don't expect," said Captain James. "I *know* you will, because you got to! And that, my young cock sparrer, is that!"

Tony did not move. He still looked at Captain James. And Captain James pushed his chair back half an inch. The eyes of Captain James seemed smaller than ever and extremely wary.

Tony put out a hand and tapped the little pile of papers before him. His eyes never left the eyes of Captain James. He said:

"I know you're foul, but I don't think you're a fool. I think I must be correct in assuming that you hold the original of this."

"As I hinted before," said Captain James, "the brains in this building must be worth their weight in gold."

Tony's hands were itching, but Tony not only looked like his father, he had his father's intelligence and perhaps more. Tony said:

"And I take it that you want to sell me the original?"

Captain James laughed. "Brains going?" he said. "Why the hell should I sell you the *original?* What I do with the original's my own business. The original," said Captain James, "is, if you want to know, Mister Benedik, reposing in the vaults of the National & Shire Bank, Felton Street branch, W. And there it's going to stay! What I've come here for—" here the face of Captain James seemed more like one of the things that peer down from the cornices of Gothic cathedrals than a human face has any right to be—"what I've come here for is just to borrow a little ready. Nothing, of course, to do with anything I've showed you just now. Just a trifling loan from one pal to another. What I should like," said Captain James, "and what I'm damn well going to have, is a couple of hundred quid just to go on with."

"You are going," said Tony slowly, each word seeming to be forced out of him, "to have a couple of hundred quid, are you? Just to be going on with?"

He got suddenly to his feet; his chair, thrust back, rocked for a moment; seemed about to fall, then settled itself.

Captain James moved his chair back another half inch.

"Now!" said Captain James. "Now, now! . . . What I mean, if you *want* a rough-house, have one. But I shouldn't, laddie. I shouldn't! Suppose, before I sent *you* to the hospital, *I* was to get some terrible injuries . . . Well, think of my doctah's bills. That two hundred quid would have to be five, and I should just hate that to happen, old chahp!"

"Has anyone," said Tony, "ever told you exactly what a blot you are on the face of the world?"

"Cut it," said Captain James.

Tony put out a groping hand behind him, found his chair, pulled it toward him, and sat. He opened a drawer at his right hand.

Captain James shot to his feet as if he had been galvanized. Captain James had seen drawers open before. Captain James's hand went to his left armpit. "Now *then!*" said Captain James.

"This," said Tony, "is not Chicago!" His hand closed the drawer and came back to the table-top bearing a check-book. He opened it, and picked up a pen. He began to write.

"A thousand apologies!" said Captain James. He sat down again.

"I am writing," said Tony, "a check payable to Inigo James——"

"Friends call me Glassy," said Captain James. "Owing to my habit of never waiting to draw a cork out of a bottle, but just cracking the neck off with my teeth." Captain James seemed in good humour.

"I am writing," said Tony again, "a check . . . payable to Inigo James . . . for the sum of . . . one . . . hundred . . . pounds. . . ."

"Oh, are you?" said Captain James. "Are you indeed? I said two."

Tony stopped writing. He looked up. "You did," said Tony, "but I'm writing a check for one hundred pounds, and I'm going to ask you, Captain James—what are you a captain in, by the way, or of?—I'm going to ask you whether you would come and see me at, let me see, four o'clock to-morrow afternoon, when we could doubtless have a nice cup of tea together—and discuss some possible permanent arrangement."

Captain James pondered. He said at last:

"Nobody can say that Glassy James is hard. My whole trouble in life, son, has been my soft heart. I accept your proposal as made from one gentleman to another."

"That," said Tony, "must be very difficult." He blotted the check, ripped it off with a little hishing sound, and threw it across the table. It landed, not upon the table edge, but upon the floor at Captain James's feet.

"I'm not proud," said Captain James. "Not too proud, at any rate, to pick up a check for a hundred. But if you wouldn't mind keeping your hand away from that drawer while I stoop down, I should be *much* obliged."

Captain James stooped down. He picked up the check, but throughout his stooping, his right hand was below his coat and beneath his left armpit.

"That," said Captain James having scrutinized the check and put it into a strangely empty seeming wallet, "is ve-ry nice!" He got to his feet. "And I'll be here, as you say, to drink a nice cup of tea with you at four to-morrow."

"Do!" said Tony. "Do!" His tone had changed. It was now very pleasant. He even smiled; with an effort which cost him, he explained afterwards to Peter, a stiff neck for three days. He even, as Captain James stood up, extended his hand. He made it of set purpose a hand as limp as a dead cod. Captain James squeezed the hand with his fur-backed, five-fingered enormity.

"Ow!" said Tony, by this time well within his part.

Captain James laughed heartily.

"I'm so frail these days," said Captain James, "that I can't do that trick any more of splitting a lioness from mouth to tail by getting her upper jaw in my right hand and her lower jaw in my left. I can only do cubs now!"

"That's too bad," said Tony. He massaged with gentle left hand the fingers of his right—an admirable piece of acting. He pressed a bell upon his desk, and presently Charles came.

"Charles," said Mr. Anthony X. Benedik, "will you show Captain James to the lift, and will you also tell Miss Pagan that Captain James is coming to see me at four o'clock to-morrow and must be admitted immediately."

Captain James slapped Charles upon the shoulder. "Unks!" said Charles, and then, "Sorry, sir, I'm sure, sir!" He looked at Tony as he spoke.

Tony smiled at him. "You needn't worry, Charles. Captain James doesn't know his own strength."

"Bye-bye!" said Captain James with another of those smiles. "We meet again at Philippi!"

2

Sergeant Bellows had been day (and half the night) porter at Croft's Hotel ever since that unfortunate day when, owing to that trifling incident of the petty cash at Halliwells he was dismissed from the Corps of Commissionaires.

Sergeant Bellows' long thin person was so unlike a sergeant's that his claim to that rank was probably genuine. He wore a dingy and bastard uniform but never succeeded in looking as if it belonged to him. He was thin and drooping and disillusioned, with weary straw-coloured moustaches and weary gin-glazed eyes.

Only once during that year had Sergeant Bellows been seen to smile, and only three times to run. But this morning Sergeant Bellows did both.

At two-thirty exactly by Sergeant Bellows' watch a taxi pulled up outside Croft's, and from it came, into the palmed but dusty "Entrance Lounge" which measured eleven-feet by thirteen, the cause of Sergeant Bellows' blitheness and activity.

Sergeant Bellows knew a lady when he saw one. He also, despite his general air of being entirely devoted to the bottle, knew beauty when he saw it. And this young lady—this young lady who had come in the taxi and was now standing in the Lounge talking to Sergeant Bellows—this young lady had both gentility and beauty in greater measure than Sergeant Bellows could remember having seen for many, many years.

The young lady smiled at him. The young lady said, after a glance round the Entrance Lounge which showed to her that there was no one else within sight, that she wished to see her brother, the name being Mornington.

Sergeant Bellows put up his right hand to scratch at his head, but snatched the hand away before it had reached its goal. He said:

"Mornington, miss? Mornington? Mornington? Mornington?"

"The name," said the young lady, "is Mornington."

"Oh! Mornington," said Sergeant Bellows. "Well, miss, I'm very sorry but I don't recollect. . . ."

"Oh, *don't!*" said the young lady. *"Please* don't tell me my brother isn't here!"

"I won't, miss," said Sergeant Bellows with fervour. "Leastways, miss," he said, "I wouldn't if I could help it. Perhaps the best thing I could do, miss, would be to look at the register. I don't remember all the names of the people that stays here. Birds of passage, you know, birds of passage. Here to-day. Gone to-morrow."

"If you would," said the young lady, smiling upon Sergeant Bellows. "I should be most *terribly* grateful."

"Certainly, miss, certainly!" said Sergeant Bellows. "Anything to oblige, I'm sure."

He then ran. He ran from just within the doors of the Entrance Lounge to the small and hutchlike office of Miss Figwell. He came out again almost immediately. He was not running now. He was walking, and his knees sagged beneath the weight of an enormous leather-bound book.

"Here we are, miss! Here we are! You can soon see if your brother's here."

He put down the register upon one of the wicker tables. He did this with a flourish which was somewhat marred by the collapse of the table. . . .

"Oh, I'm *so* sorry," said Miss Mornington, "I'm afraid I'm giving you an *awful* lot of trouble."

"No trouble, miss," said Sergeant Bellows, now upon his knees and looking up with a craning of his long neck which made him seem more like an ostrich than ever. "No trouble at all. A pleasure!"

He rose at last to his feet, the register securely clasped. He tried another table this time, stouter than its fellow. It swayed on its cane legs but remained upright. Together Sergeant Bellows and Miss Mornington peered at the register. . . .

Sergeant Bellows straightened himself; shook his head sadly; his moustache seemed to droop even more than usual. There came to his face a look so intensely lugubrious that Miss Mornington gazed at him with compassion not altogether concealing incipient mirth. He shook his head woefully.

"It's no good, miss. He's not here."

Any signs of vivacity and the joy of living which might have been in evidence upon Miss Mornington's face were now obliterated. Her lower lip trembled. Her eyes seemed bright with unshed tears. Sergeant Bellows could hardly bear it. He stretched out a hand to pat Miss Mornington tenderly upon the shoulder; snatched it back only just in time.

"There, miss, there," said Sergeant Bellows, "don't you take on——"

"I think," said the young lady faintly, "I think—if I might sit down . . . Such a disappointment. . . . If I could sit down somewhere . . . No, no, not here— Some one might see me. . . ."

"Certainly, miss. Certainly," said Sergeant Bellows in anguish. "Certainly, miss. Certainly. Certainly. Certainly. This way, miss!" And again Sergeant Bellows ran. He ran now from the centre of the Entrance Lounge to the door marked Reading and Writing Room. This door he held open.

With a handkerchief pressed to her mouth—a little handkerchief which bravely endeavoured to conceal her agitation—Miss Mornington passed through the Entrance Lounge into the Reading and Writing Room.

This was a chamber some nine feet by six. It seemed, certainly, that no one could ever read in it; if they had, they had certainly taken away with them what they were reading. That someone, however, might at one time or another have been expected to write there, was proved conclusively by the presence of a small and dusty and much battered bureau. Upon this bureau lay a piebald piece of blotting paper, a crusted inkstand, and a partitioned wooden box holding paper and envelopes.

Sergeant Bellows pushed forward the one delapidated armchair, and into this Miss Mornington sank with a sigh of relief and closed her eyes. The tiny handkerchief was still pressed to her lips.

"Can I get you anything, miss?" said Sergeant Bellows, his moustaches agitated by a fervent pity.

"If I might," said Miss Mornington faintly from behind the handkerchief, "have a glass of water."

"*Water,* miss?" said Sergeant Bellows incredulously. And then having collected himself: "Certainly, miss. You just sit there, and I'll get you a glass of water. Certainly, miss." Sergeant Bellows was gone. When he came back, a thick tumbler between maculate, careful hands, Miss Mornington was sitting upon the arm of her chair. She seemed much revived. She said:

"I'm feeling *so* much better. I can't think what made me so silly!" She took the glass of water from Sergeant Bellows outstretched hands. "Thank you *very* much," she said. "You *have* been kind." She sipped at the water and, rising, set the glass down upon the mantelpiece. "I can't think," she said again, "what made me so silly. Except—well, you see, my brother is all I have in the world, and I haven't seen him for four or five years—and—and—" a return of Miss Mornington's distress seemed imminent but was bravely mastered—"and I'm afraid . . . well, I'm afraid he's been getting himself into trouble. . . . I wish you'd do something for me. Would you?"

"*Would* I?" said Sergeant Bellows with tremendous emphasis. "You just try me, miss!"

Miss Mornington tried him. Miss Mornington stammered at first, but, warming to her work, asked Sergeant Bellows whether, should her brother come, under whatever name, he would let her know. Miss Mornington then gave him her telephone number—which she seemed to have some slight difficulty in remembering—and a description of her brother.

"He's tall," said Miss Mornington, "a very tall man; rather slim; very broad shoulders; very well dressed. He would have been," added Miss Mornington, "very good-looking if it hadn't been for his accident. I don't think you could *possibly* miss him! His nose is very crooked, and one side of his mouth goes up much higher than the other."

"Just so soon, miss," said Sergeant Bellows earnestly, "as the gentleman comes, I'll ring up."

"Thank you," said Miss Mornington, "you are very, very good." She rose to her feet. With unobtrusive fumbling in her bag, she produced coins. She said, so charmingly that even a prouder man could not have refused: "I wonder whether you would be so nice as to drink my health some time."

"I will that, miss!" said Sergeant Bellows, taking the money, "and I give you me solemn word, miss, that if your brother comes here I'll look after him."

Again Miss Mornington smiled.

"Good-bye," said Miss Mornington, "and thank you very, very much!"

For the last time that afternoon Sergeant Bellows ran. He ran, not only out from Reading and Writing Room, but across the Entrance Lounge and out of the Entrance Lounge into the street, to return very soon, puffing triumphantly, upon the running board of a taxi.

3

"I really don't know," said Mr. Butters to his chief lad, Richards, "what's coming over this branch. Why, I can remember the time, boy, when I'd sixteen lads here and could of done with twenty more. We was that pushed."

Richards, a youth who would get on, smiled sympathetically. "You're such a one for work, sir!" he said.

"Well," said Mr. Butters complacently, "I do hate being idle. No day is too hard for me. I like to feel I go to bed with something attempted something done. A night's repose well earned. Always have been that way."

The telephone bell at the other end of the counter rang shrilly. Mr. Butters leapt for it. Mr. Butters whipped the receiver to his ear with a deft click of his stiff-cuffed wrist.

"Yers?" said Mr. Butters interrogatively.

"Is this," said the telephone, "the District Messenger Office?" A man's voice, deep and pleasing.

"Yers," said Mr. Butters, "District Mersengers speakin'."

"I want," said the telephone, "to know whether you can place a messenger at my disposal for the remainder of the day. I have no specific message for him to deliver yet, but I want a boy to come round to my house now"—here the telephone gave a most select address which Mr. Butters wrote down upon his little yellow pad with a graceful flourish—"so that he can be at hand if I want to send any messages. I have a very busy afternoon in front of me. I don't know whether you do that kind of thing. . . ."

"Cer-tain-ly, sir, cer-tain-ly!" said Mr. Butters. "We're very busy at the moment, of course, but we always do our best to oblige. I think I can get a lad round to you—a trustworthy, intelligent lad —within, shall we say, a quarter of an hour? Would that suit, sir?"

"Admirably," said the telephone.

"The lad, sir," said Mr. Butters, "will tell you, at the end of his time, what the necessary fee will be. Is that all, sir? . . . Thank you, sir. . . . The lad will be there within fifteen minutes."

Mr. Butters delicately snipped the receiver back on to its hook. Mr. Butters turned.

"Richards!" said Mr. Butters loudly.

"Sir!" said Richards.

"I want you," said Mr. Butters, tearing the top sheet off his little yellow pad, "to go to this address at once. You are to 'old—hold yourself at the disposal of this gentleman. He wants your services for running messages this afternoon. Now that's a very, very nice little job, Richards; one that may broaden you a lot. You have never had such a job before, I don't think. We don't often get 'em nowadays."

Richards shook his round, clipped bullet of a head upon which was perched, like some neat but untimely growth, the pill-box hat of the messenger service.

"No, sir," said Richards briskly.

"Well, I hope you will find it an int*erest*ing afternoon," said Mr. Butters, to-day in benevolent mood. "Now slip off and if it's after six when you get away, report in the morning as usual. If you get off before six come back here. Understand?"

"Yes, sir," said Richards smartly.

"Right, then," said Mr. Butters. "Off with you." He had the manner of a Marèchal Ney hurling four regiments of cuirassiers into action on the right flank.

"What'll I do, sir?" said Richards looking at the buff slip. "Take a bus, sir, or walk?"

"Walk," said Butters, "walk, walk, walk. I told the gentleman a quarter of an hour, and you should be there five minutes early if you use those fat legs of yours. Off with you now."

So Richards walked. Richards went on his way whistling. It was a sunny afternoon, and he had, the day before, attained the sunny age of fifteen. It may be that on his melodious way he pondered upon what the afternoon held in store for him. If he did, it is quite certain that any answer he may have given himself to this question was wrong. Many things may have been in his mind, but certainly it did not occur to him that he would spend the rest of that day, clad only in his underclothes, reading, very comfortably, a wonderful book called *The Coral Island,* and eating, for at least an hour of that afternoon, the biggest and most splendid tea for which any boy could wish.

4

Captain James laid down a new and rustling five-pound note with a slap upon the counter. It splashed in a little glittering pool of beer.

"Dirty thing!" said Gwen, snatching the note.

Captain James smiled upon her. A smile to which Gwen responded with a challenging toss of the head which showed that, to her at least, the odious qualities of this smile were not too marked.

"Never mind about dirty thing," said Captain James. "You take for that last round out of it and give me the change, ducky. And what about a nice sip of port for yourself?"

Now Gwen smiled upon Captain James in her turn. They had

all, Gwen and Mr. Titchfield and the elegant Mr. Fawcett and three other unnamed customers in this bar of Croft's, been smiling upon Captain James, and smiling steadily, ever since half-past three that afternoon.

"I don't reelly mind," Gwen said, "if I do . . ." and then, a moment or so later: "Well, cherriliho!"

"Good-night, Nurse!" said Captain James. He drained his own glass and set it down upon the counter with a ringing smack.

"I," said he, "am going to knock the pills about a bit. Anyone comin'?"

Without waiting for reply he swaggered off, rolling his thick, short bulk in the direction of the swing doors leading to the Billiard Room.

And presently, in the Billiard Room, he was playing a hundred up with Mr. Titchfield. Mr. Fawcett was acting as marker, delicately moving the indicators with the tip of his amber-hilted stick. Two of the unnamed cronies were watching. Every shot played by Captain James was applauded by one of them with loud suckings of his deficient teeth; by the other with a curious snorting chuckle. . . . And Albert the pot-boy kept running in and out of the Billiard Room with tray after tray of brimming glasses. Every now and then Captain James would give Albert money. . . .

Captain James, with a break of forty-six, ran out.

"Too hot for me!" said Mr. Titchfield. "Lucky I didn't have any money on it."

"*I*," said Captain James, "didn't have any money on it because I knew I'd best you and I knew you couldn't pay. Have a drink? BOY!"

Albert came on the heels of the cry, but this time he came without his tray.

"Excuse me, Cabted," said Albert, "bud there's a Bessenger boy. Got a parcel for you, Cabted. Says he bust have it sighed for."

"Well, my Spanish Catarrh," said Captain James, "sign for the thing yourself and then give it to me."

"Please, sir," said Albert, "the boy says it bust be sighed by you, sir."

"A lot of nonsense," said Captain James. "Send the brat here. I'll sigh 'im!"

"Certeddly, sir," said Albert and was gone, reappearing almost immediately followed by a District Messenger who bore beneath his thin right arm a large square box wrapped in brown paper.

"That," said Albert, "is Cabted Jabes."

Captain James surveyed the messenger, very smart in his uniform with its jaunty cap.

"You are Captain James, sir?" said the boy. His voice was determinedly deep, his enunciation almost painfully precise.

"You know," said Captain James, "you'll be wanting my birth certificate next, son."

The boy set down the parcel upon the edge of the billiard table. It was addressed in bold characters to:

> Captain Inigo James,
> Croft's Hotel,
> Milady Street,
> Strand.

The boy produced from his satchel a large, flat receipt book. He opened it and presented it, with a pencil, to Captain James.

"If you wouldn't mind, sir," he said, "signing at the foot here."

Captain James took the pencil and signed with a heavy-handed flourish.

"And who the hell," said Captain James, "is sending me parcels, I can't think." He turned to Mr. Titchfield. "Here, you've got a knife. Open that, will you? . . . Here, sonny. . . ."

The messenger boy, escorted by Albert, went out the richer by a shilling. Captain James, this night, was in a mood unusually generous. . . .

"It's a box," said Mr. Titchfield through the rustlings of brown paper, "of cigars."

Captain James came to his shoulder and peered over it.

"Any message?" he said.

Mr. Titchfield conducted an exhaustive search but shook a mournful head. "None," he said, "so far as I can see."

"*Too* marvellously mysterious!" said Mr. Fawcett.

Captain James inspected the square box.

"Floriala Regias," he read. "Well, they may be smokable or they may not." He turned to Mr. Fawcett. "Here, you shove one of those into your face and tell us what it's like." He advanced upon Mr. Fawcett, determination in every line of him, and a cigar between his fingers.

Mr. Fawcett backed nervously away. "Oh, really, Ay couldn't!" said Mr. Fawcett. "Ay never smoke anything except cigarettes."

"You are going," said Captain James, "to smoke this Floribloodyala. Oh, yes, you are, Mary! Oh, yes, you are! . . . Hi! Someone stop him!"

There was subsequently much merriment over Mr. Fawcett and the cigar.

CHAPTER ELEVEN

4th October: 9:30 A. M. *to 9:15* P. M.

The Manager was away, a victim to the latest and most fashionable form of influenza, and therefore the management of the bank was in the hands of his assistant, Mr. Bernard Ponsonby.

Mr. Ponsonby was young, impeccably tailored and by no means unaware of his own attractions. He was also, in spite of earnest determination to appear blasé, highly impressionable in regard to that division of humanity which he called, according to his mood or company, either "The Fair Sex" or, more simply, "the girls, God bless 'em."

Mr. Ponsonby was also a snob of snobs, and the impressionability mentioned above therefore increased in direct ratio to the apparent wealth, breeding and habiliments of the impression-giver. So that the immediate effect upon him of Miss Patricia Maltravers was, to say the least, seismic . . .

Except for her clothes, which included a sable coat and other appurtenances which, in eminent taste though they were, would have been most remarkably out of tune with the decor and surroundings of Croft's Hotel, Miss Maltravers bore a marked resemblance to Miss Mornington; and, from the moment she was shown into the managerial office, she proceeded (though with a completely different technique) to enslave Mr. Ponsonby as Sergeant Bellows could never have been enslaved.

In the first place she addressed Mr. Ponsonby, throughout her visit, with a tone and manner which accepted him as a fellow member of the haut monde to which she obviously herself belonged. In the second, she made Mr. Ponsonby subtly aware, throughout every moment of their all too short meeting, that she was far from unaware of his charm and manhood.

Mr. Ponsonby, of course, was from the start in a state of euphoria. He floated. So rapt was he in what Miss Maltravers was *not* saying, that he found it difficult as well as tedious to pay more than the necessary minimum of attention to the simple, if somewhat unusual, matter of business she had come to discuss.

"Not that it's really *business*," said Miss Maltravers, with one of the smiles that turned Mr. Ponsonby's knees to water. "It's just an *errand* really. For that black sheep uncle of mine. Don't you adore black sheep, Mr. Ponsonby—really rugged, rascally, *romantic* black sheep? *I* do. I bet you have one in your family . . . Our sort of people always do," she added, to Mr. Ponsonby's eternal and gratified wonder.

The errand for the darkly ovine relative *was* a simple matter. Having received a letter which Miss Maltravers produced from the faintly but deliciously perfumed depths of her handbag, Mr. Ponsonby read it and was immediately ready to do his part.

Taking as long as he could over the far from arduous task, Mr. Ponsonby (whose kin were all sheeplike indeed but none of them even tinged with black) kept conversation going as long as he could, but all too soon was compelled to usher Miss Maltravers out of the office, and through the main hall of the bank, and so to the outer doors of glittering glass and metal.

He stood for a timeless moment looking after the departing vision, wondering how he might conceivably bring about another meeting . . .

2

At the sound of the door opening, Miss Pagan looked up. She saw, around the edge of the door, at a matter of only some six inches above its handle, the bright face of Charles.

"Mr. Benedik," said Charles, "told me to tell you, Miss Pygan, that he don't want any tea to-day. When Capting Jymes arrives, he wants me to show him straight along. . . . No, don't you fret, Mr. 'Arris, he's not going to ask you to deal with him!" Charles shut the door rapidly upon this last shaft. You never knew when people might throw things.

Harris, his ears flaring banners of embarrassment, bent over his work, muttering. Miss Pagan smiled.

"I don't know," said Miss Pagan, "what's come over that boy to-day. Seems to be even more sure of his own importance than usual!"

"Brat!" said Harris savagely. "If I had *my* way . . ."

"Your way, Mr. Harris," said Miss Pagan, "is so different always from what you say it's going to be."

Harris subsided.

"I must say," said Miss Pagan, who seemed this morning in a mood unusually loquacious, "that I do wonder at Mr. Benedik seeing that awful man again."

Harris muttered.

"It does seem very odd!" said Miss Pagan. "All I hope is that he doesn't come in here."

Harris muttered.

Miss Pagan's hopes were realized. Captain James did not enter the outer office. Captain James was met just inside the main doors by Charles.

"'Afternoon, sir!" said Charles brightly.

"Good-afternoon, my lord!" said Captain James, who seemed in a mood most expansive. He smiled upon the world with his unpleasing teeth. His eyes were more notably red-rimmed even than before. The miasma was to-day an aggressive miasma.

"I want," said Captain James, "to see Mr. Benedik."

"Yes, sir. Mr. Benedik's instructions were to show you stryte along to his room. If you would come this way, sir?" Charles, a small and strutting figure, strode down the carpeted corridor, Captain James rolling in his wake like a tanker towed by a tug.

Charles halted; behind him Captain James. Charles rapped smartly upon the door.

"Come in!" said Tony's voice.

Charles opened the door. "Capting Jymes, sir," he said and stood aside.

Captain James, preceded always by the miasma, rolled into the room; rolled up to the room's owner with outstretched paw. . . .

"All right!" said Captain James a moment later. "If we want to be haughty and exclusive, haughty and exclusive let's be. It matters, I might tell you, son, very little to me."

Captain James still smiled. Unasked, he dropped into the big leather chair which, it seemed to Tony looking at him, he had never left since the interview of yesterday morning.

Captain James crossed his legs and leaned the back of his head against the top of the chair and looked up at Tony.

Tony, standing in the middle of the room, his hands clasped behind his back, looked down at Captain James. . . .

The silence, combined with Tony's attitude and Tony's hard,

cold, steel-gray stare—might well have discommoded ninety-five men out of a hundred. But Captain James was the ninety-sixth. He began to laugh. Not so loudly nor so raucously as yesterday but even more objectionably.

"Well!" said Captain James. "Come to any decision, mister?"

Tony crossed to the table; twisted his chair to him and sat. Tony put his elbows on the table and continued to stare at Captain James. Tony said at last:

"Oh, yes! I thought, you know, Captain, that this was going to be a very serious and difficult matter for me and my firm. . . ."

"*Thought?*" said Captain James. "Ought to say *think,* oughtn't you?"

"I was using," said Tony, "the perfect tense. It perfectly describes my perfect peace of mind over this whole matter."

Captain James' smile faded from his face. His lips disappeared. He uncrossed his legs and sat, quite rigid now, leaning forward. His eyes narrowed to glittering pin points under the craggy brows.

"The hell you say!" said Captain James. With a movement obviously subconscious, his left hand came up and stroked with soft fingers something which bulged a little beneath his coat and his left armpit.

"The hell," said Tony cheerfully, "I *do* say!" He took his elbows from the table. He sat back in his chair. He smiled at Captain James. If Rickworth or Woolrich had come in at that moment and looked at that figure in the chair, they would have thought for a full half minute that they were seeing a ghost. Always strong, the likeness between Tony and F. X. at this moment seemed something more than likeness. This Benedik said:

"Suppose, before we go any further, that you tell me just how you came into possession of that letter."

Captain James pondered, closing red-rimmed lids over the almost invisible eyes. "I don't see," said Captain James, "any harm in that. That letter was given to me by a bloke who used to be in the F. M. S. Name of Carruthers—Pinkey Carruthers they used to call him because he could drink more Pink Gins to the square minute than any other man, even out there: and that, sonny," said Captain James, who seemed to have recovered some of his good-humour, "is *drinking.*"

"Why," said Tony not moving, "did Carruthers give you this letter?"

"Because," said Captain James with an evil leer, "Pinkey Carruthers was cashing in his checks. Fever, plus knife, plus, I've always said, chopped bamboo in his curry. I happened to drop in on Pinkey—he lived so many miles away from anywhere that the bloody fellow must have been mad anyhow—I happened to drop in on him when he was almost on the last lap. He hadn't got anyone he could trust, and I don't wonder, and he gave this to me to deliver." Here Captain James laughed one of his laughs. "Mind you," said Captain James, "he didn't trust me, but there wasn't anyone else to hand who could do the job for him . . ."

"The job?" said Tony.

"Your head," said Captain James, "doesn't seem to be as clear as it was yesterday. The job of delivering this letter to you. Or, in the case of your death, to one of the other partners of Rynox."

"And how," said Tony, "did Pinkey Carruthers originally obtain the letter?"

"If you've read it," said Captain James, "and I know you have because I bloody well sat here and watched you do it, you know. Pinkey Carruthers got it by the mail, inside another letter saying how Pinkey was to post this one six months from the day he got it. When I ran across Pinkey and he gave it to me, five of the months had gone. . . . So, seeing there was something funny about this, I did as nine hundred and ninety-nine men out of a thousand men would do, I opened the thing. And when I'd read it, I thought to myself, 'Ah-*hah!*' . . ."—here Captain James laughed again, most heartily. He let the laughter rumble into silence before he went on:

"And there, as you might say, mister, we are! I've got the goods. You've got to pay. All merry. All above board. You don't quarrel with me, I shan't quarrel with you." Captain James once more lay back in his chair and once more crossed one leg over its fellow.

"*You,*" said Tony in an odd voice, "have the goods. . . . Are you sure of that, Captain?"

"Oh, stop it!" said Captain James. "Don't make me laugh. You ought, by this time, mister, to know me well enough to know that when I say I've got the goods, got the goods I have."

"All right," said Tony. "I'll tell you what I propose to do—"

Captain James, scenting business at last, uncrossed his legs and once more leaned forward, each knee supporting a fur-backed paw.

"I propose," said Tony, "to give you a check, for services rendered, for the sum of one hundred and fifty pounds. This makes, with the one hundred I gave you yesterday, two hundred and fifty pounds. For carrying a letter—especially when you've copied that letter and tried to make blackmailing capital out of it—I think that's good pay."

An extraordinary sound, half grunt, half roar, came from the visitor. "Do I understand," said Captain James, "that you think, you poor fresh-water, soft-roed young skate, that you are going to fob me off with a mere two hundred and fifty quid? Oh, don't, *please* don't, make me laugh!"

Tony said nothing. Instead he put his hand to his breast-pocket. Immediately, with this action, Captain James' right hand shot beneath his coat in the direction of his left armpit.

Tony brought from his own pocket a folded envelope. This he laid upon the table so that it and its superscription were easily visible to the eye of Captain James as he lolled in the big chair. It bore, this envelope, the words: Captain Inigo James.

"In there," said Tony, "is the check for one hundred and fifty pounds which I mentioned just now. Are you going to take it, James?"

"Am I going to *what?*" said Captain James. He reached out a hand; engulfed the envelope; rammed it into the now bulging wallet. "I am going to take it," said Captain James, and as he said this he looked, though unsmiling, even more repulsive than Tony's worst memory of him. "But," said Captain James, "I am going to take, sonny, a whole hellova lot more. . . ."

Tony interrupted. "And that," he said, "is where we disagree. You are *not* going to take one penny more. You are going to take nothing more. There is not, if you follow me, any more for you to take."

"Oh, fresh!" said Captain James. "Very, very fresh! And as green as the bleeding grass! What the hell do you take me for? Somebody's Aunt Susie?"

"I shudder to think," said Tony, still smiling, "of your being anybody's aunt. Or, for that matter, anybody's relation at all. Any human being's relation, that is. I can, however, think of many animals to which you not only bear a resemblance but a probable blood kinship."

"Oh, funny! Very amusing!" said Captain James, again out of a lipless mouth. "But see here, sonny, I've got your piddling two-fifty, and if I don't get more—one whole holy hell of a lot more!—*as* I want it and *when* I want it, the original of that letter—gets to places where you don't want it."

"Oh, no!" said Tony, shaking his head.

"What the hell do you mean, 'Oh, no'?" demanded Captain James.

"Exactly," said Tony, "what I say. In no circumstances will the original of that letter be shown by you to anybody."

Captain James stared. At last, with what was doubtless intended for a pitying smile, he raised his forefinger and touched his rock-like mahogany forehead. He said:

"Daft! Bugs! Flooey! Bats dashing themselves to death against the belfry walls. . . ." Captain James broke off. "What the *hell!*" he said suddenly in a sort of hissing whisper. He stared as if pulled by some invisible force. He got to his feet, thrusting back the deep armchair. He stared, as a snake might stare who suddenly has found a rabbit better at hypnotism than he is himself, at something which Tony held between his fingers . . .

"This," said Tony, "is the original letter." He held the thing up between the thumb and forefinger of each hand, a thick wad of foolscap pages clipped together at the left-hand corner with a rusty brass clip; pages covered with a neat, small-charactered handwriting.

"Look!" said Tony. "That's it, you know! No mistake! No deception! Nothing, ladies and gentleman, up my sleeve! . . ."

"How—*what the hell!*" said Captain James again.

To Tony's left rear, as he stood behind his table, was the fireplace, and in it there crackled a fire of coals and logs.

"Look!" said Tony. Under his fingers the pile of sheets tore, ripped in half across their length, and then in his hands the torn sheets were crushed into a ball, and then the ball was tossed, before Captain James's horrified gaze, unerringly into the fire. . . .

A strange sound burst from Captain James. A sound which was a cross between oath and prayer and the roaring of an injured animal.

The right hand of Captain James came up and disappeared beneath the left lapel of his bulging coat. . . .

"Oh, no, you don't!" Tony's right hand came up from the table, in it a heavy silver inkstand. . . . The hand jerked. . . . There struck Captain James, across his eyes, a stream of blue-black liquid.

From Tony's right hand the inkpot dropped with a clatter. His left hand came down on the desk and he vaulted. As his feet touched the floor on the desk's other side, his right hand caught the right wrist of Captain James, now (despite the gasping splutters to which its owner was giving vent), grasping a stubby automatic. Tony's left hand came up to Captain James's right elbow. There was a sudden flurry of straining bodies . . . a twist . . . a wrench. . . . The automatic was in Tony's hands.

"That," said Tony, drawing a deep breath, "is downright naughty!" He tossed the pistol from him, half turning his body. It slid in a brown arc through the air to smash the glass of a window and fall with a hideous clattering on to the jutting roof of the storey below.

Tony stepped back from Captain James. Tony ripped off his jacket and threw it to lie in a corner. He backed away from Captain James until he was at the door; then turned, and with one swift movement locked the door and thrust the key into his hip pocket.

"Gord Ormighty!" said Captain James. He had cleared the ink from his eyes with the back of his left hand. His face was a skewbald mask. . . .

"If it's a rough-house you're wanting——" said Captain James.

He stood stock-still; his arms, tremendously long for his height, raised themselves, the broad squat fingers crooked. He leapt . . .

The door of Miss Pagan's room opened with a crash through which hurtled an electrified Charles. He stood in the doorway and beckoned wildly.

"Here, cummere quick!" stuttered Charles. "Here, cummere quick! Here, cummere quick!"

"Whatever," said Miss Pagan, "is the——"

"Here, cummere quick!"

"What," said Harris heavily, "do you mean, Charles, by——"

"Here, cummere quick! No, not you. You're no damn good. Miss Pygan, it's the Guv'nor. He's scrapping in there with that Jymes. You never 'eard such a dust-up! Here, cummere quick!"

Miss Pagan, for probably the first time and certainly the last in that office, not only did as she was bidden by Charles, but did it with a celerity quite shattering. Losing for once her determined pose of shock-proof calmness, Miss Pagan flew down the passage on small and beautifully shod feet which seemed hardly to touch the carpet. Miss Pagan leaned against the wall, having vainly tried the door of the room and found it locked, and put a hand to her heart.

"Oh, my *God!*" said Miss Pagan.

"Didjever," said Charles, coming up a bad second, "'ear anythink like it in all your life?"

"Quick, quick!" said Miss Pagan, clutching Charles by the shoulder and shaking him in her agitation. "Quick! Run out and fetch a policeman. *Quickly!* Oh, listen to that! Oh, my God! Go and get the other men and then send someone for a policeman. Hurry, Charles, hurry!"

Charles scratched his head but stayed where he was.

"I'm not so sure, Miss Pygan, . . ." he said.

"Oh, hurry, Charles, *hurry!*"

"Now, then," said Charles with kindly tolerance, "you take a holt of yourself, Miss Pygan. This is the Guv'nor's job, this is. Now, I know somethink about the Guv'nor and Jymes and I'm not so sure that the Guv'nor'd thank us for interruptin'. *Blimey!* Listen to *that!*"

Miss Pagan leaned against the wall again, covering her face with her hands. That last crash, a sound as if all the tables in Rynox House had, of their own accord, suddenly and simultaneously hurled themselves against their respective walls, still rang with its dreadful sound in her ears. And still in her ears were other sounds. Hissing breaths; grunts—awful, animal-like yet human grunts; gasps; the thudding of feet upon the soft carpet; and other thuddings, reminiscent to Miss Pagan, who had never in her well-ordered life heard fist meeting flesh, of meat and butchers' blocks.

Along the passage, leading a charge of fellow clerks, came Harris. In each of Harris's hands was a heavy ruler. Harris stopped outside the door. He listened. Behind him his three adherents clustered. They looked at each other with awe-stricken and yet joyous faces. Happenings like this were, alas, far too rare in New Bond Street. . . .

Another crash within the room. A crash which was father to all the other crashes. And then—dead, utter silence. . . .

"O-oh!" said Miss Pagan faintly and once more covered her face.

Harris, very pale, stepped up to the door and beat upon it with his rulers. "Here!" said Harris in a tone which was meant to be deep and manly and official. "What's all this? What's all this? Are you there, Mr. Benedik? Are you there, sir?"

Then faint sounds within the room. A stirring; a rattle of the key in the lock; the turning of the key; the door opening. . . .

"I am," said Tony on the threshold. "But what the hell are all you people playing at? Buzz off back to your work. Go on! Sharp!"

Miss Pagan, looking up with joy at the sound of this voice, screamed a little scream, instantly repressed, as her eyes took in the spectacle. Tony was, in this place and at this time, fit matter for a woman's cries. Not only was he coatless, but waistcoatless. His collar had gone, and the most part of the right sleeve of his shirt. This gaped to show his chest, and down the chest were angry scratches, some of them bleeding. His mouth was a mashed blur. His left eye, darkening rapidly, was closed. His nose—the imperious Benedik nose—was swollen like a clown's, and all over his face were replicas of the scratches on his chest. . . .

"Blimey!" said Charles in Harris's ear. "Just look at that arm, will you! There's a arm for you! He's O. T., the Guv'nor."

The shapeless mouth of the figure in the doorway opened again. "I said buzz off back to your work. All of you except Charles. Come in here, Charles."

The whole lot buzzed back to their work. *Buzzed* is the right word, for their talk was like the storming of a thousand bumble bees. Charles, swollen with pride, entered the room. The door banged to. Charles looked round the room, and a smile of unholy joy brightly illumined his face.

"Oh, *crikey,* sir!" said Charles.

Tony looked round and put up a hand to feel tenderly at his jaw. "Yes," he said, "bit of a mess, Charles, isn't it? But it was worth it."

Once more Charles looked around him. "But I sye, sir, where's —where's——Oh, Lord love a duck!"

He had been looking for Captain James, and now, quite suddenly, he saw Captain James' feet. They were sticking out from under the overturned mahogany desk. Charles, borne upon the wings of curiosity, took three strides and a jump. He saw—stretched neatly upon his back, breathing heavily to show that he was indeed alive but otherwise with no signs of life—Captain James. He lay very tidily, his legs together, his arms stretched neat and trim by his sides. He had, except for his collar, all his clothes on. But his face made Tony's seem a thing of beauty.

"Oh, *blime,* sir," said Charles. "You 'aven't half messed him up proper." He looked round at his employer with the words. His employer was seated on the window sill, writing with a pencil on a slip of paper.

"Charles!" said Charles's employer, "nip off and get all these things on this list as quickly as you damn well like. I have to make myself presentable. Look slippy, now!"

With one more delighted glance at the body beneath the desk, Charles looked slippy, and was gone.

Tony, with a heave, righted the desk, sat upon its top, and, with tender care for his battered mouth, lit a cigarette. He sat immediately above the prostrate Captain James and smoked; and waited. . . .

Captain James stirred at last. Though he might indeed be always half full of Holland's gin, he was made of hard stuff. Captain James opened an eye with difficulty. Tony watched while into this red-rimmed orb intelligence came flooding back.

Captain James sat up. As he moved he let out a grunt like a pig in agony.

Tony stood up. He said, looking down at Captain James:

"Had enough?"

Captain James looked up at him and mumbled: "By God, son, I have!" His tone seemed to carry no resentment. Only a dazed wonder. He got slowly and with difficulty to his feet and stood swaying. He eyed Tony up and down, the remains of his mouth twisted in painful effort to produce a smile. "But I marked you, son, I marked you!" said Captain James.

Tony laughed. "But have a look at yourself in some mirror when you pass one, will you?"

"I never," said Captain James, "look at myself in a glass. Not even when I'm shaving." He shrugged. He bent his left arm stiffly and searched in his breast pocket. It came away holding the envelope containing the check which Tony had given him half an hour before.

"This," said Captain James, anxiously waving the envelope, "this all right, eh? This is O. K.?"

Tony nodded.

Captain James put the envelope back in his pocket. "Well," he said with philosophic resignation, "that's that!" Once more he eyed his conqueror. "I must say," he said—there was wonder now in his voice—"I knew they kept smart men in the City of London, but I didn't know they kept bear-cats with brains. Where did you learn to handle yourself, mister?"

Tony shrugged. "Here and there," he said.

"Well," said Captain James, stiffly and unsteadily trying the action of his legs, "I better be going."

"You had," said Tony grimly.

Captain James went, only to come back through the door a moment after it had closed behind him.

"See here," said Captain James, "there's one thing."

"And what the hell," said Tony, "is that?"

"Just this," said Captain James. "How in the name of God did you manage to get hold of that letter? If I don't find out, I'll never get any more sleep all my life, and you couldn't bear that to happen to Glassy James, now could you, mister?"

Tony stood up and threw away his cigarette and went to the corner and picked up his coat. He slipped it on. He stood buttoning it and turning up the collar. He said:

"You practically gave me the letter yourself. You showed me the way to it. When you were in here yesterday afternoon, you told me that the letter was with your bank. You told me what the bank was and what the branch was and you said, 'And don't you forget it!' Well, I didn't. What I did was to talk the matter over with a friend of mine, and what happened then was that this friend of mine went to your hotel and managed to get hold of some of the hotel notepaper. We then got a messenger boy and paid him to lend his uniform to our boy here. You didn't recognize him, did you? That will teach you something, Glassy! That'll teach you to look at faces."

"*God Almighty!*" said Captain James. "Do you mean to tell me . . ."

"I do!" said Tony. "A messenger boy, who was my boy here, went to your hotel last night with a box of cigars. He gave you the box and made you sign for it at the foot of a printed form. Under the form was a piece of carbon paper, and under that piece of carbon paper was a sheet of Croft's Hotel notepaper with a typewritten letter from you on it. When you signed the form, you signed a carbon reproduction on the letter. Charles brought the book back to us, and with due care we inked in the signature. The letter was a masterpiece, I think. It was badly typed, but not too badly. It was just the sort of letter that might be typed by a man of your type who used a portable typewriter.

"This morning my friend took this letter to the bank and had no difficulty in getting your envelope out. The only risk, Glassy, was that you might have had more than one envelope in the bank's keeping, but I had to take that risk, and it worked out all right."

"May God," said Captain James fervently, "strike me a beautiful, bloodstained, ruby pink!"

3

"Your *poor* face, darling!" said Peter.

"Forget my face," said Tony. "If you want to see faces, you'd better take a squint at the one my friend Captain Inigo James is wearing. Or p'raps I should call him Glassy."

"But was it necessary?" said Peter. "All the strong-arm stuff, I mean?"

"Well, I had to do *something!*" Tony's expostulation came near to the querulous. "Didn't I, now? There was that great stiff thinking he had me on toast and scaring Christmas out of my staff. Well, after I'd got what I wanted, I had to have the odd word or so with him." He started to grin in pleasurable retrospect, but the grin didn't get far. It hurt to grin. "It *was* a scrap," he said, "a good scrap!" He looked across the table of the William Pitt Street dining room at Peter. "The sort of scrap," he said slowly, "that F. X. would have liked."

"Dear F. X. . . ." said Peter. "Tony, I want to read that letter again. Now, dear. Got it?"

Tony nodded. From the breast pocket of his dinner jacket he pulled the folded sheets of Captain James' copy and handed them across the table. Peter took them and unfolded them and smoothed out their creases with a gentle touch. Across the table—F. X.'s table —she looked at her lover and F. X.'s son. She raised her glass. She did not speak, but Tony raised his too. In silence they drank a toast.

Peter set down her glass and sat back in her chair and once more began to read that letter, which is really:—

PROLOGUE

MY DEAR ANTHONY:

So far as I can calculate, you will receive this letter about six months after I have been murdered.

I shall have been murdered by half-past ten to-morrow night. This will be, I daresay, distressing for me and I am sure damn painful for you and perhaps one or two other people. My one consolation about you is that I know you will be so busy with Rynox, owing to my death, that you won't have time to be as put out about it as you would in ordinary circumstances.

Before I go any farther, there is one thing I ought to tell you: a thing which, when I have told it you, will make you a good deal easier in your mind and far more likely to agree with me as to the desirability of my own death. I discovered a little over eighteen months ago—do you remember the time when we were over in Vienna and I had to go to hospital with what I told you was some sort of nervous gastritis?—that I had got cancer. I have seen a good few specialists about it, and they all tell me that whatever they do and however much carving and treatment they give me, the thing is bound to kill me in the end. They didn't say as much, but that was what they meant. I am sure you will agree with me that that sort of death is most undesirable. Frankly, from the time I was first *sure* that nothing could be done—that was almost a year ago—I started to think of getting rid of myself in a clean and decent and orderly and untroublesome way. At the beginning I only thought along the lines of suicide, with an explanation to you. But then—it was in February last when we decided, you remember, to go up to the neck and a bit more over Paramata—I suddenly saw that I could, if I played my cards properly, kill a whole flutter of birds with one stone. Mind you, I knew right from the beginning that to pull off Paramata was not going to be nearly such an easy job as I had told old Sam Rickworth. I'd hinted to you that we were going to have trouble, but even to you I didn't say how absolutely certain I was as to the probable extent, in terms of time and money, of that trouble. I knew, for instance, almost to a penny what we should be pushed for to-day. And I knew, almost as certainly, that we shouldn't, by ordinary means, be able to get it. And I knew, quite certainly, that if we *did* get it and did tide over, then we stood a very, very good chance of knocking 'em all edgeways.

I think you know that you and Rynox and Peter, and a grossly over-developed sense of humour, have been the four big things, almost the four only things, in my life. When, therefore, I found that that life was a rotting and shaky and, from my point of view anyhow, a most unpleasing concern, I began to try and find a way by which, in ending it, I could serve the interests of the three other things. I found it like this:

Two years before I discovered there was anything the matter with me, I had, as you know, insured my life—with that colossal endowment policy—for nearly £300,000. (What an awful job I had to get these poor insurance fish to realize that I was serious over my sevens! If I could, I'd have made the damn thing not only £277,777, but I'd have put seven shillings and sevenpence onto it. Seven's always been pretty lucky for me.) I began, almost as soon as I started to plan, to see how this insurance policy might fit in with all requirements. I had taken it out with no ulterior motives whatsoever—save the great tax-saving ramp, which is what I did it for—but now I saw how the thing could be more than trebly useful. I saw the time coming, and not far off, when Rynox would want—would have to have—at least a hundred and ninety thousand, and I saw how, serving all my ends, I could get that money. (It would have been hopeless to attempt to borrow it, even using the policy. You know that as well as I do. We might have got fifty or sixty thousand, but not more.)

My plan in rough came to this:

To get rid of myself in such a way that the question of suicide could not enter the minds of the insurance people or anyone else on earth. The full amount of the insurance would then be paid to you at once and without question.

If I could do this I *knew* that you would immediately put all the money into Rynox and then proceed to run Rynox better than it had ever been run before. I knew, in other words, that you'd weather the Paramata business until Rynox and Paramata were rolling along on top of the world. I knew also that if I left instructions for you—leaving them in such a way that they could not too soon give away my plans—to pay back the insurance, pay back the insurance you would. I knew also that if I played my cards properly I could get out of life, in leaving it, one last colossal joke.

I began to scheme. I've schemed, as you know, all my life, but never have I produced a better scheme than this one.

Listen! I am going to be, as I said, murdered to-morrow night. I am going to be murdered by a man named Marsh. That makes you sit up! You've heard of Marsh, haven't you? Sick of the sound of his name! And when I've been murdered by Marsh, the police, try as they will, are going to be completely unable, although they will know that Marsh killed me, to find Marsh. This will annoy them. Marsh is so distinctive a person—not at all the sort of needle one could lose even in the largest haystack.

But they won't find him! They won't find him because at precisely the same moment and by the same means that Francis Xavier Benedik meets his death, so will Boswell Marsh meet his!

In other words Boswell Marsh and Francis Xavier Benedik are one and the same! Marsh, whom everyone, yourself included, will be prepared quite honestly to swear was a man with whom I became acquainted many years ago in South America, actually only came into being six months ago.

You see, Tony, it is absolutely essential to make my death not an accident but a murder. Accidents, when such large sums are at stake, are always viewed with suspicion by insurance companies; and when an insurance company gets suspicious, God knows what may not be revealed. And so I created Marsh, the man who is going to kill me. It was fun, that creation. My one regret was that I couldn't share the joke with you.

The first thing I did was to buy the ancient diary which is going to prove that Marsh's enmity toward me existed many years ago. Then, a little bit at a time, I began to fake it up. I covered years with that diary, writing up about five years a week. I was full of cunning—most of the stuff was *actual* stuff! I mean, most of it referred to actual and provable incidents. The only real fake in the whole thing was Marsh, and I did him so cleverly that after all this time it would be quite impossible for anyone to say no man called Marsh was ever in such a place at such a time; that no man called Marsh ever quarrelled with F. X. Benedik. Quite impossible! After the diary I began to teach myself Marsh's handwriting; very soon I had got it not only so that it was utterly different from my own but so that it could be written by me as quickly as my own. And then I set out to *make* Marsh *in propria persona*.

It took, to make him:

1   black sombrero
1   walking stick
1   pair imitation horn-rimmed dark-glassed spectacles
5   pounds'-worth of moustache and imperial
1   limp
1   guttural voice
2   million Latin r's

The actual delivery of Marsh was easy. He first saw the light in the public lavatory at Piccadilly Circus. F. X. Benedik, that spruce, alert, free-striding, and athletic business man, went in, carrying a parcel which contained a sombrero-type hat. There came out, limping and gutturally cursing, Boswell Marsh. In Boswell Marsh's pocket was, folded up flat, F. X. Benedik's hat; otherwise all the clothes of Boswell Marsh were the clothes of F. X. Benedik. But clothes do not go even a small way toward making the man!

One of the first things that Mr. Marsh did, Anthony, was to take a cottage; a little cottage in a village where Mr. Marsh's eccentricity and Mr. Marsh's unpleasant ways would secure a very full measure of attention from the village gossips. Mr. Marsh paid for his cottage, which he was careful to rent from an easy-going farmer, in untraceable notes and, *at the time of signing the lease,* and Mr. Marsh's visits to his country seat (after all, if you're going to make a man, you must show him) will explain all those weekends of mine which, I know, used to make you wonder. From his cottage, Mr. Marsh, as you will remember, wrote insulting letters to F. X. Benedik. And F. X. Benedik, from his palatial offices, wrote back even more insulting letters to Mr. Marsh. Presently the office began (and the office included yourself!) to *accept* Mr. Marsh.

Then Mr. Marsh began to telephone. I don't suppose that any-one will ever comment upon the fact that Marsh always rang up when F. X. Benedik happened to be out, but of course he did. If it should, however, come to her being questioned on this point, Miss Pagan will swear that there was one occasion upon which Mr. Benedik rang up Mr. Marsh from the office, because Miss Pagan heard Mr. Benedik talking over the telephone to Mr. Marsh. I did that to-day—and got a great deal of fun out of it—rather macabre fun, doubtless, but fun, nevertheless. I left the house in the morning to walk to the office, as usual, and on the way to the office I rang up twice, using Marsh's voice. I wanted to speak very, very, very urgently to Mr. Benedik. Mr. Benedik, having delivered, as Marsh, this message, walked on to his office, and once there, not only heard about the telephone calls which Marsh had been making, but *appeared* to make one to the telephone number which Marsh had left. How was poor Miss Pagan—who is my witness, and a very good one, I should say—to see that while I, F. X. Benedik, appeared to be talking to Boswell Marsh, I had my right forefinger pressed down upon the receiver hook and was therefore talking into an unconnected telephone?

Once—I daren't make it more—Marsh visited the office. I chose a day when I knew both you and Woolrich would be out. You probably heard all about the visit. Marsh was extraordinarily offensive. I can tell you, when I saw Pagan looking at me as I came in, I nearly passed away. I had to think very hard of how well my specially built little imperial was stuck on and how satisfyingly well the dark glasses, which were so dark that they would not allow anyone to see anything at all of my eyes, really altered me. I can tell you, Anthony, Mr. Marsh's visit, although part of this greatest of all great jokes, put the wind up me. Time and again I thought I'd be spotted, and time and again somebody—bless 'em!—did or said something that made me realize that I hadn't been. After all, you mustn't forget—as I very nearly forgot at the time—that I had already *planted* Marsh on everyone in the office. I don't think you saw me forcing Marsh down your throat, and I don't think the others saw me forcing him down theirs, but force him down I did; so that by the time the actual visit came along they *knew* Marsh existed.

This seems to be turning out a much more ponderous epistle than I had intended. I'd better cut the cackle and explain exactly *how* I am going to get murdered by my very much altered ego. So here we go:

To-day, as I have told you, I, F. X. Benedik, have made an appointment (Miss Pagan heard me making it) with Mr. Marsh, the appointment being for ten o'clock P. M. to-morrow, Friday, at my house. You will remember that I wasn't at the office this morning. I couldn't be at the office, because F. X. Benedik was temporarily nonexistent while Mr. Boswell Marsh made his presence felt very considerably over quite a large portion of London. You will also remember that I wasn't at home last night, being on one of those mysterious flying visits to what I have always supposed you to think was a woman but was really Marsh's cottage at Little Ockleton. The climax began this morning, when Mr. Marsh got up.

It worked like this:

	Time	Point	Remarks
1.	8:45 A. M.	Mr. Marsh receives an unstamped letter from Mr. Benedik. Mr. Marsh makes a hell of a fuss with postman.	Posted this letter unstamped on purpose to give Marsh a chance to show himself.
2.	9:00 A. M.	Mr. Marsh makes himself unpleasant at Little Ockleton station.	General principles of trail blazing. No particular point.
3.	11:30 A. M.	Mr. Marsh, more unpleasant than ever, buys three stalls at Royal Theatre. Leaves indelible impression on booking clerk.	See below.
4.	11:55 A. M.	Mr. Marsh enters District Messenger Office: very unpleasant. Insists on letter addressed to "Housekeeper and Staff, 4, William Pitt Street" being delivered at a certain time.	Certain time adopted as additional memory provoker.
5.	12:15 P. M.	Mr. Marsh, upon the emergency stairs Dover Street Station, becomes again F. X. Benedik.	
6.	1:30 to 3:30 P. M.	F. X. B. lunches with A. X. B. and Peter Rickworth. F. X. B. sends A. X. B. to Paris.	Thus removing A. X. B. from scene of crime and any possible implication in same.

So much for what I have done. Now for what, to-morrow, I'm going to do. I'm going to put this in the same tabular form as to-day's activities, like this:

	Time	Point	Remarks
1.	9:30 A. M.	I am going to give old Fairburn and the two women permission to go to the theatre. She is sure to ask me.	See how bad this will look for Marsh, who presented, anonymously, the tickets.
2.	10:00 A. M.	Shall leave the house as Benedik and somewhere *en route* become Marsh.	

3. 11:00 A. M.   As Marsh shall go and   More trail blazing.
                     buy at Selsinger's the   (Shall probably make it
                     gun with which I am   a German automatic,
                     going to be murdered.   this being the most dif-
                                                ferent thing I can think
                                                of from my own re-
                                                volver which I am also
                                                going to use.)

4. 12 noon to   As Benedik, shall carry   Anything to avoid any
    7:30 P. M.   on in a usual—a very,   subsequent suspicion
                     very usual—way.   that I knew that any-
                                                thing untoward was to
                                                happen.

5. 7:30 to 8:30 P. M. F. X. Benedik will dine.   See how bad it is look-
                     The house will be   ing for Marsh. He has
                     empty except for Prout.   got rid of the female
                     After dinner I shall tell servants and will be as-
                     Prout that a man called   sumed to know that be-
                     Marsh is coming to see   tween ten and eleven
                     me at ten; that I, in the every night Prout goes
                     meantime, am going   out.
                     down to see Rickworth;
                     that if Marsh should
                     come before I return he
                     is to be let in; that once
                     Marsh is in, Prout can,
                     as he has been in the
                     habit of doing for the
                     last two or three years,
                     "slip round to the Fox-
                     hound for a small one."

6. 8:30 P. M.   Shall leave for Rick-   Trail blazing.
                     worth's. Will probably
                     take a taxi, but will get
                     out of taxi round about
                     Knightsbridge.   And
                     then (having changed
                     to Marsh in some con-
                     venient place) will for
                     a moment or two—prob-
                     ably in some pub—be-
                     have in a most extraor-
                     dinary manner.

7. 9:00 P. M.   Sam's house and once   Very useful. Sam will
                     more in my own ap-   make a nice, solid, un-
                     pearance. Shall talk to   shakable,   roast-beef-
                     Sam on business, prob-   and-baked-potatoes wit-
                     ably using the Car-   ness.
                     ruthers-Blackstone tan-
                     gle as a pretext. Shan't
                     stay very long, but long
                     enough to say that I've
                     got to get back to settle
                     with Marsh.

8. 10:00 P. M.

Shall enter 4, William Pitt Street as Marsh. Shall be (I don't think I shall like this part much: Prout's a good old sort) most unpleasant to Prout. Prout, you can bet your last boot, won't forget Marsh in a hurry, but Prout, having had permission from me, is sure to go out. He doesn't drink much, but can't do without that nightly gossip.

9. 10:20 P. M. (or so soon as Prout has thoroughly left!)

Setting stage. This, Anthony, is really damned good. Listen! Marsh is in the house, to everybody's knowledge. Benedik, since shortly he will be found dead there, must have come in at some later time, letting himself in with his key. (Problem: how to kill Benedik, leaving it clear that Marsh has killed him and got away?) I shall (a) smash the dark spectacles into minute pieces and flush these down the toilet; (b) deal the same way with the moustache and imperial; (c) wash my face thoroughly to get traces of spirit gum right off it; (d) leave Marsh's most distinctive sombrero prominently in the room; (e) get out of the window, cross the path, tie a bit of string on to a tough, long enough shoot of one of the yews on the other side of the path from the house, go back to the study and fix the bit of string so that the shoot is within my reach from the window; (f) have a lovely duel between Marsh and Benedik, leaving plenty of signs of it. (I shall stand by the window and blaze away with the Luger as Marsh. I shall then go over to the other side of the room and blaze away with my own gun as Benedik. There will be a nice lot of bullet-holes all telling their own lying story); (g) quickly, because people may come in at any moment after the shooting, I shall then set the last scene! The setting will prove that Marsh having started to run away, got through the window, shot Benedik and then escaped across the path, through the shrubbery and out at the other side of the gardens. This will be done like this, ladies and gentlemen—pure deception! I shall go to the window, which will be open at the bottom. I shall take the piece of string off the yew shoot, keep hold of the shoot and slip the string into my pocket.

I shall then slip the end of the shoot of yew through the trigger guard of the Luger. I shall then take my own gun in my right hand and lean my torso out of the window. With my left hand I shall put the Luger which has, don't forget, the yew shoot through the trigger guard straining at it, up close to my head, but not too close, and blow out my brains. What must happen, because

Thank the Lord it hasn't been raining and no footprints could be expected to show.

Anyone might have a bit of string in his pocket.

I've worked it out very
carefully, is that I shall
be found lying across
the window with my
own gun in my right
hand, shot through the
head with Marsh's gun,
while Marsh's gun will
be found feet—perhaps
yards—away from the
house, because the yew
shoot will have pulled it
back and dropped it
somewhere.   Pretty nice, what?

And that, Anthony, is the end of Boswell Marsh and F. X. Benedik. Don't—I know you won't—curse me for this. In time you will even see the joke. I'm a rotten life, so I'll make a good death of it. *You* wouldn't like to find that *your* body was going bad on you, would you? You'd do just the sort of thing I'm doing, but you'd probably make an even better joke of it than I have of this.

Look after yourself, boy, and Peter. And run Rynox for all you're damn well worth until you're sick of it. When you're sick of it, chuck it, but I don't think you will get sick of it. We've had many good times together, and I'm most grateful to you for all of them, and for a lot of other things.

You won't get this letter until long after you've done what I know you'll do, and that is, using the money which you'll make the insurance wallahs pay you out as quick as you damn well can, see Rynox out of the bad times and into the high lights. (I'm prepared to bet you have a tough time with old Sam, who will immediately want to throw himself upon the very doubtful mercies of Carey Street without another word, but I'm equally prepared to bet you'll stop him from doing it.)

You'll get this letter in about seven months from this minute. I'm posting it to-night to Carruthers in the F. M. S. (I don't think you know old Carruthers—a very good friend of mine.) I shall tell him I want it mailed at such-and-such a time to you. He's a stout old fellow and won't let me down, and he's unlikely to die. He's as tough as I used to think I was once. When you get it, perhaps you'll get a shock; perhaps you won't. But, anyhow, you'll realize that what I've *done* is to borrow £277,777 for Rynox from the Naval, Military & Cosmopolitan. If Rynox goes big, pay it back. If Rynox doesn't go big, you can't, and so I should forget it. But if you do repay, I should give them interest at the prevailing rate. I leave it to you as to the manner in which you do it. I bet it will be damned funny!

Good-bye, son, and give my love to Peter.

Hoping this will find you as it leaves me at present (very happy),

We remain, dear sir,

Your humble and obedient servants,

FRANCIS XAVIER BENEDIK.

BOSWELL MARSH.